ZITA THE SPACEGIRL

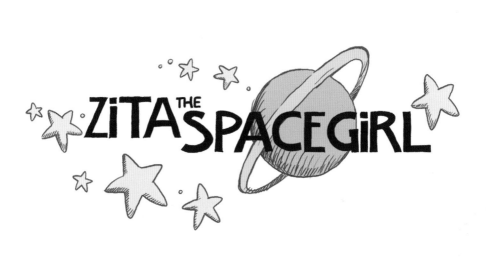

First Second

New York & London

Text and illustrations copyright © 2010 by Ben Hatke

Published by First Second
First Second is an imprint of Roaring Brook Press, a division of Holtzbrinck Publishing
Holdings Limited Partnership
120 Broadway, New York, NY 10271

Distributed in the United Kingdom by Macmillan Children's Books, a division of Pan
Macmillan.

Cover and interior design by Colleen AF Venable

Cataloging-in-Publication Data is on file at the Library of Congress

Paperback ISBN: 978-1-59643-446-2
Hardcover ISBN: 978-1-59643-695-4

First Second books are available for special promotions and premiums.
For details, contact: Director of Special Markets, Holtzbrinck Publishers.

First Edition February 2010

Printed in China by Toppan Leefung Printing Ltd.,
Dongguan City, Guangdong Province

Paperback: 20 19 18
Hardcover: 20 19 18 17 16 15 14

ZITA THE SPACEGIRL

by Ben Hatke

Book one: FAR FROM HOME

First Second

New York & London

THERE ARE TWO WAYS OF GETTING HOME; AND ONE OF THEM IS TO STAY THERE.

THE OTHER IS TO WALK ROUND THE WHOLE WORLD TILL WE COME BACK TO THE SAME PLACE.

-G.K. CHESTERTON

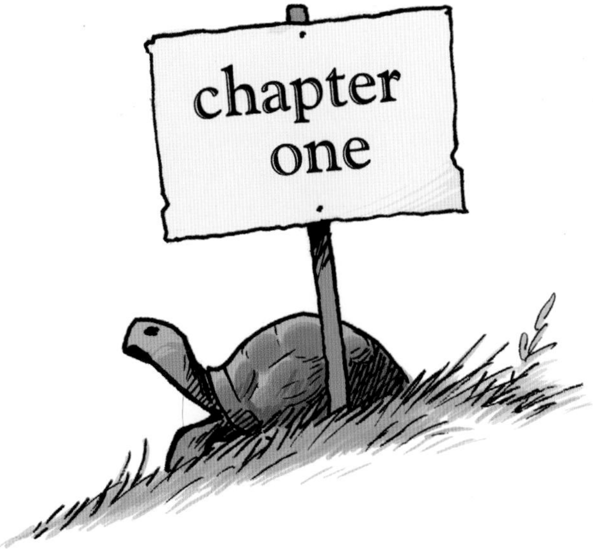
chapter
one

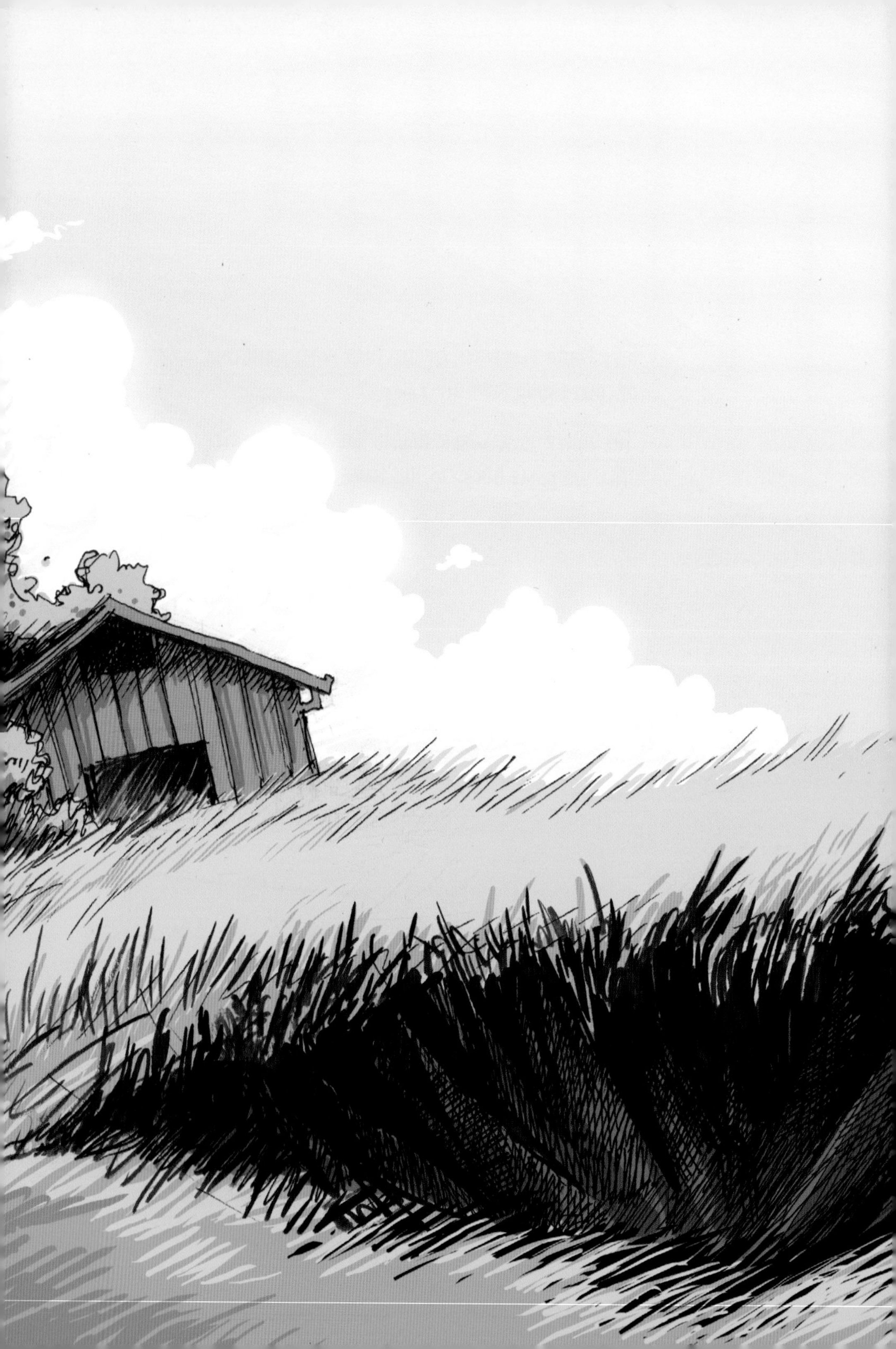

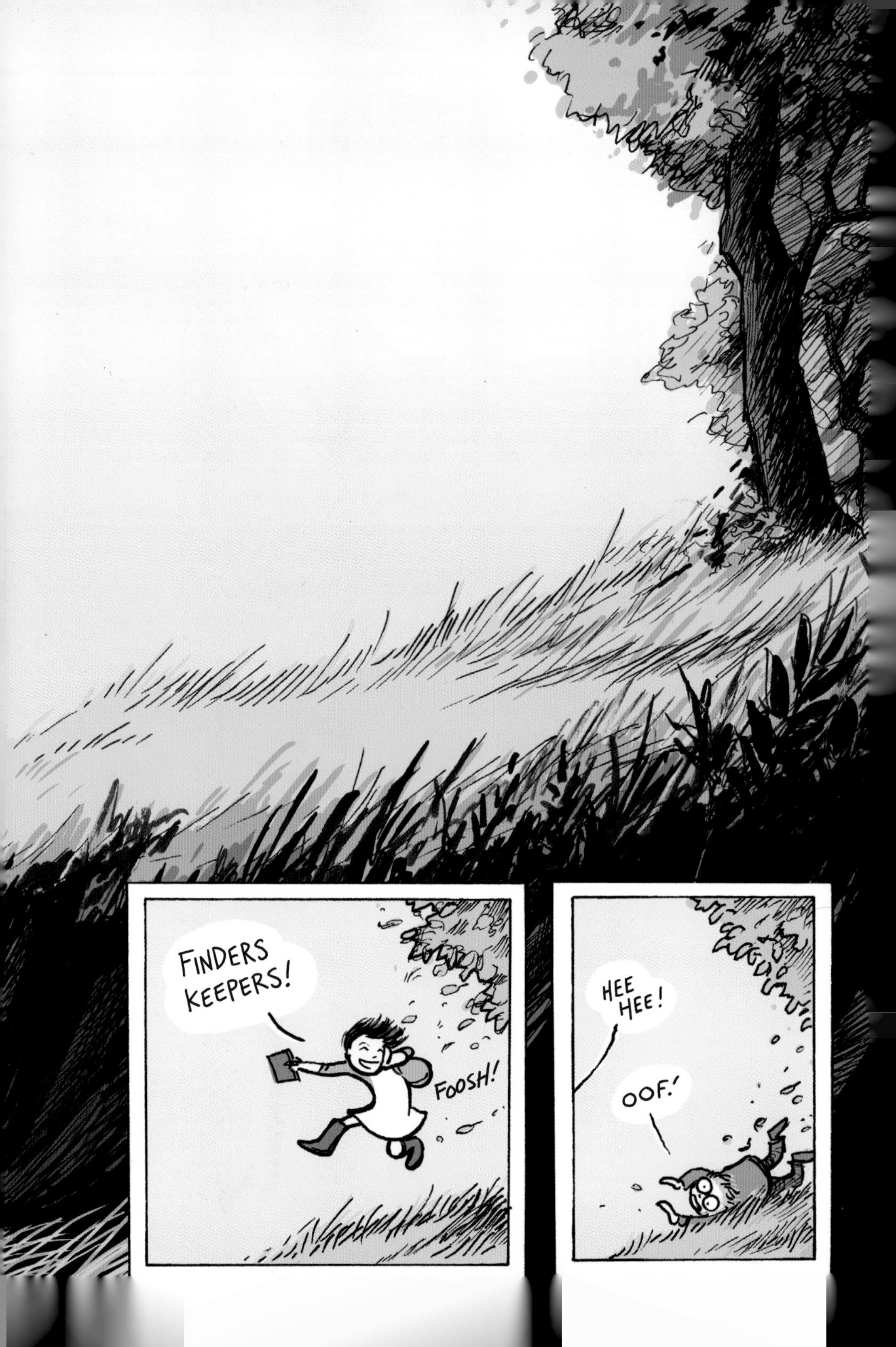
FINDERS KEEPERS!
FOOSH!
HEE HEE!
OOF!

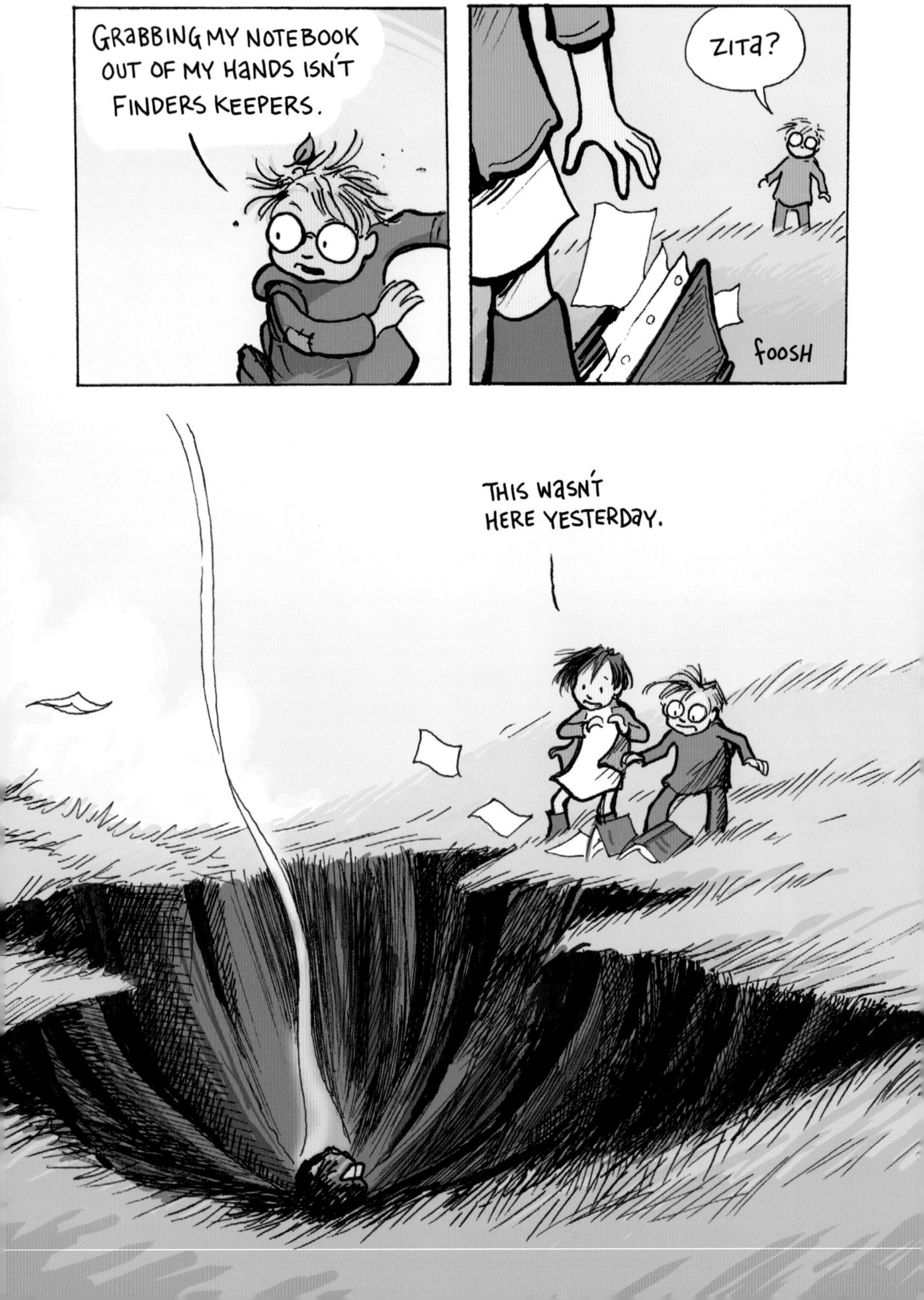
GRABBING MY NOTEBOOK OUT OF MY HANDS ISN'T FINDERS KEEPERS.
ZITA?
FOOSH
THIS WASN'T HERE YESTERDAY.

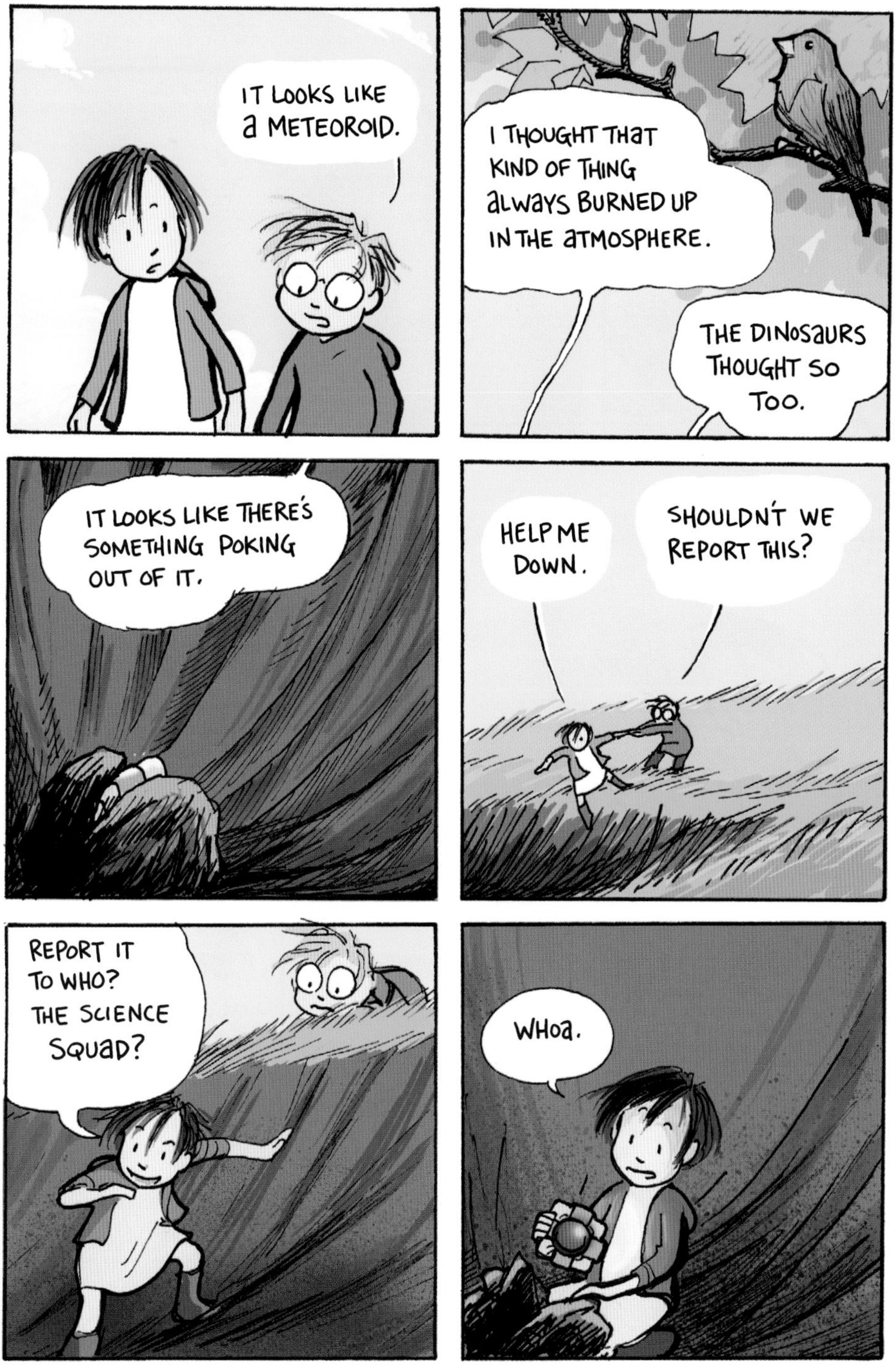
IT LOOKS LIKE a METEOROID.
I THOUGHT THAT KIND OF THING always BURNED UP IN THE atMOSPHERE.
THE DINOSaURS THOUGHT SO TOO.
IT LOOKS LIKE THERE'S SOMETHING POKING OUT OF IT.
HELP ME DOWN.
SHOULDN'T WE REPORT THIS?
REPORT IT TO WHO? THE SCIENCE SQUaD?
WHOa.

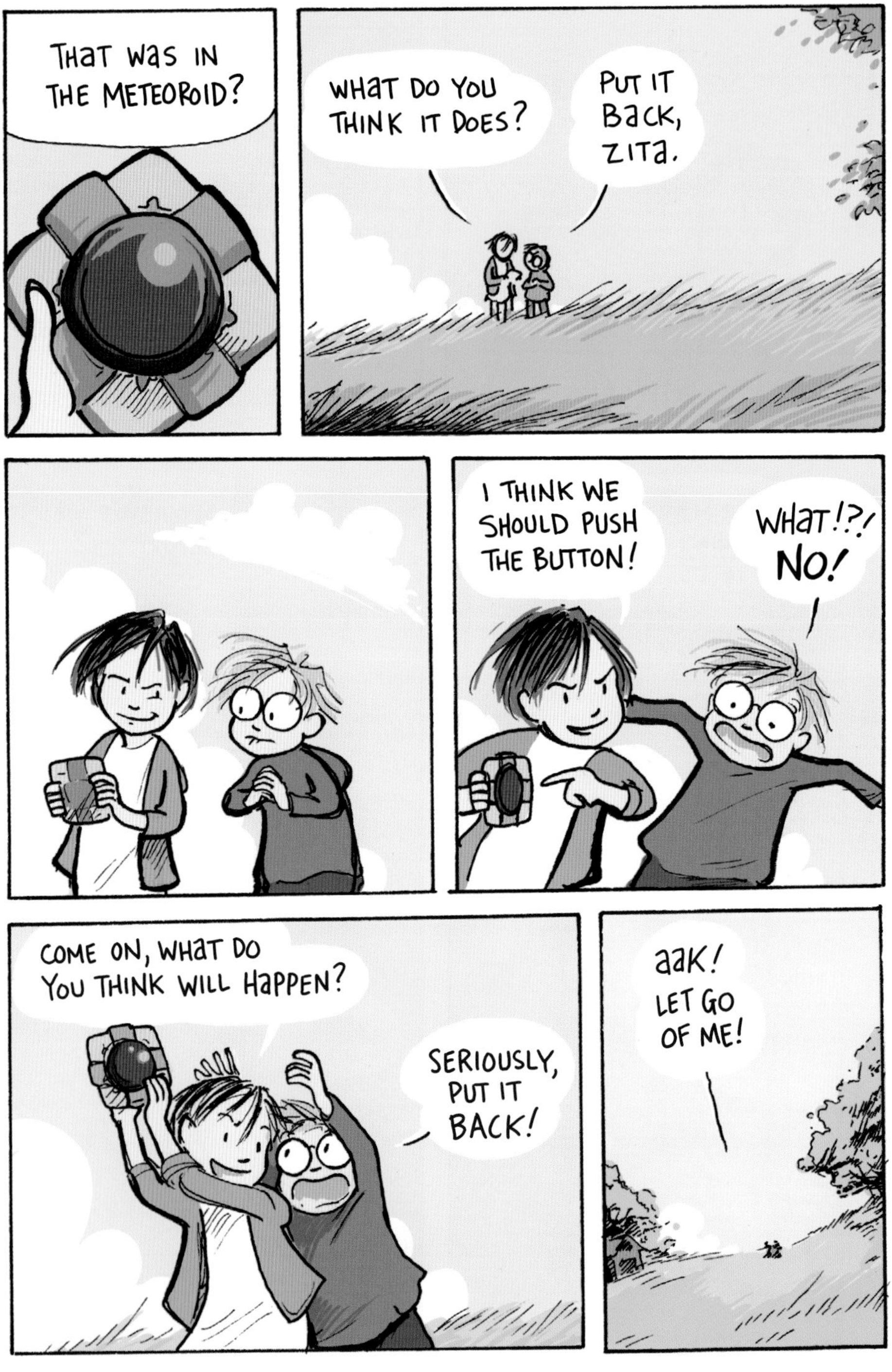
THAT WAS IN THE METEOROID?
WHAT DO YOU THINK IT DOES?
PUT IT BACK, ZITA.
I THINK WE SHOULD PUSH THE BUTTON!
WHAT!?! NO!
COME ON, WHAT DO YOU THINK WILL HAPPEN?
SERIOUSLY, PUT IT BACK!
AAK! LET GO OF ME!

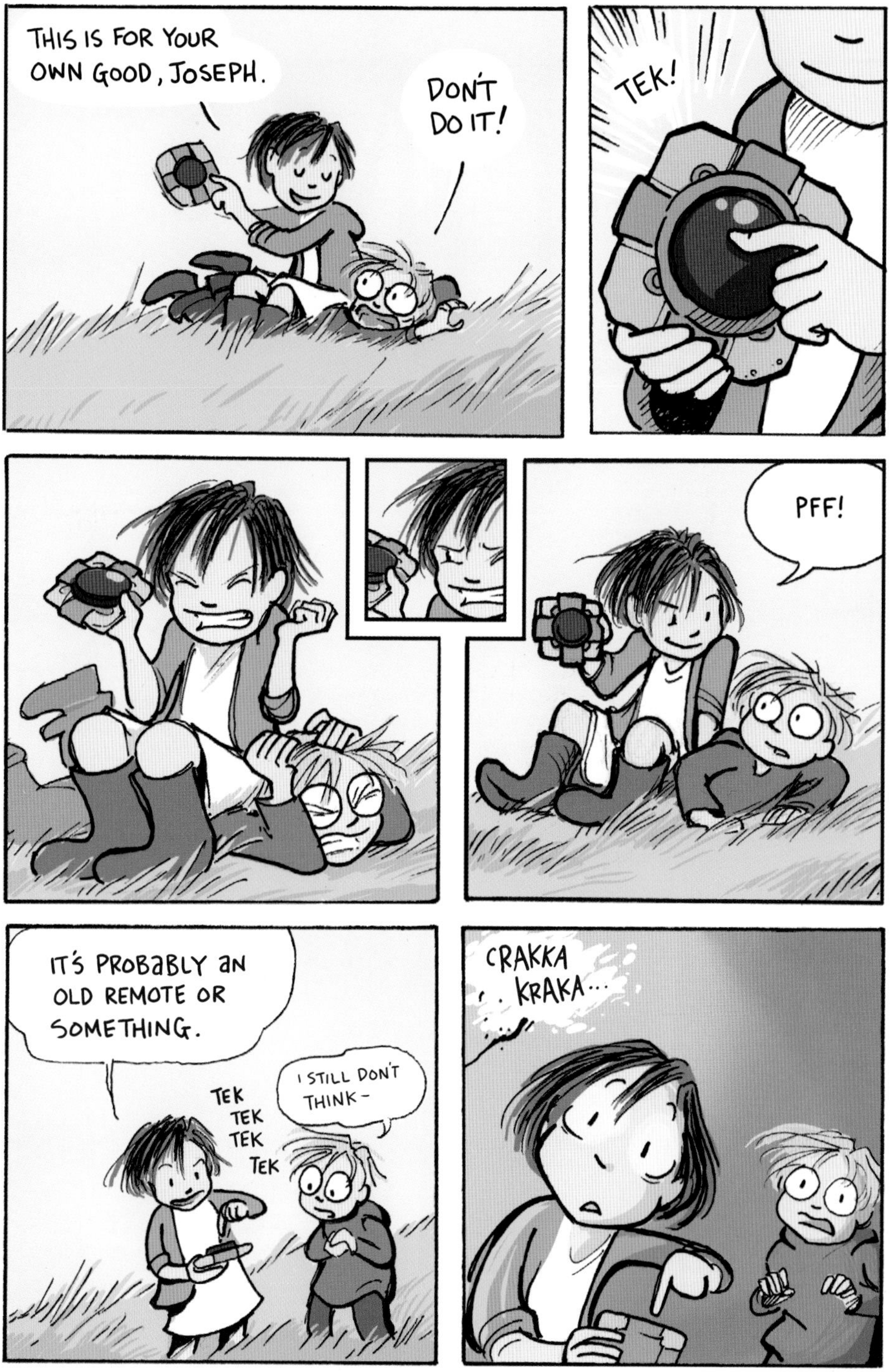
THIS IS FOR YOUR OWN GOOD, JOSEPH.
DON'T DO IT!
TEK!
PFF!
IT'S PROBABLY AN OLD REMOTE OR SOMETHING.
TEK TEK TEK TEK
I STILL DON'T THINK-
CRAKKA . . KRAKA...

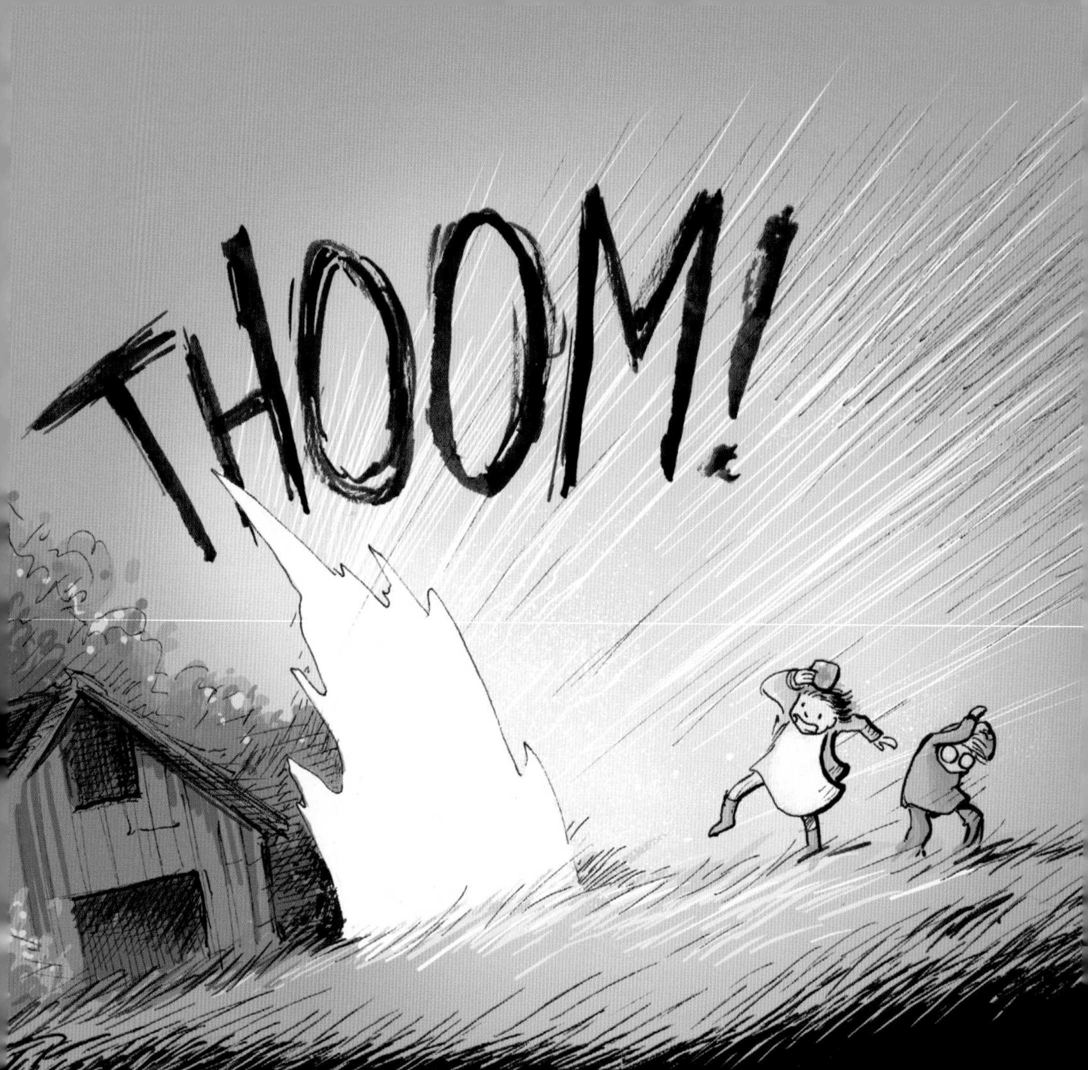
THOOM!
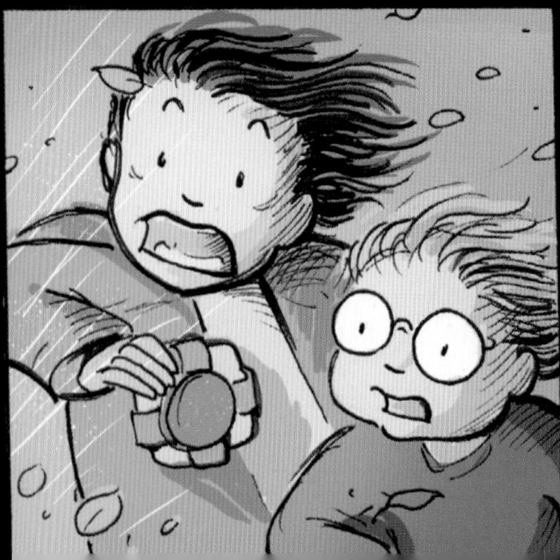
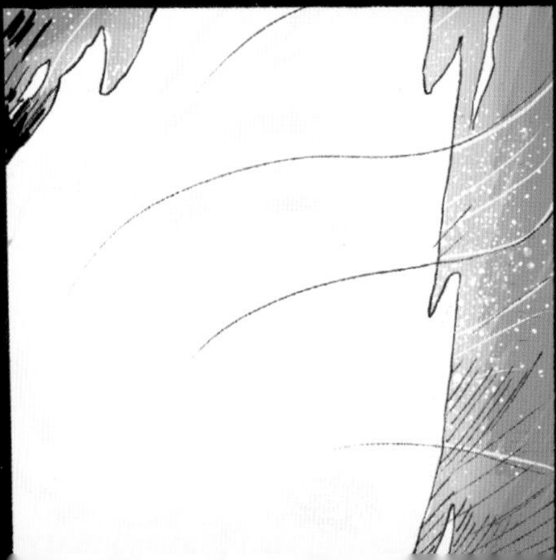

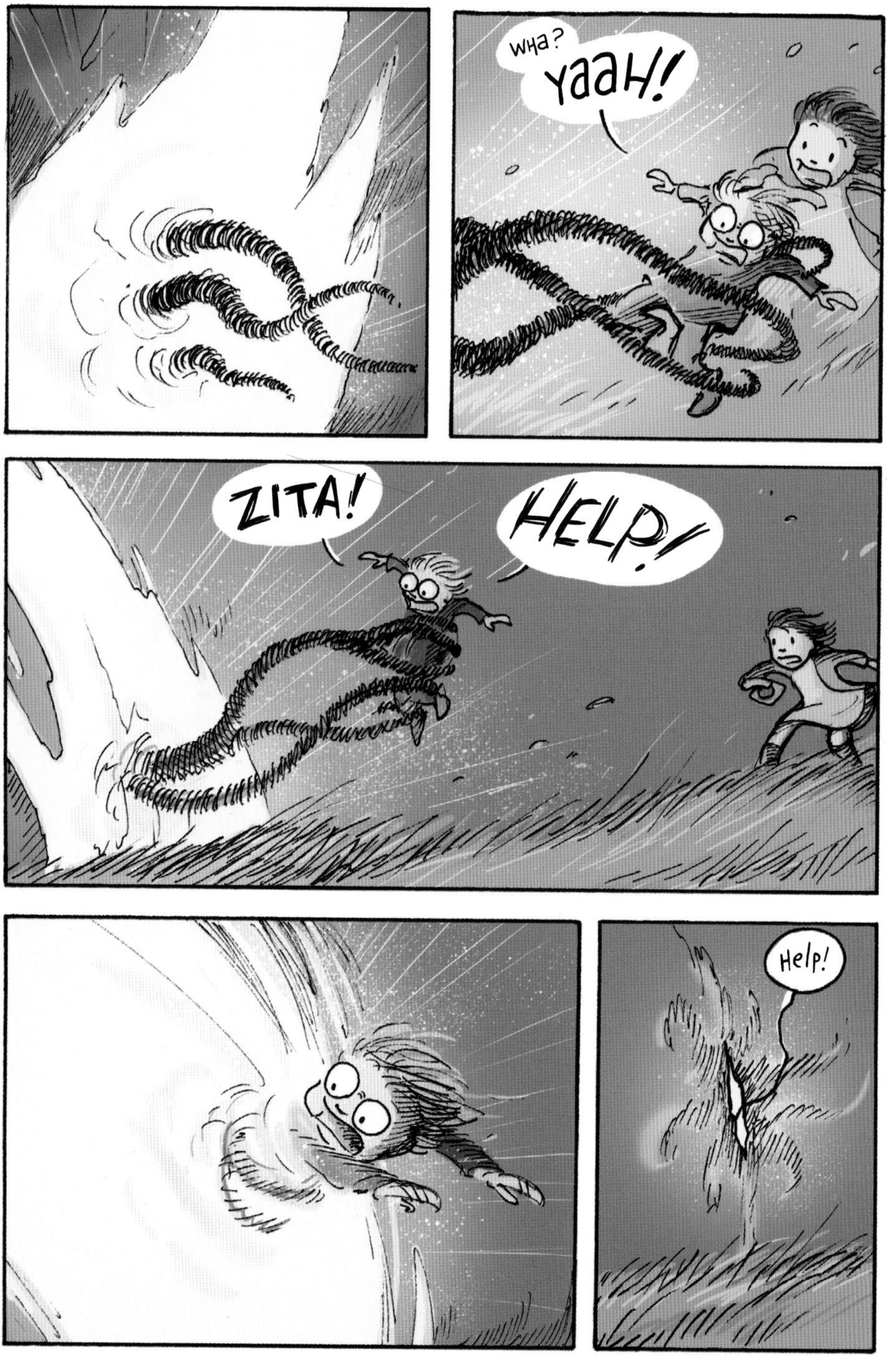
WHA?
YAAH!
ZITA!
HELP!
Help!

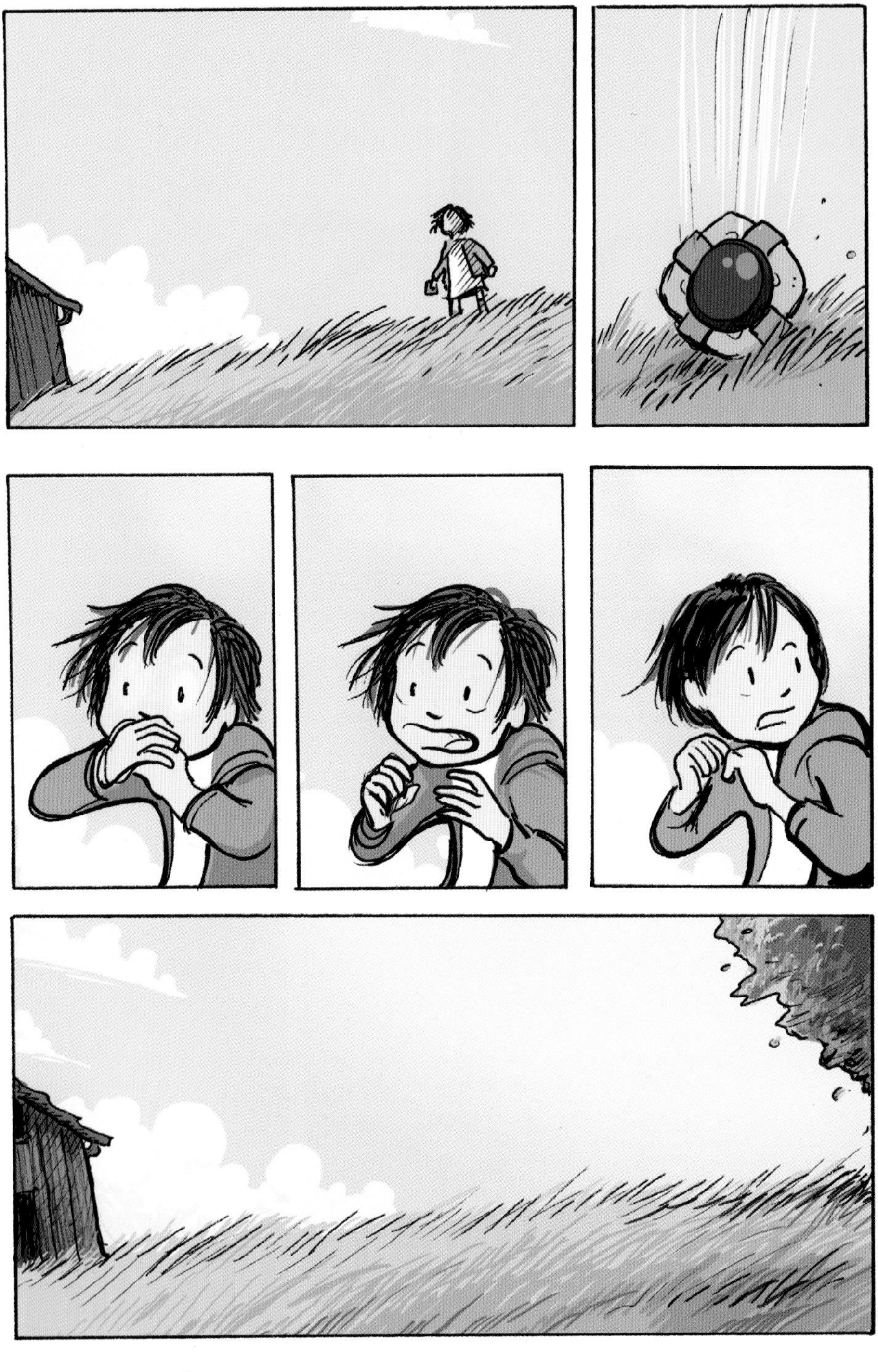

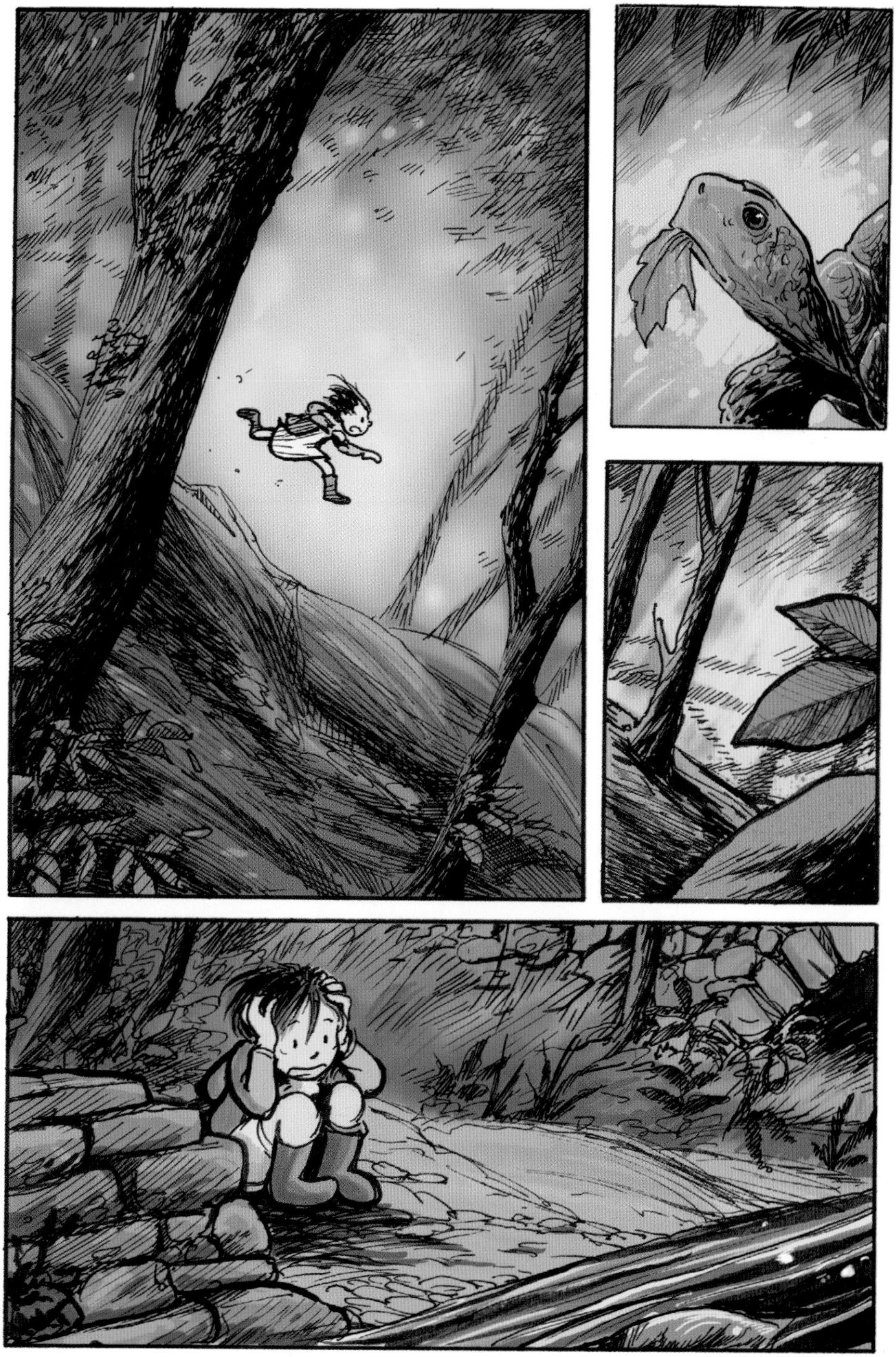

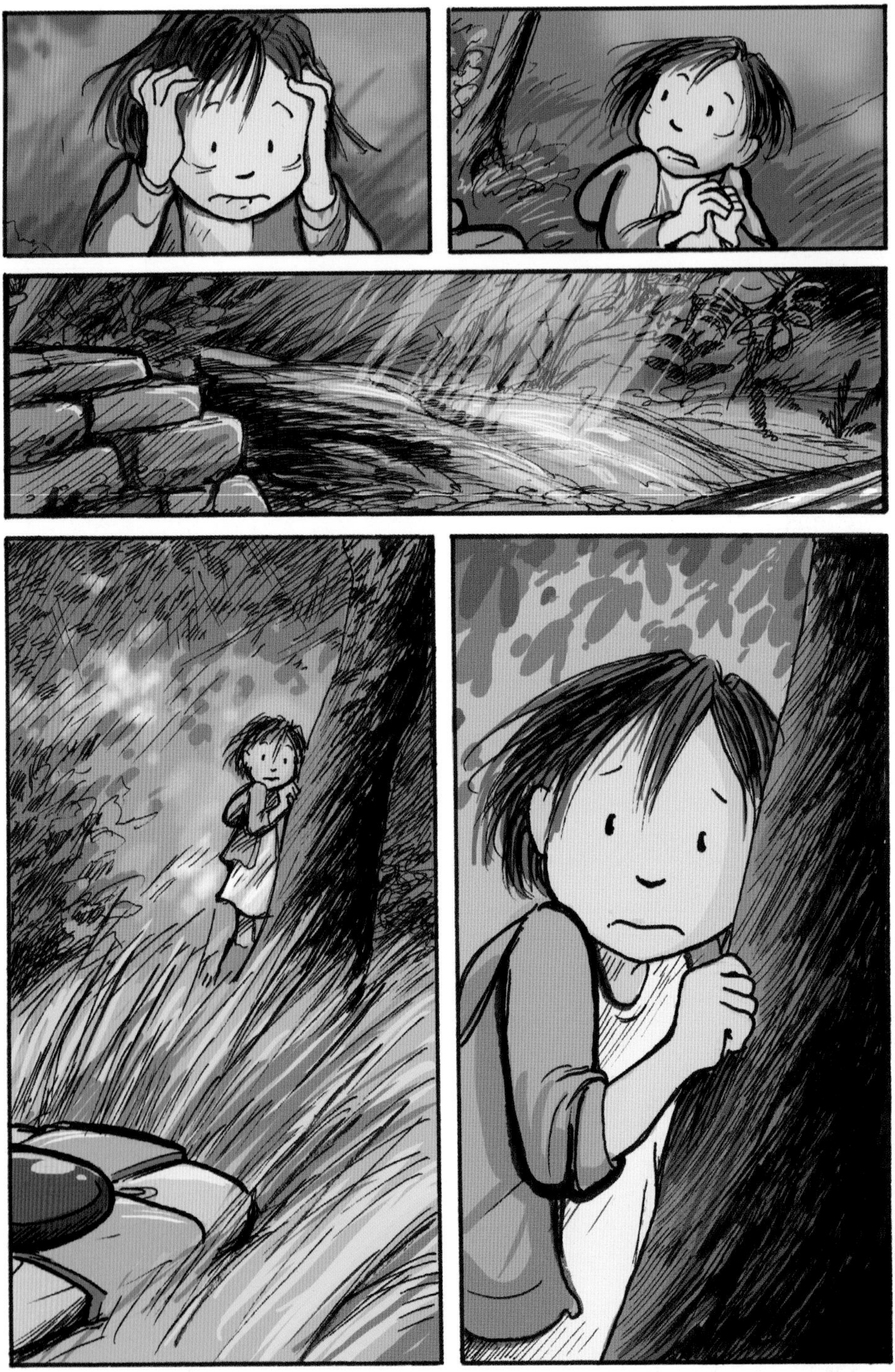

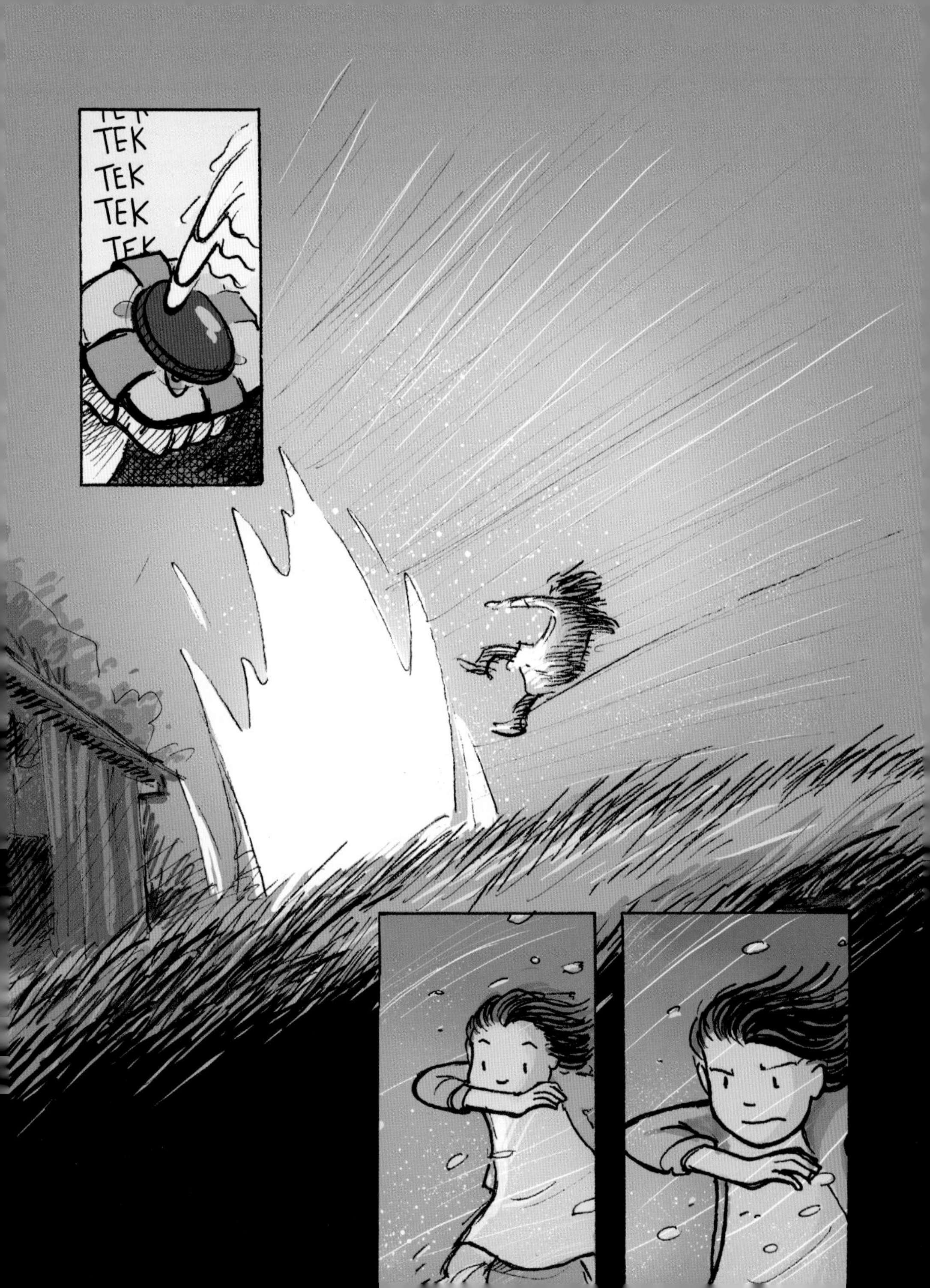
TEK
TEK
TEK

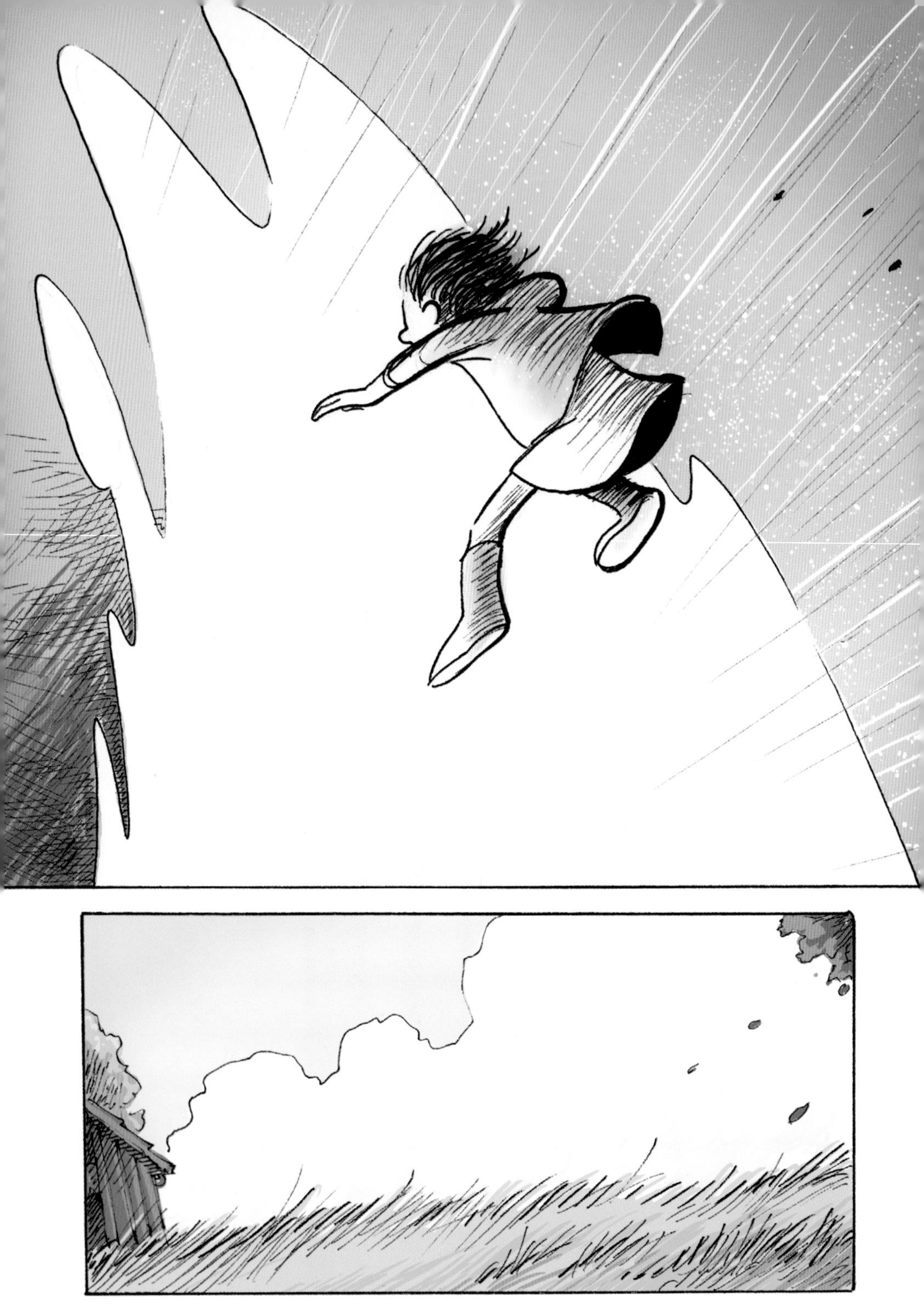

chapter
two

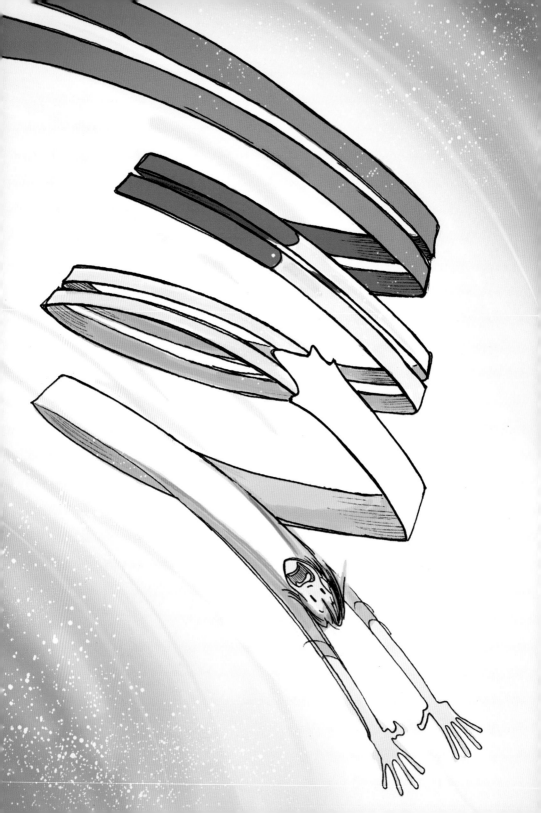

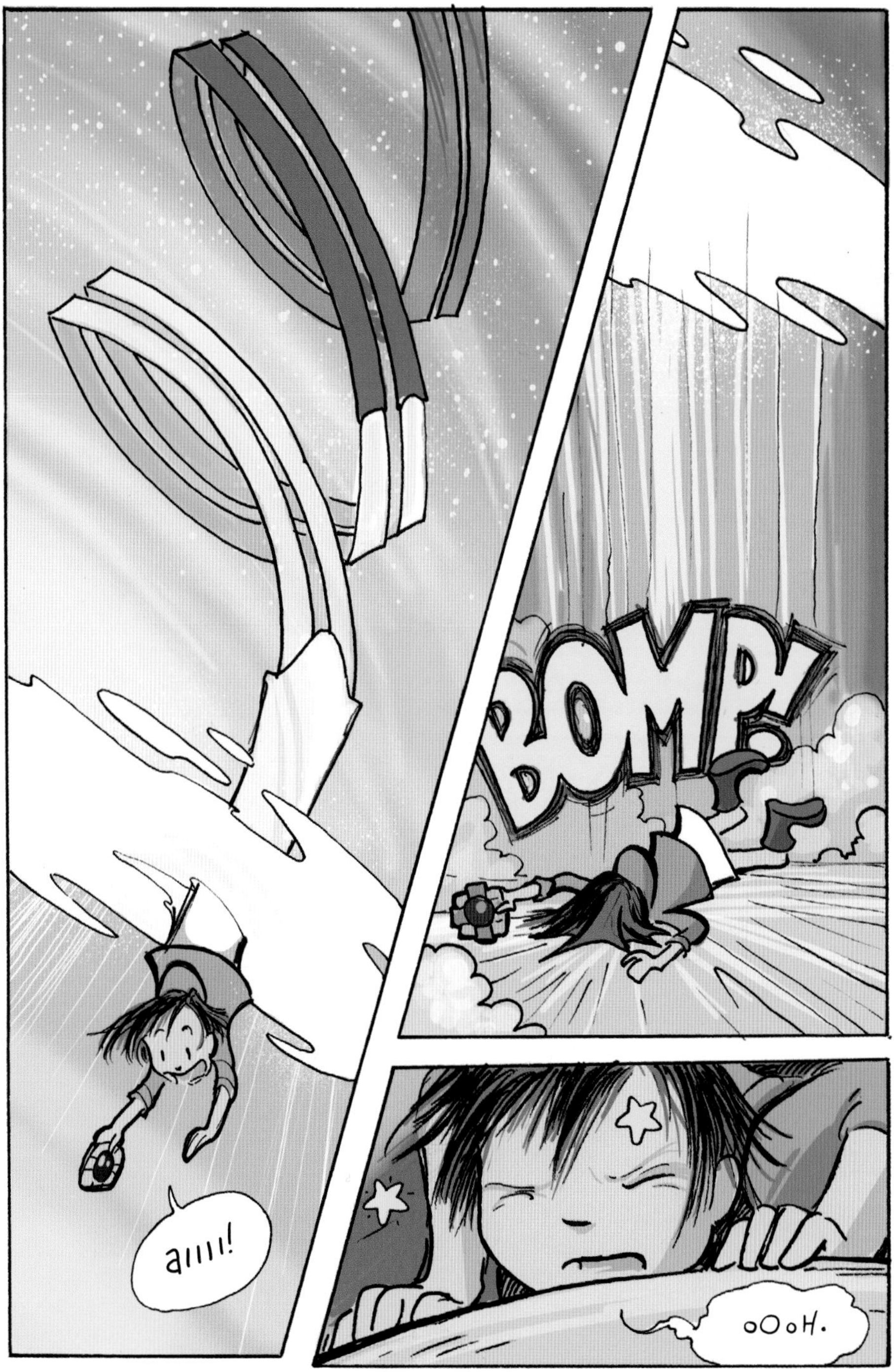

aiiii!
BOMP!
oOoH.

where...

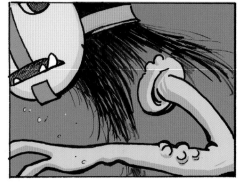

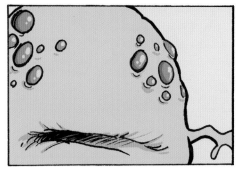

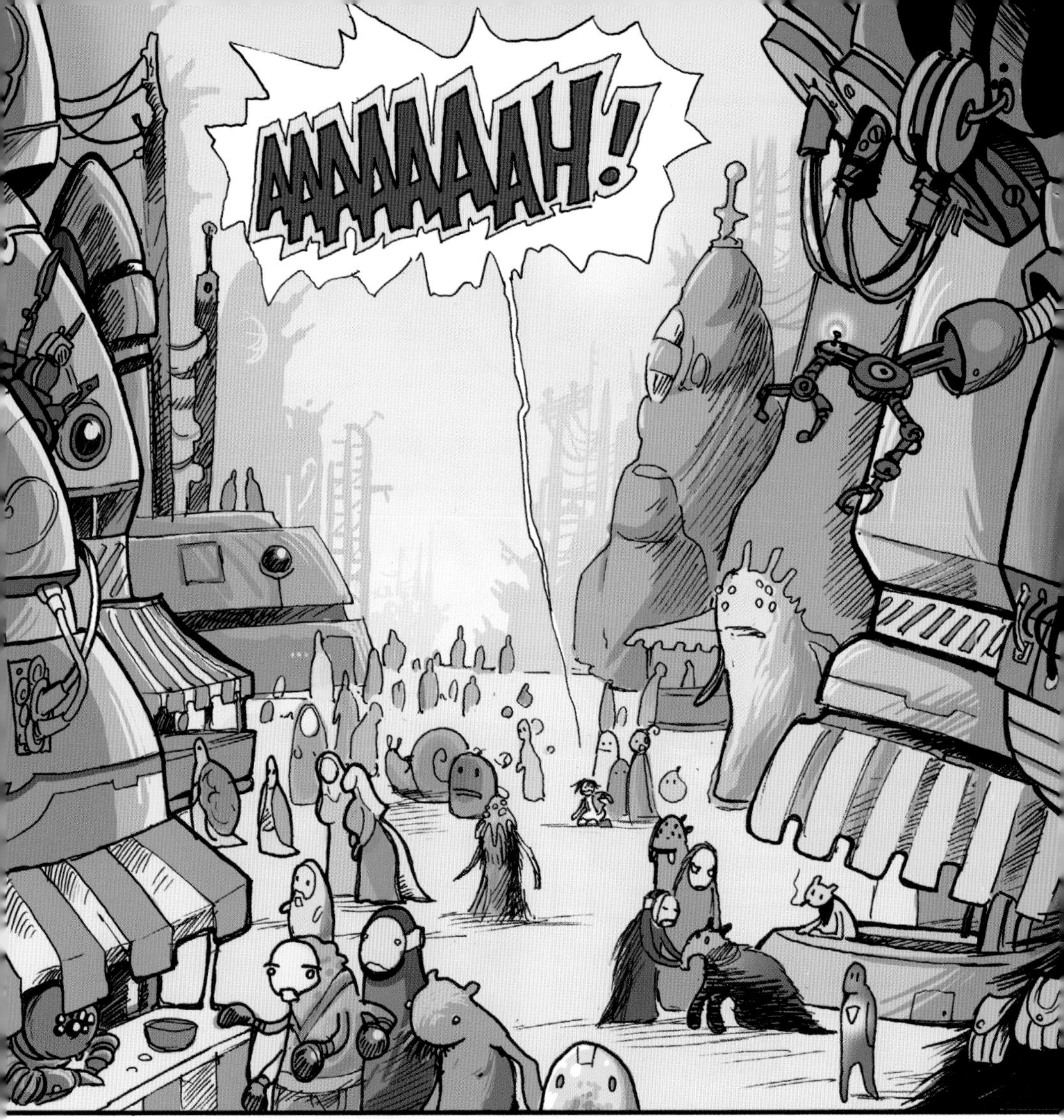
AAAAAAAH!

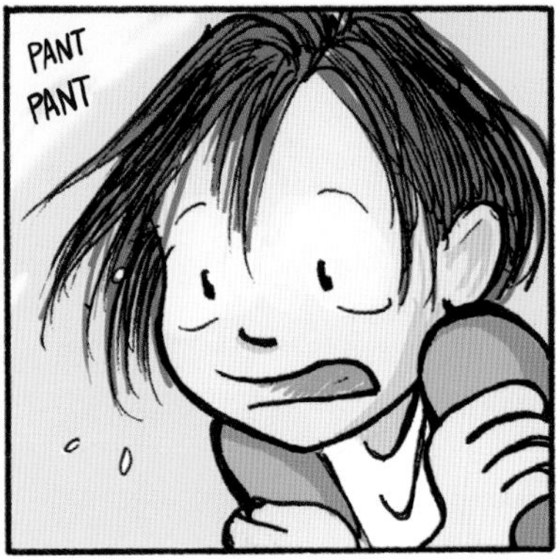
PANT
PANT

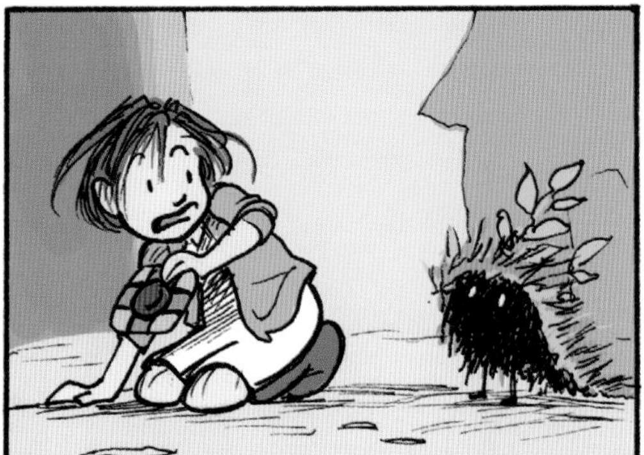

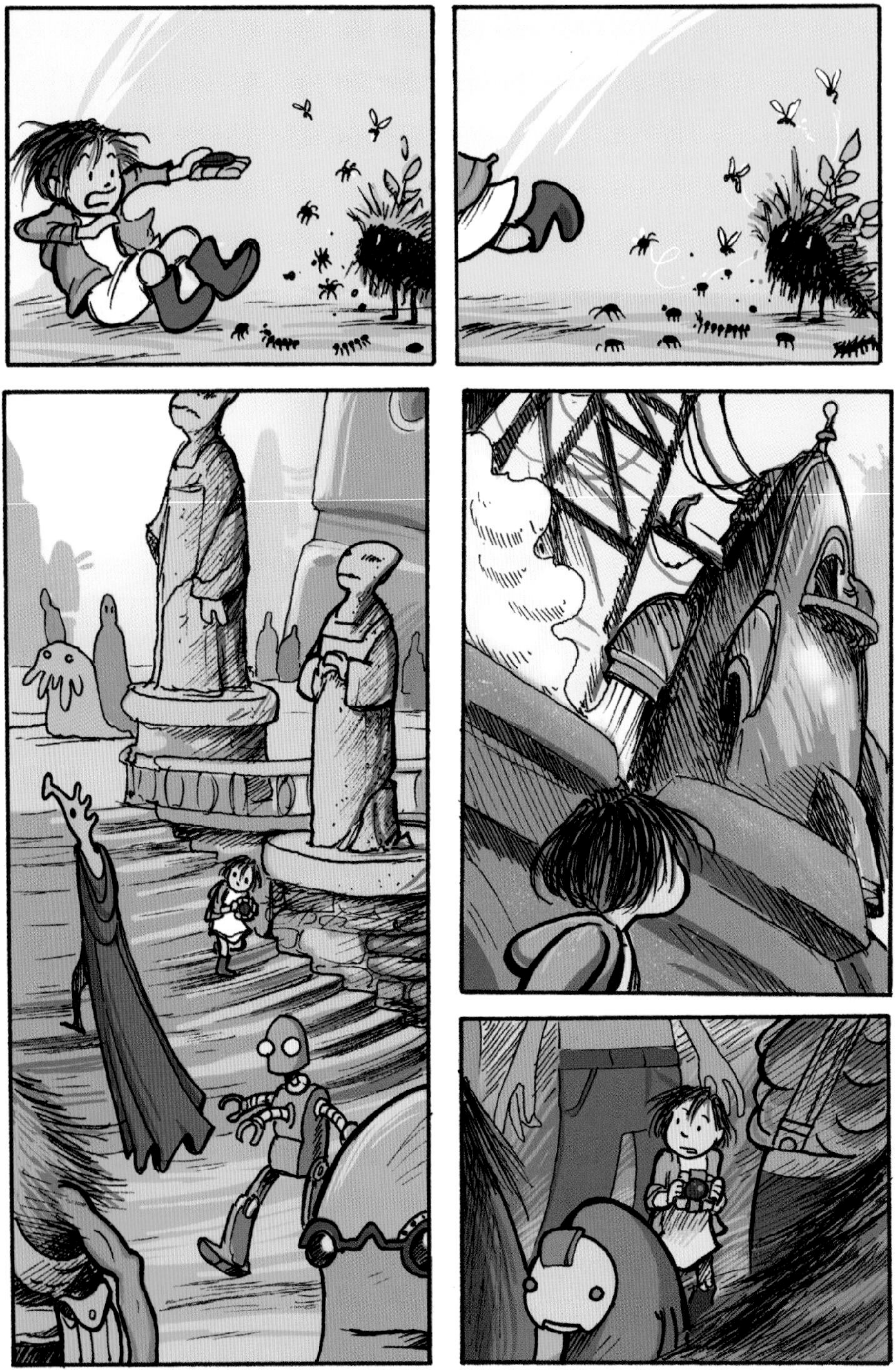

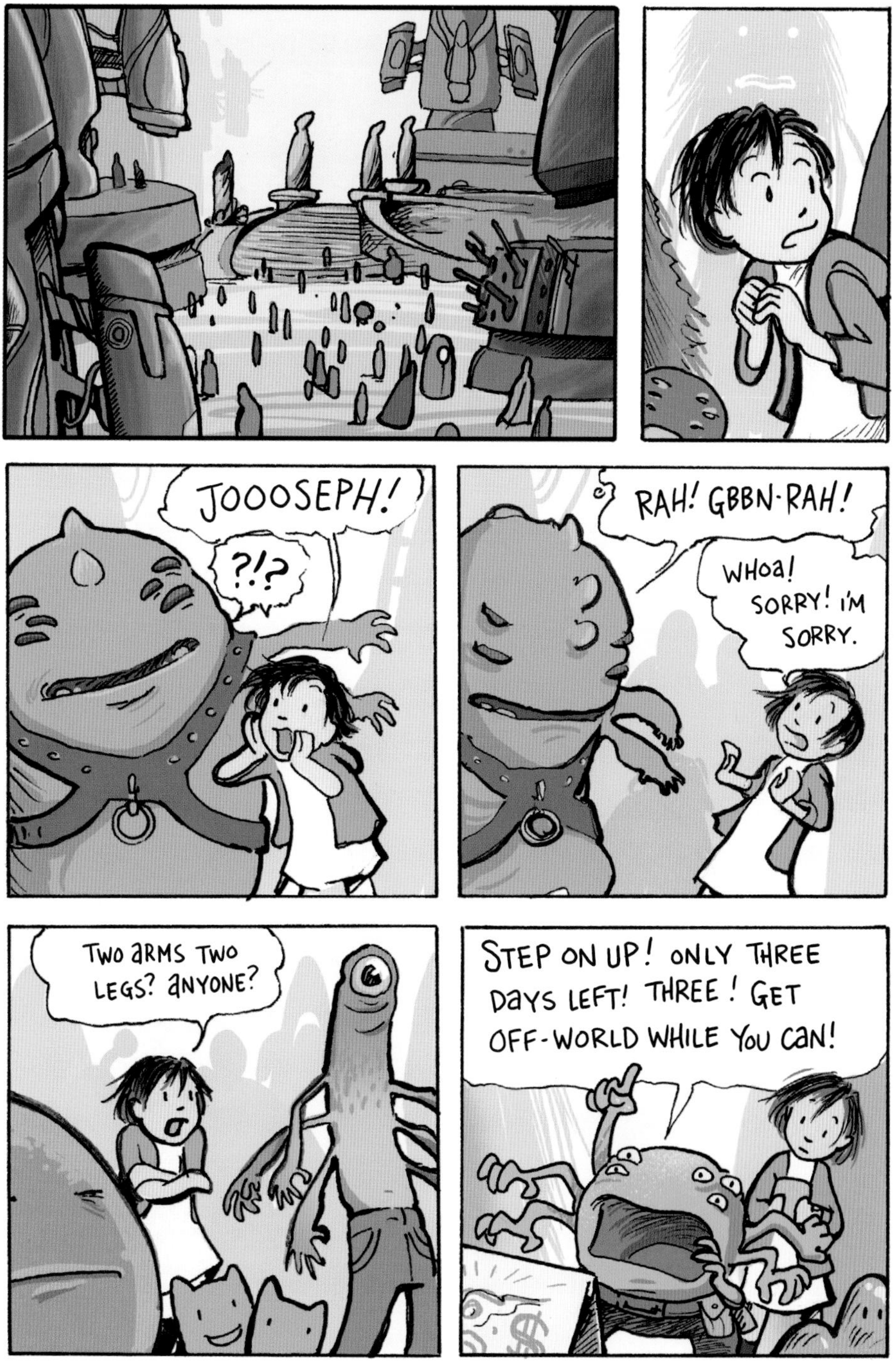
JOOOSEPH!
?!?
RAH! GBBN-RAH!
WHOA! SORRY! I'M SORRY.
TWO ARMS TWO LEGS? ANYONE?
STEP ON UP! ONLY THREE DAYS LEFT! THREE! GET OFF-WORLD WHILE YOU CAN!

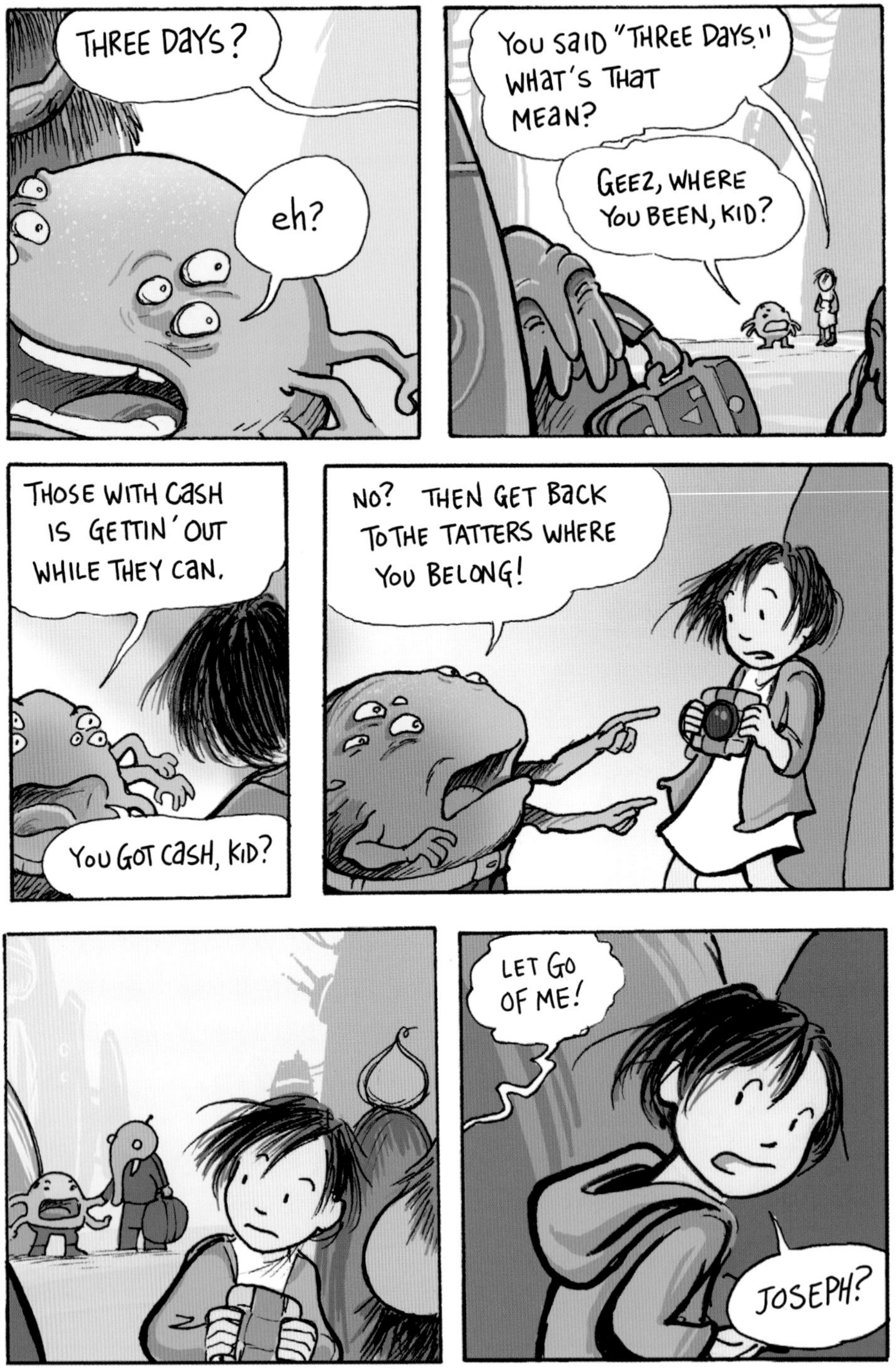
THREE DAYS?
eh?
YOU SAID "THREE DAYS." WHAT'S THAT MEAN?
GEEZ, WHERE YOU BEEN, KID?
THOSE WITH CASH IS GETTIN' OUT WHILE THEY CAN.
YOU GOT CASH, KID?
NO? THEN GET BACK TO THE TATTERS WHERE YOU BELONG!
LET GO OF ME!
JOSEPH?

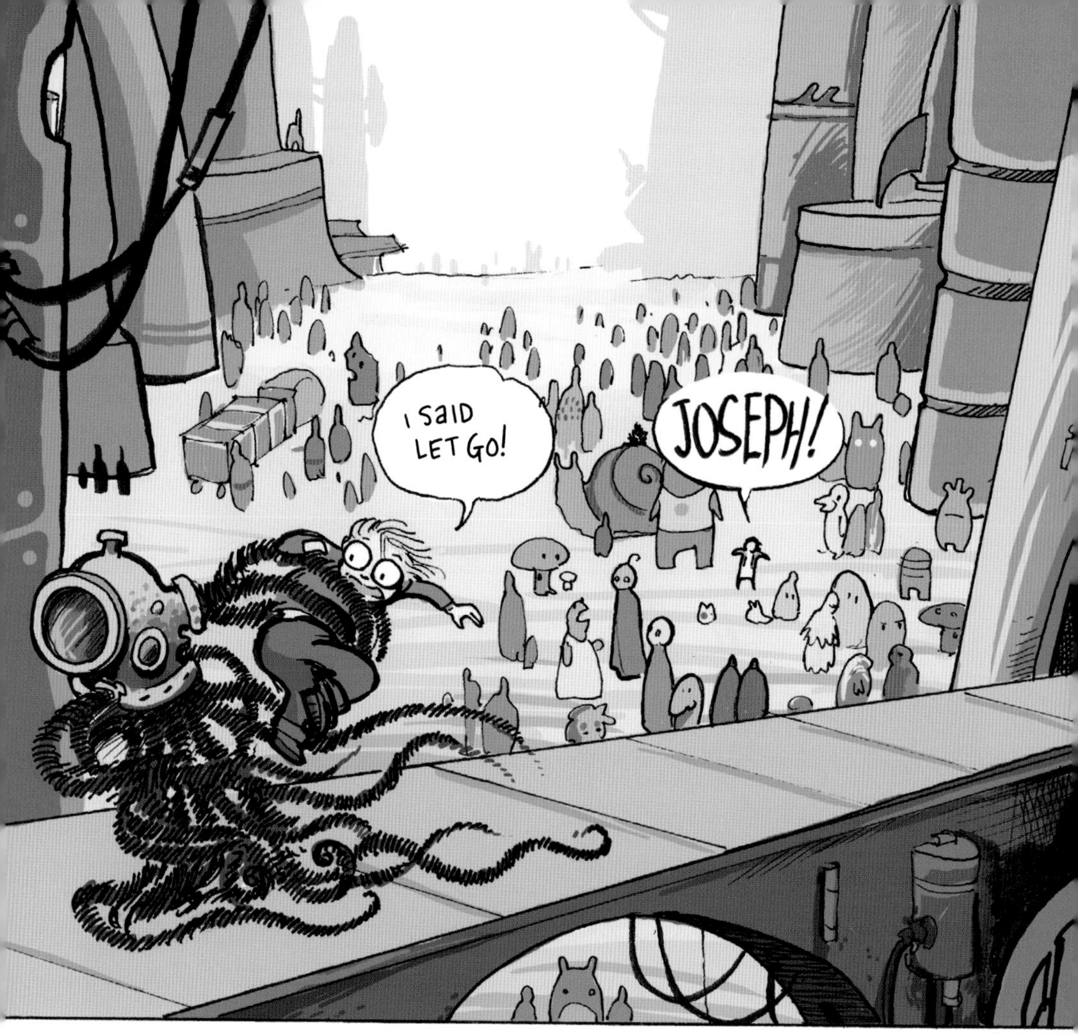
I SAID LET GO!
JOSEPH!

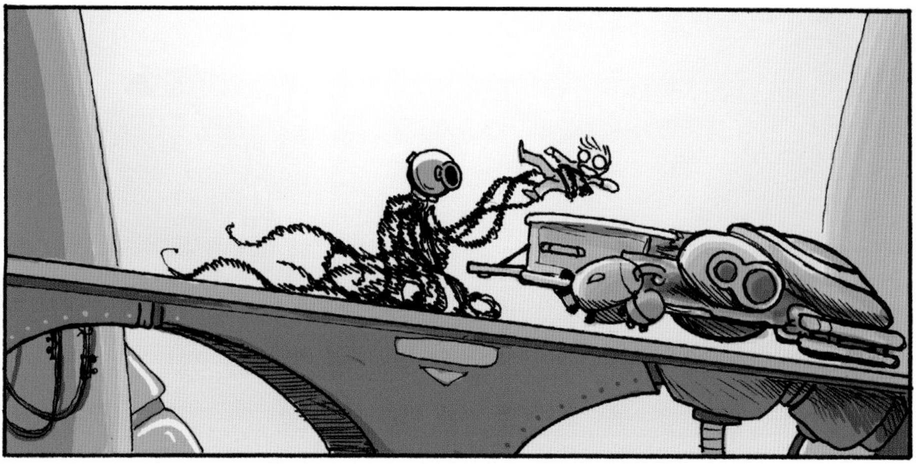

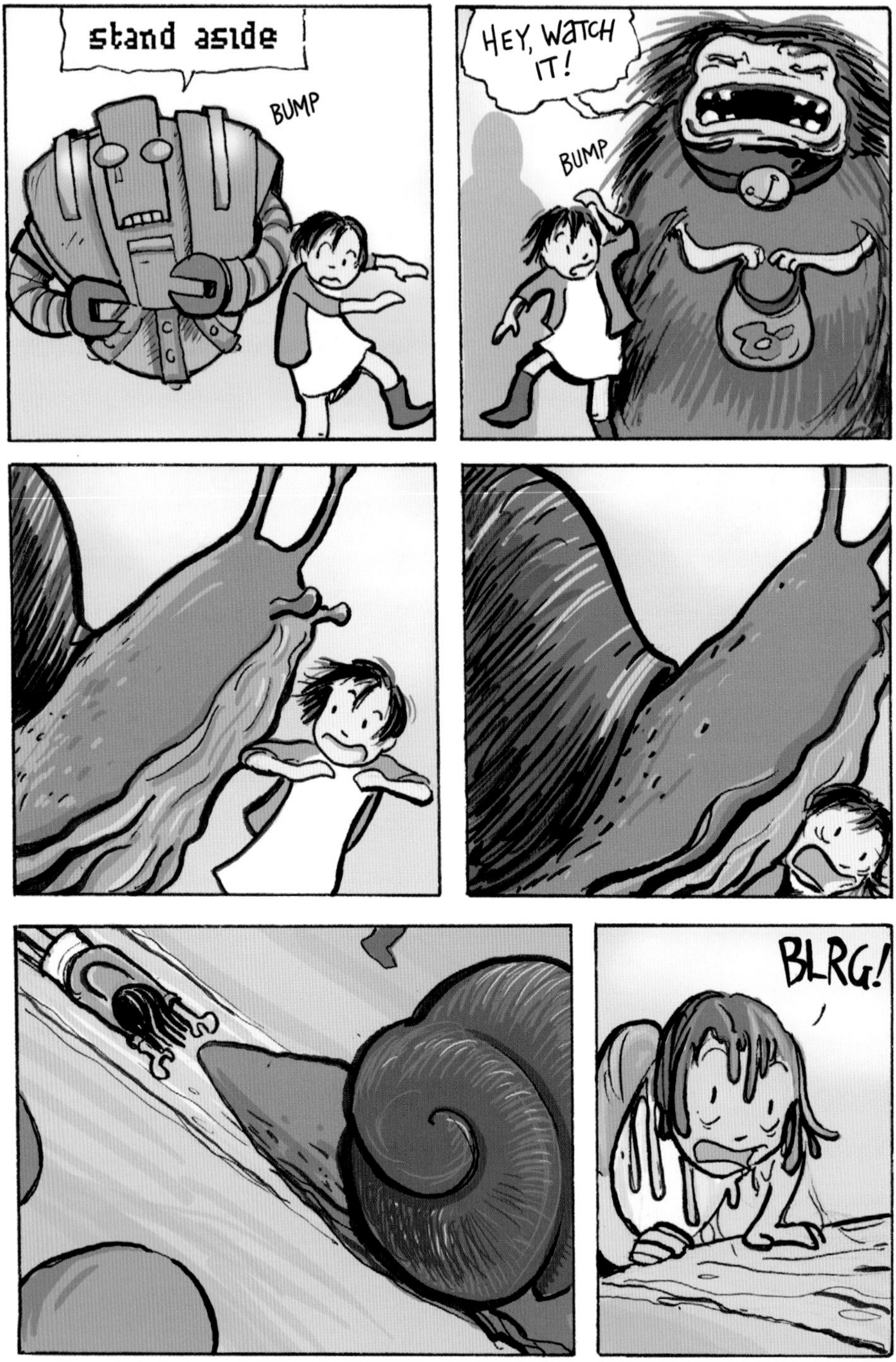
stand aside
BUMP
HEY, WATCH IT!
BUMP
BLRG!

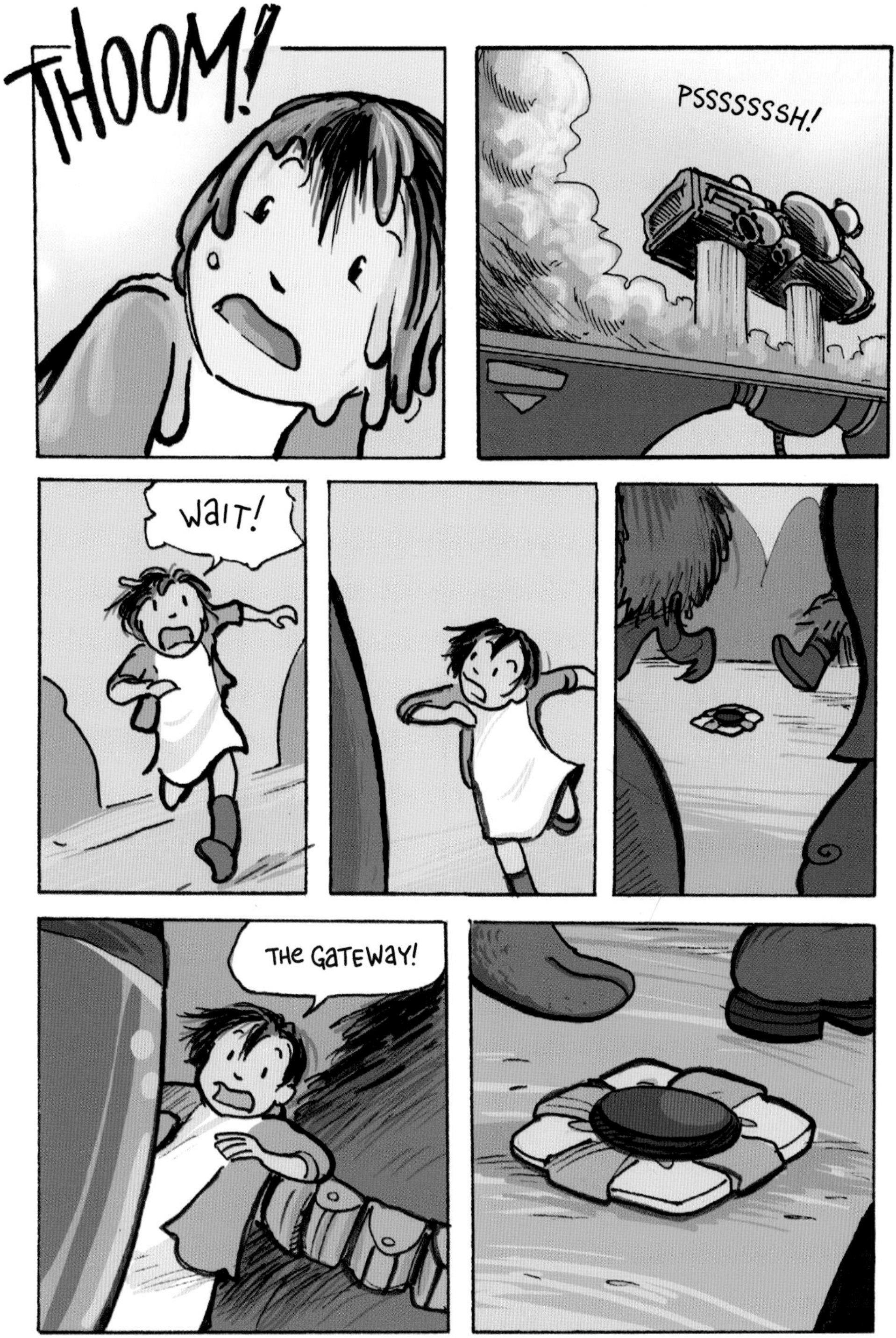
THOOM!
PSSSSSSSH!
WAIT!
THE GATEWAY!

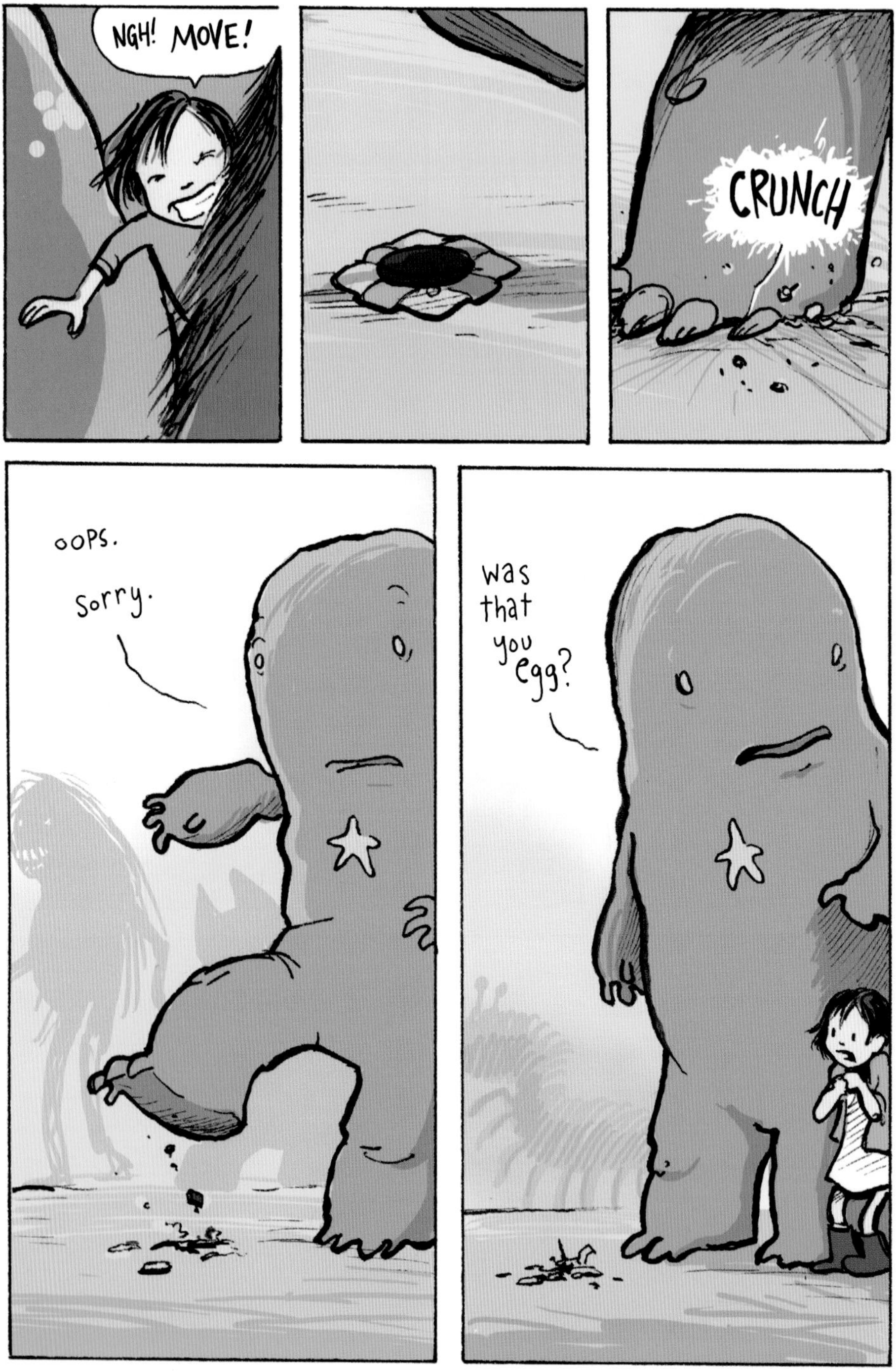
NGH! MOVE!
CRUNCH
oops.
sorry.
was that you egg?

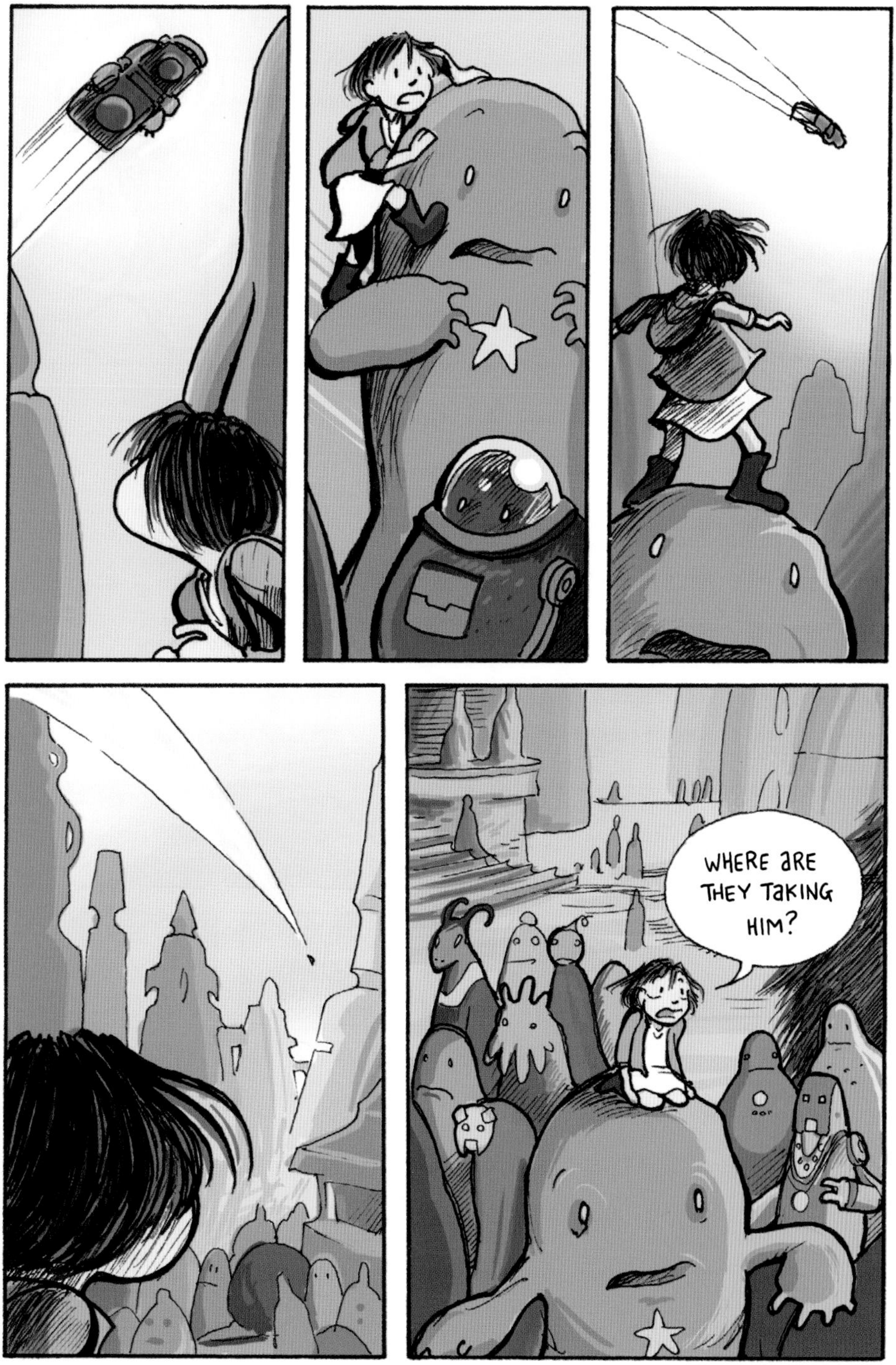
WHERE ARE THEY TAKING HIM?

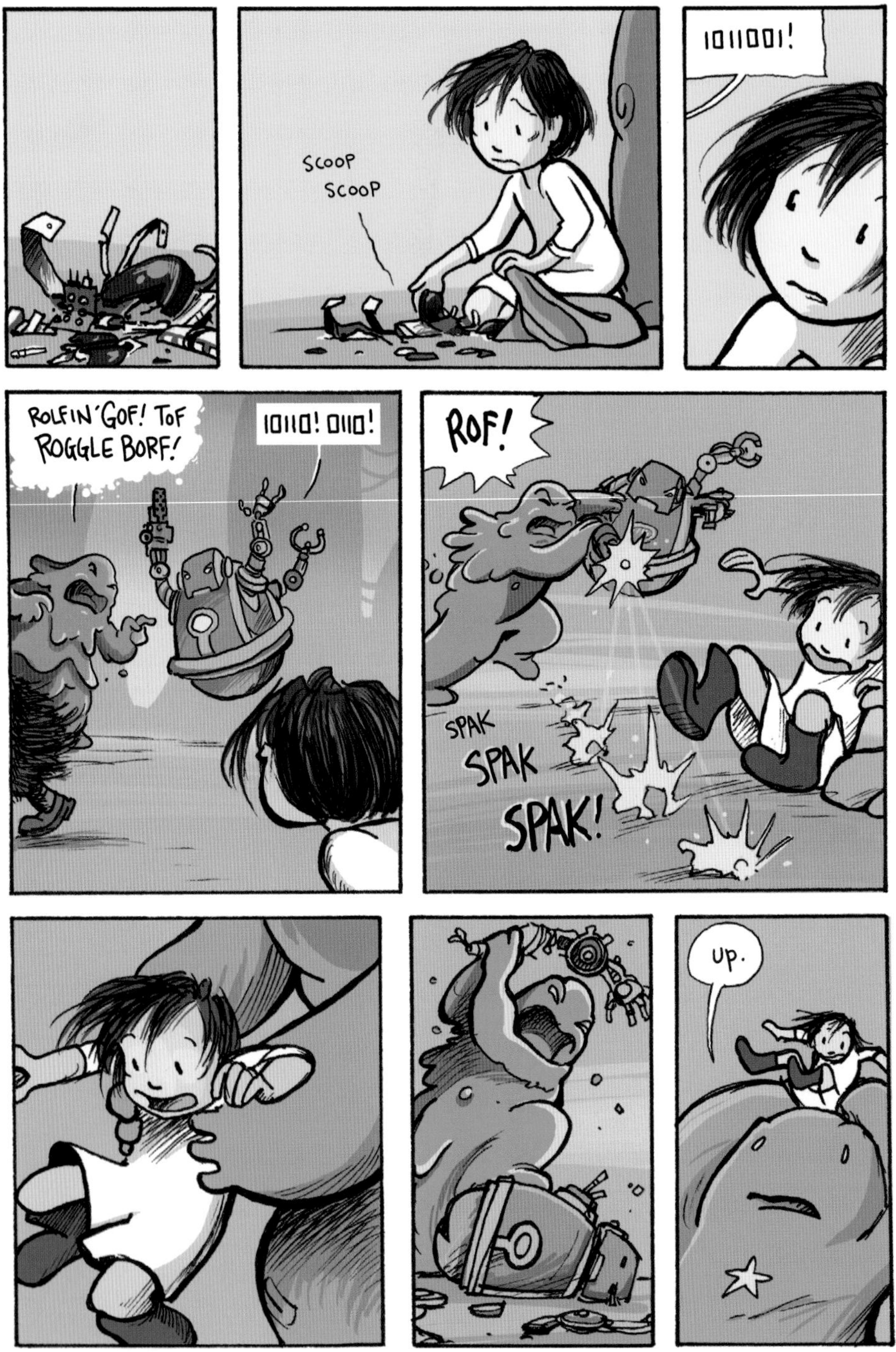
SCOOP
SCOOP
1011001!
ROLFIN' GOF! TOF ROGGLE BORF!
10110! 0110!
ROF!
SPAK
SPAK
SPAK!
Up.

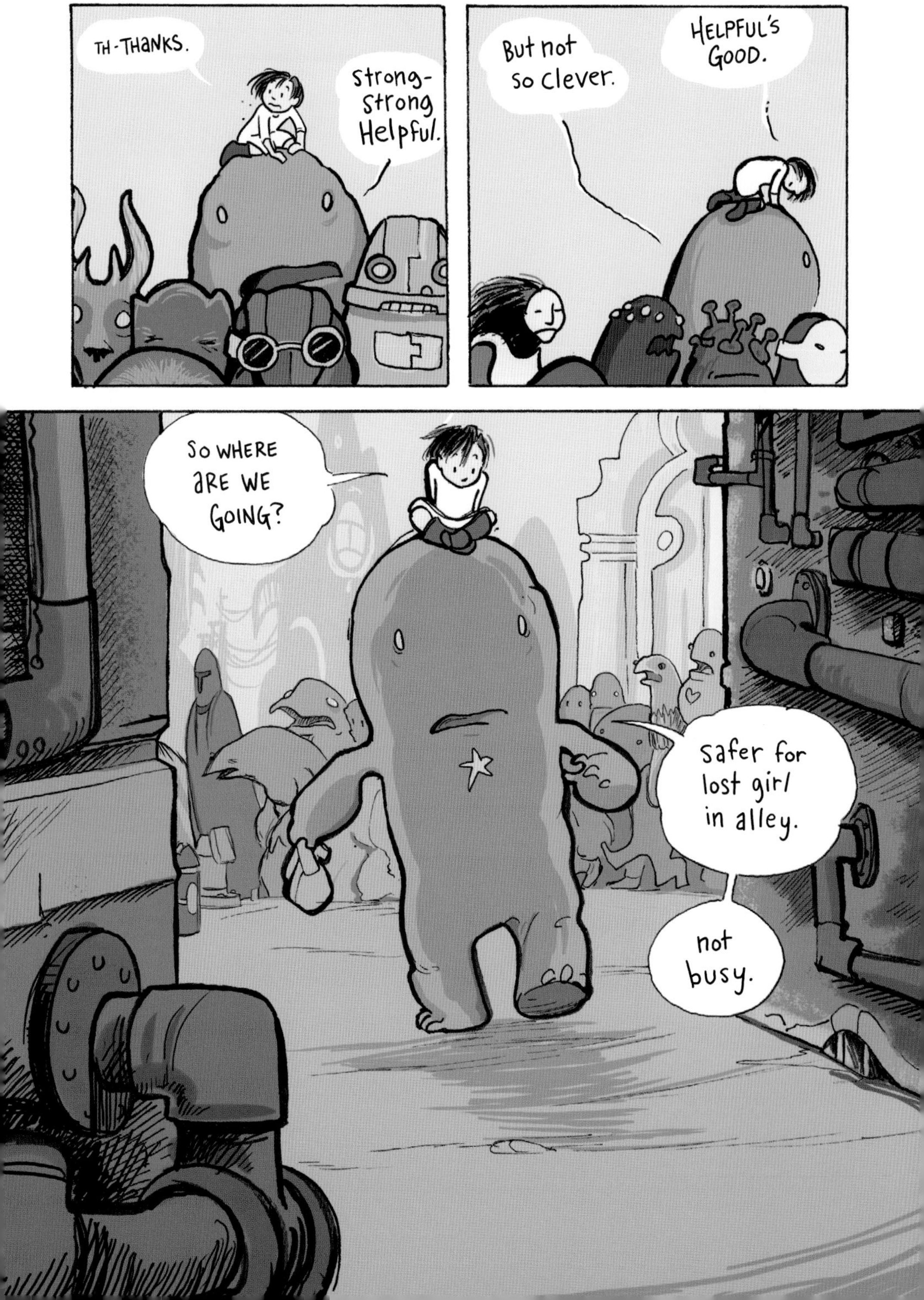
TH-THANKS.
strong-strong Helpful.
But not so clever.
HELPFUL'S GOOD.
SO WHERE ARE WE GOING?
safer for lost girl in alley.
not busy.

down for
you.

PIECES of
you egg.

RIGHT.

UM, STRONG-STRONG?
I'M LOOKING FOR MY
FRIEND WHO WAS
TAKEN AWAY.

I DON'T
THINK I
CAN FIND
HIM WITH-
OUT HELP.

So I WAS
KIND OF
WONDERING –

THERE YOU
aRE, **OAF!**

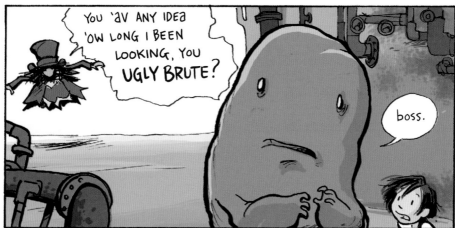

YOU 'av ANY IDEa
'OW LONG I BEEN
LOOKING, YOU
UGLY BRUTE?

boss.

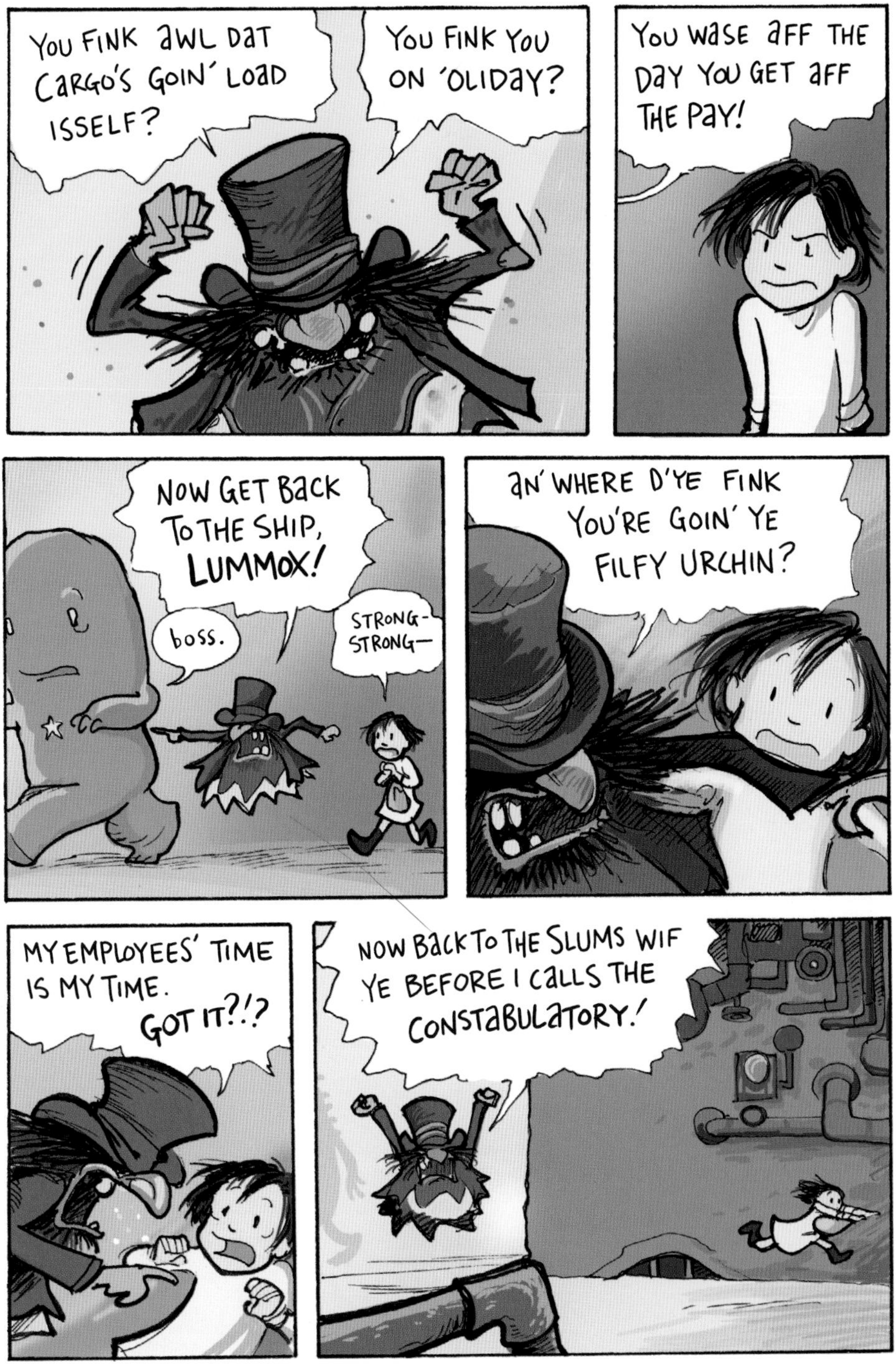

YOU FINK AWL DAT CARGO'S GOIN' LOAD ISSELF?
YOU FINK YOU ON 'OLIDAY?
YOU WASE AFF THE DAY YOU GET AFF THE PAY!
NOW GET BACK TO THE SHIP, LUMMOX!
boss.
STRONG-STRONG—
AN' WHERE D'YE FINK YOU'RE GOIN' YE FILFY URCHIN?
MY EMPLOYEES' TIME IS MY TIME.
GOT IT?!?
NOW BACK TO THE SLUMS WIF YE BEFORE I CALLS THE CONSTABULATORY!

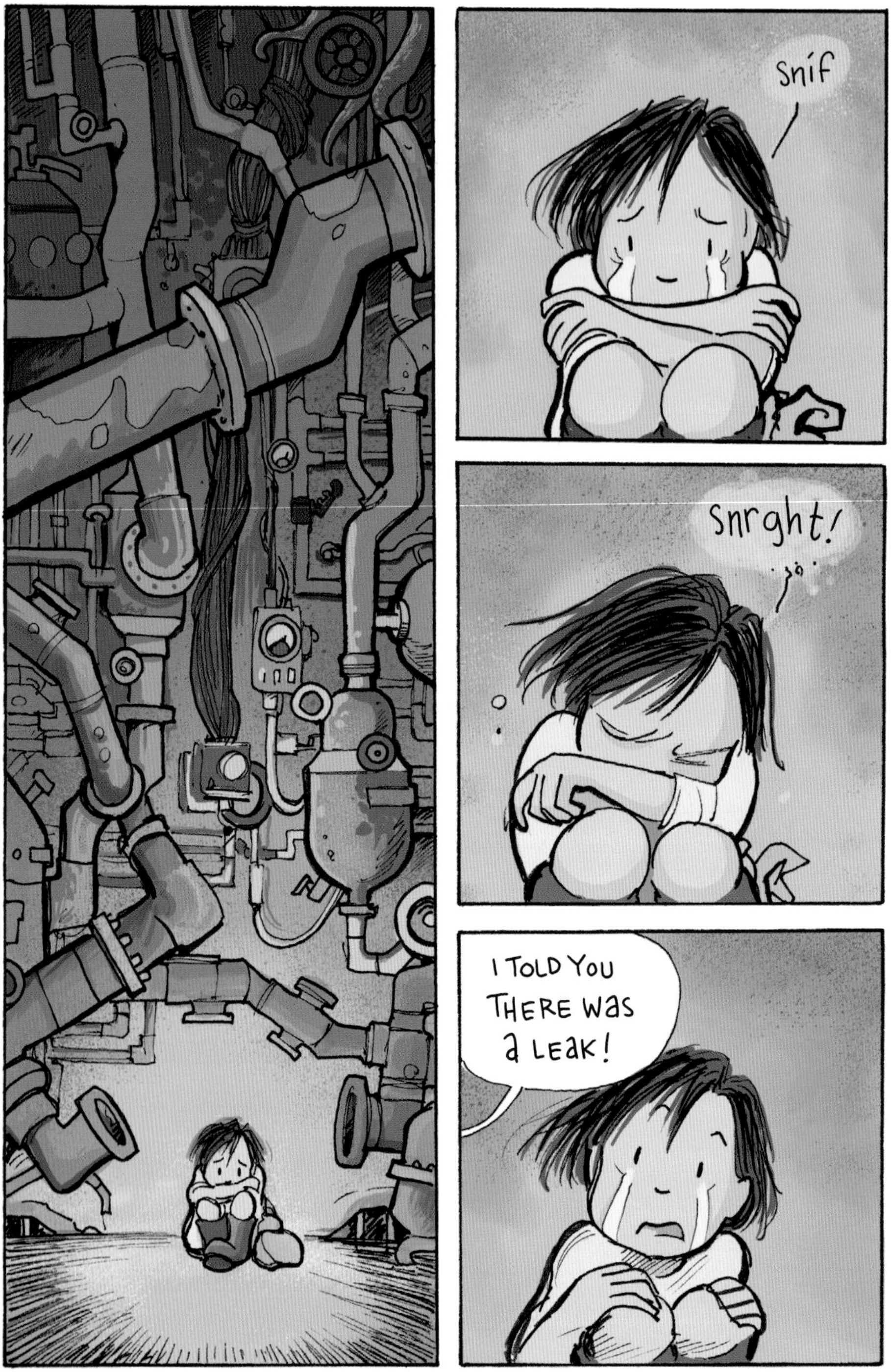
Snif
Snrght!
I TOLD YOU THERE WAS A LEAK!

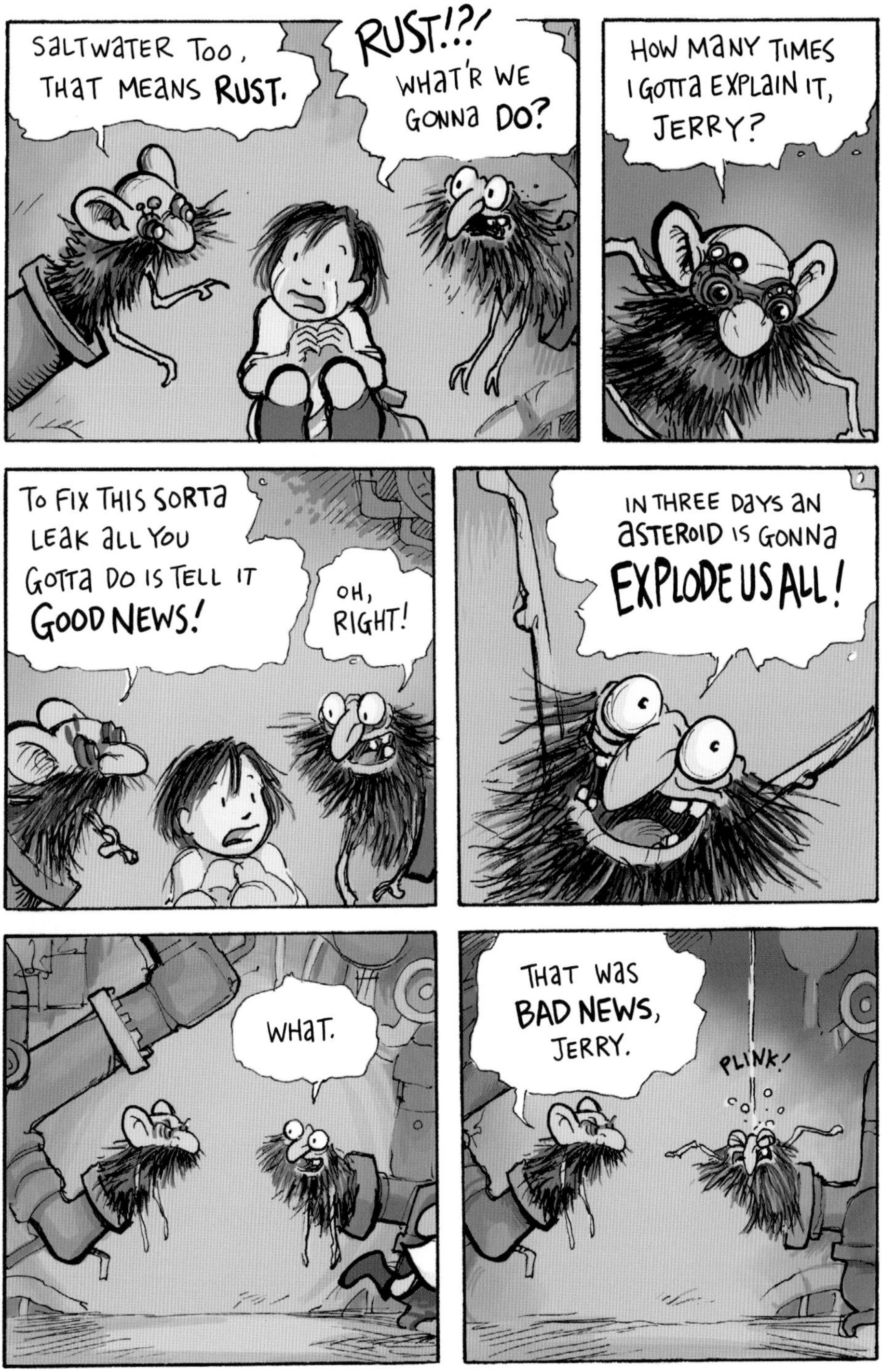
SALTWATER TOO, THAT MEANS RUST.
RUST!?!
WHAT'R WE GONNA DO?
HOW MANY TIMES I GOTTA EXPLAIN IT, JERRY?
TO FIX THIS SORTA LEAK ALL YOU GOTTA DO IS TELL IT GOOD NEWS!
OH, RIGHT!
IN THREE DAYS AN ASTEROID IS GONNA EXPLODE US ALL!
WHAT.
THAT WAS BAD NEWS, JERRY.
PLINK!

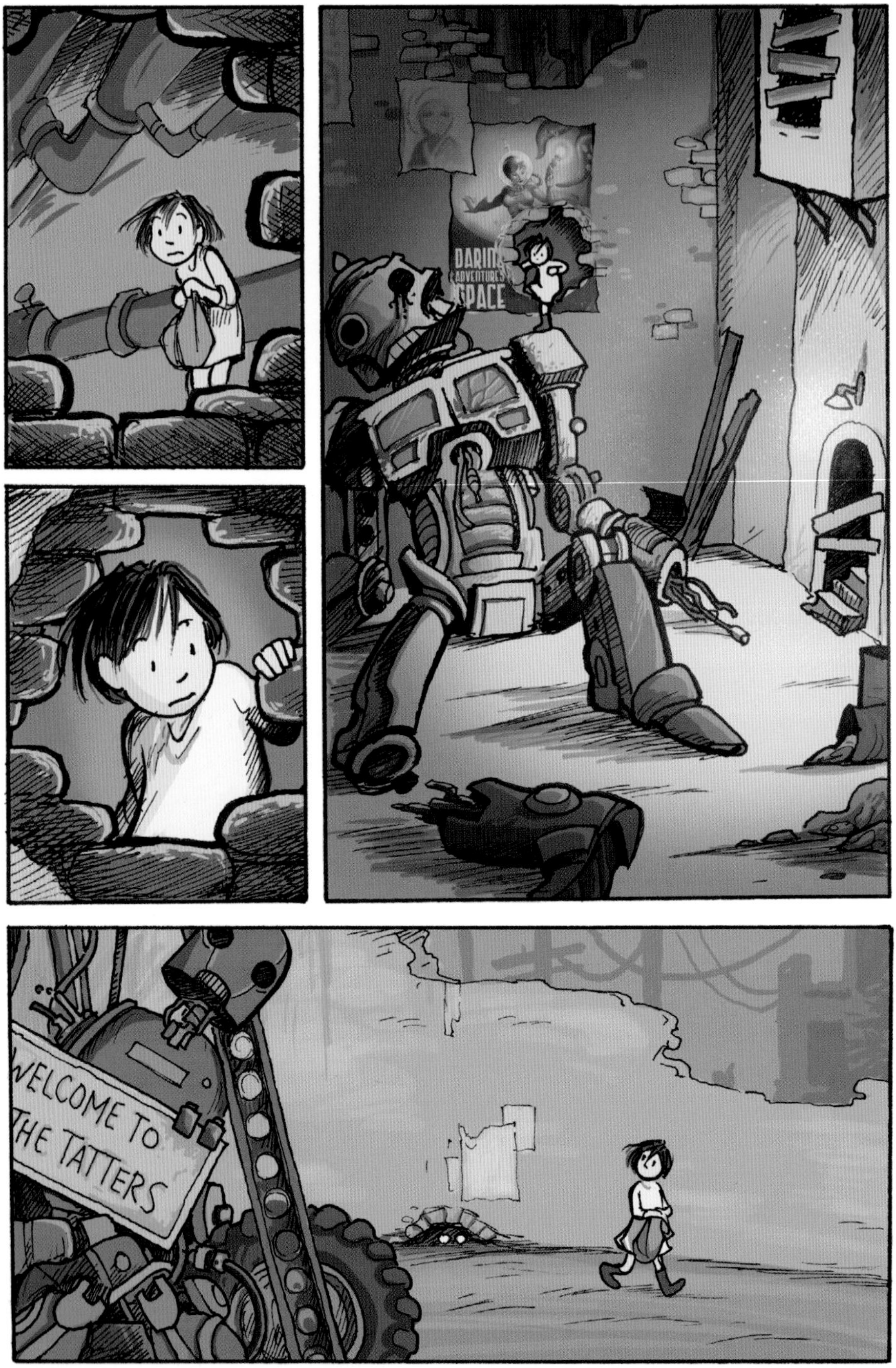
DARIN
ADVENTURES
SPACE
WELCOME TO
THE TATTERS

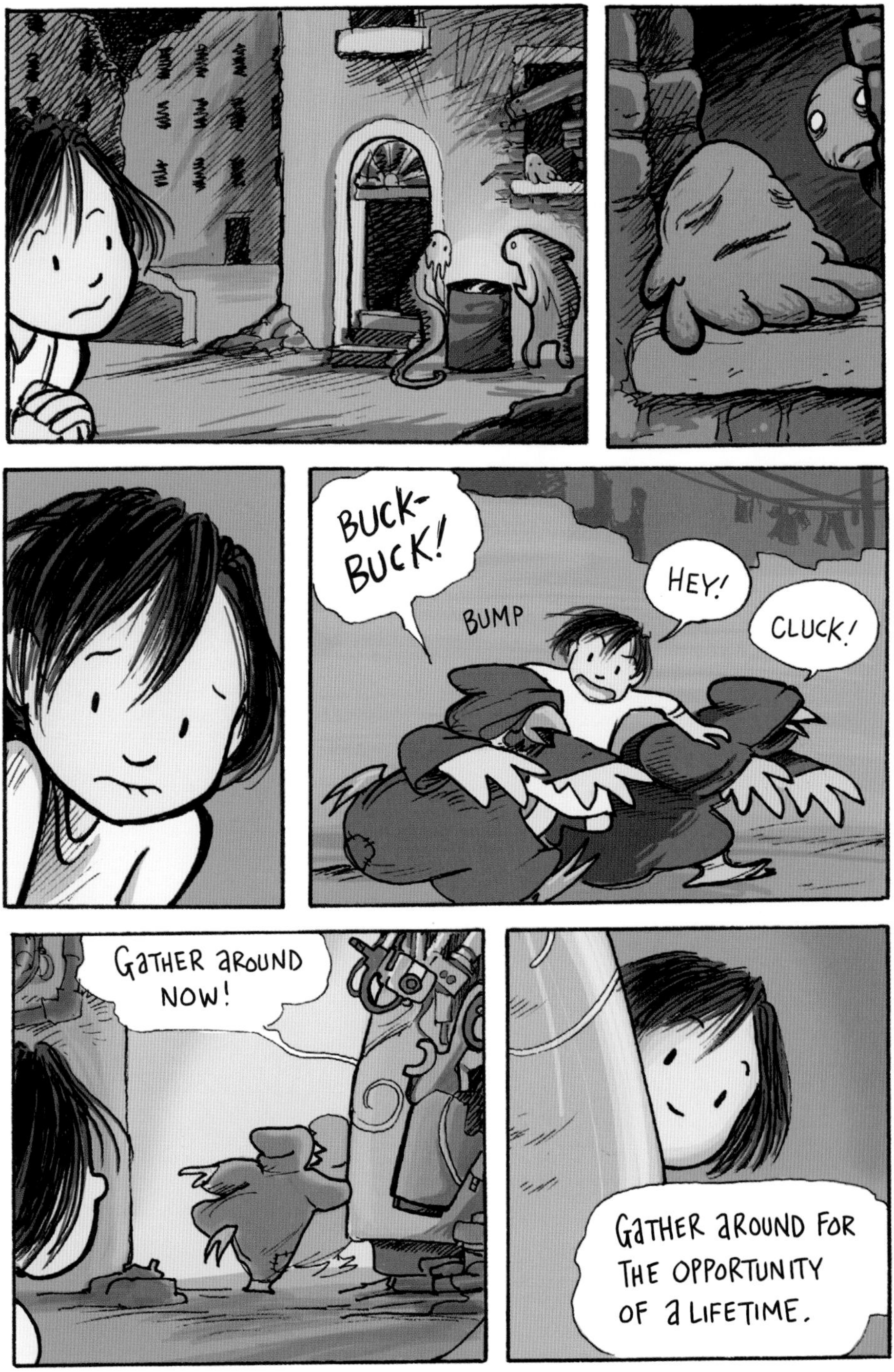
BUCK-BUCK!
BUMP
HEY!
CLUCK!
Gather around now!
Gather around for the opportunity of a lifetime.

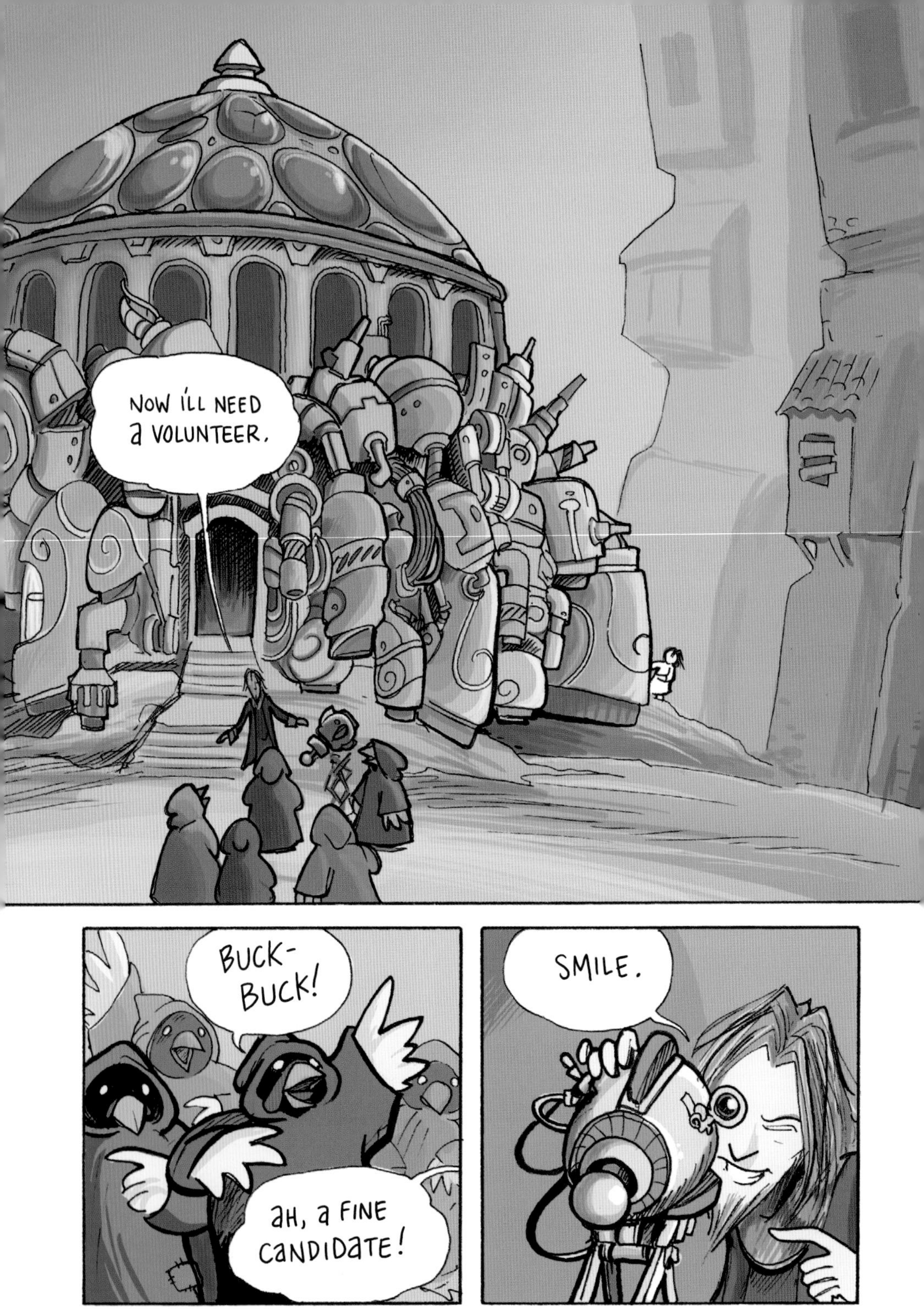
NOW I'LL NEED A VOLUNTEER.
BUCK-BUCK!
AH, A FINE CANDIDATE!
SMILE.

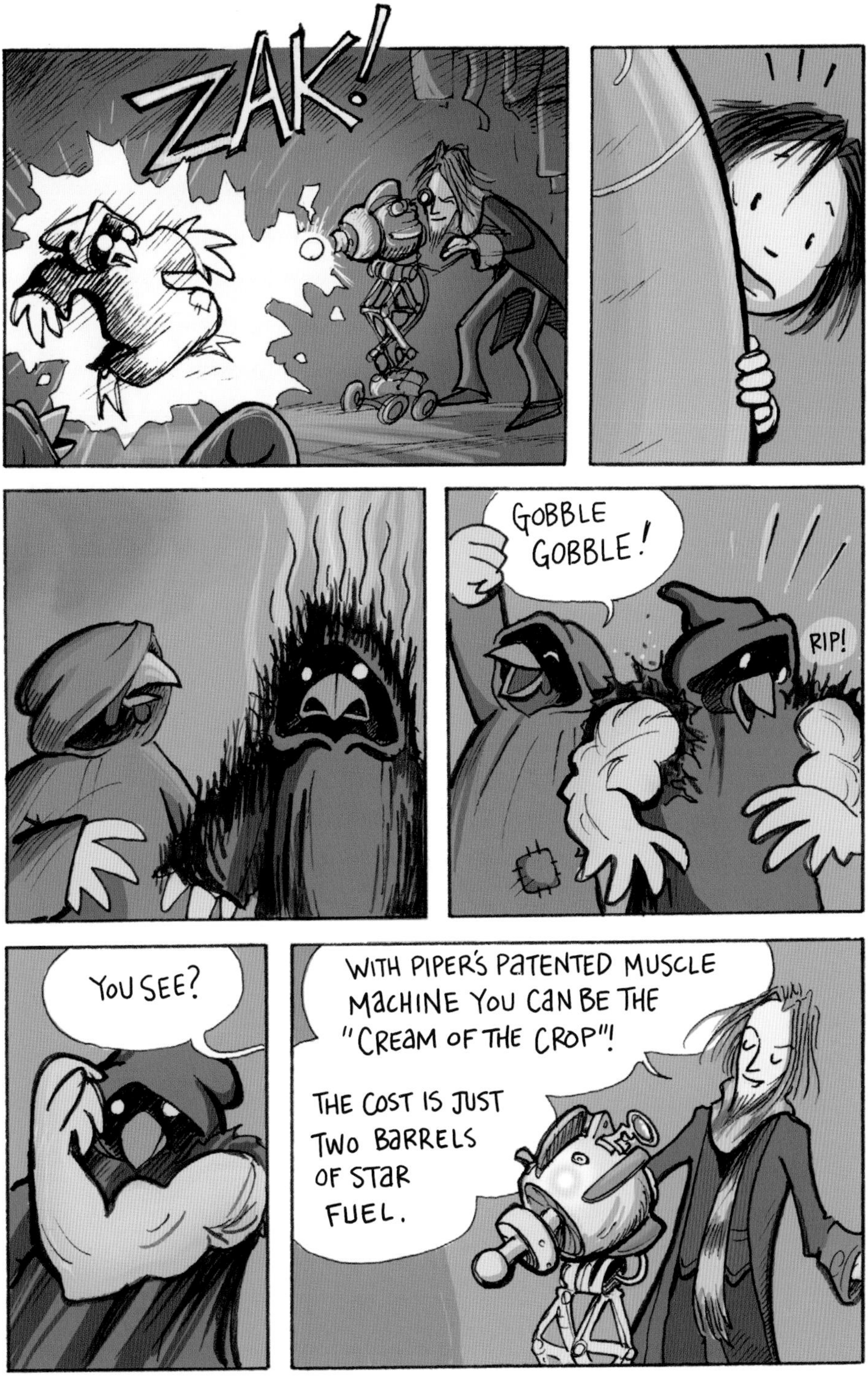
ZAK!
GOBBLE GOBBLE!
RIP!
YOU SEE?
WITH PIPER'S PATENTED MUSCLE MACHINE YOU CAN BE THE "CREAM OF THE CROP"!
THE COST IS JUST TWO BARRELS OF STAR FUEL.

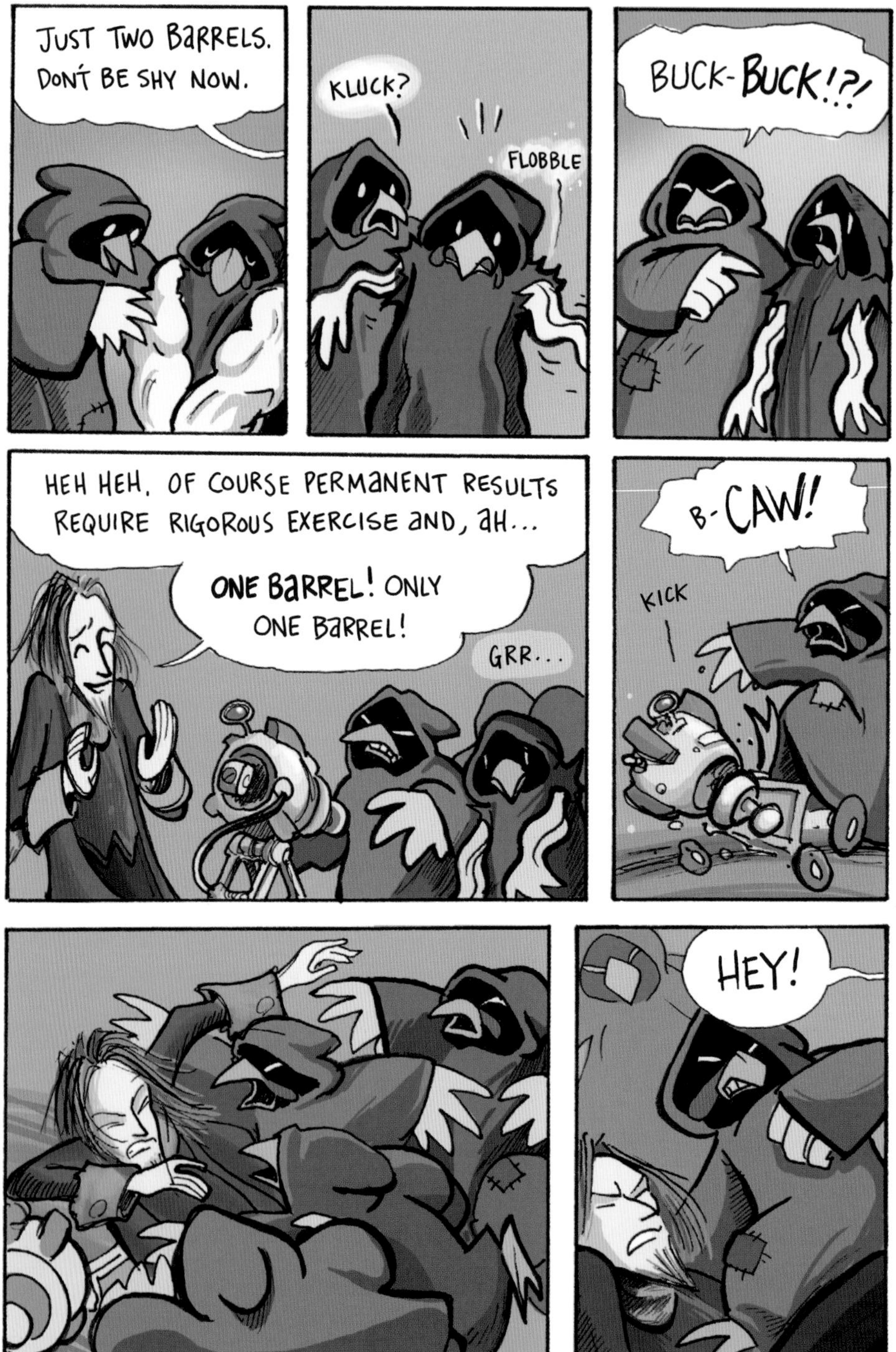
JUST TWO BARRELS. DON'T BE SHY NOW.
KLUCK?
FLOBBLE
BUCK-BUCK!?!
HEH HEH. OF COURSE PERMANENT RESULTS REQUIRE RIGOROUS EXERCISE AND, AH...
ONE BARREL! ONLY ONE BARREL!
GRR...
B-CAW!
KICK
HEY!

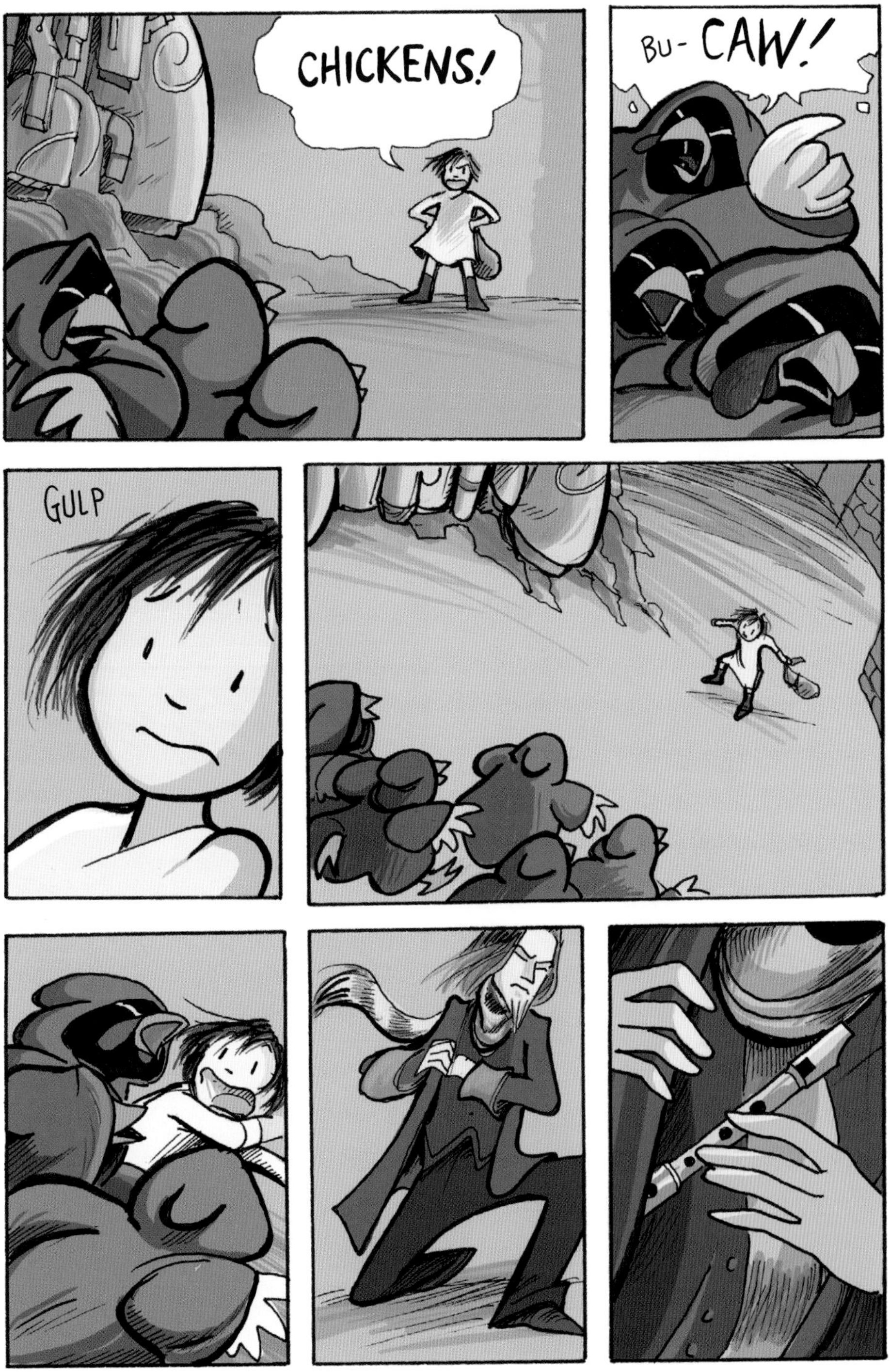
CHICKENS!
BU- CAW!
GULP

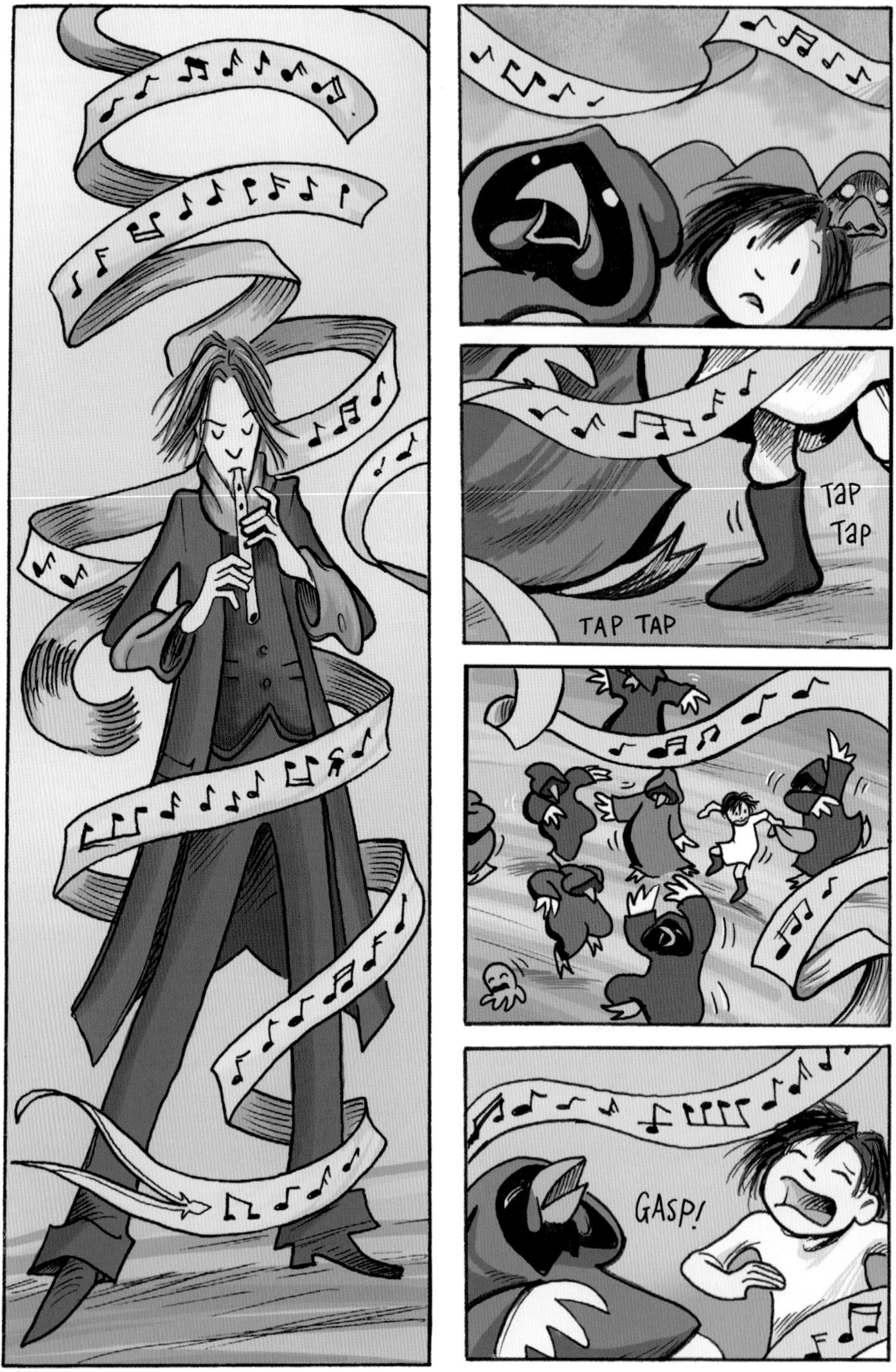
Tap
Tap
TAP TAP
GASP!

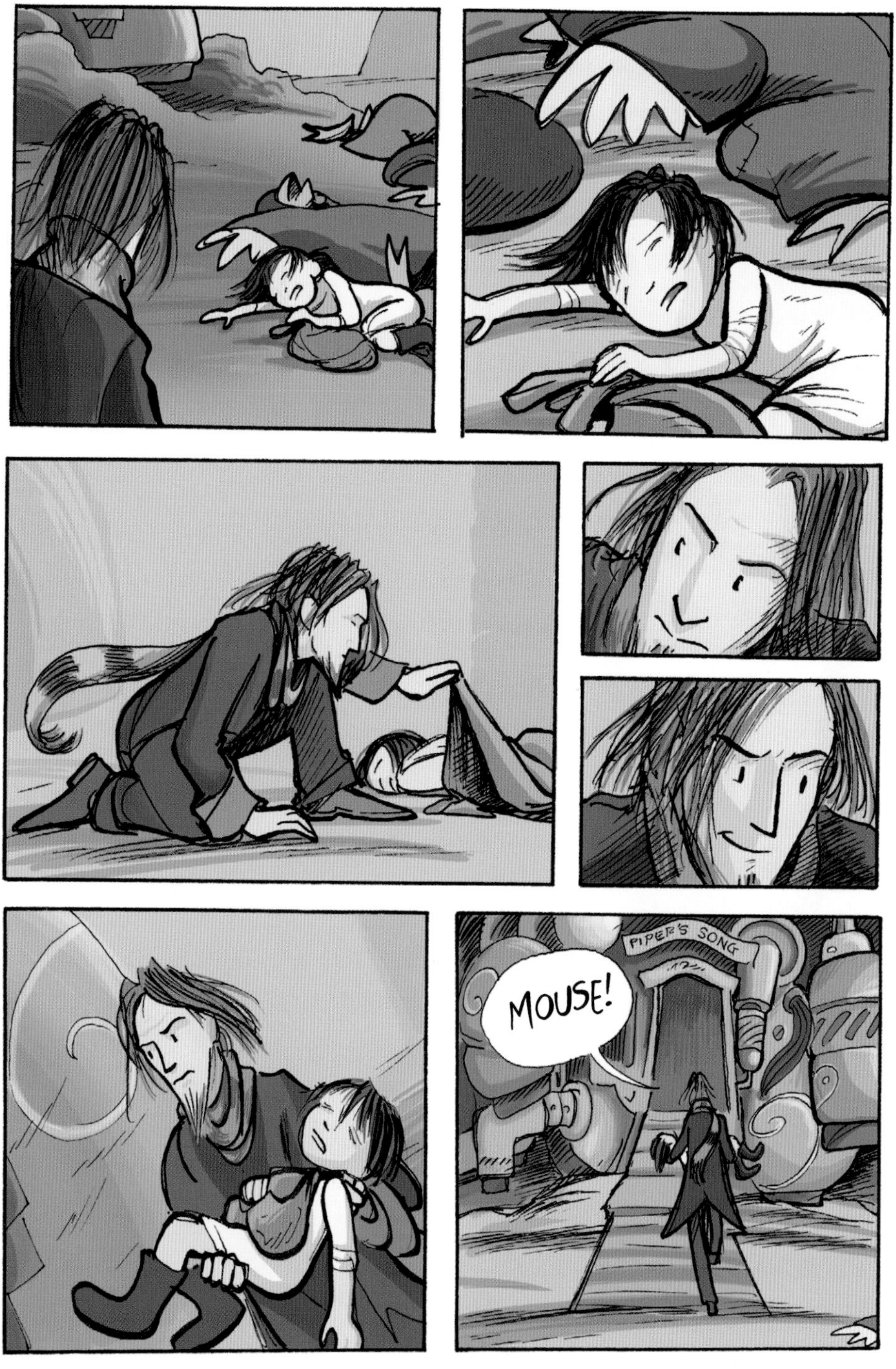
PIPER'S SONG
MOUSE!

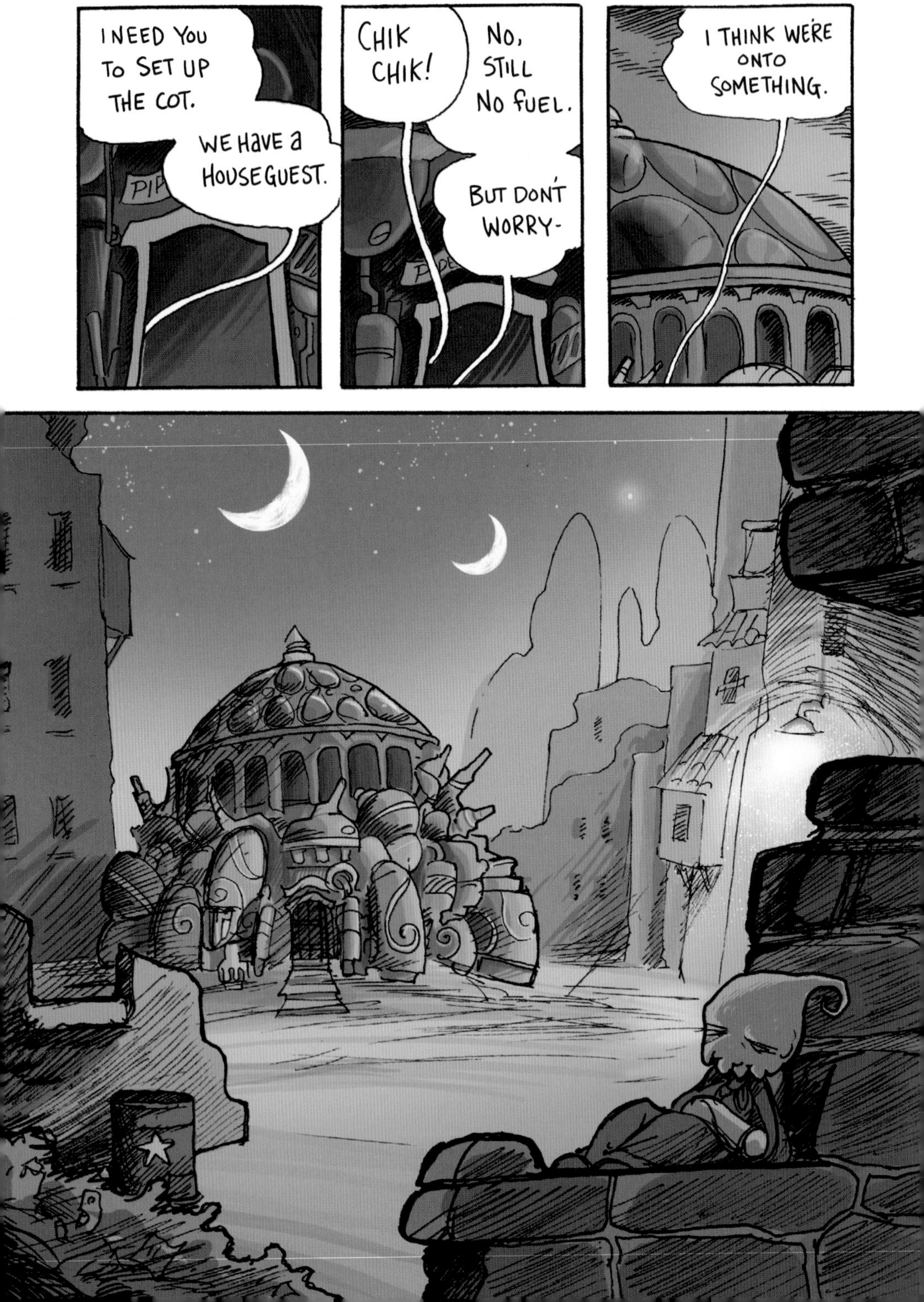
I NEED YOU TO SET UP THE COT.
WE HAVE A HOUSEGUEST.
CHIK CHIK!
NO, STILL NO FUEL.
BUT DON'T WORRY-
I THINK WE'RE ONTO SOMETHING.

chapter
three

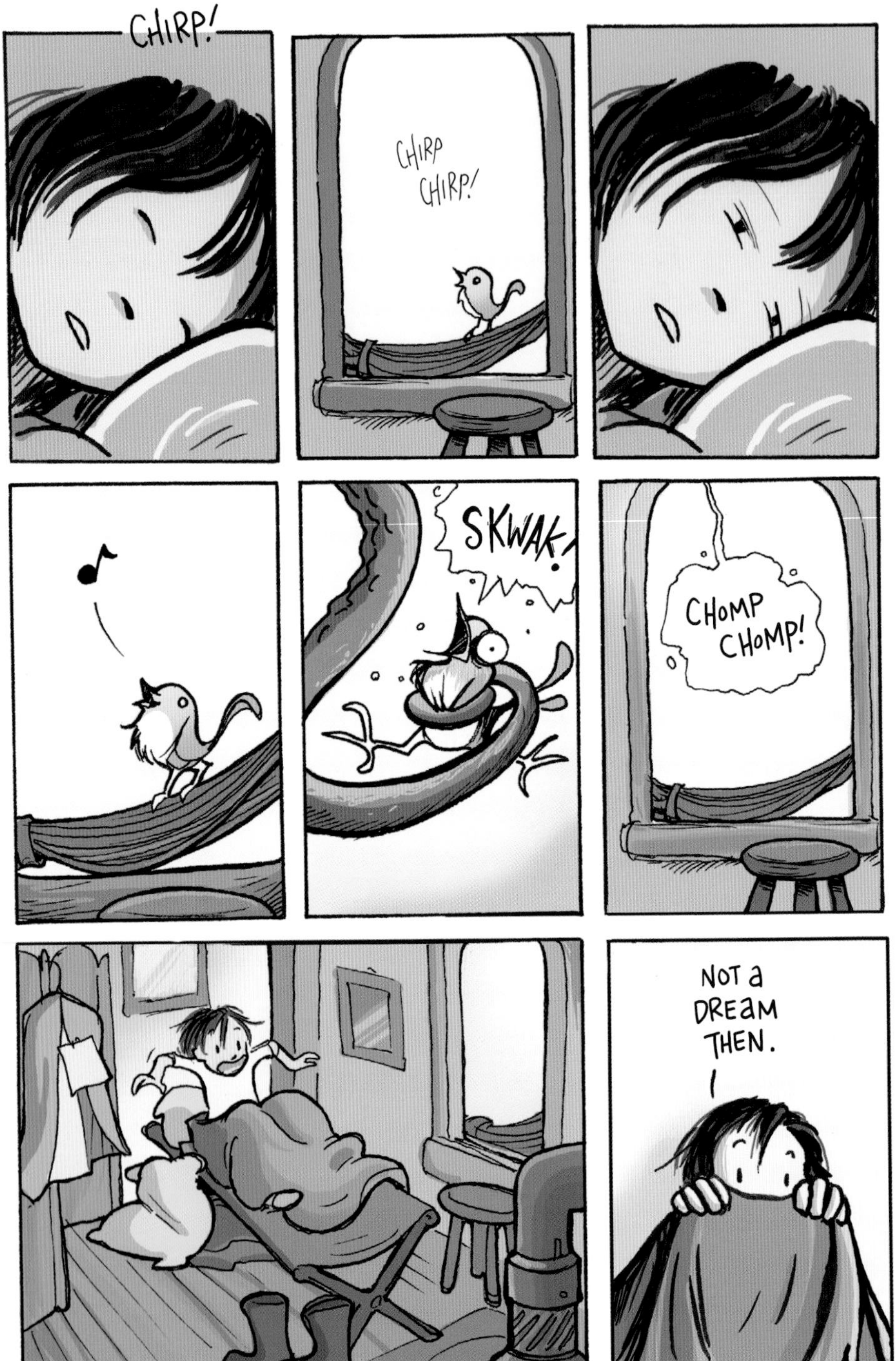
CHIRP!
CHIRP
CHIRP!
SKWAK!
CHOMP
CHOMP!
NOT a
DREAM
THEN.

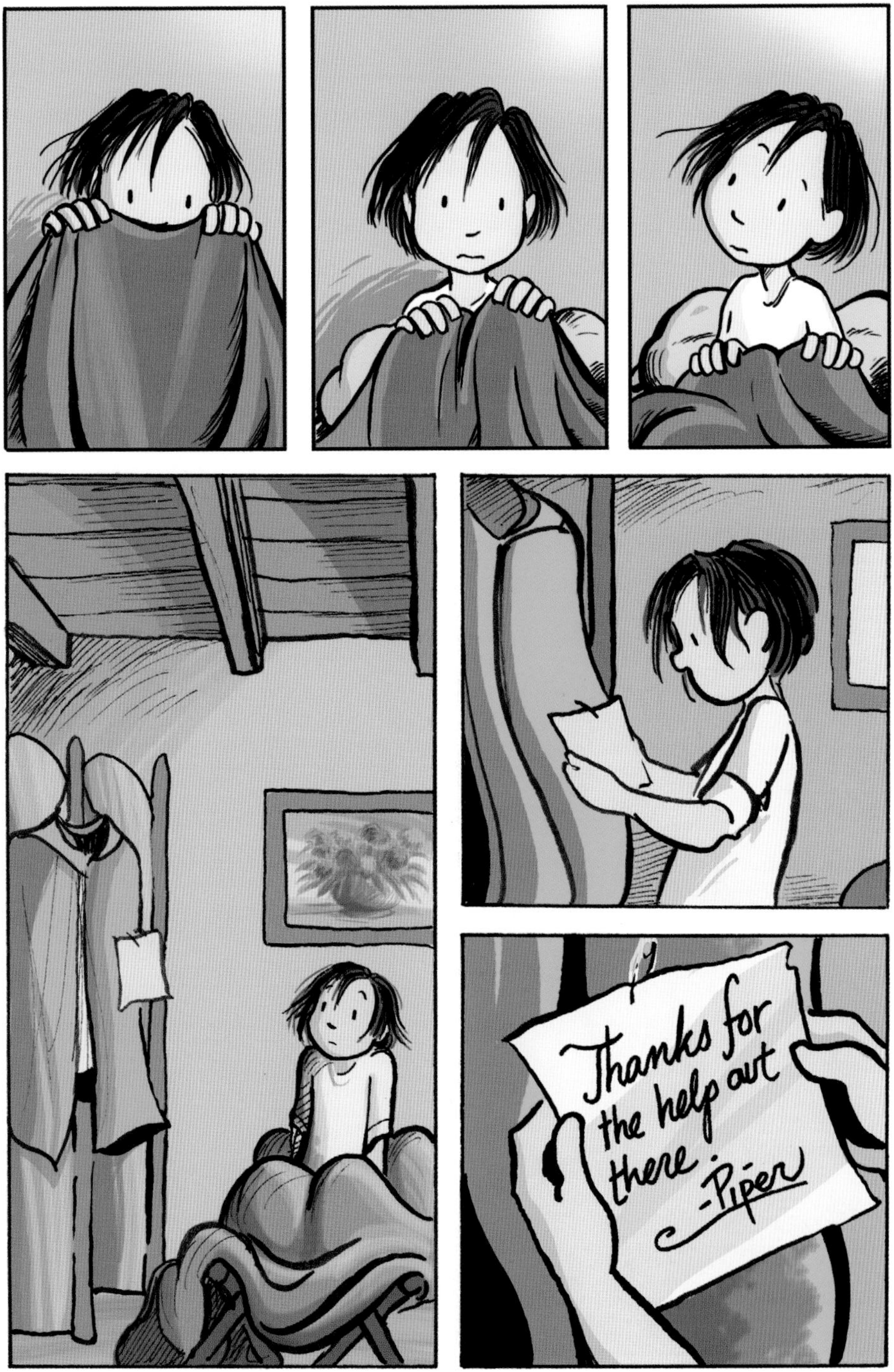
Thanks for the help out there. -Piper

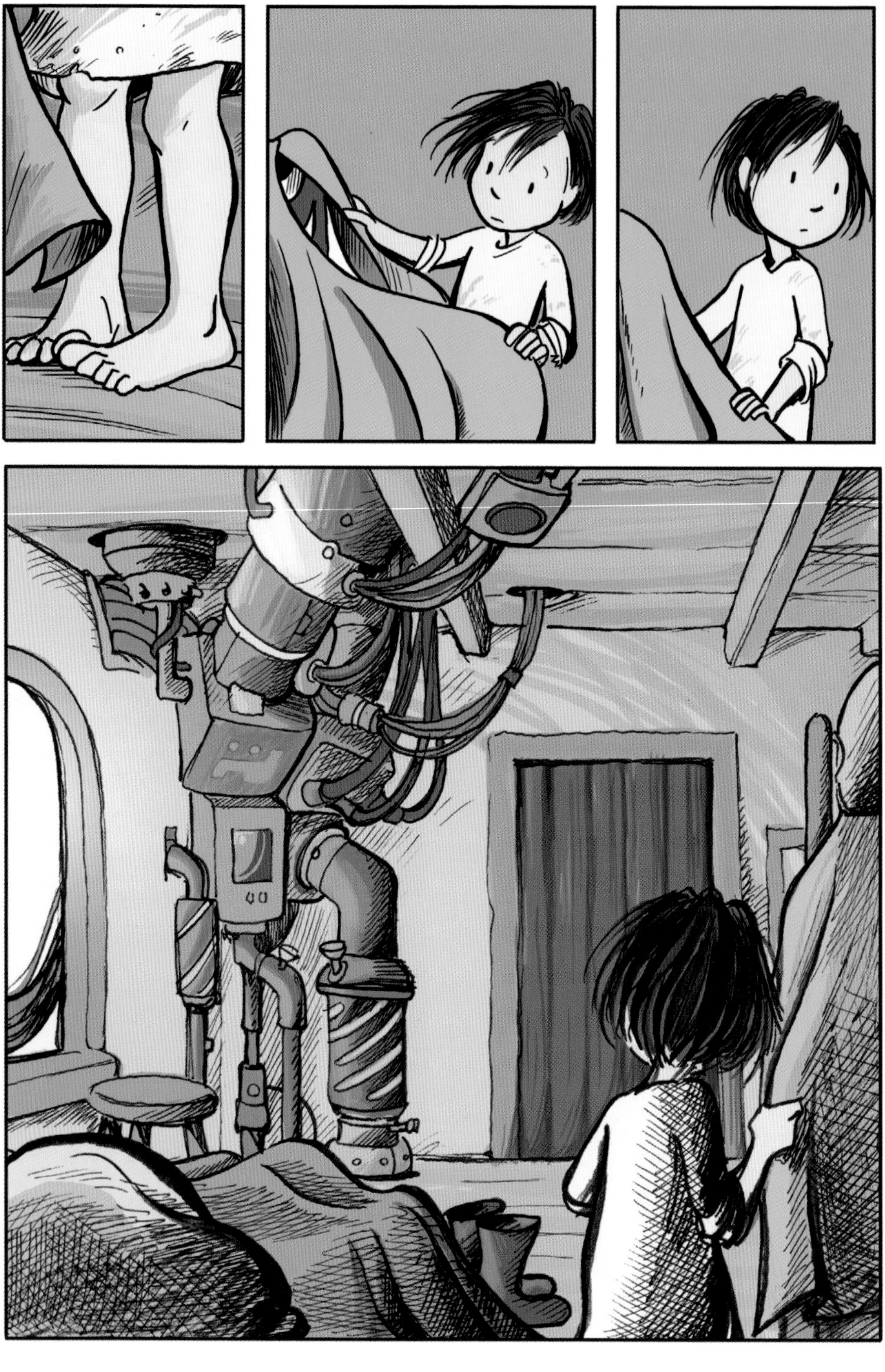

Sniff
floof
ha!

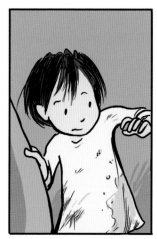

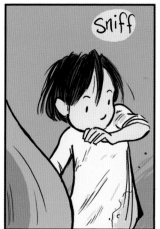

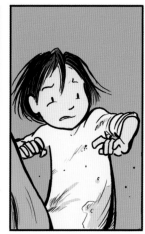

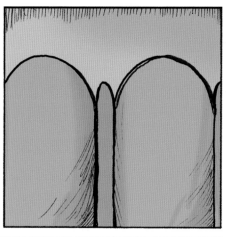

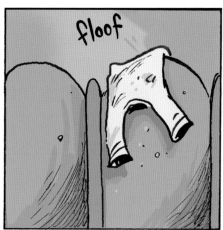

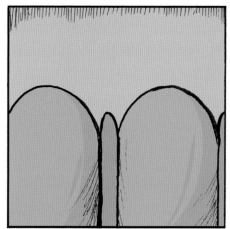

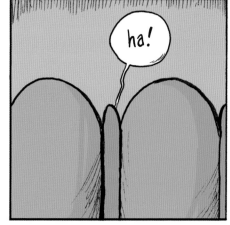

SKRITCHa
SKRITCH

SKRTCH

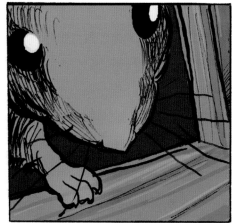

48

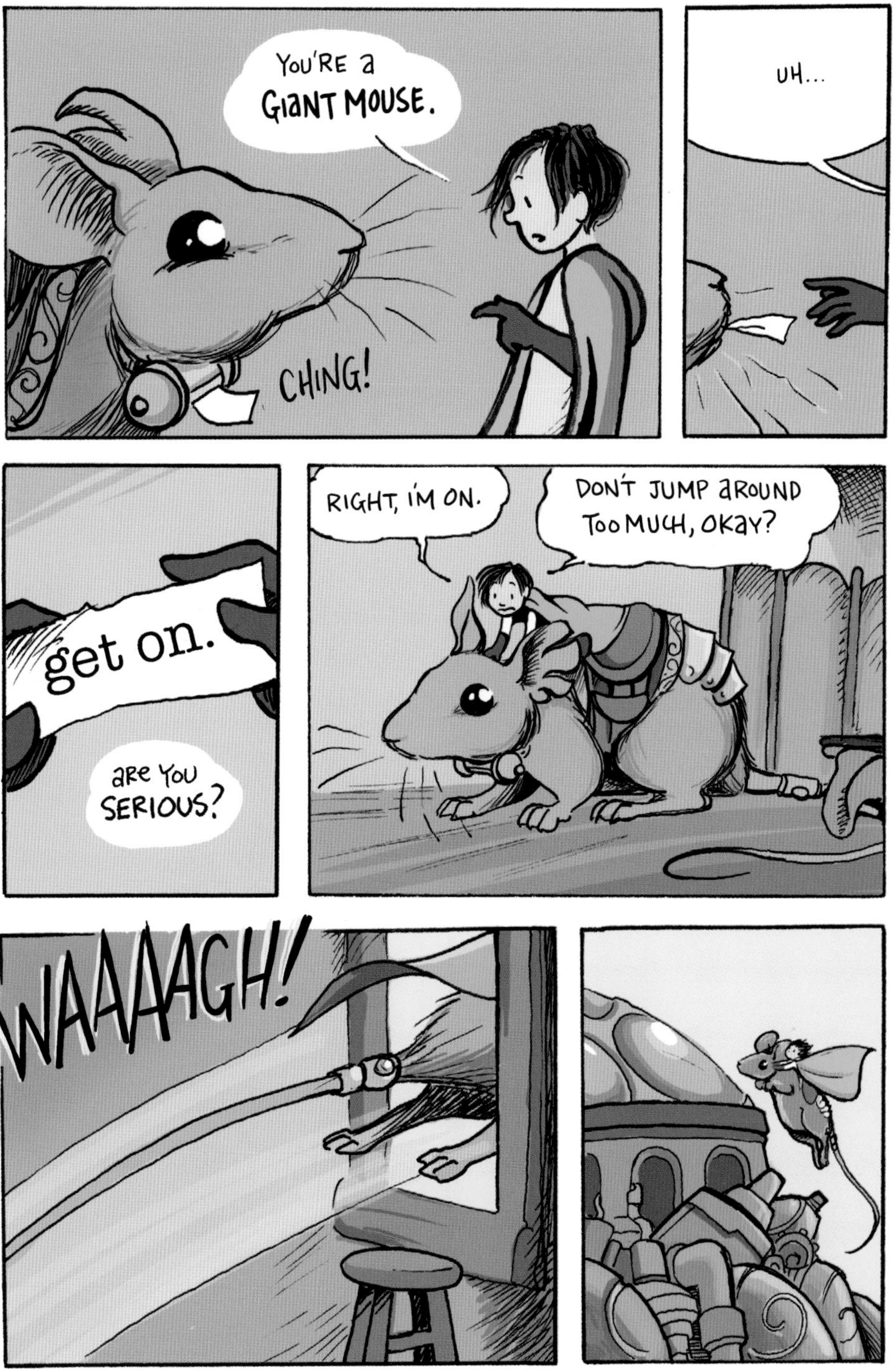

YOU'RE A GIANT MOUSE.
CHING!
UH...
get on.
are YOU SERIOUS?
RIGHT, I'M ON.
DON'T JUMP AROUND TOO MUCH, OKAY?
WAAAAGH!

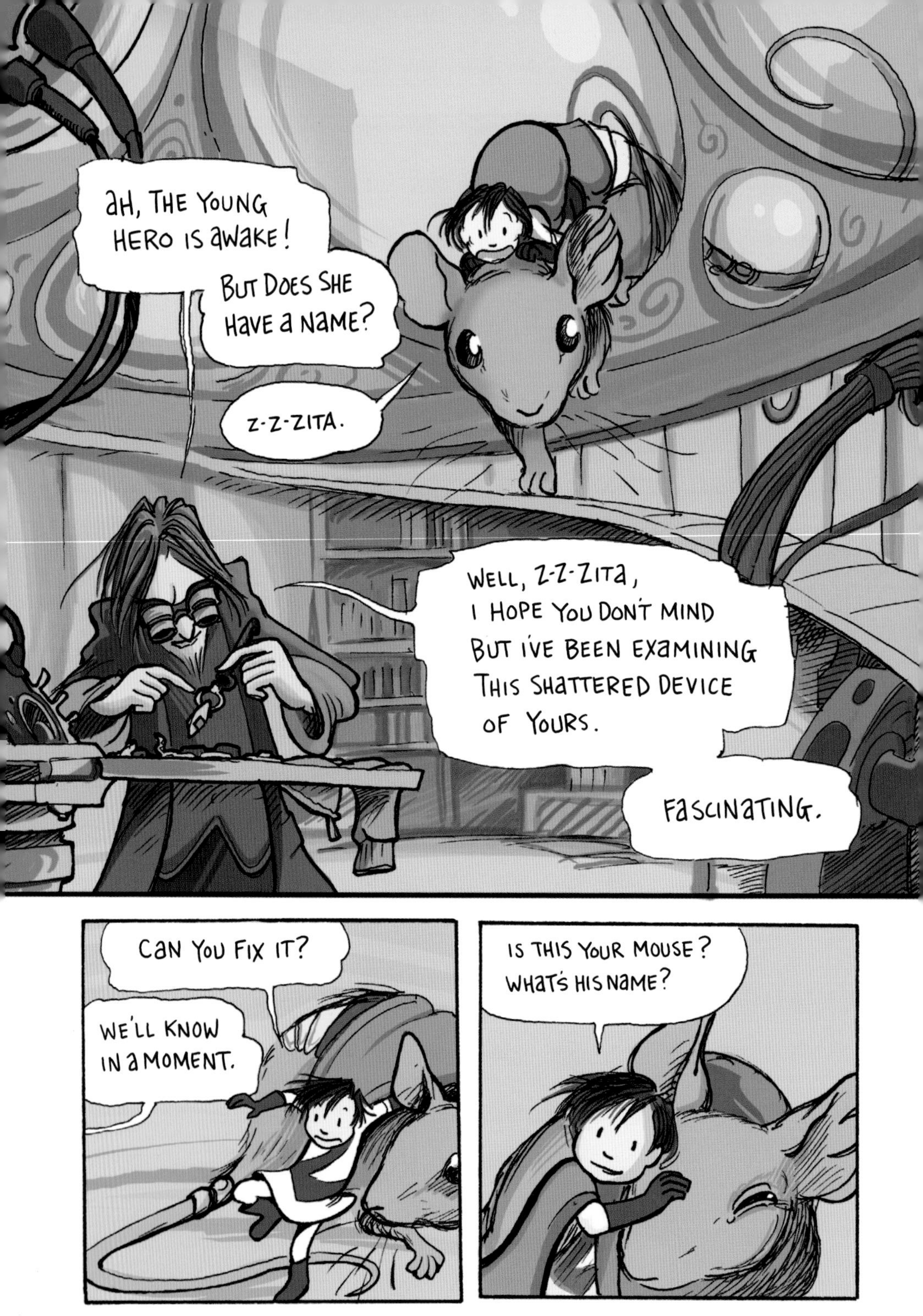
AH, THE YOUNG HERO IS AWAKE!
BUT DOES SHE HAVE A NAME?
Z-Z-ZITA.
WELL, Z-Z-ZITA, I HOPE YOU DON'T MIND BUT I'VE BEEN EXAMINING THIS SHATTERED DEVICE OF YOURS.
FASCINATING.
CAN YOU FIX IT?
WE'LL KNOW IN A MOMENT.
IS THIS YOUR MOUSE? WHAT'S HIS NAME?

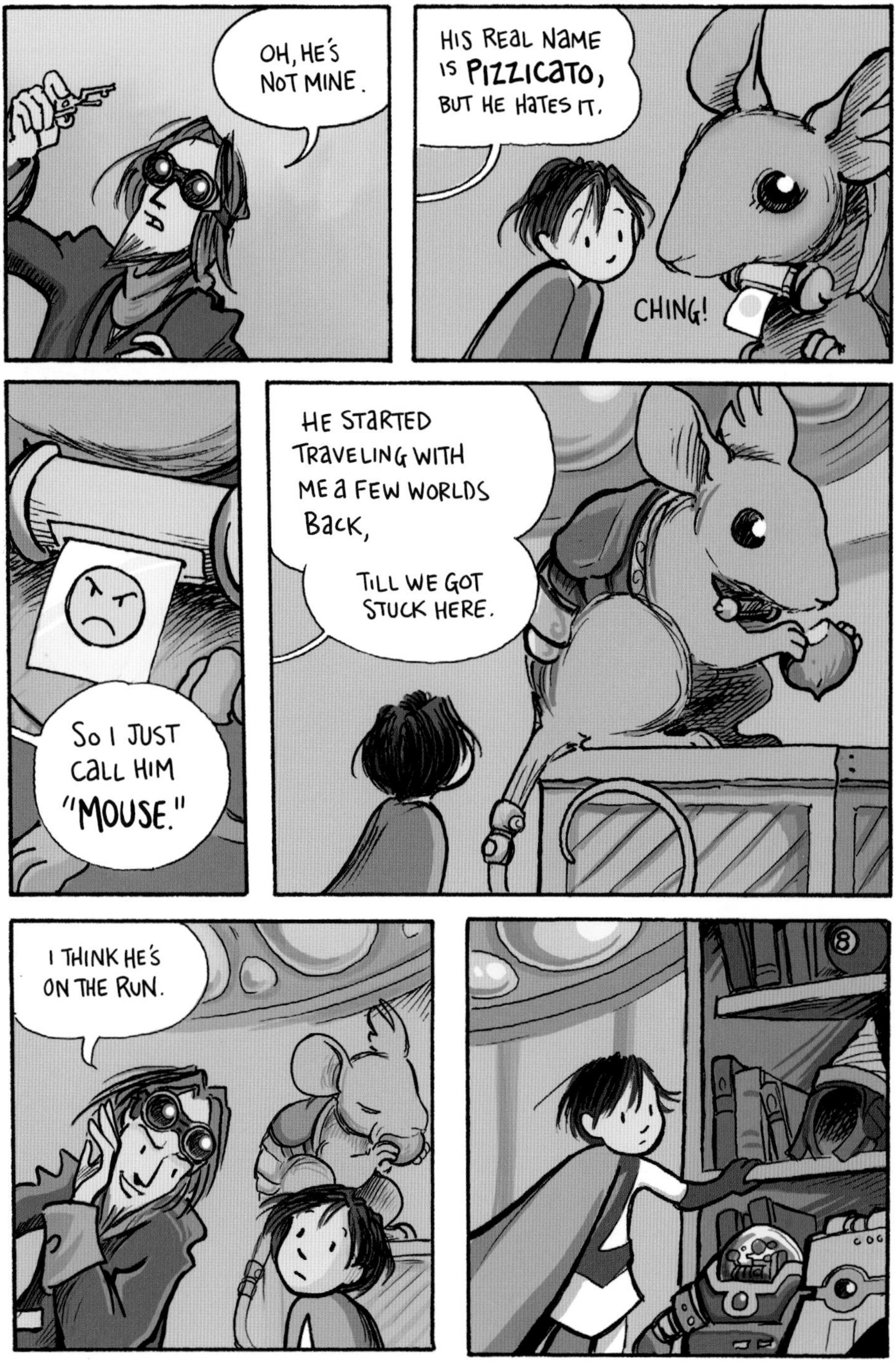
OH, HE'S NOT MINE.
HIS REAL NAME IS PIZZICATO, BUT HE HATES IT.
CHING!
So I JUST CALL HIM "MOUSE."
HE STARTED TRAVELING WITH ME A FEW WORLDS BACK,
TILL WE GOT STUCK HERE.
I THINK HE'S ON THE RUN.

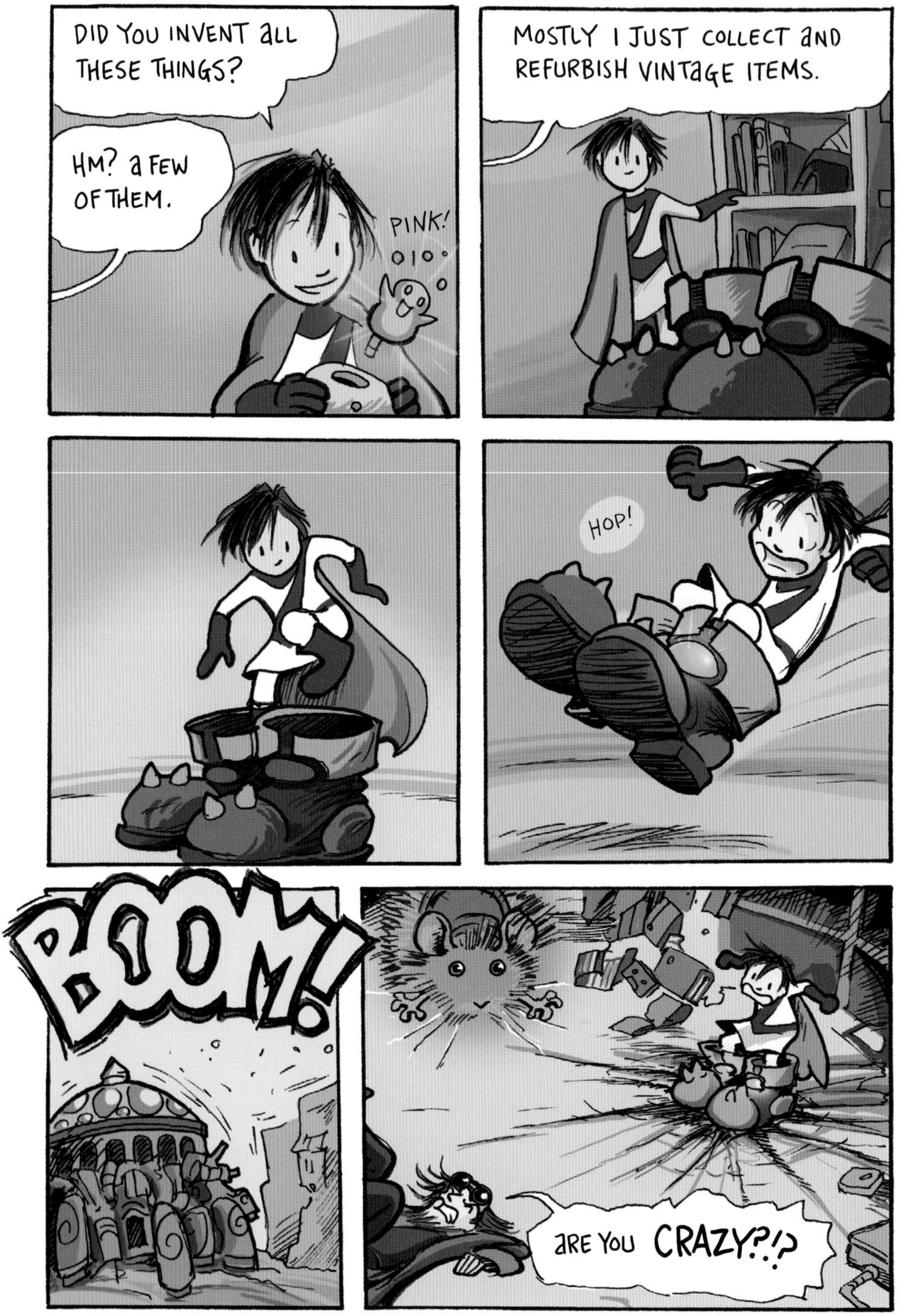
DID YOU INVENT ALL THESE THINGS?
HM? A FEW OF THEM.
PINK!
MOSTLY I JUST COLLECT AND REFURBISH VINTAGE ITEMS.
HOP!
BOOM!
ARE YOU CRAZY?!?

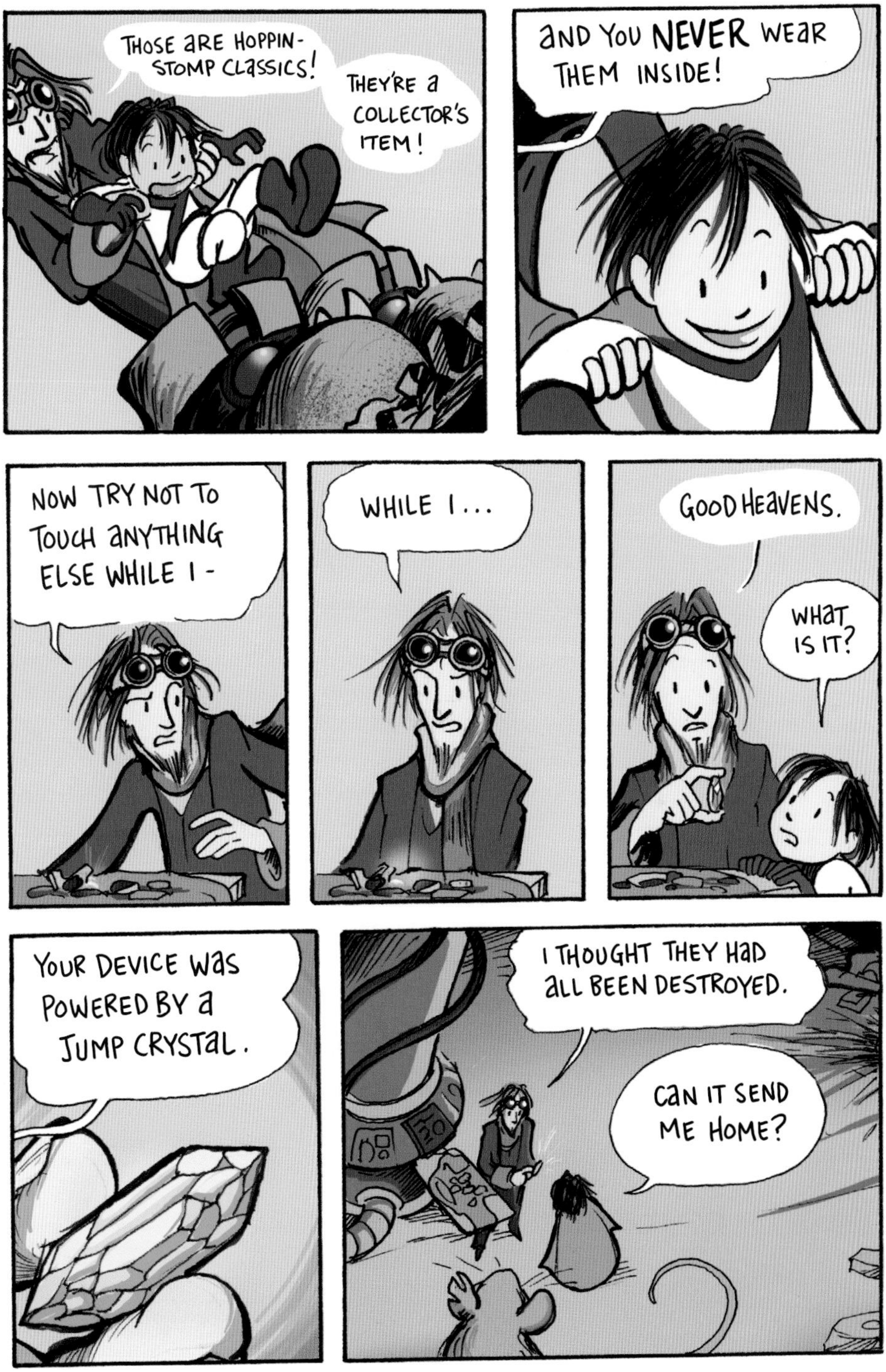
THOSE ARE HOPPIN-STOMP CLASSICS!
THEY'RE A COLLECTOR'S ITEM!
AND YOU NEVER WEAR THEM INSIDE!
NOW TRY NOT TO TOUCH ANYTHING ELSE WHILE I -
WHILE I...
GOOD HEAVENS.
WHAT IS IT?
YOUR DEVICE WAS POWERED BY A JUMP CRYSTAL.
I THOUGHT THEY HAD ALL BEEN DESTROYED.
CAN IT SEND ME HOME?

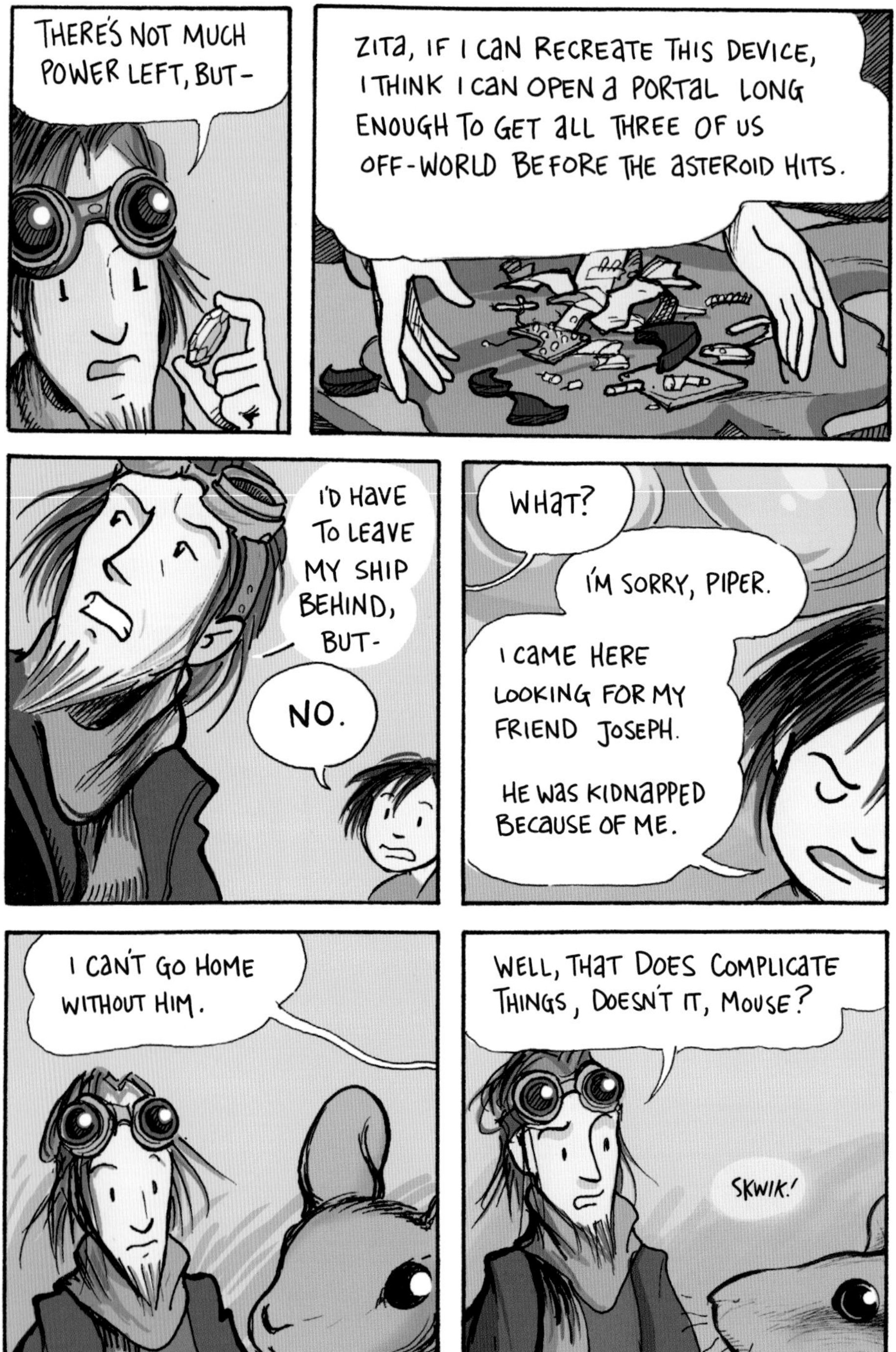
THERE'S NOT MUCH POWER LEFT, BUT-
ZITA, IF I CAN RECREATE THIS DEVICE, I THINK I CAN OPEN A PORTAL LONG ENOUGH TO GET ALL THREE OF US OFF-WORLD BEFORE THE ASTEROID HITS.
I'D HAVE TO LEAVE MY SHIP BEHIND, BUT-
NO.
WHAT?
I'M SORRY, PIPER.
I CAME HERE LOOKING FOR MY FRIEND JOSEPH.
HE WAS KIDNAPPED BECAUSE OF ME.
I CAN'T GO HOME WITHOUT HIM.
WELL, THAT DOES COMPLICATE THINGS, DOESN'T IT, MOUSE?
SKWIK!

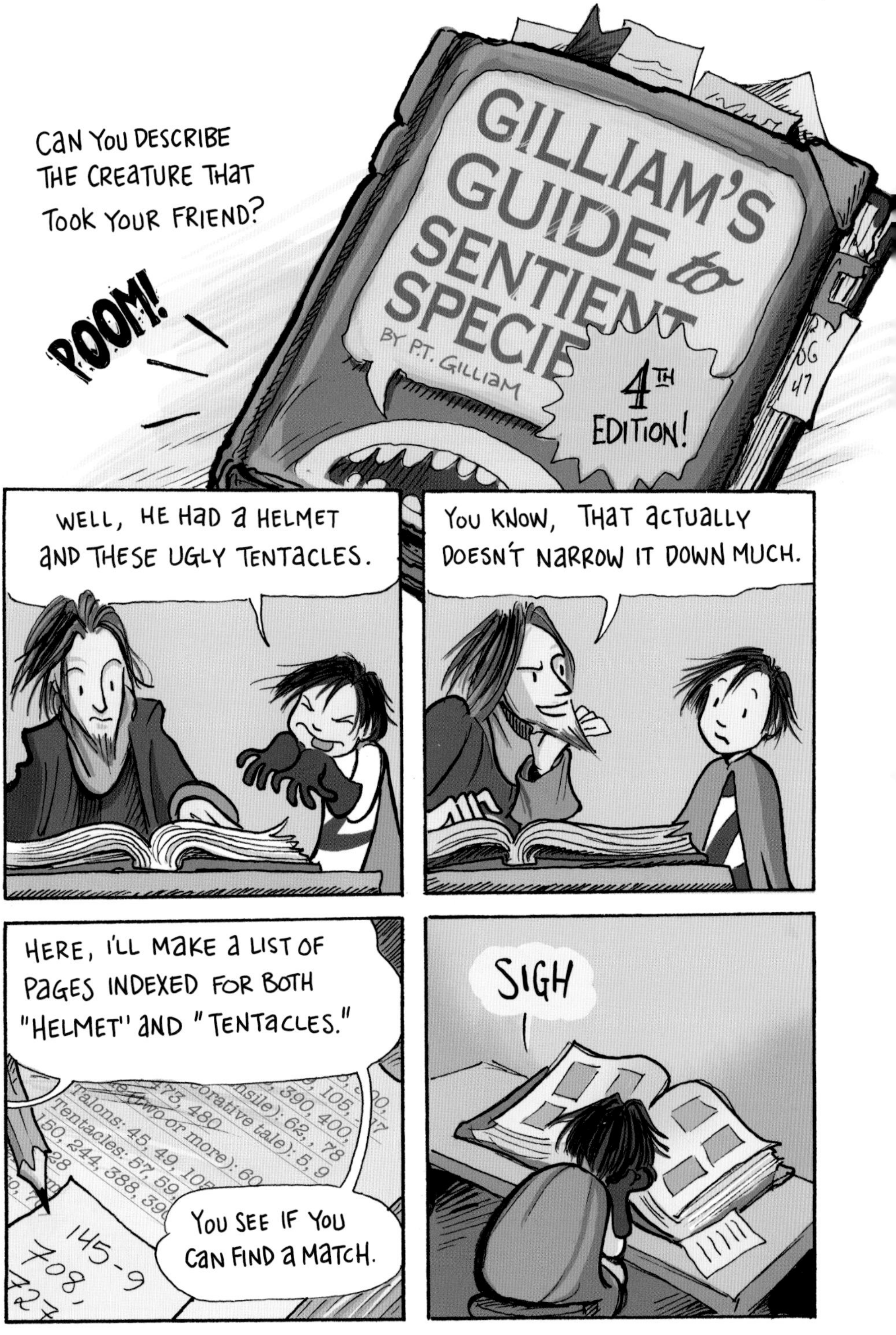

CAN YOU DESCRIBE THE CREATURE THAT TOOK YOUR FRIEND?
POOM!
GILLIAM'S GUIDE to SENTIENT SPECIE
BY P.T. GILLIAM
4TH EDITION!
WELL, HE HAD A HELMET AND THESE UGLY TENTACLES.
YOU KNOW, THAT ACTUALLY DOESN'T NARROW IT DOWN MUCH.
HERE, I'LL MAKE A LIST OF PAGES INDEXED FOR BOTH "HELMET" AND "TENTACLES."
YOU SEE IF YOU CAN FIND A MATCH.
145-9
708-
SIGH

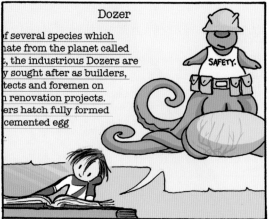

Dozer

f several species which
nate from the planet called
t, the industrious Dozers are
y sought after as builders,
tects and foremen on
n renovation projects.
ers hatch fully formed
cemented egg

flip

flip
flip

Whiskersmith

as composers
the armless
sters sport a
beard-like
n. They
n travel
ly stray
ir home
rba, and
y-seven
g moons.

flip

Tentacled Tubb

n without a
g televisor,
seen
habitable
and video
ions.
y
ation
cled
w

flip *flip*
flip
flip *flip*

IT'S HIM.

PIPER! PIPER!
I FOUND HIM!

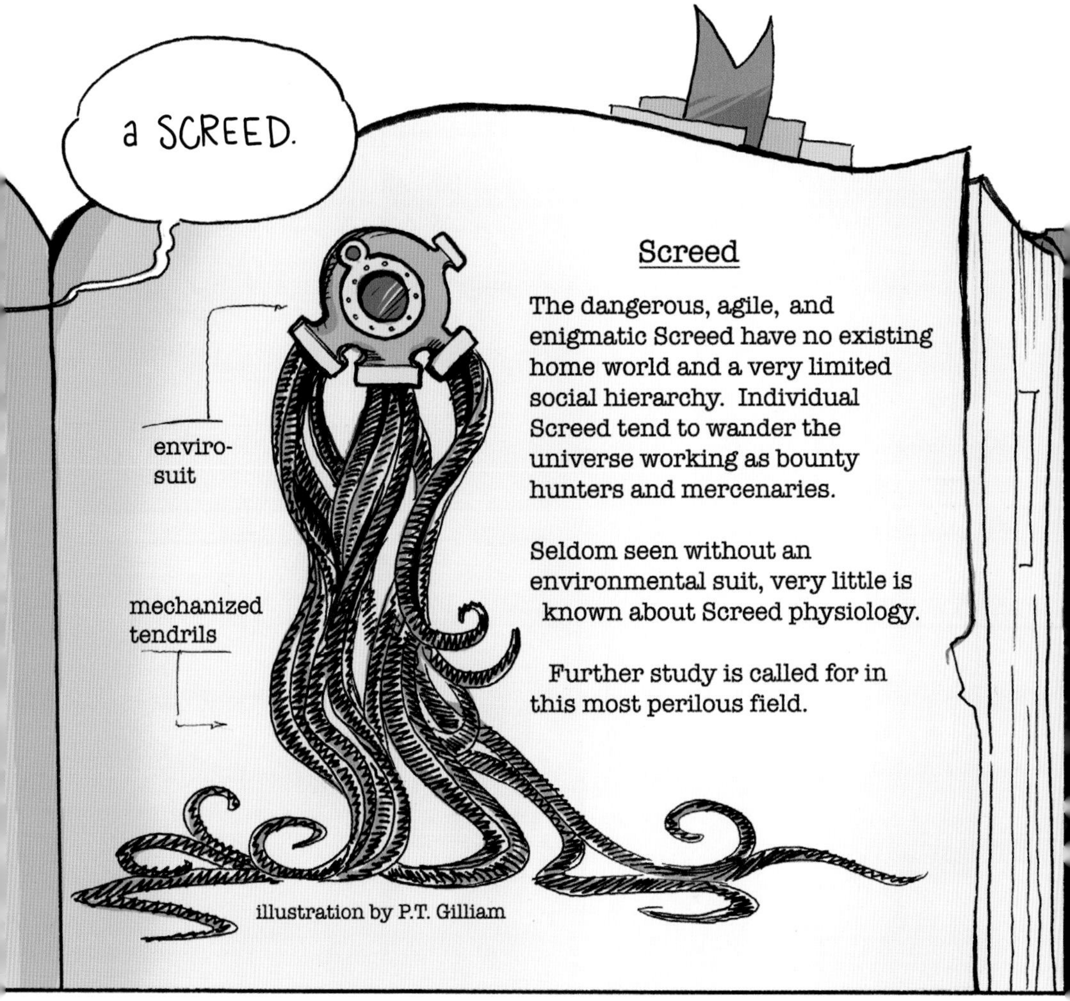
a SCREED.
Screed
The dangerous, agile, and enigmatic Screed have no existing home world and a very limited social hierarchy. Individual Screed tend to wander the universe working as bounty hunters and mercenaries.
Seldom seen without an environmental suit, very little is known about Screed physiology.
Further study is called for in this most perilous field.
enviro-suit
mechanized tendrils
illustration by P.T. Gilliam

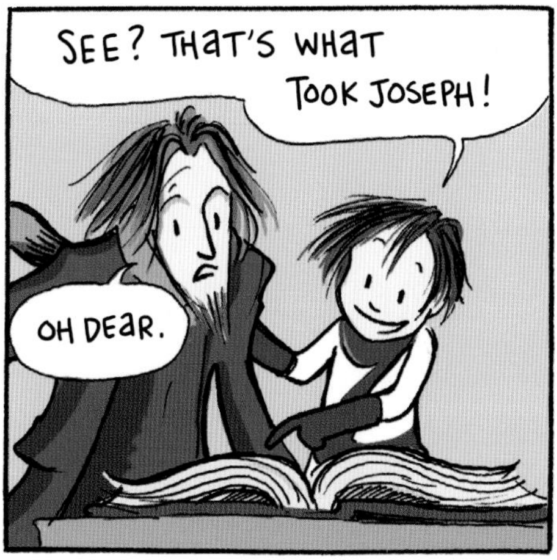
SEE? THAT'S WHAT TOOK JOSEPH!
OH DEAR.

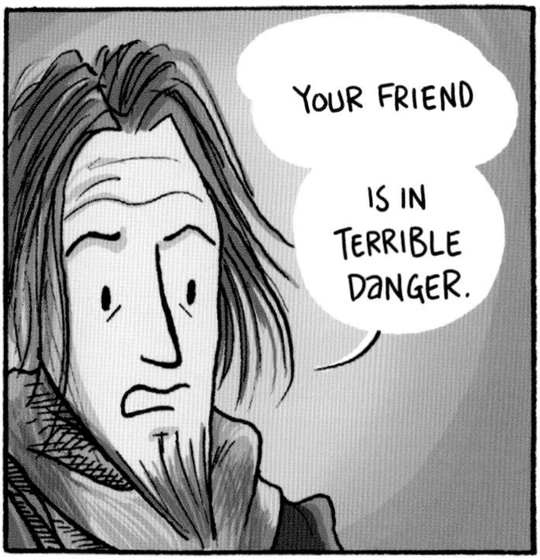
YOUR FRIEND
IS IN TERRIBLE DANGER.

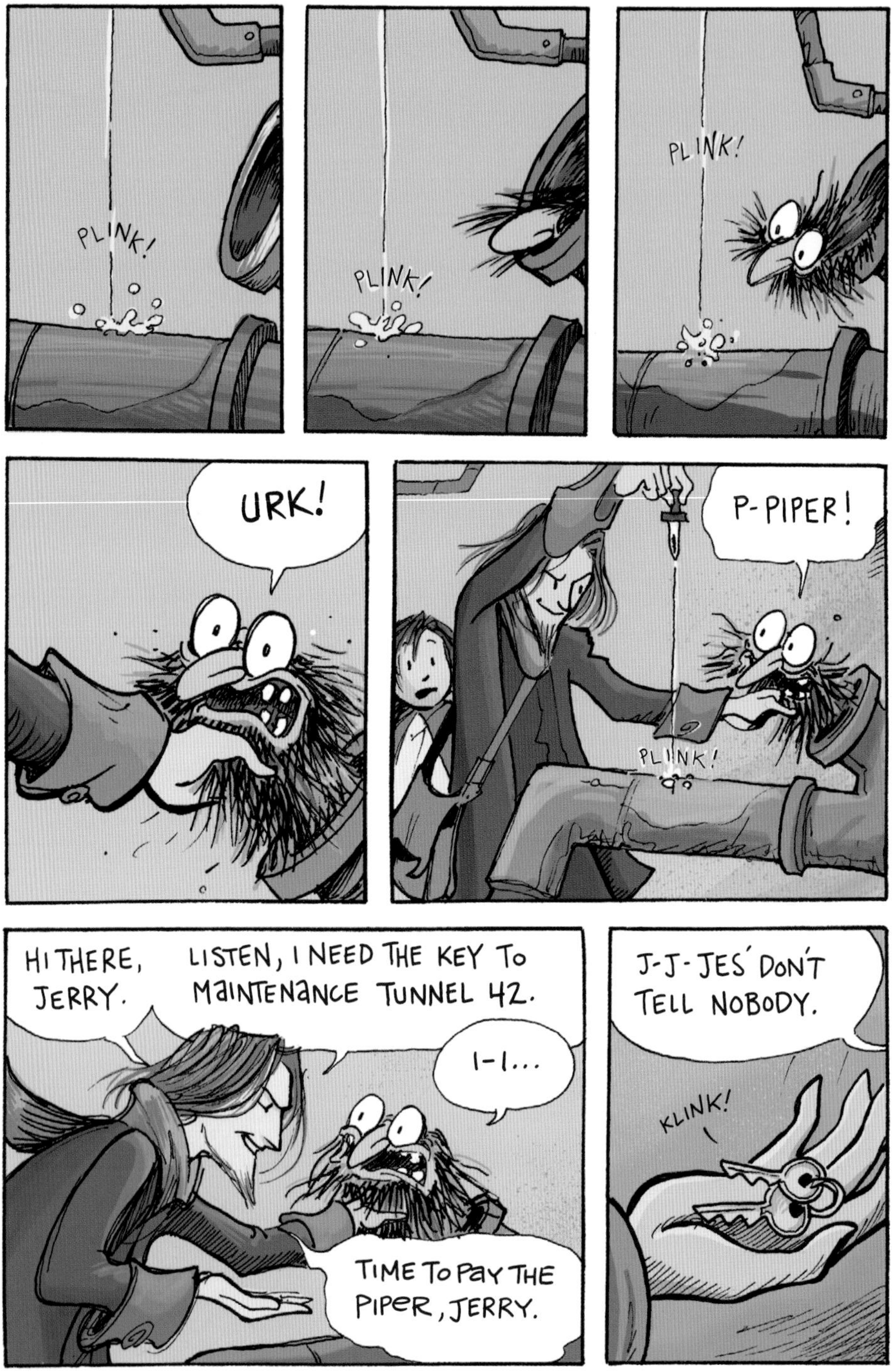
PLINK!
PLINK!
PLINK!
URK!
P-PIPER!
PLINK!
HI THERE, JERRY.
LISTEN, I NEED THE KEY TO MAINTENANCE TUNNEL 42.
I-I...
TIME TO PAY THE PIPER, JERRY.
J-J-JES' DON'T TELL NOBODY.
KLINK!

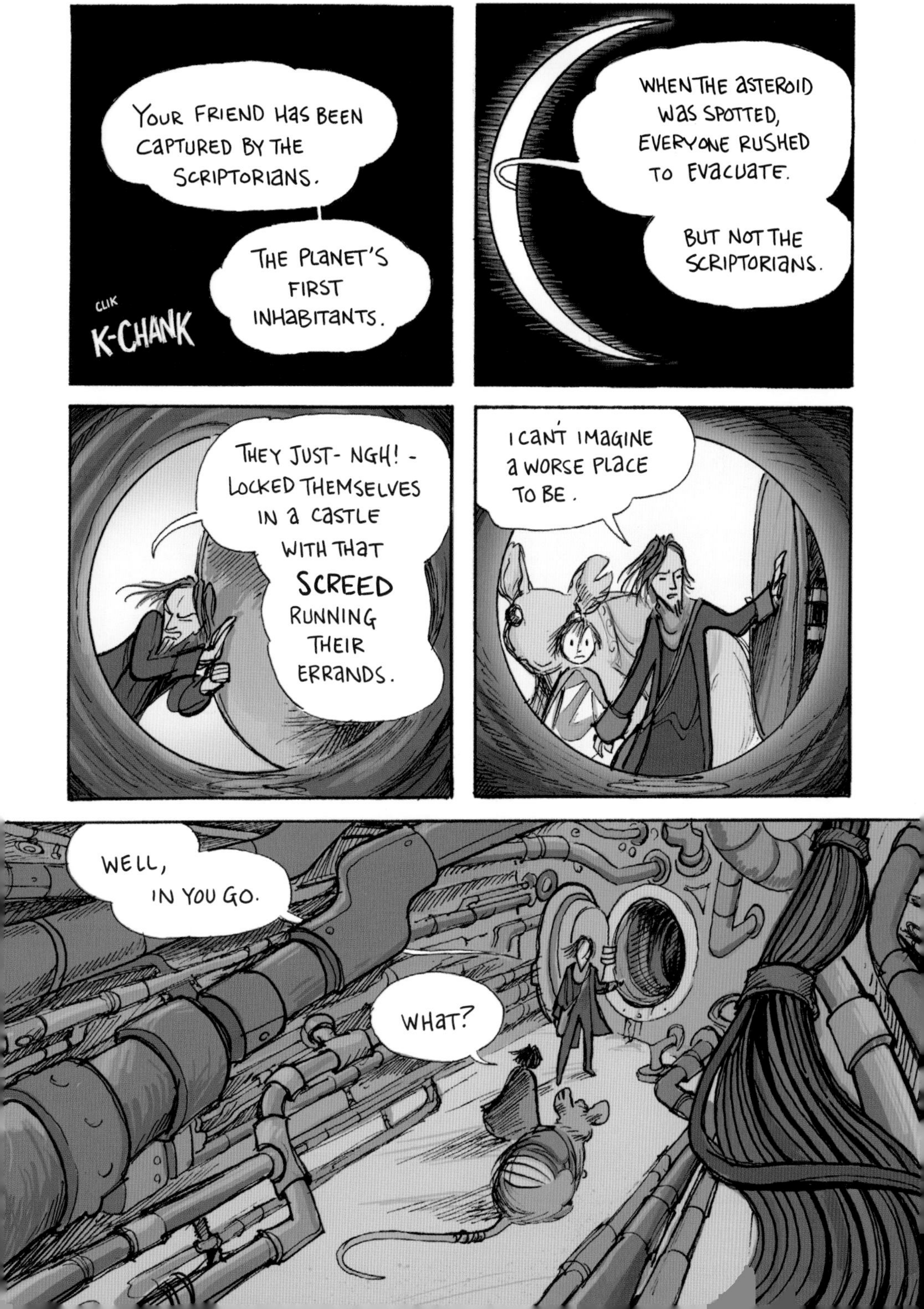
YOUR FRIEND HAS BEEN CAPTURED BY THE SCRIPTORIANS.
THE PLANET'S FIRST INHABITANTS.
CLIK
K-CHANK
WHEN THE ASTEROID WAS SPOTTED, EVERYONE RUSHED TO EVACUATE.
BUT NOT THE SCRIPTORIANS.
THEY JUST- NGH! - LOCKED THEMSELVES IN A CASTLE WITH THAT SCREED RUNNING THEIR ERRANDS.
I CAN'T IMAGINE A WORSE PLACE TO BE.
WELL, IN YOU GO.
WHAT?

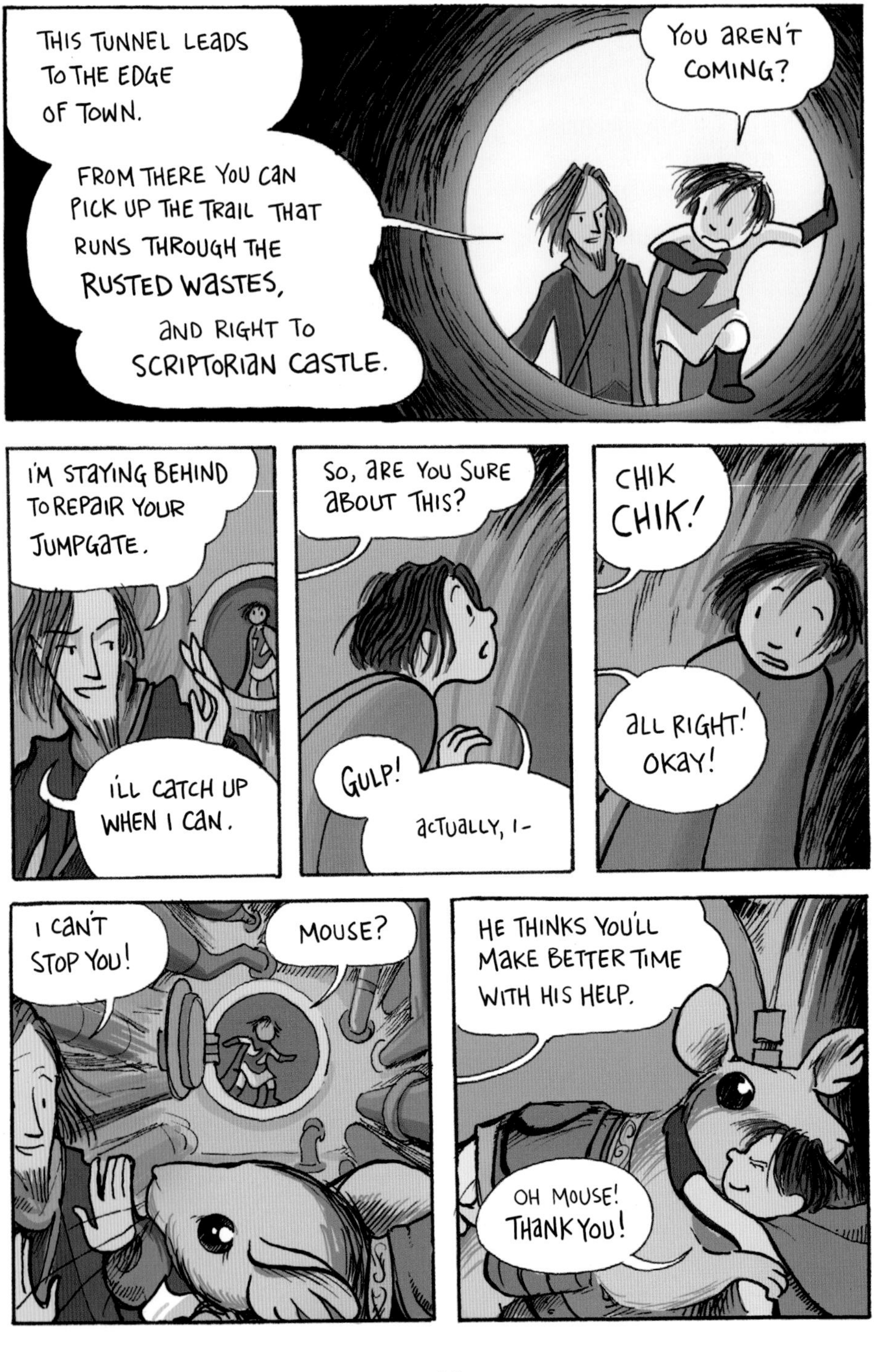
THIS TUNNEL LEADS TO THE EDGE OF TOWN.
FROM THERE YOU CAN PICK UP THE TRAIL THAT RUNS THROUGH THE RUSTED WASTES,
AND RIGHT TO SCRIPTORIAN CASTLE.
YOU AREN'T COMING?
I'M STAYING BEHIND TO REPAIR YOUR JUMPGATE.
I'LL CATCH UP WHEN I CAN.
SO, ARE YOU SURE ABOUT THIS?
GULP!
ACTUALLY, I-
CHIK CHIK!
ALL RIGHT! OKAY!
I CAN'T STOP YOU!
MOUSE?
HE THINKS YOU'LL MAKE BETTER TIME WITH HIS HELP.
OH MOUSE! THANK YOU!

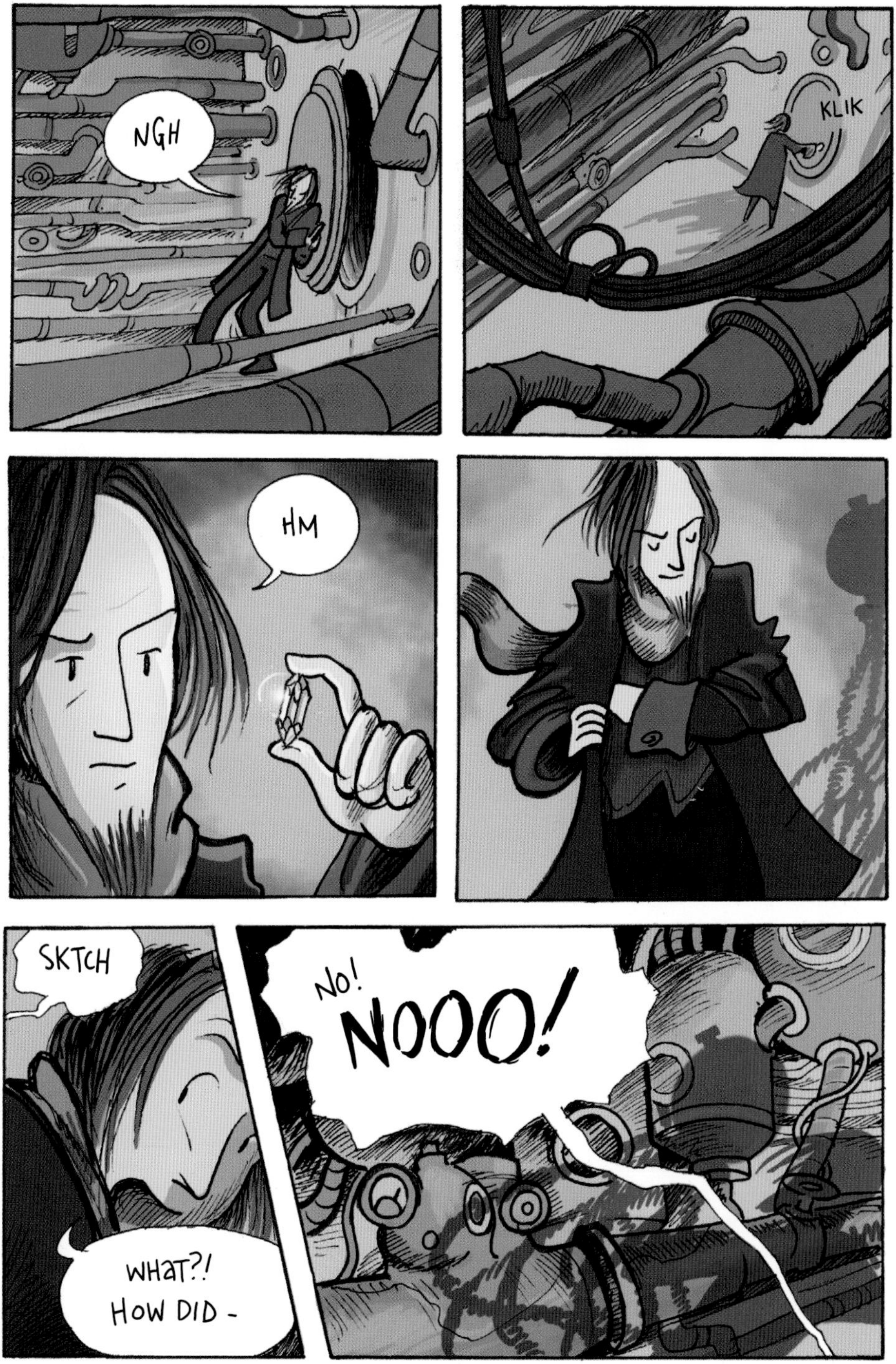
NGH
KLIK
HM
SKTCH
WHAT?!
HOW DID -
No!
NOOO!

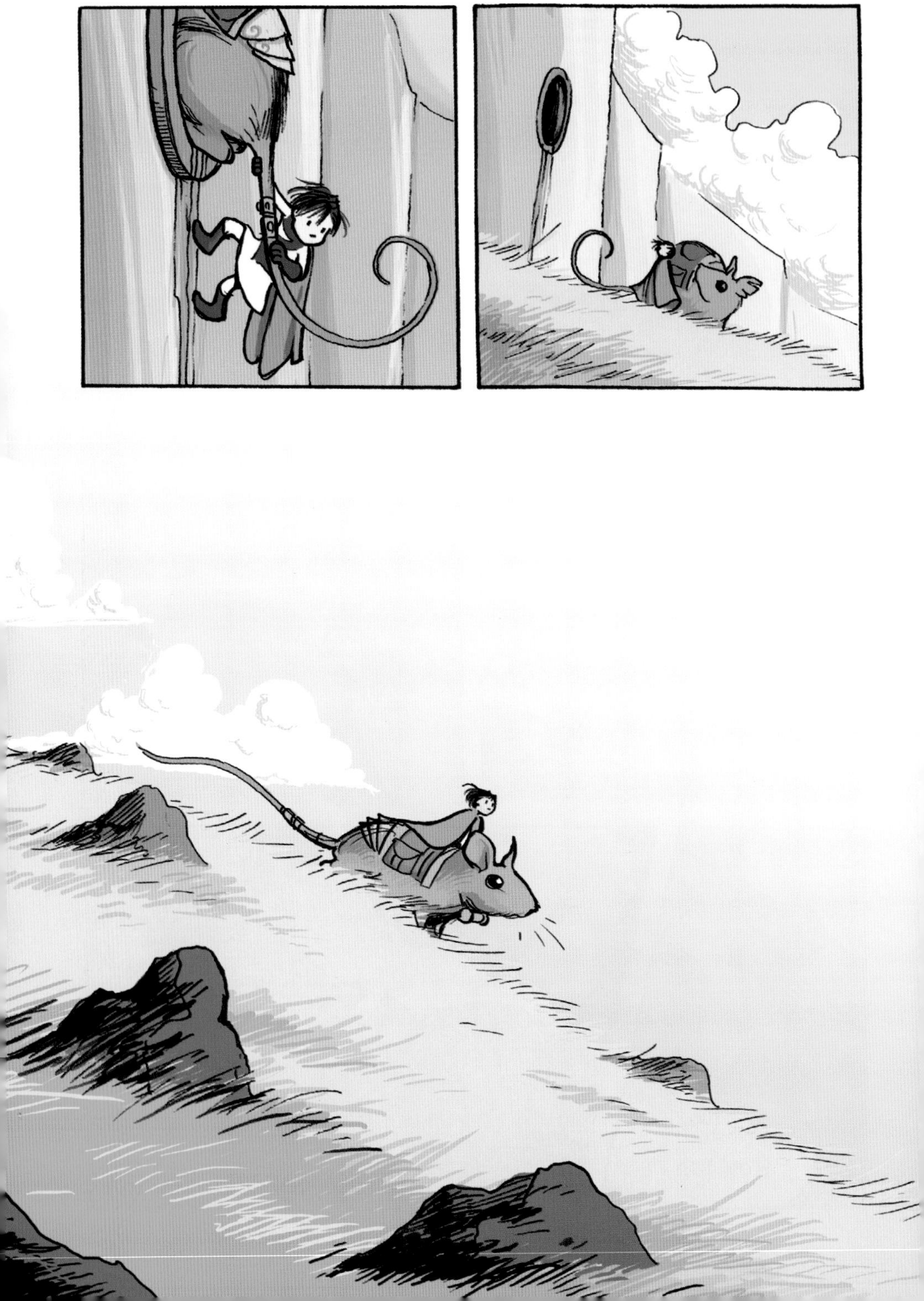

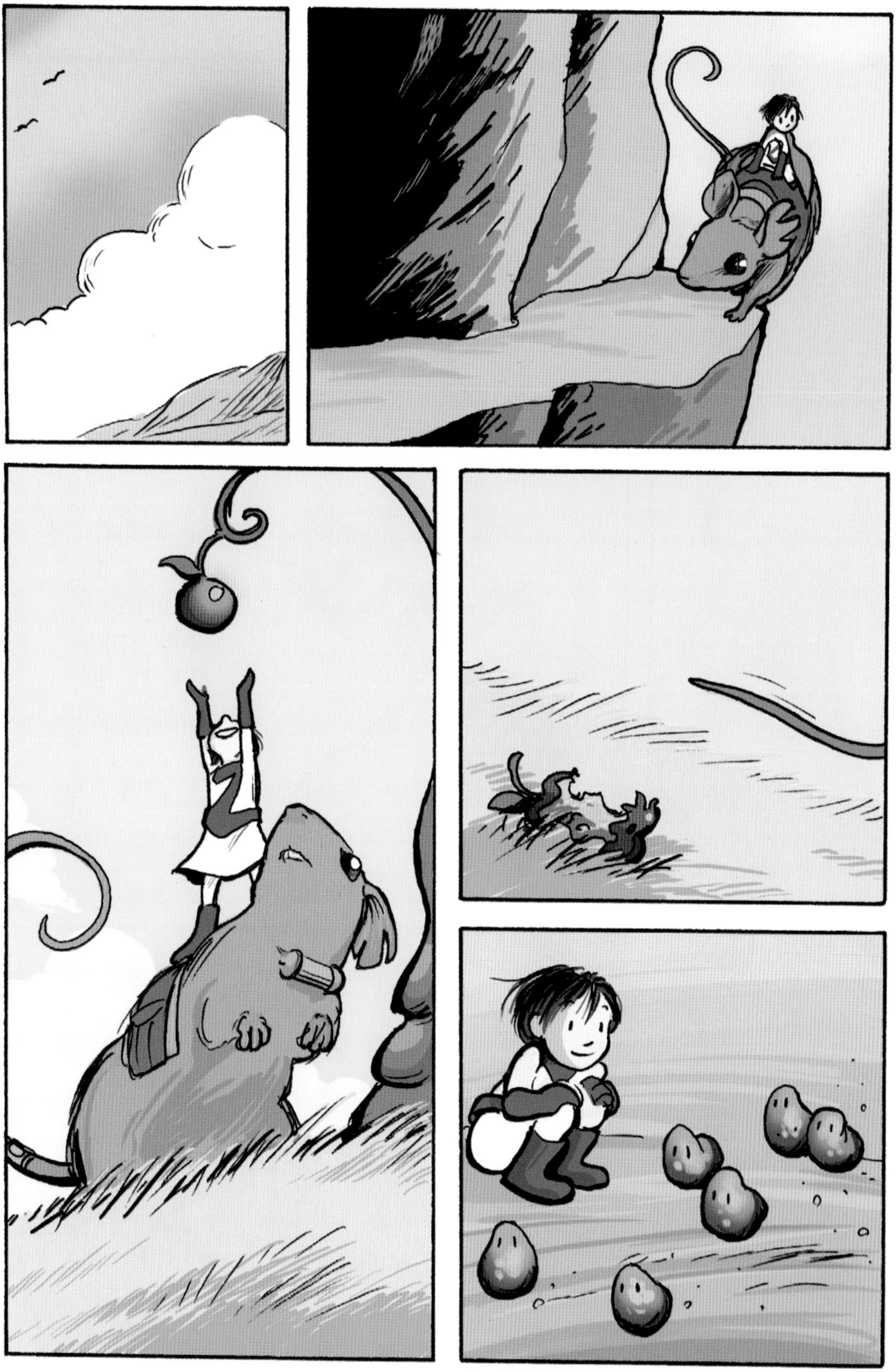

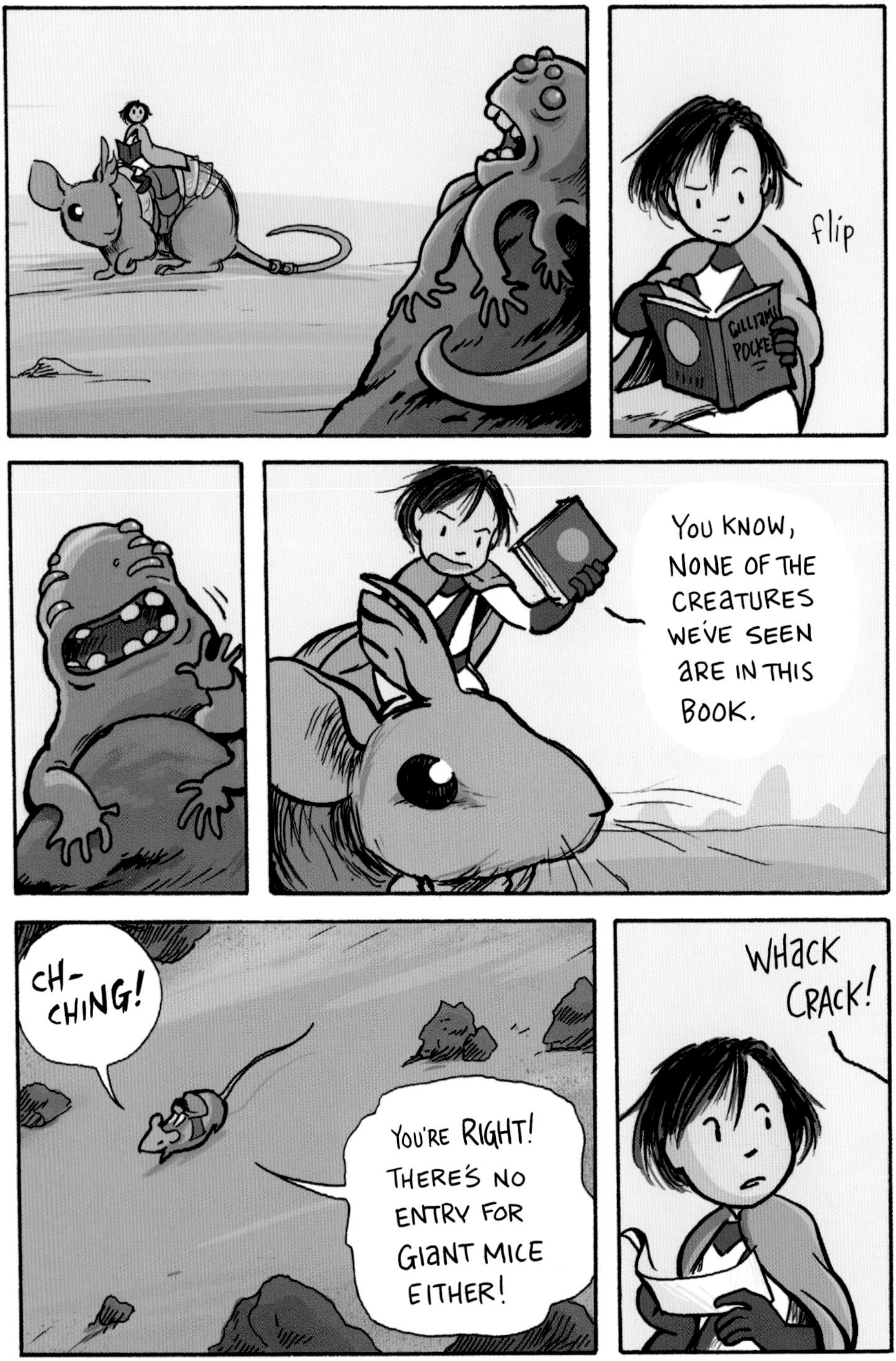
flip
YOU KNOW, NONE OF THE CREATURES WE'VE SEEN ARE IN THIS BOOK.
CH-CHING!
YOU'RE RIGHT! THERE'S NO ENTRY FOR GIANT MICE EITHER!
WHACK CRACK!

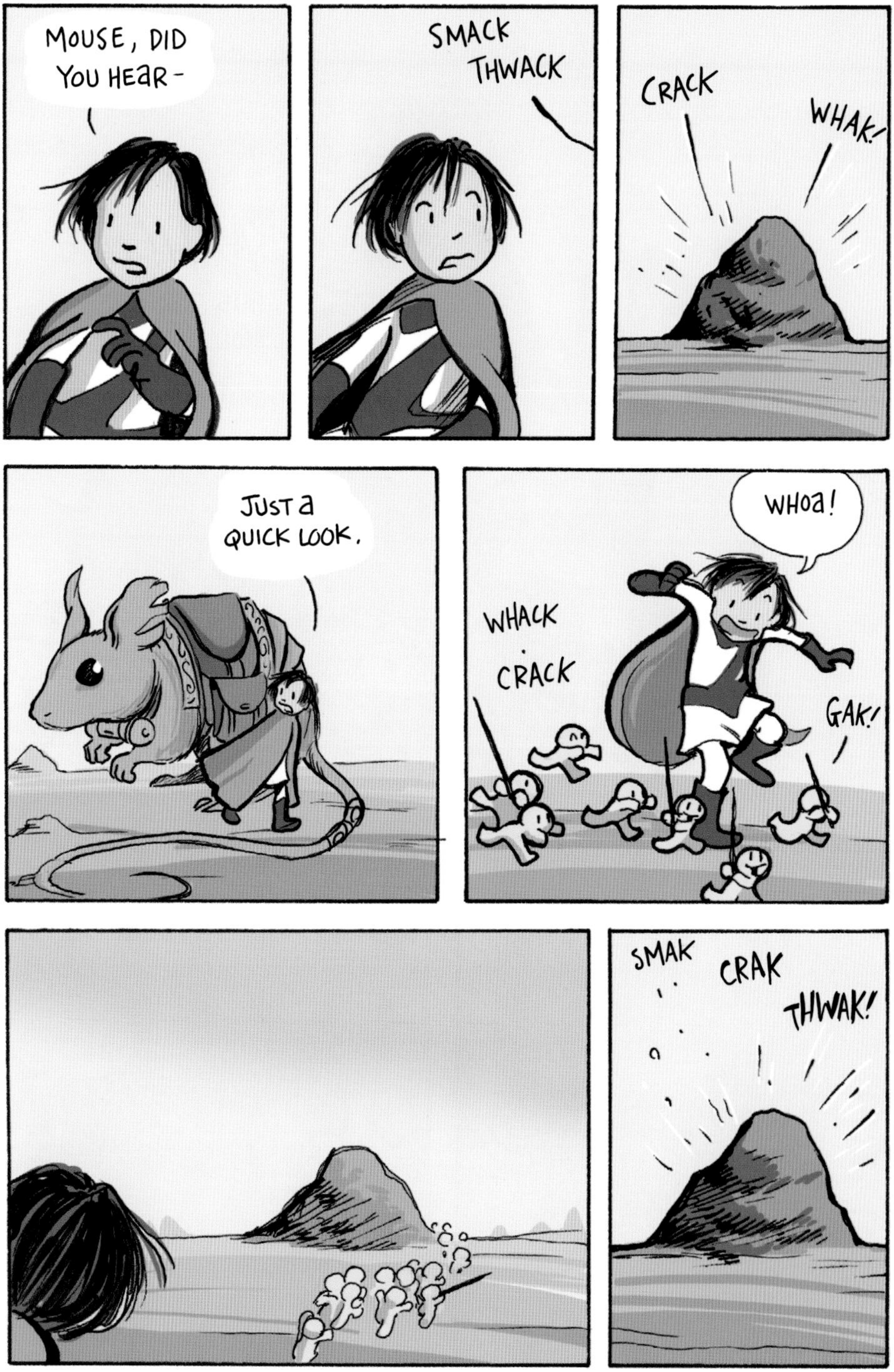
MOUSE, DID YOU HEAR -
SMACK
THWACK
CRACK
WHAK!
JUST A QUICK LOOK.
WHOA!
WHACK
CRACK
GAK!
SMAK
CRAK
THWAK!

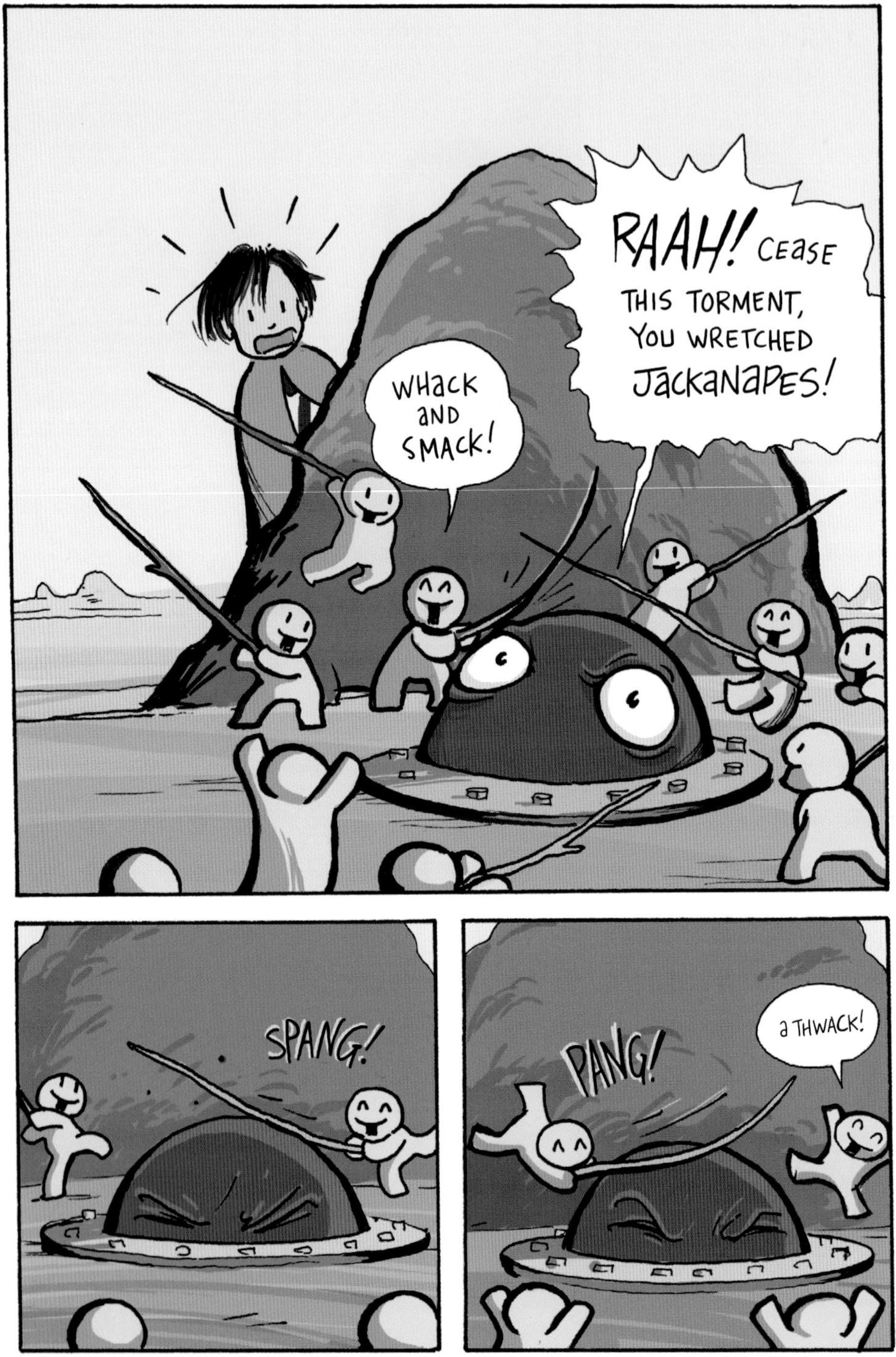
RAAH! CEASE THIS TORMENT, YOU WRETCHED JACKANAPES!
WHACK AND SMACK!
SPANG!
PANG!
A THWACK!

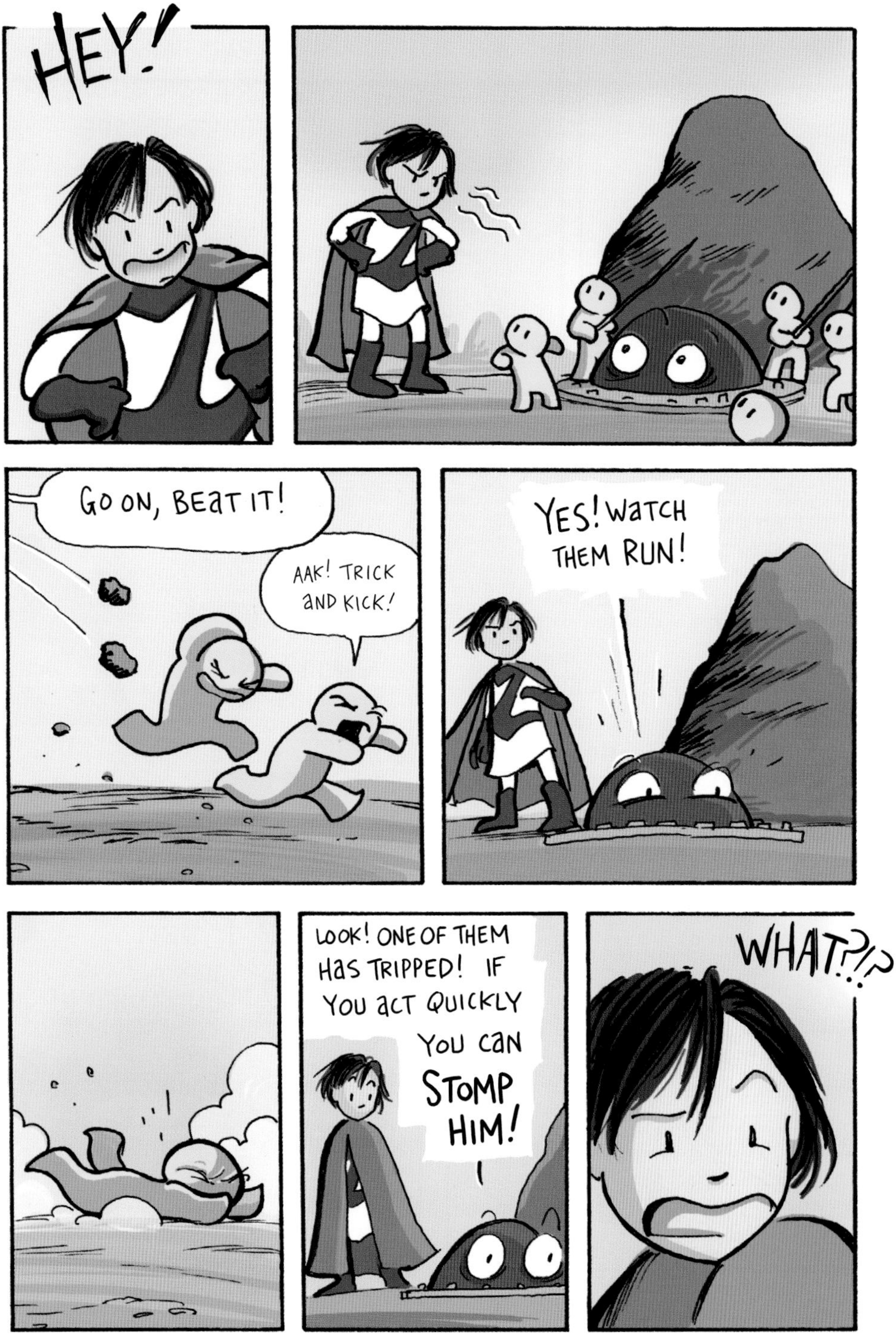
HEY!
GO ON, BEAT IT!
AAK! TRICK AND KICK!
YES! WATCH THEM RUN!
LOOK! ONE OF THEM HAS TRIPPED! IF YOU ACT QUICKLY YOU CAN STOMP HIM!
WHAT?!?

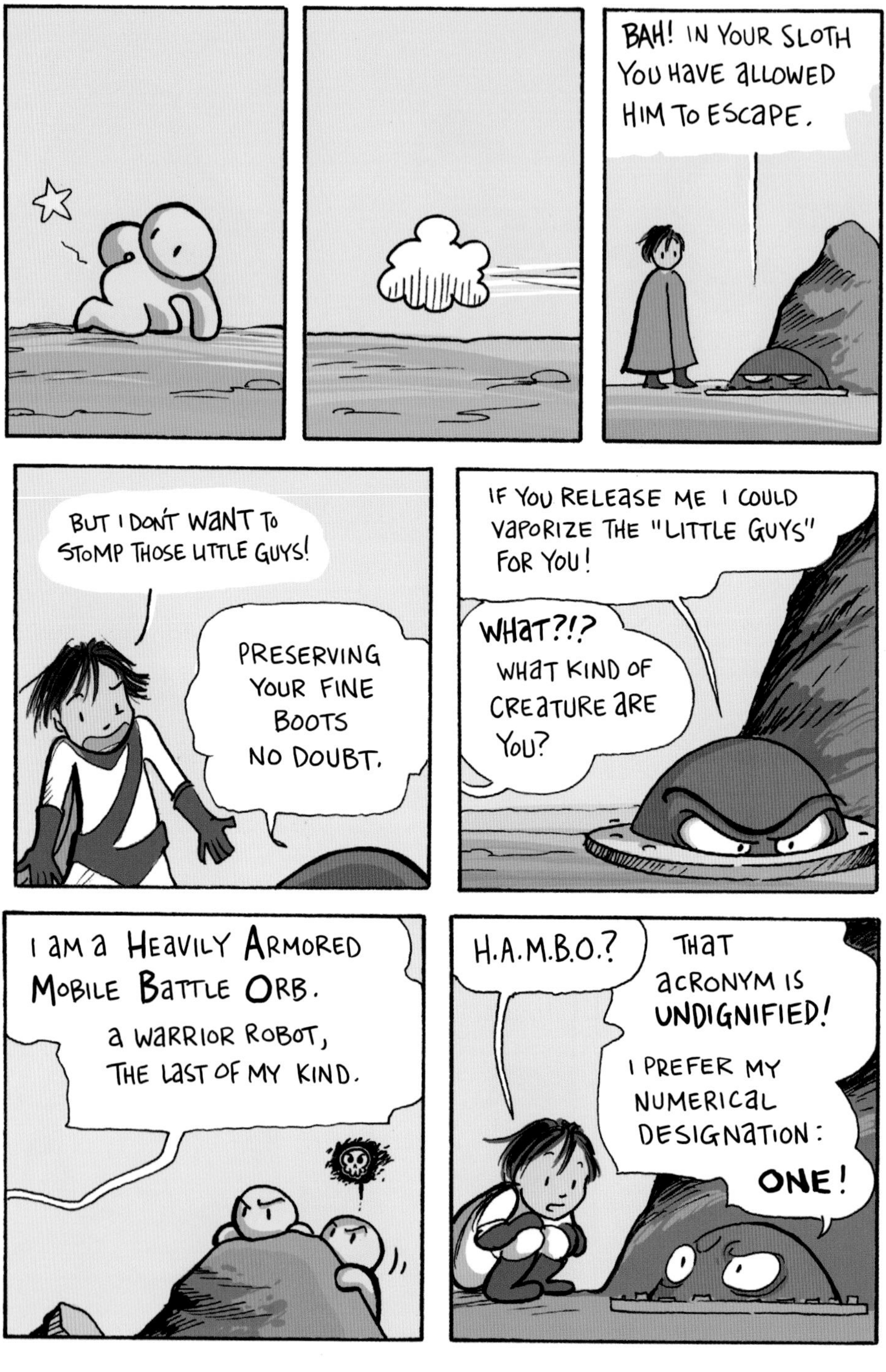

BAH! IN YOUR SLOTH YOU HAVE ALLOWED HIM TO ESCAPE.
BUT I DON'T WANT TO STOMP THOSE LITTLE GUYS!
PRESERVING YOUR FINE BOOTS NO DOUBT.
IF YOU RELEASE ME I COULD VAPORIZE THE "LITTLE GUYS" FOR YOU!
WHAT?!?
WHAT KIND OF CREATURE ARE YOU?
I AM A HEAVILY ARMORED MOBILE BATTLE ORB.
A WARRIOR ROBOT, THE LAST OF MY KIND.
H.A.M.B.O.?
THAT ACRONYM IS UNDIGNIFIED!
I PREFER MY NUMERICAL DESIGNATION:
ONE!

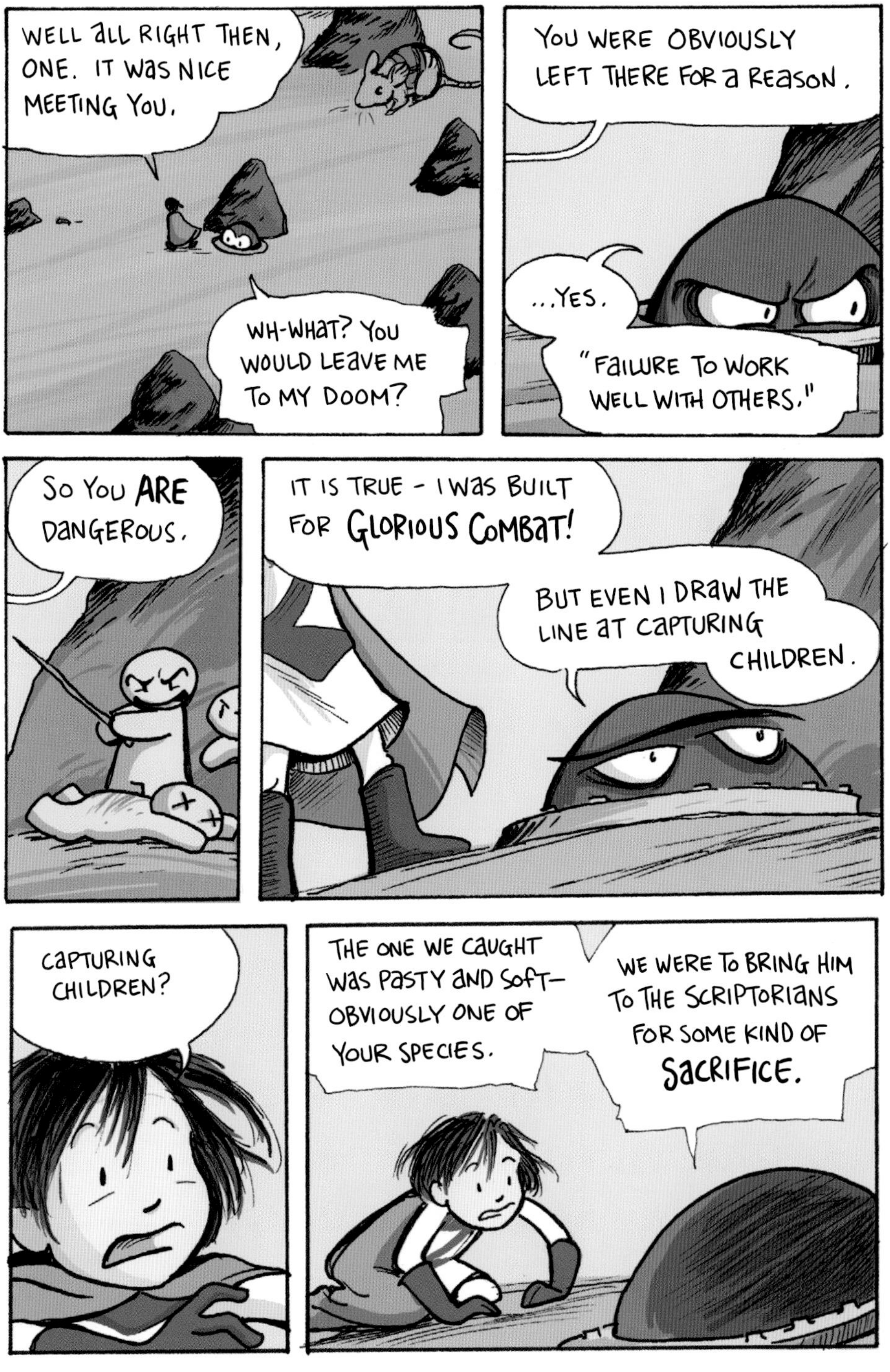
WELL ALL RIGHT THEN, ONE. IT WAS NICE MEETING YOU.
WH-WHAT? YOU WOULD LEAVE ME TO MY DOOM?
YOU WERE OBVIOUSLY LEFT THERE FOR A REASON.
...YES.
"FAILURE TO WORK WELL WITH OTHERS."
SO YOU ARE DANGEROUS.
IT IS TRUE - I WAS BUILT FOR GLORIOUS COMBAT!
BUT EVEN I DRAW THE LINE AT CAPTURING CHILDREN.
CAPTURING CHILDREN?
THE ONE WE CAUGHT WAS PASTY AND SOFT— OBVIOUSLY ONE OF YOUR SPECIES.
WE WERE TO BRING HIM TO THE SCRIPTORIANS FOR SOME KIND OF SACRIFICE.

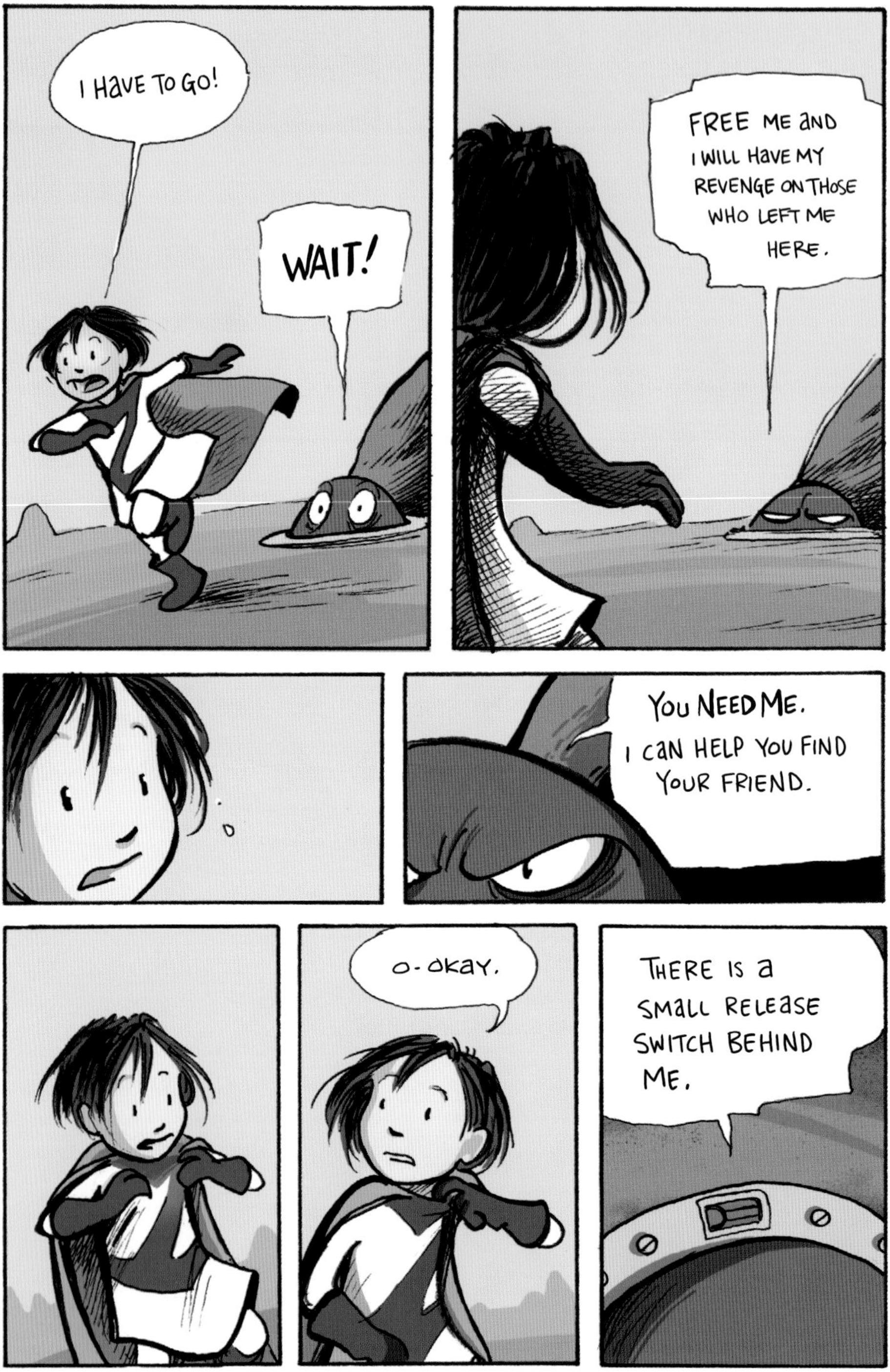
I HAVE TO GO!
WAIT!
FREE ME AND I WILL HAVE MY REVENGE ON THOSE WHO LEFT ME HERE.
YOU NEED ME.
I CAN HELP YOU FIND YOUR FRIEND.
O-OKAY.
THERE IS A SMALL RELEASE SWITCH BEHIND ME.

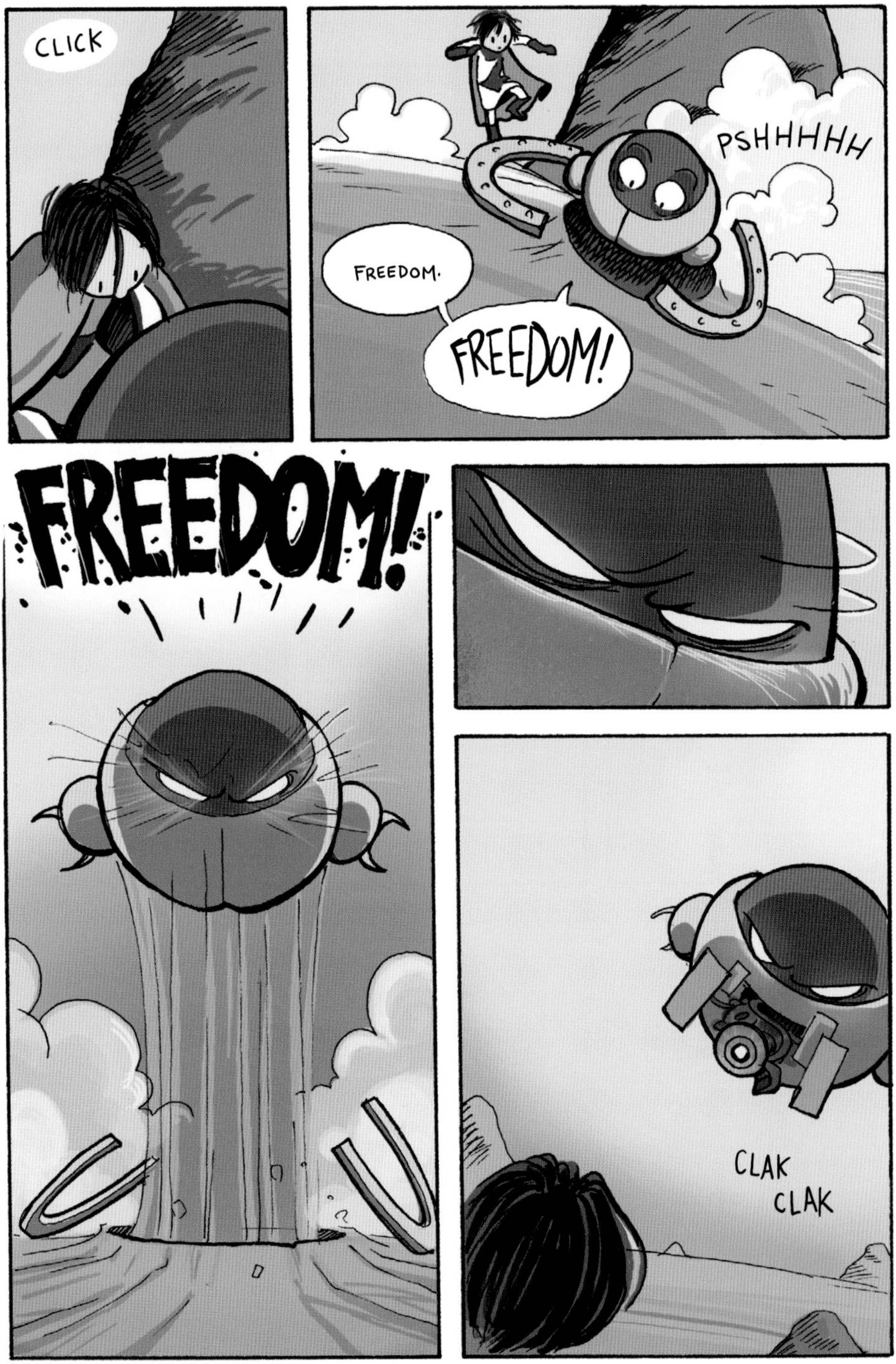
CLICK
PSHHHHH
FREEDOM.
FREEDOM!
FREEDOM!
CLAK
CLAK

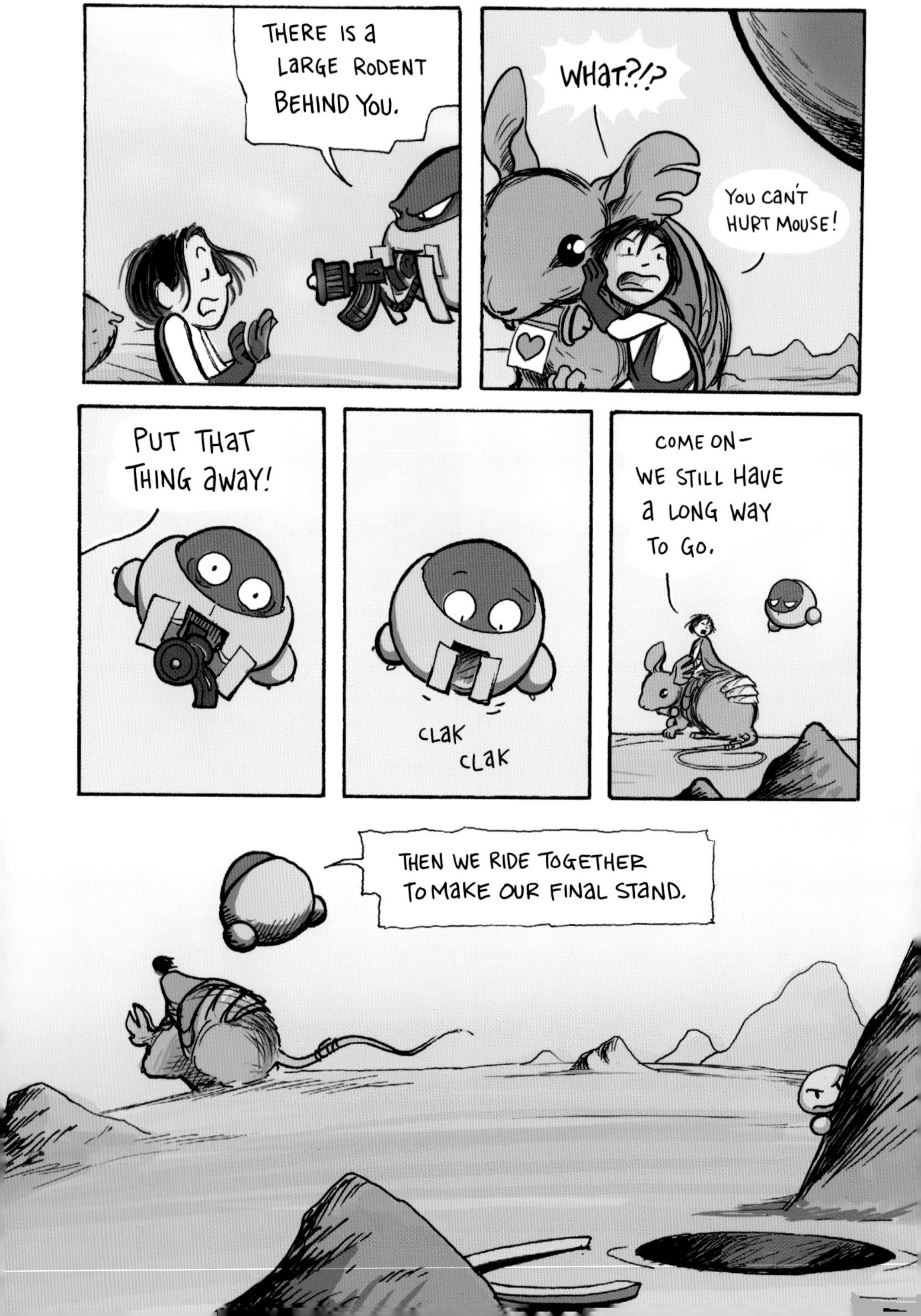
THERE IS a LARGE RODENT BEHIND YOU.
WHAT?!?
YOU CAN'T HURT MOUSE!
PUT THAT THING away!
CLAK
CLAK
COME ON— WE STILL HaVE a LONG WaY TO GO.
THEN WE RIDE TOGETHER TO MAKE OUR FINAL STAND.

chapter
four

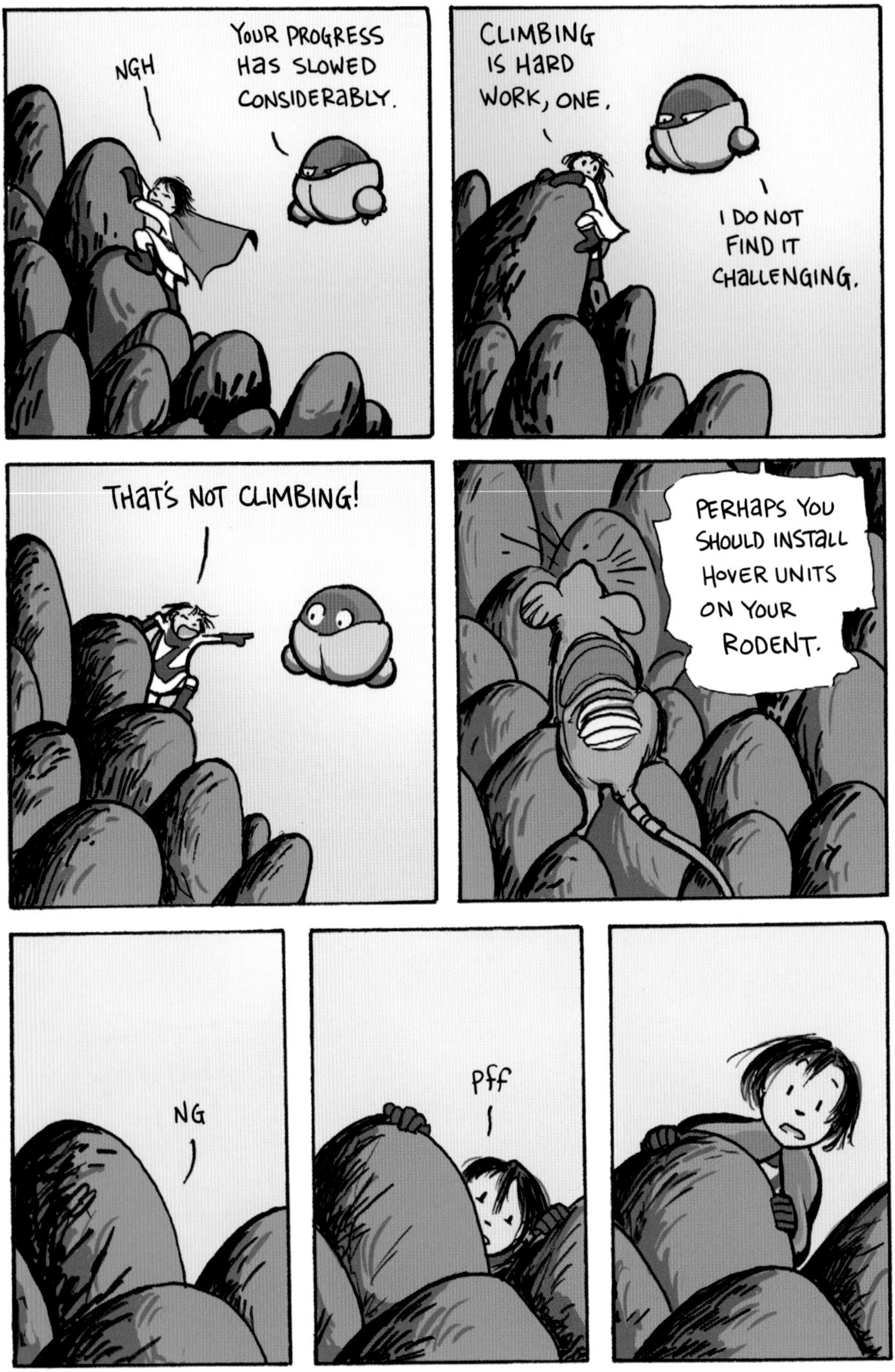
NGH
YOUR PROGRESS HAS SLOWED CONSIDERABLY.
CLIMBING IS HARD WORK, ONE.
I DO NOT FIND IT CHALLENGING.
THAT'S NOT CLIMBING!
PERHAPS YOU SHOULD INSTALL HOVER UNITS ON YOUR RODENT.
NG
pff

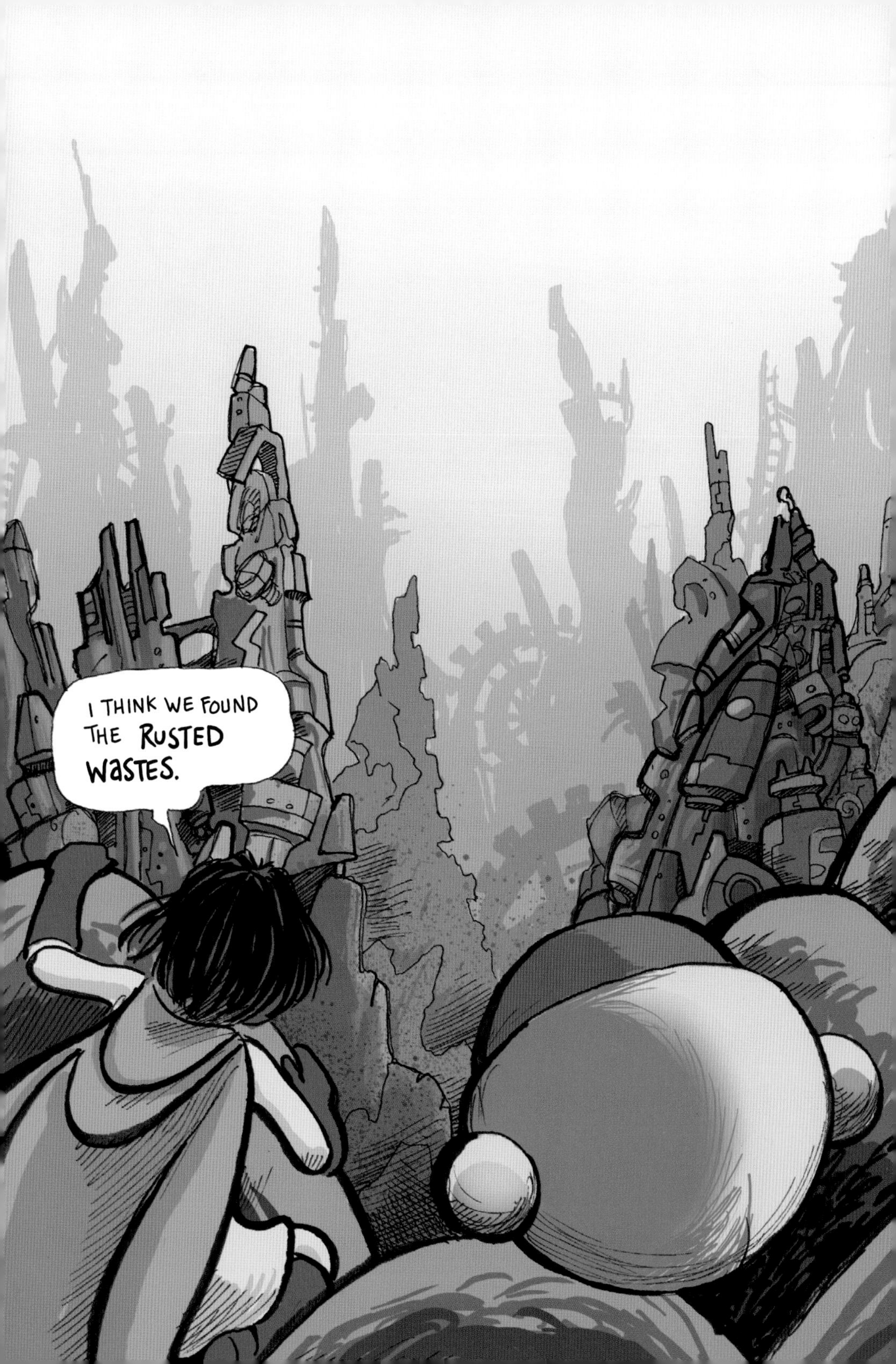
I THINK WE FOUND THE RUSTED WASTES.

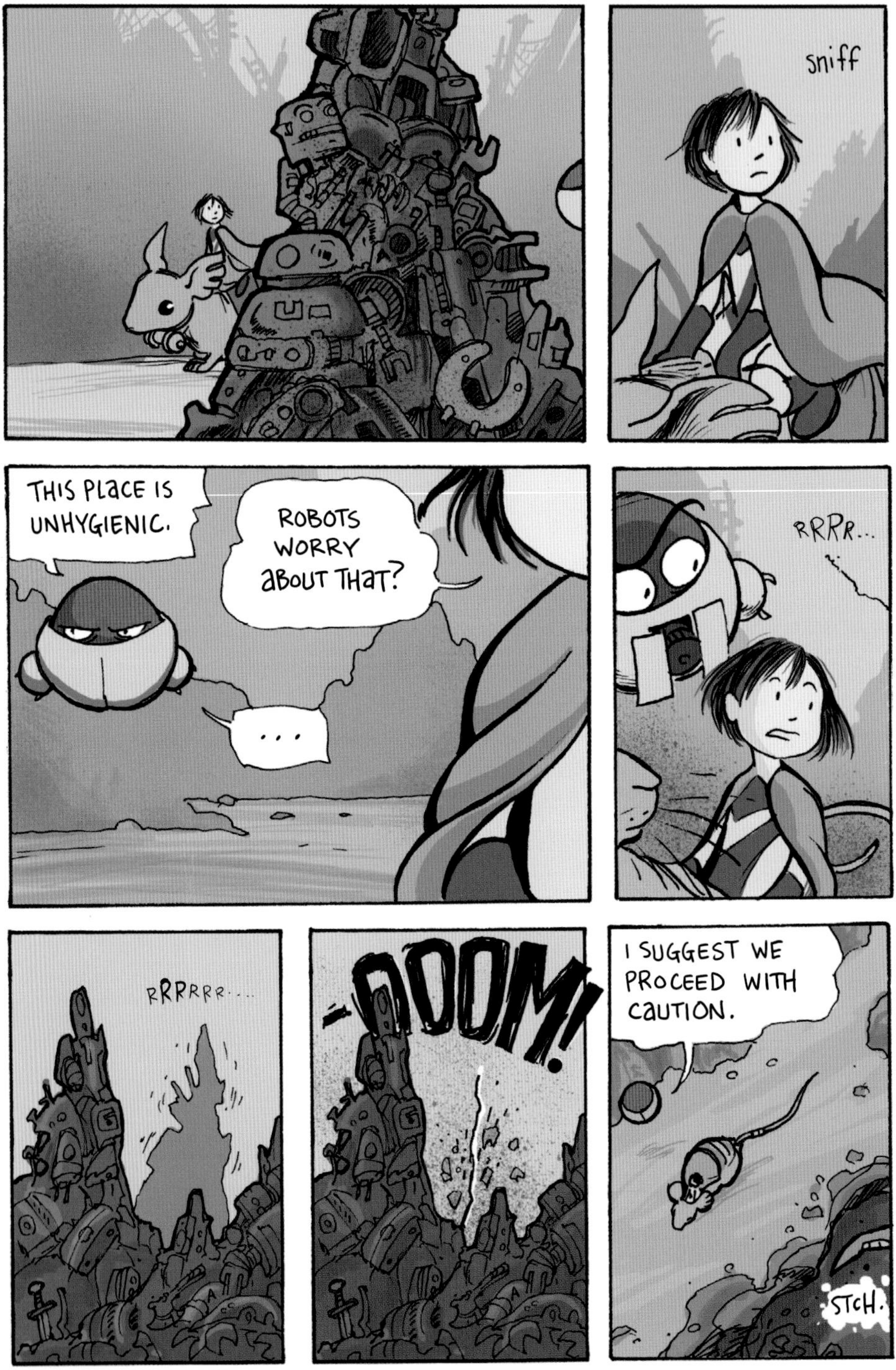
sniff
THIS PLACE IS UNHYGIENIC.
ROBOTS WORRY ABOUT THAT?
...
RRRR...
RRRRRR....
-DOOM!
I SUGGEST WE PROCEED WITH CAUTION.
STCH.

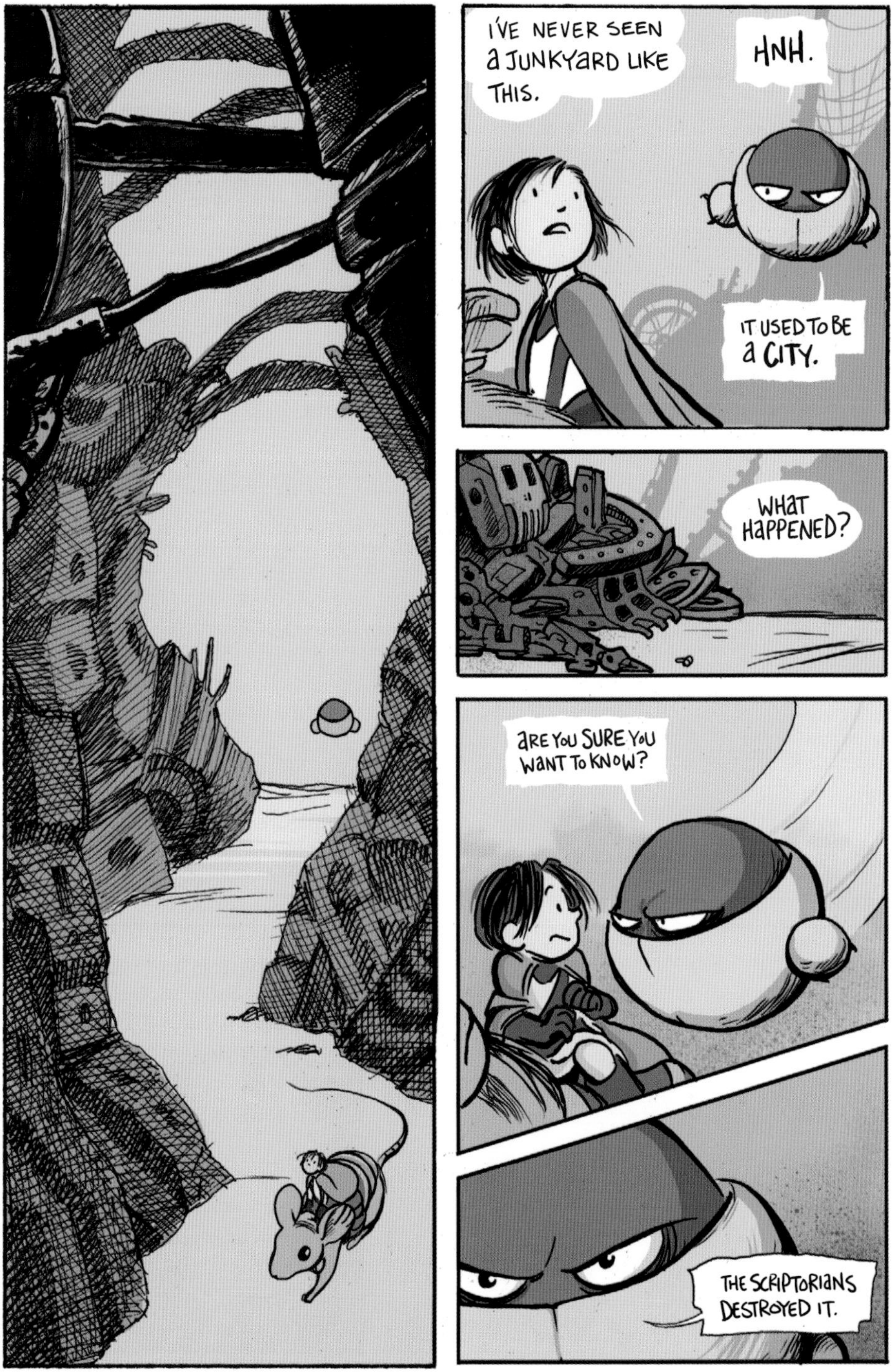
I'VE NEVER SEEN A JUNKYARD LIKE THIS.
HNH.
IT USED TO BE A CITY.
WHAT HAPPENED?
ARE YOU SURE YOU WANT TO KNOW?
THE SCRIPTORIANS DESTROYED IT.

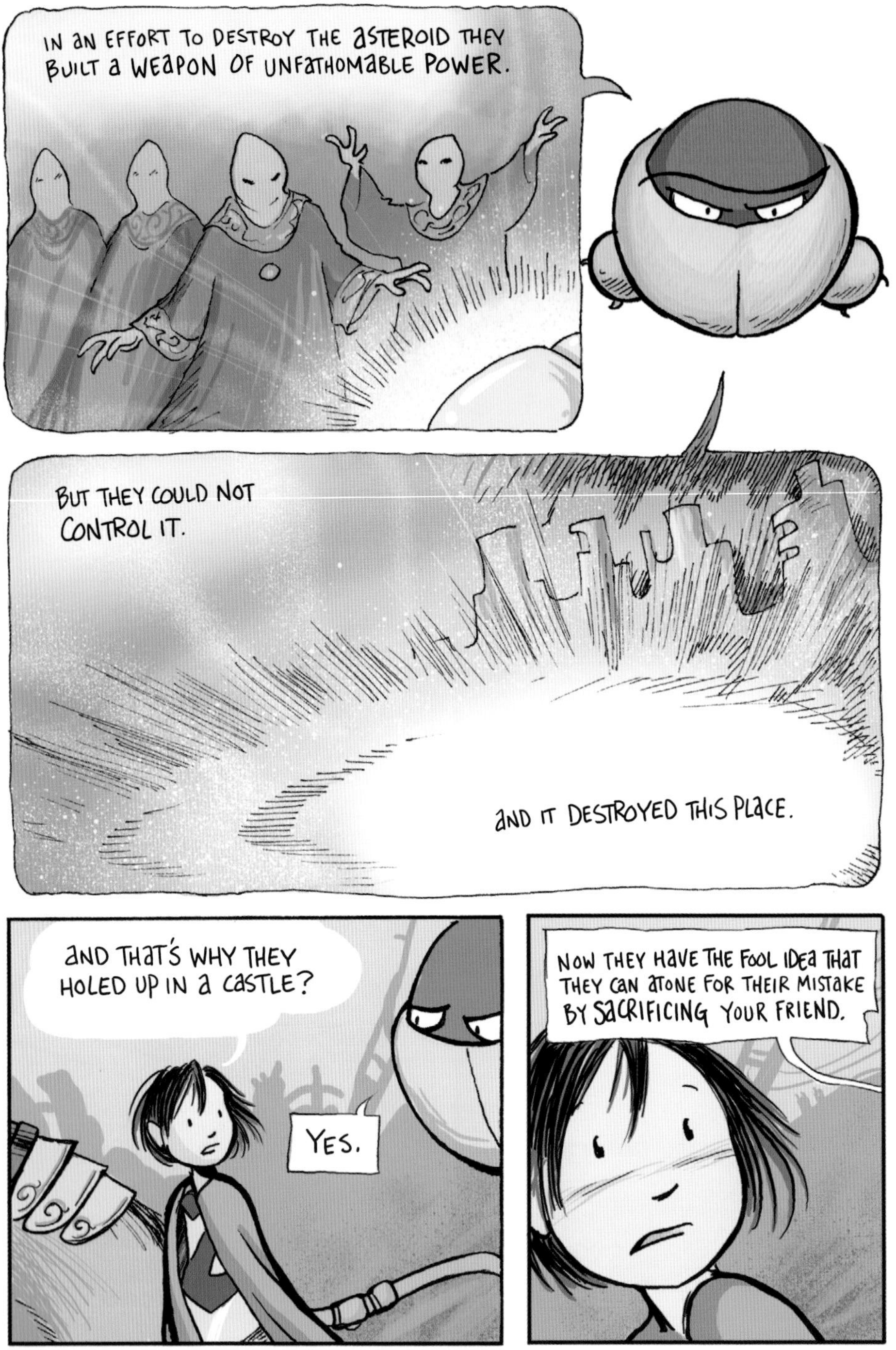
IN AN EFFORT TO DESTROY THE ASTEROID THEY BUILT A WEAPON OF UNFATHOMABLE POWER.
BUT THEY COULD NOT CONTROL IT.
AND IT DESTROYED THIS PLACE.
AND THAT'S WHY THEY HOLED UP IN A CASTLE?
YES.
NOW THEY HAVE THE FOOL IDEA THAT THEY CAN ATONE FOR THEIR MISTAKE BY SACRIFICING YOUR FRIEND.

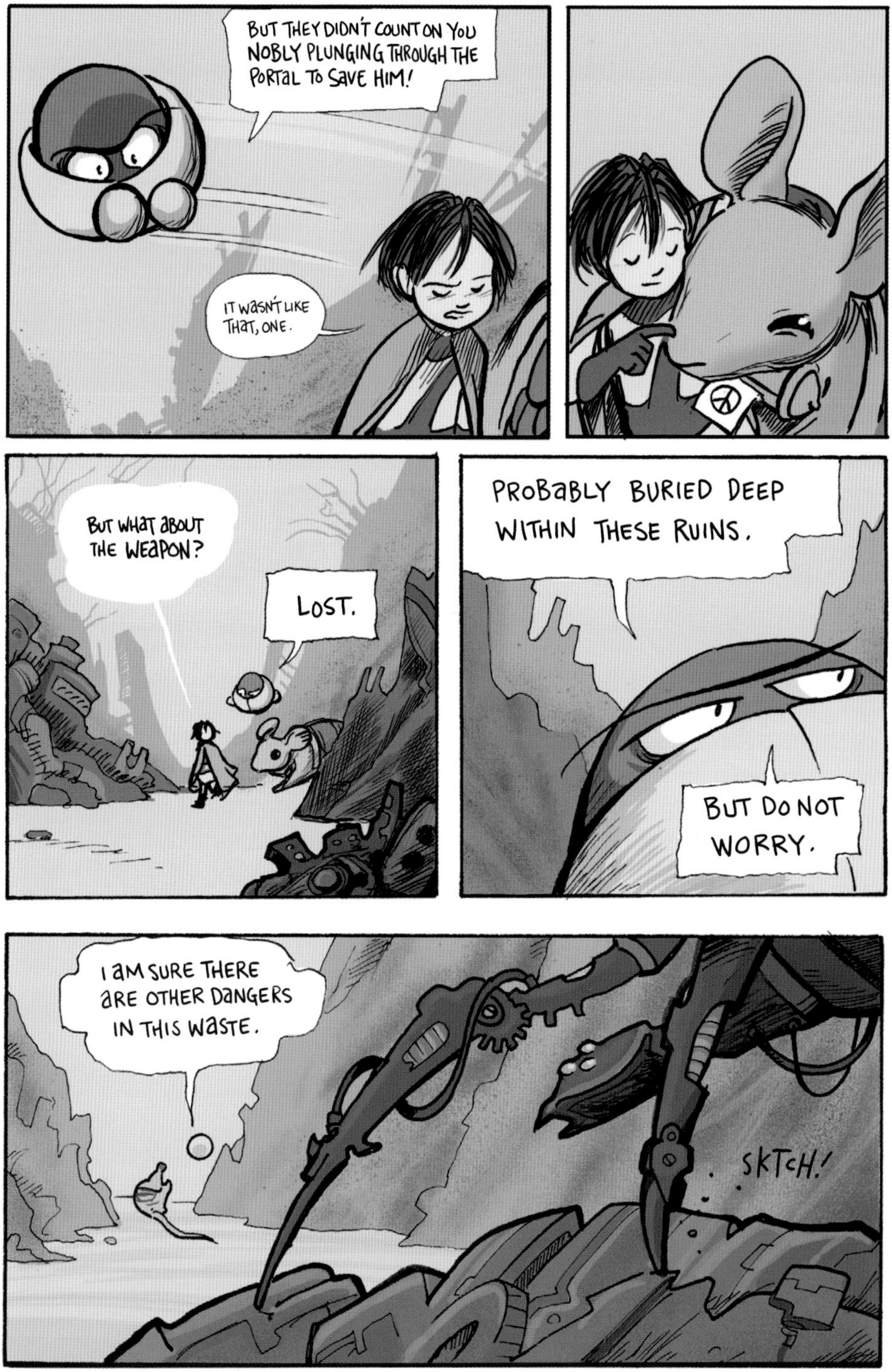
BUT THEY DIDN'T COUNT ON YOU NOBLY PLUNGING THROUGH THE PORTAL TO SAVE HIM!
IT WASN'T LIKE THAT, ONE.
BUT WHAT ABOUT THE WEAPON?
LOST.
PROBABLY BURIED DEEP WITHIN THESE RUINS.
BUT DO NOT WORRY.
I AM SURE THERE ARE OTHER DANGERS IN THIS WASTE.
SKTCH!

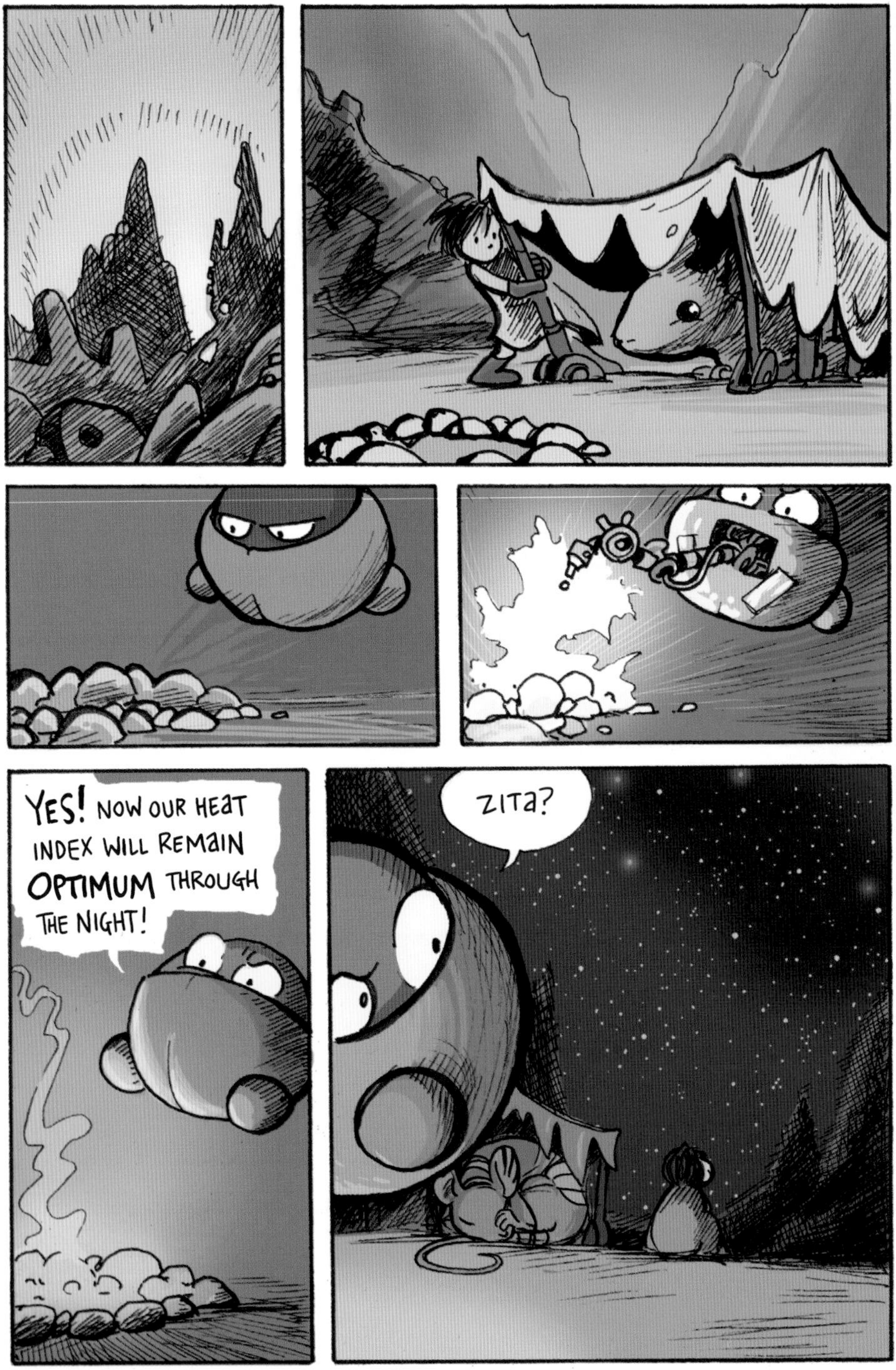

YES! NOW OUR HEAT INDEX WILL REMAIN OPTIMUM THROUGH THE NIGHT!
ZITA?

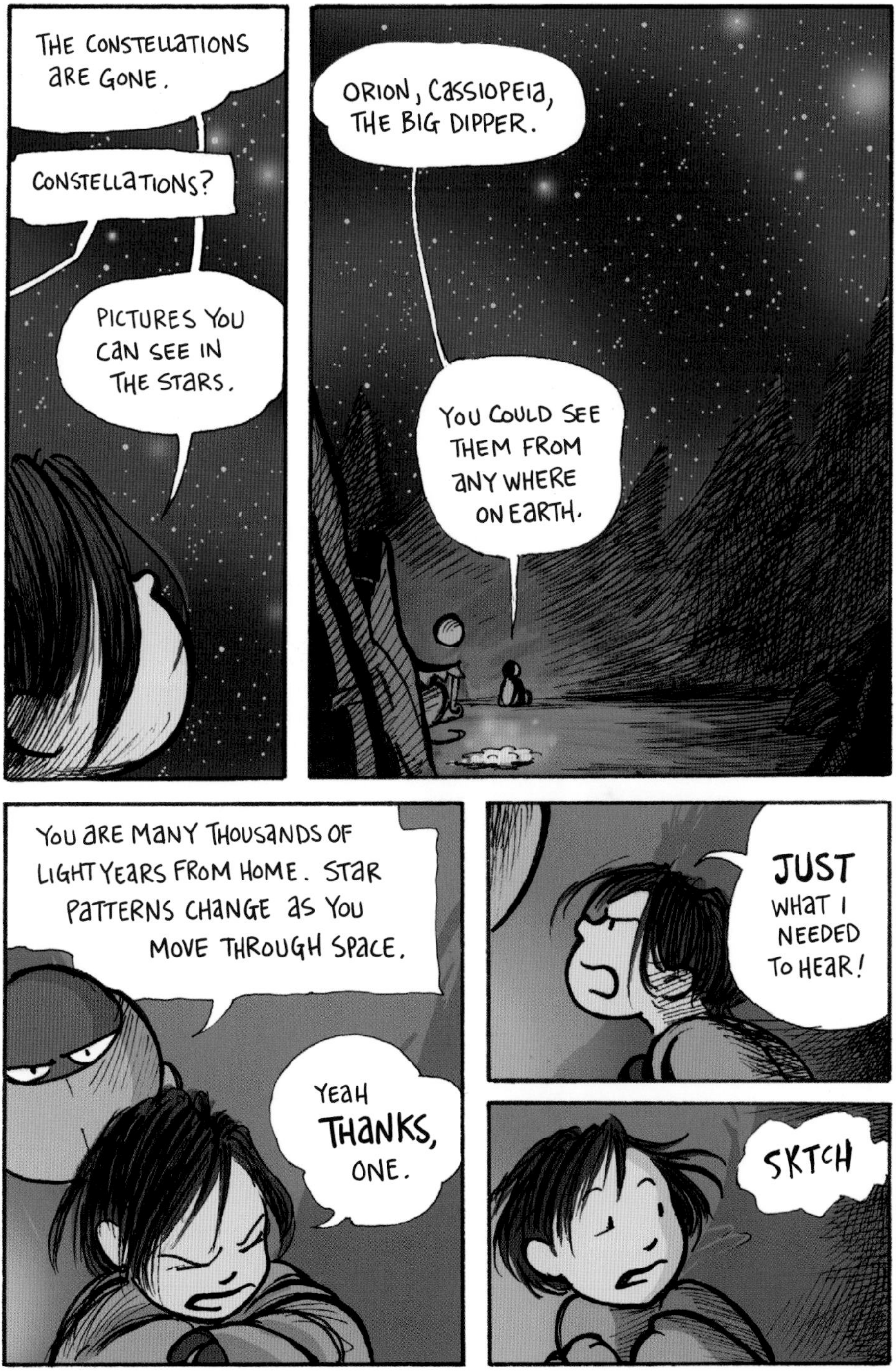
THE CONSTELLATIONS ARE GONE.
CONSTELLATIONS?
PICTURES YOU CAN SEE IN THE STARS.
ORION, CASSIOPEIA, THE BIG DIPPER.
YOU COULD SEE THEM FROM ANY WHERE ON EARTH.
YOU ARE MANY THOUSANDS OF LIGHT YEARS FROM HOME. STAR PATTERNS CHANGE AS YOU MOVE THROUGH SPACE.
YEAH THANKS, ONE.
JUST WHAT I NEEDED TO HEAR!
SKTCH

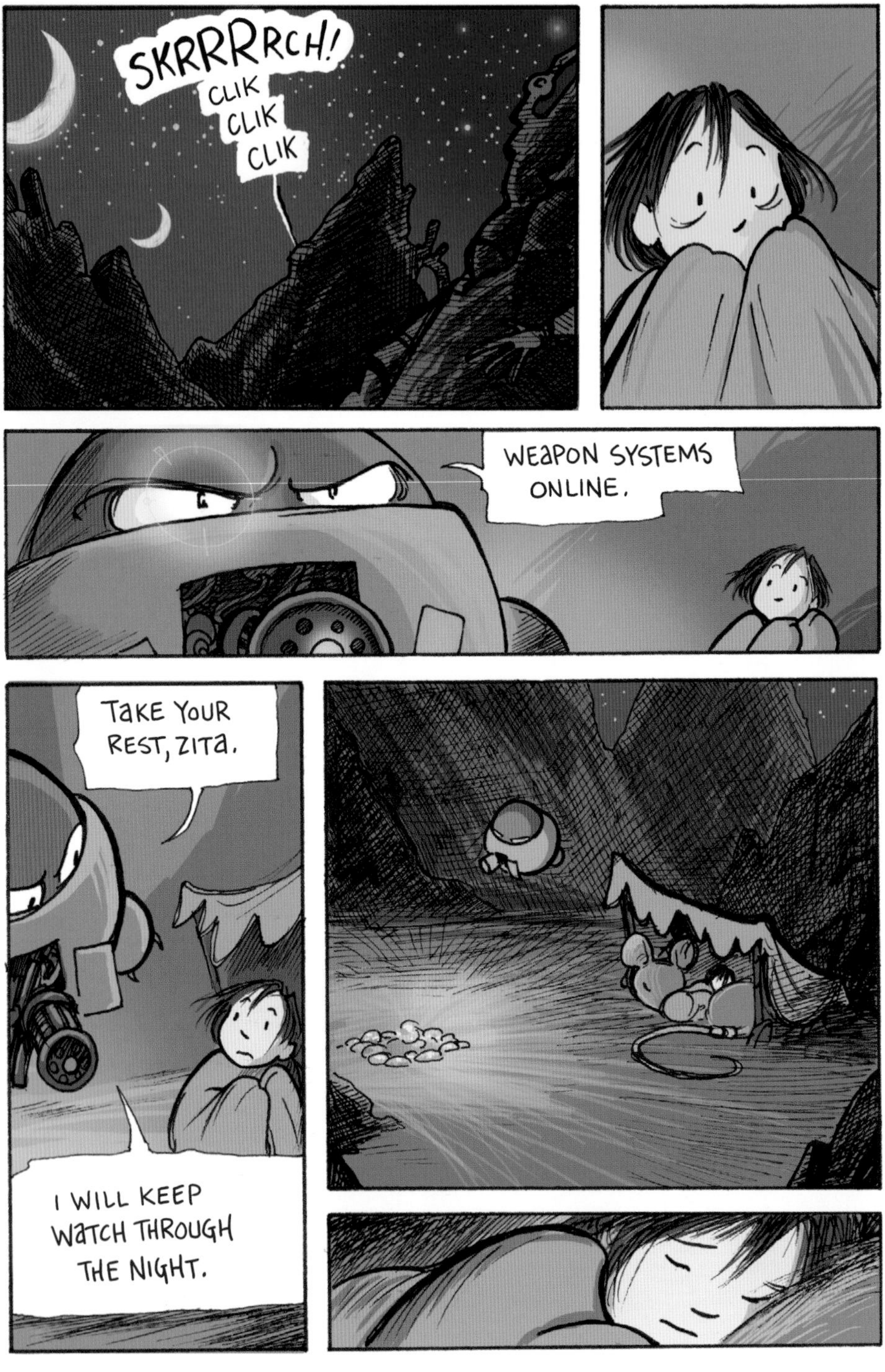
SKRRRRCH!
CLIK
CLIK
CLIK
WEAPON SYSTEMS ONLINE.
TAKE YOUR REST, ZITA.
I WILL KEEP WATCH THROUGH THE NIGHT.

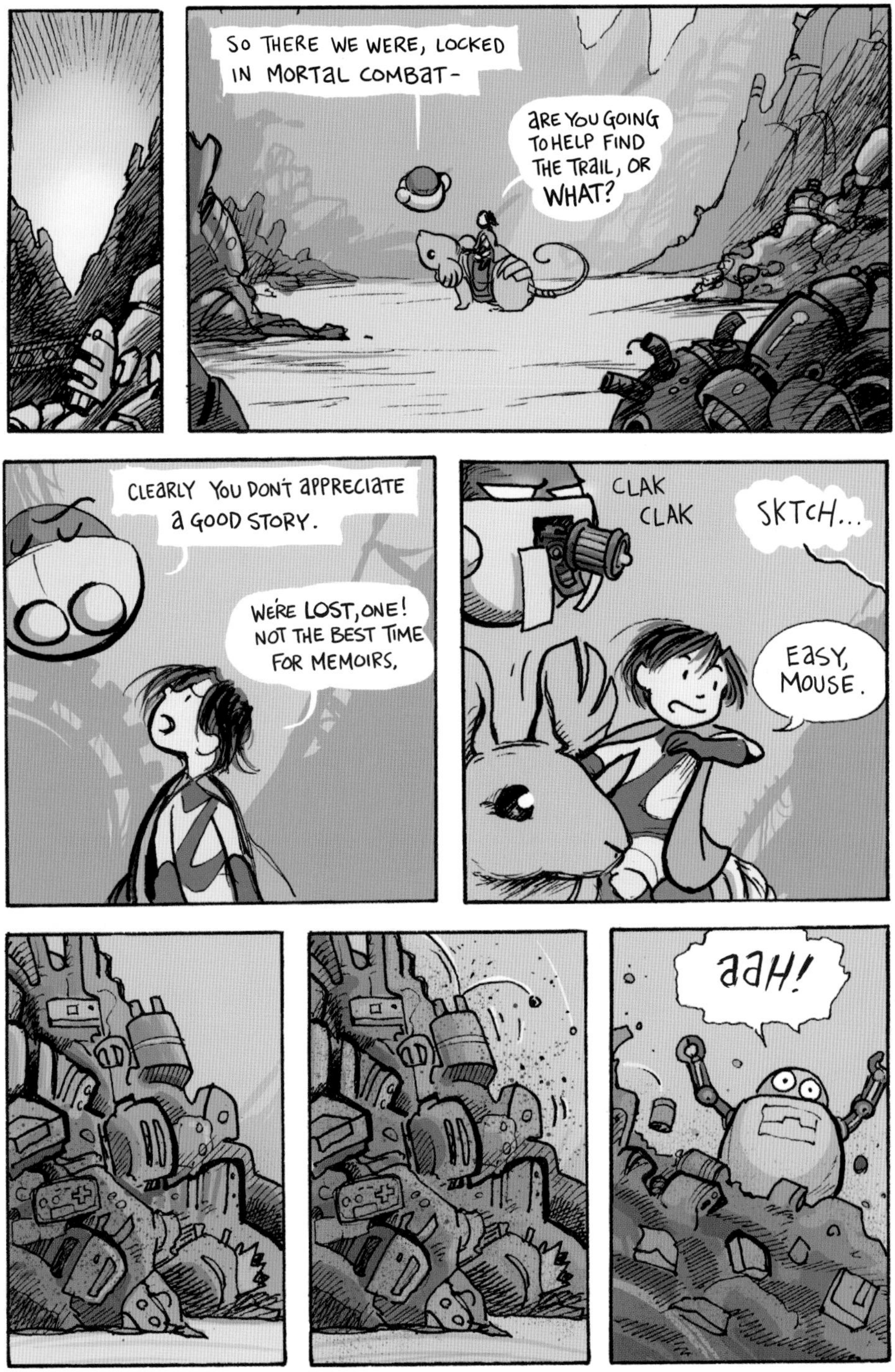
SO THERE WE WERE, LOCKED IN MORTAL COMBAT-
ARE YOU GOING TO HELP FIND THE TRAIL, OR WHAT?
CLEARLY YOU DON'T APPRECIATE A GOOD STORY.
WE'RE LOST, ONE! NOT THE BEST TIME FOR MEMOIRS.
CLAK CLAK
SKTCH...
EASY, MOUSE.
AAH!

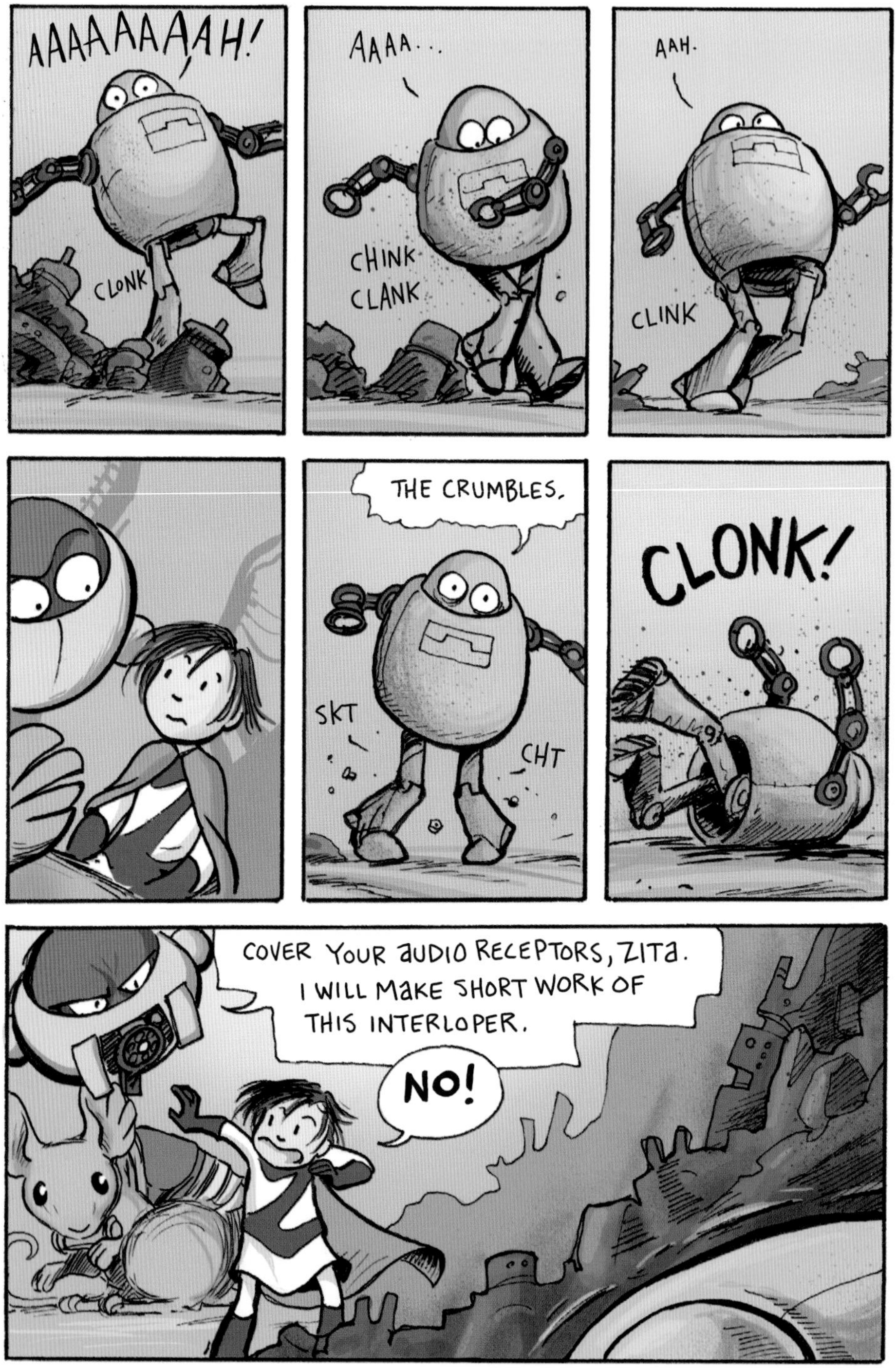
AAAAAAAAH!
CLONK
AAAA...
CHINK
CLANK
AAH.
CLINK
THE CRUMBLES.
SKT
CHT
CLONK!
COVER YOUR AUDIO RECEPTORS, ZITA. I WILL MAKE SHORT WORK OF THIS INTERLOPER.
NO!

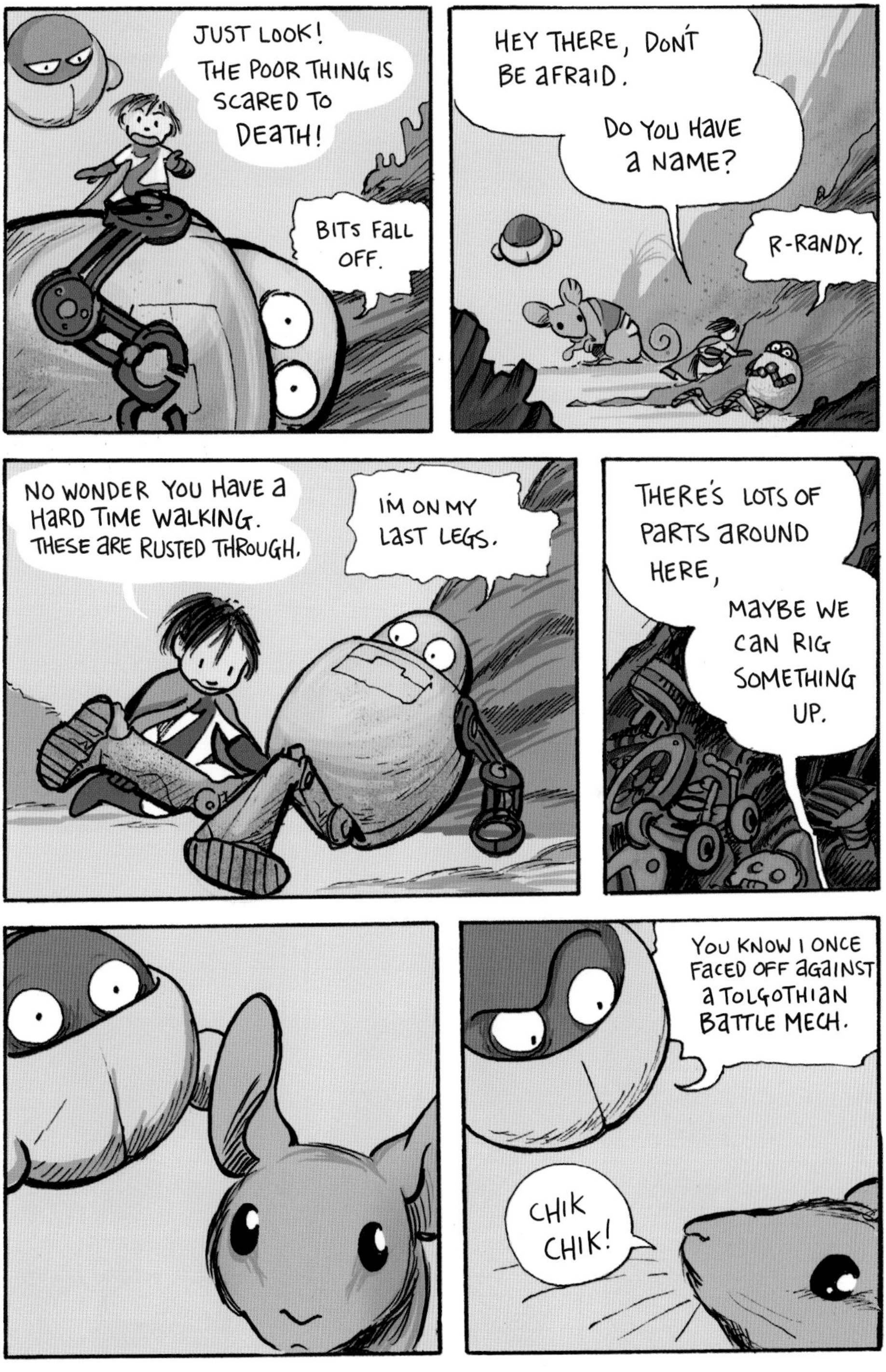
JUST LOOK! THE POOR THING IS SCARED TO DEATH!
BITS FALL OFF.
HEY THERE, DON'T BE AFRAID.
DO YOU HAVE A NAME?
R-RANDY.
NO WONDER YOU HAVE A HARD TIME WALKING. THESE ARE RUSTED THROUGH.
I'M ON MY LAST LEGS.
THERE'S LOTS OF PARTS AROUND HERE,
MAYBE WE CAN RIG SOMETHING UP.
YOU KNOW I ONCE FACED OFF AGAINST A TOLGOTHIAN BATTLE MECH.
CHIK CHIK!

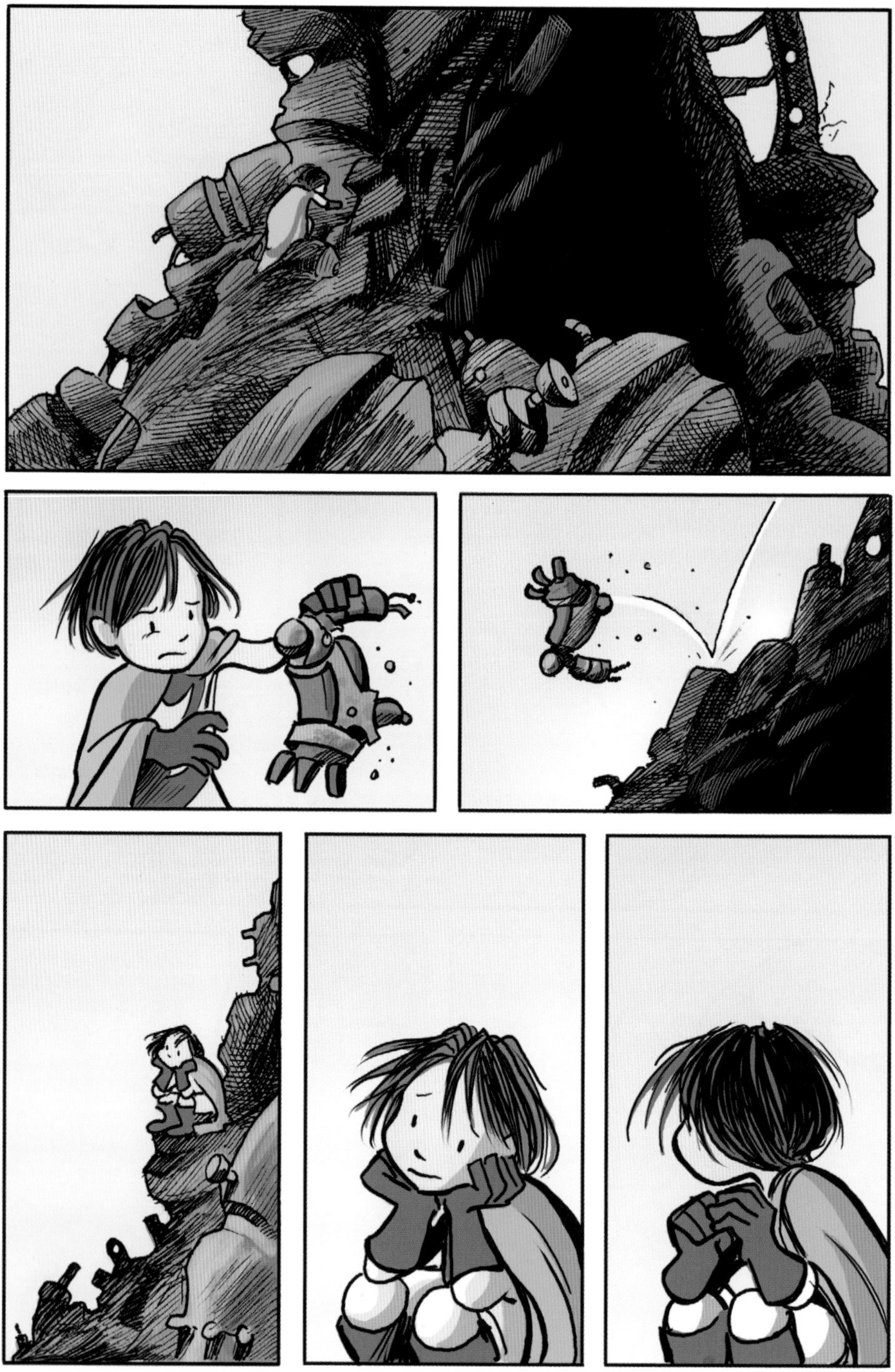

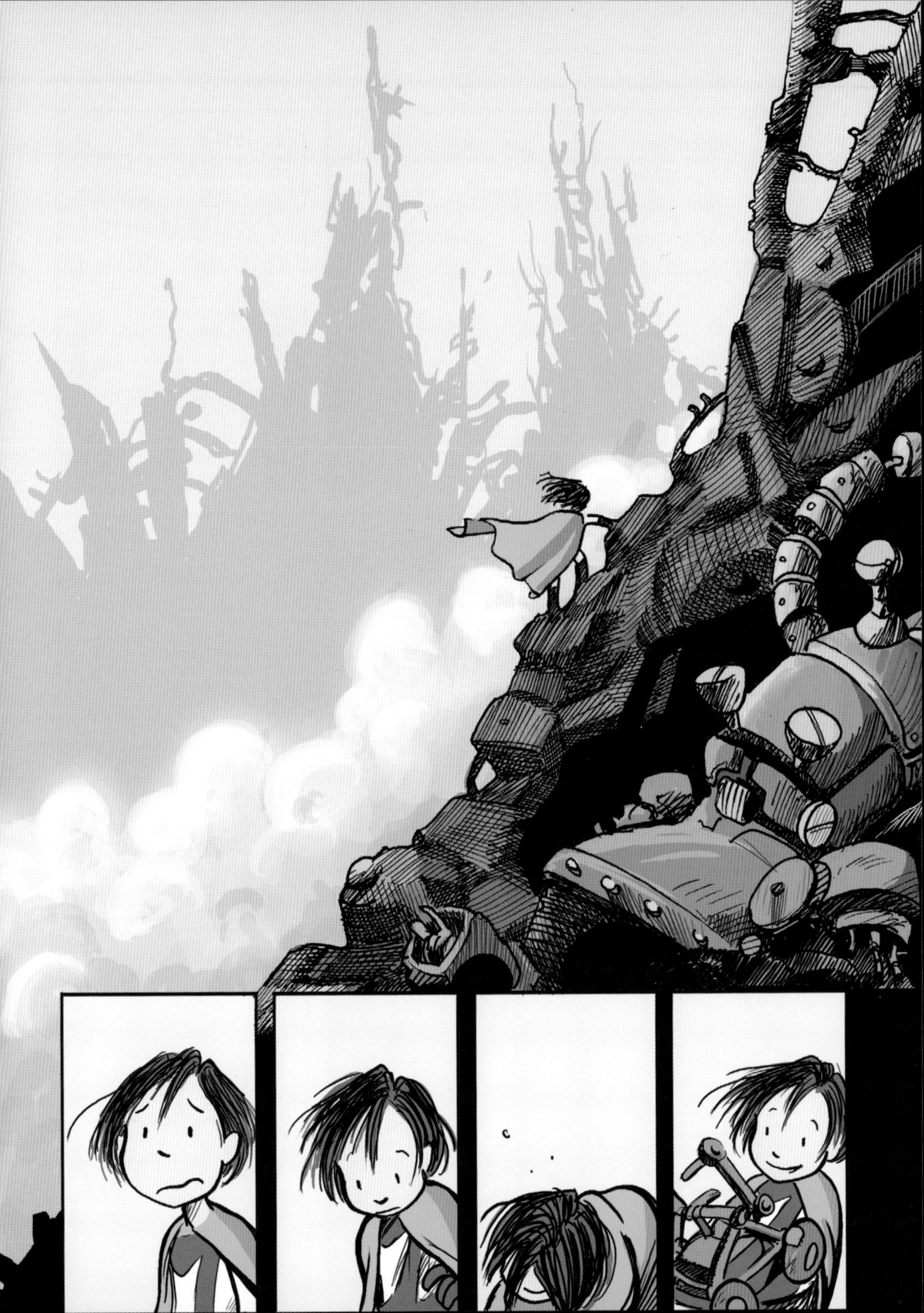

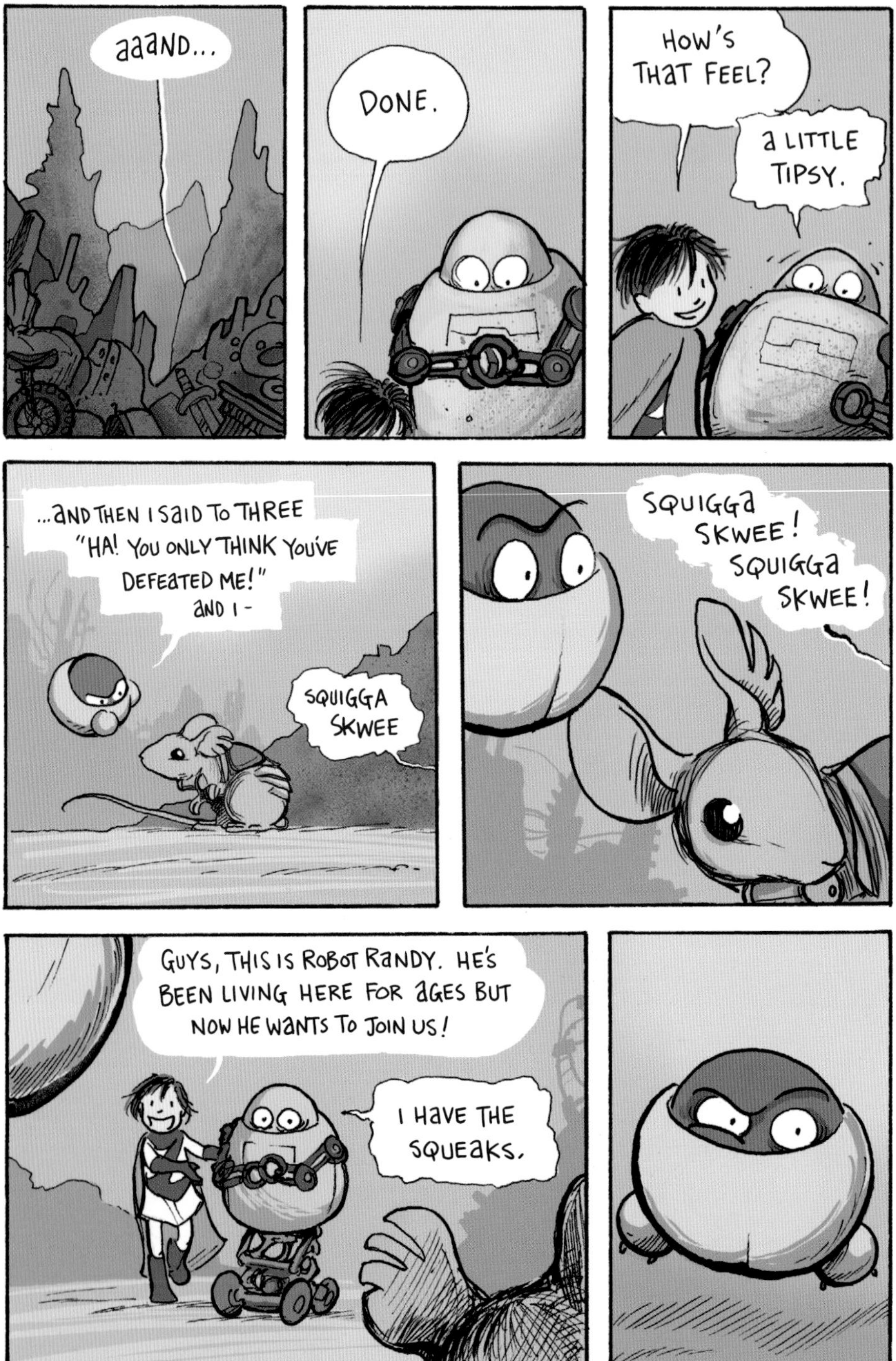
aaaND...
DONE.
HOW'S THAT FEEL?
a LITTLE TIPSY.
...aND THEN I SaID TO THREE "HA! YOU ONLY THINK YOU'VE DEFEaTED ME!" aND I -
SQUIGGA SKWEE
SQUIGGa SKWEE! SQUIGGa SKWEE!
GUYS, THIS IS ROBOT RaNDY. HE'S BEEN LIVING HERE FOR aGES BUT NOW HE WaNTS TO JOIN US!
I HaVE THE SQUEaKS.

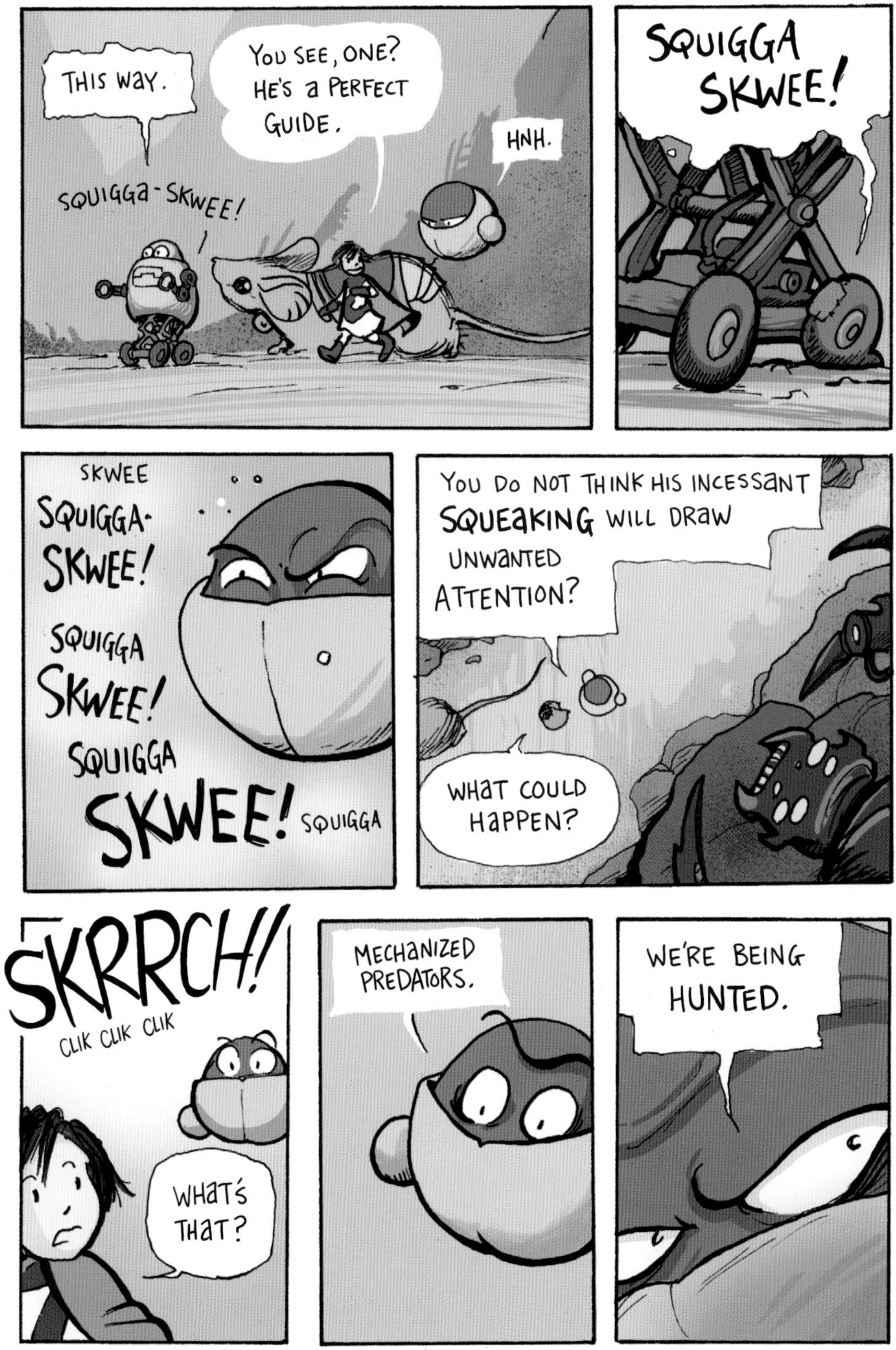
THIS WAY.
YOU SEE, ONE? HE'S A PERFECT GUIDE.
HNH.
SQUIGGA-SKWEE!
SQUIGGA SKWEE!
SKWEE
SQUIGGA-SKWEE!
SQUIGGA SKWEE!
SQUIGGA SKWEE!
SQUIGGA
YOU DO NOT THINK HIS INCESSANT SQUEAKING WILL DRAW UNWANTED ATTENTION?
WHAT COULD HAPPEN?
SKRRCH!
CLIK CLIK CLIK
WHAT'S THAT?
MECHANIZED PREDATORS.
WE'RE BEING HUNTED.

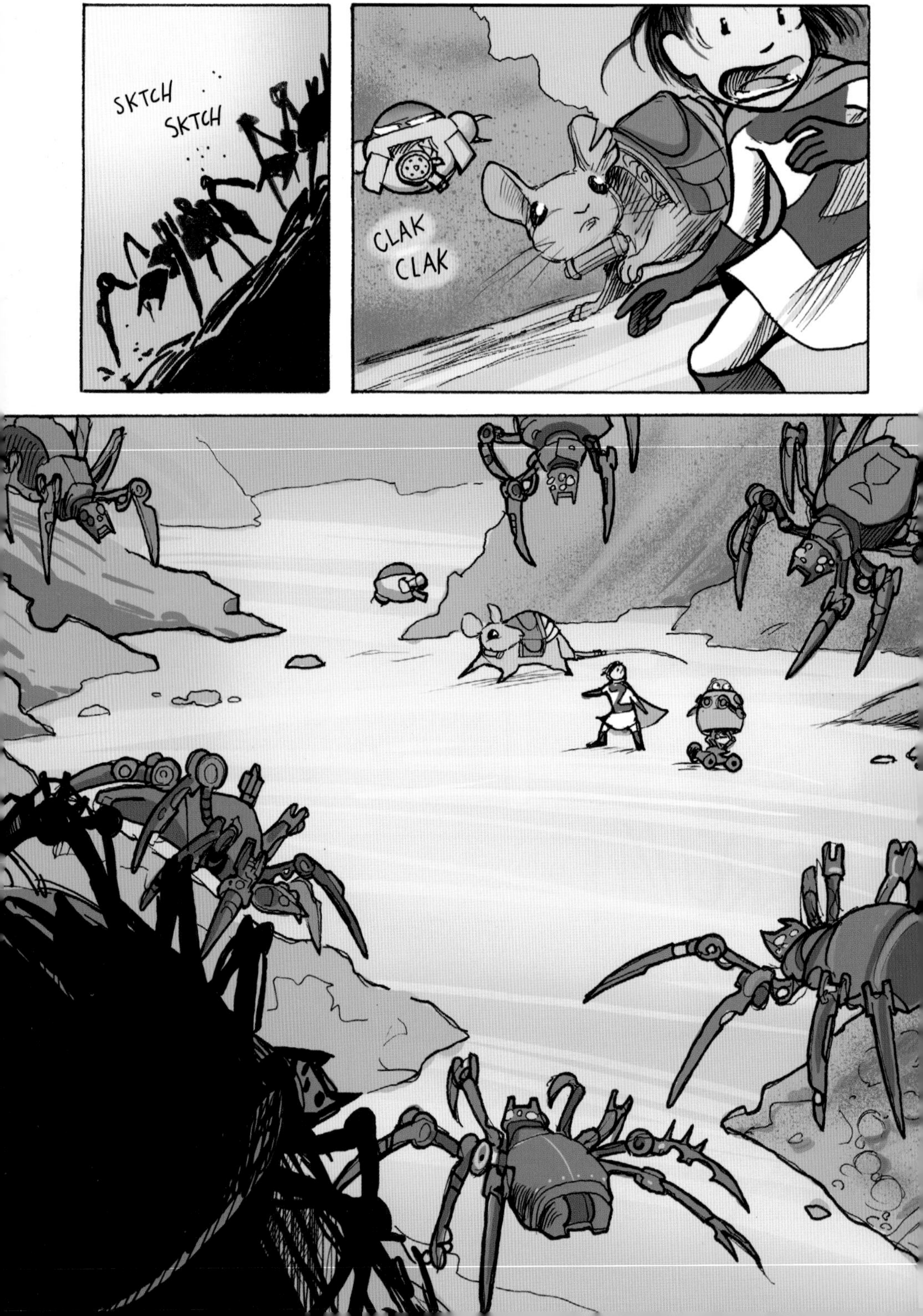
SKTCH
SKTCH
CLAK
CLAK

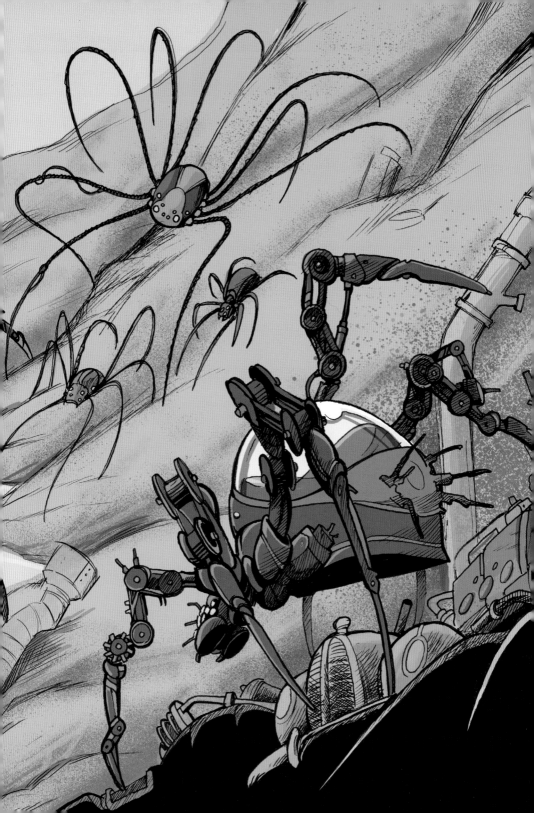

SKREEE!

MOUSE?

SKREEK!

MOUSE, NO!

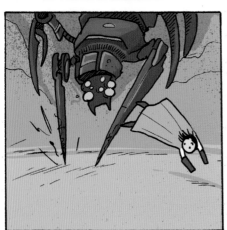

ONE! DO SOMETHING!

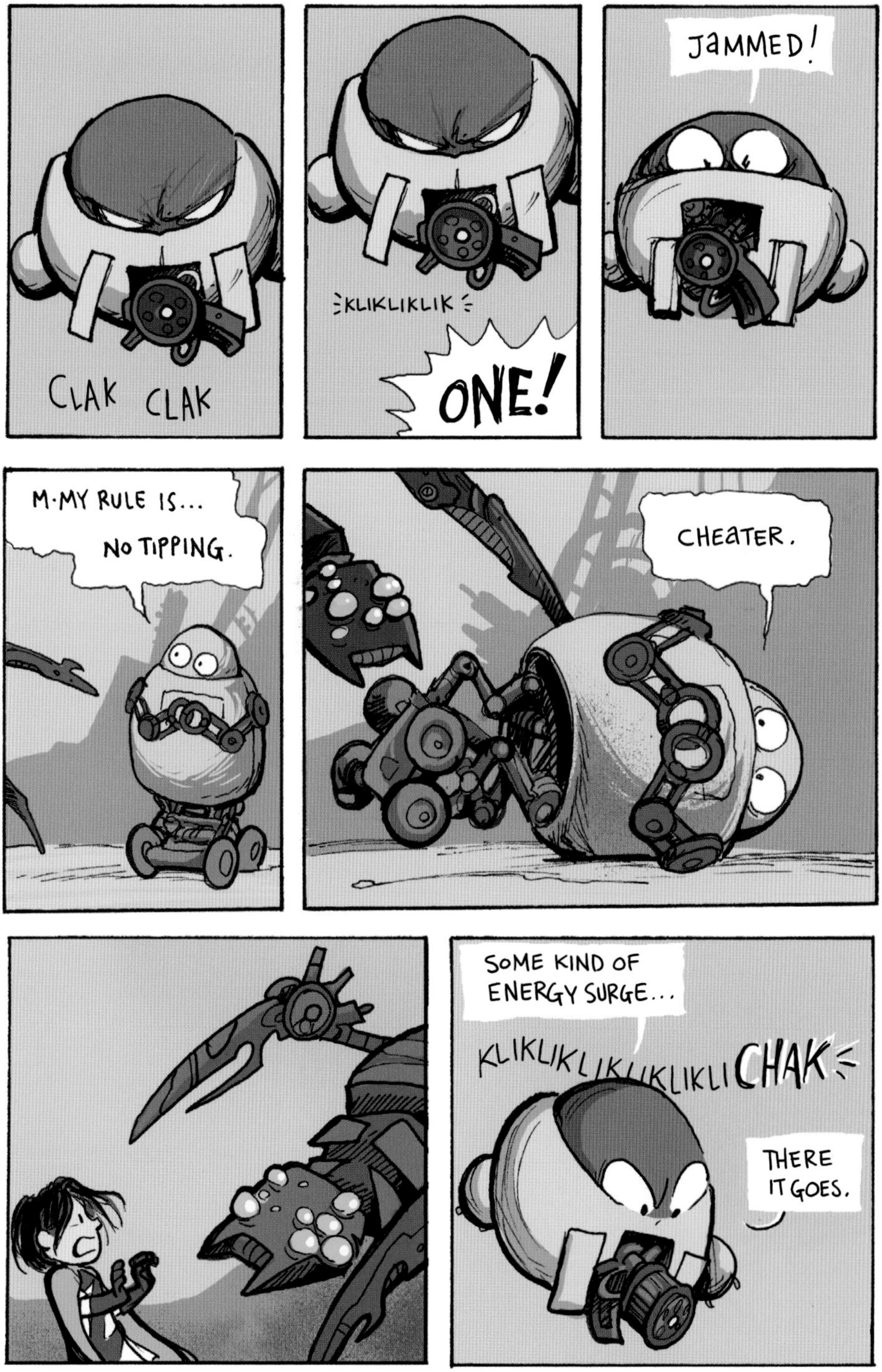
CLAK CLAK
KLIKLIKLIK
ONE!
JAMMED!
M-MY RULE IS...
NO TIPPING.
CHEATER.
SOME KIND OF ENERGY SURGE...
KLIKLIKLIKLIKLIKLIKLI CHAK
THERE IT GOES.

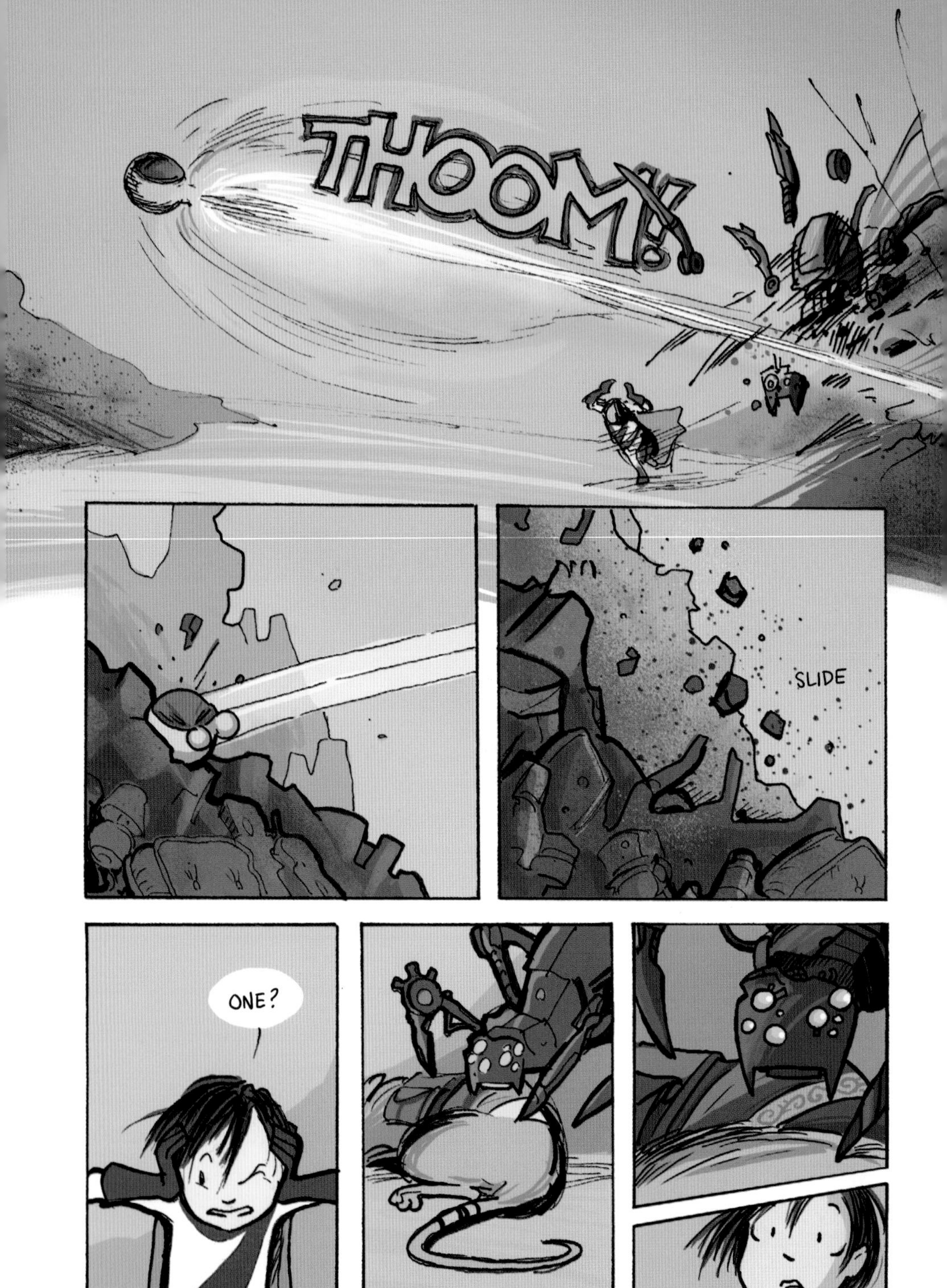
THOOM!
SLIDE
ONE?

SKITTR!

SKITTR!

SKITTR!

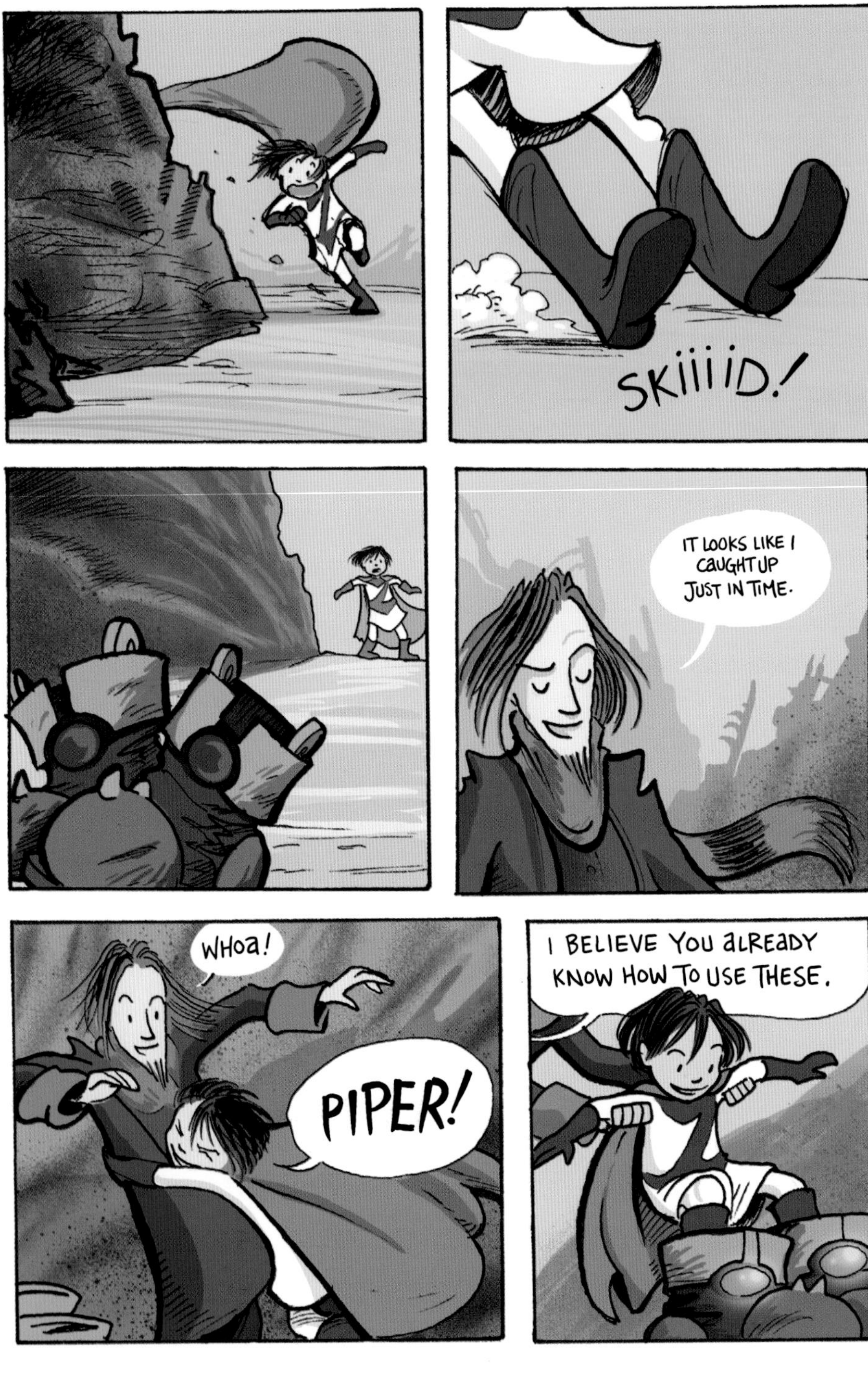
SKIIIID!
IT LOOKS LIKE I CAUGHT UP JUST IN TIME.
WHOA!
PIPER!
I BELIEVE YOU ALREADY KNOW HOW TO USE THESE.

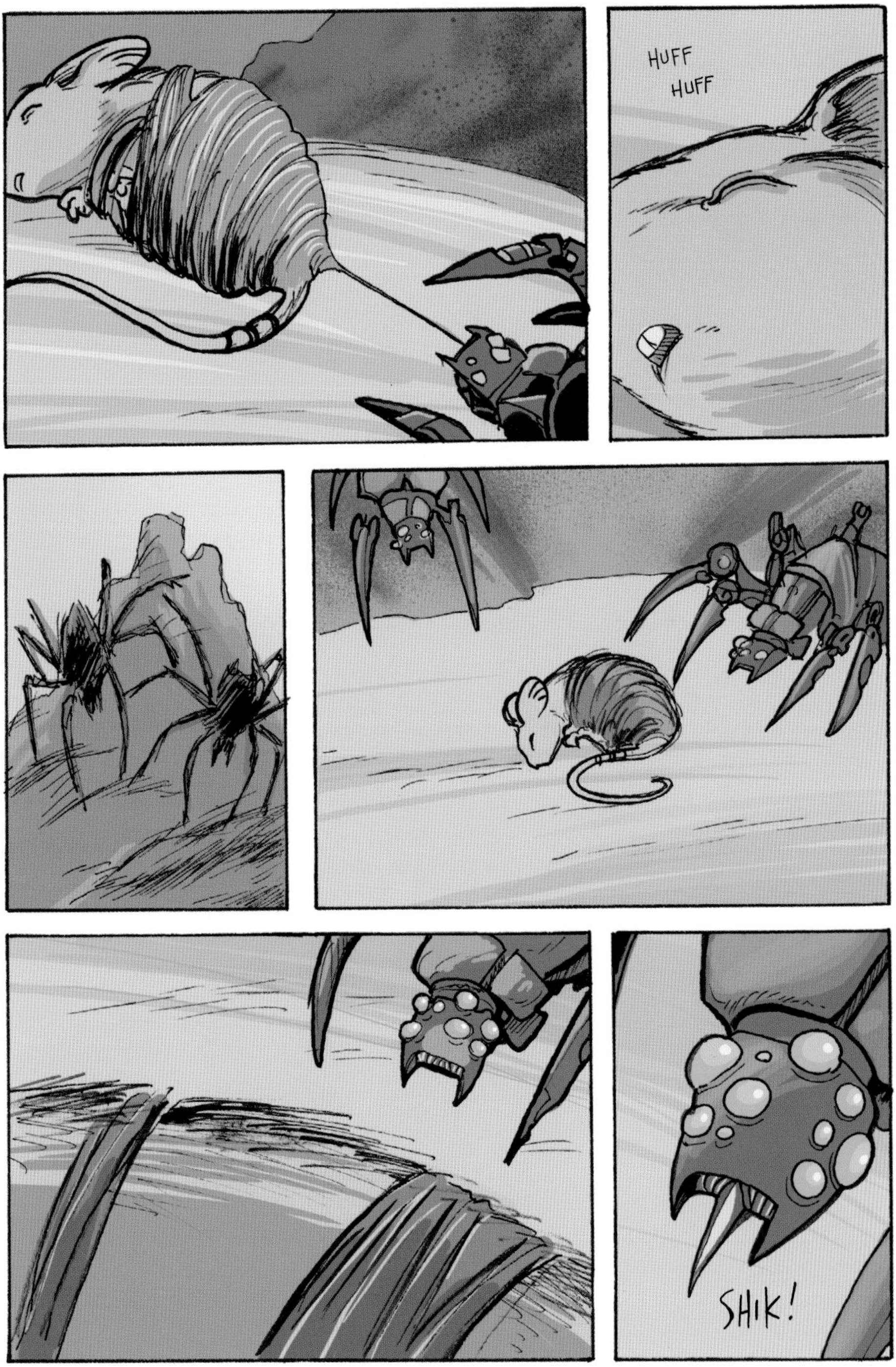
HUFF
HUFF
SHIK!

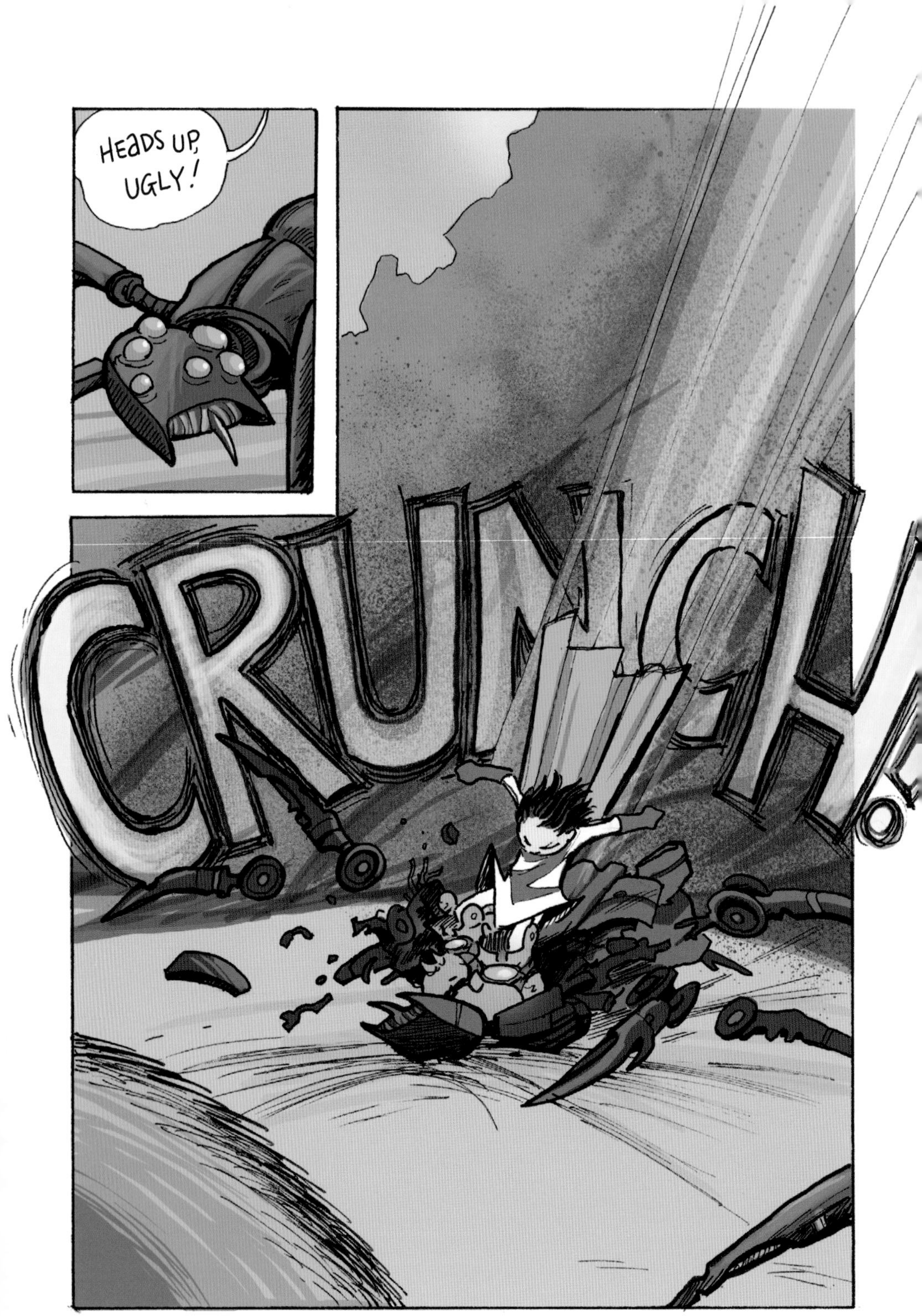
HEADS UP, UGLY!
CRUNCH!

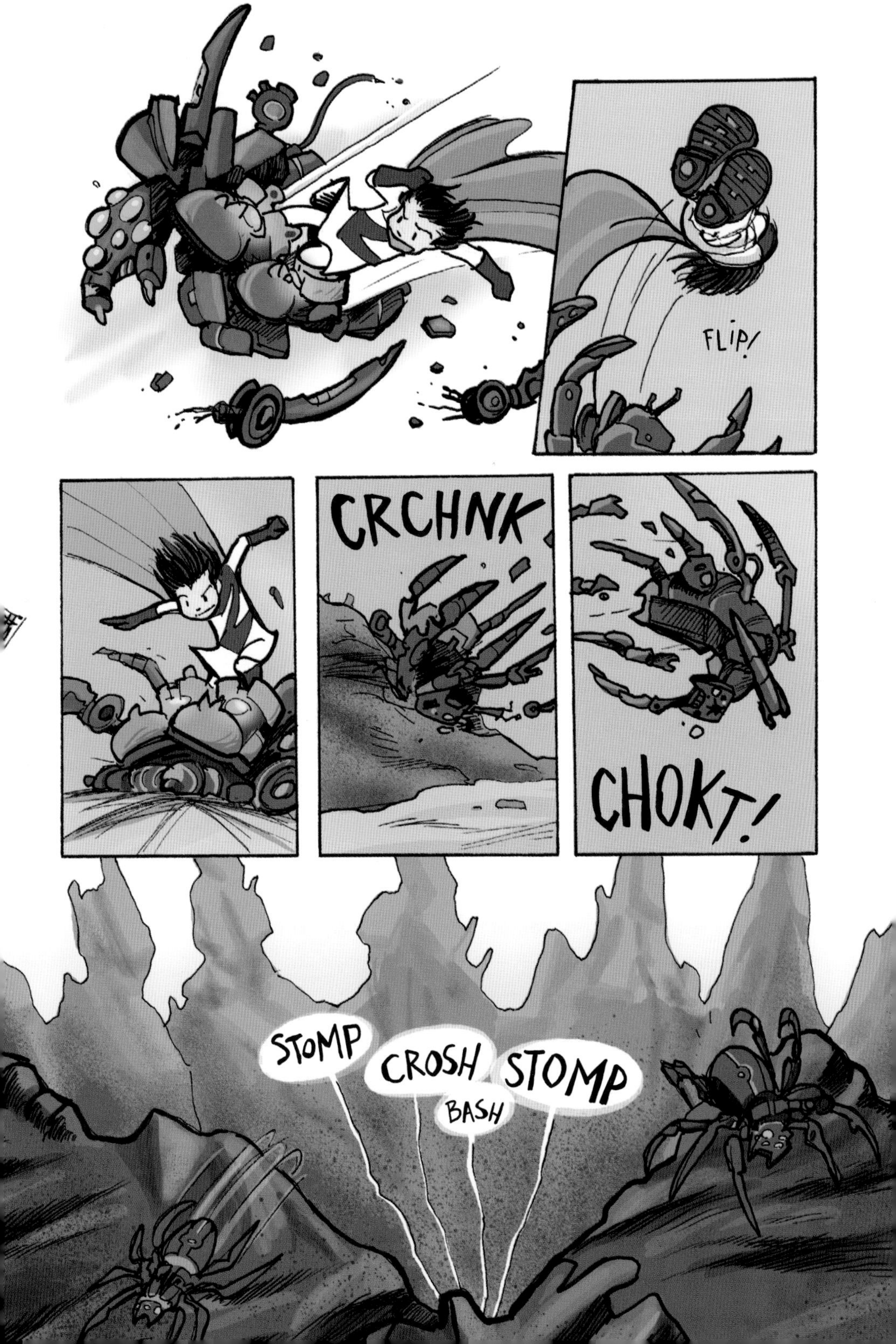
FLIP!
CRCHNK
CHOKT!
STOMP
CROSH
BASH
STOMP

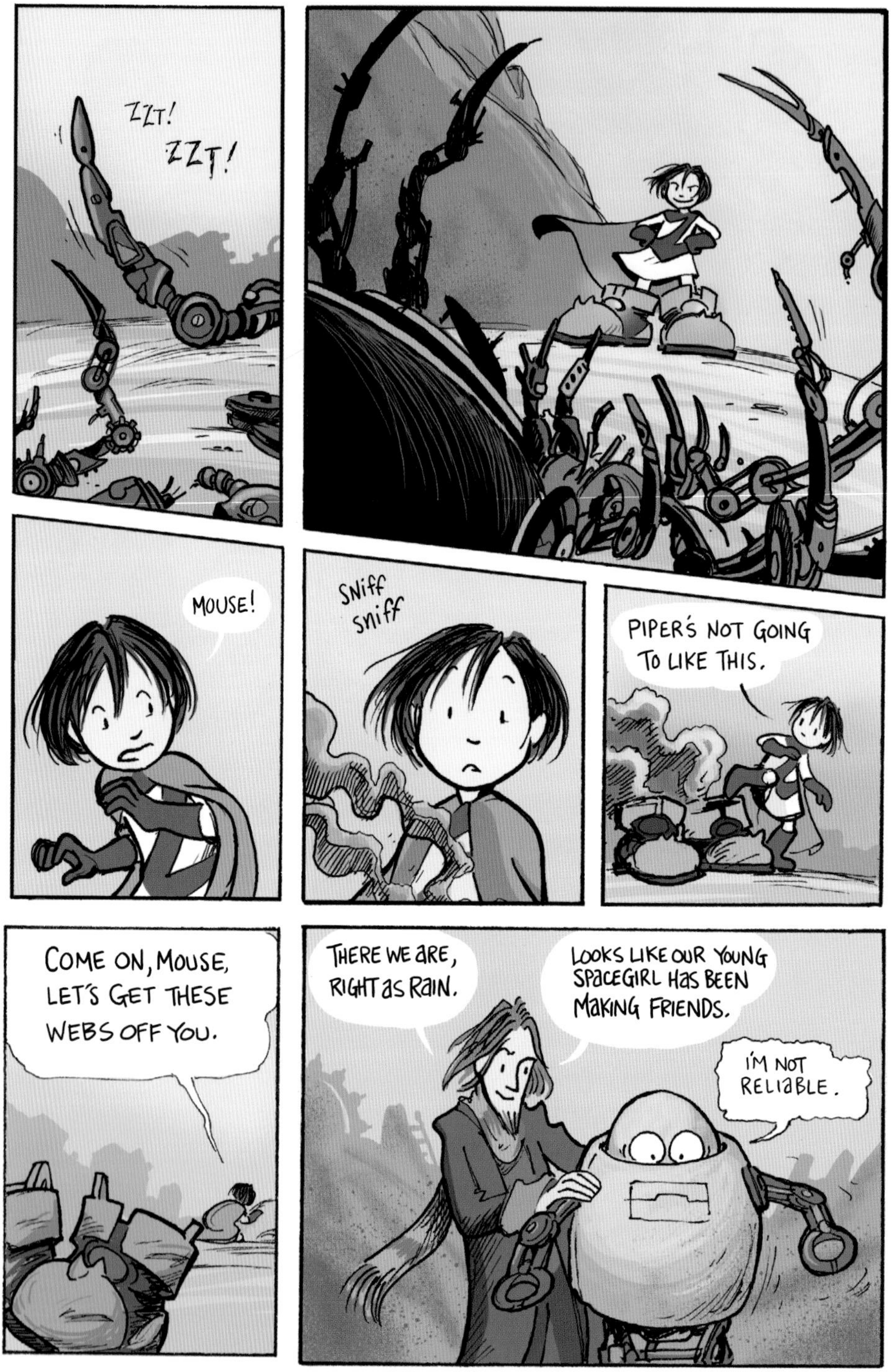
ZZT!
ZZT!
MOUSE!
SNIFF SNIFF
PIPER'S NOT GOING TO LIKE THIS.
COME ON, MOUSE, LET'S GET THESE WEBS OFF YOU.
THERE WE ARE, RIGHT AS RAIN.
LOOKS LIKE OUR YOUNG SPACEGIRL HAS BEEN MAKING FRIENDS.
I'M NOT RELIABLE.

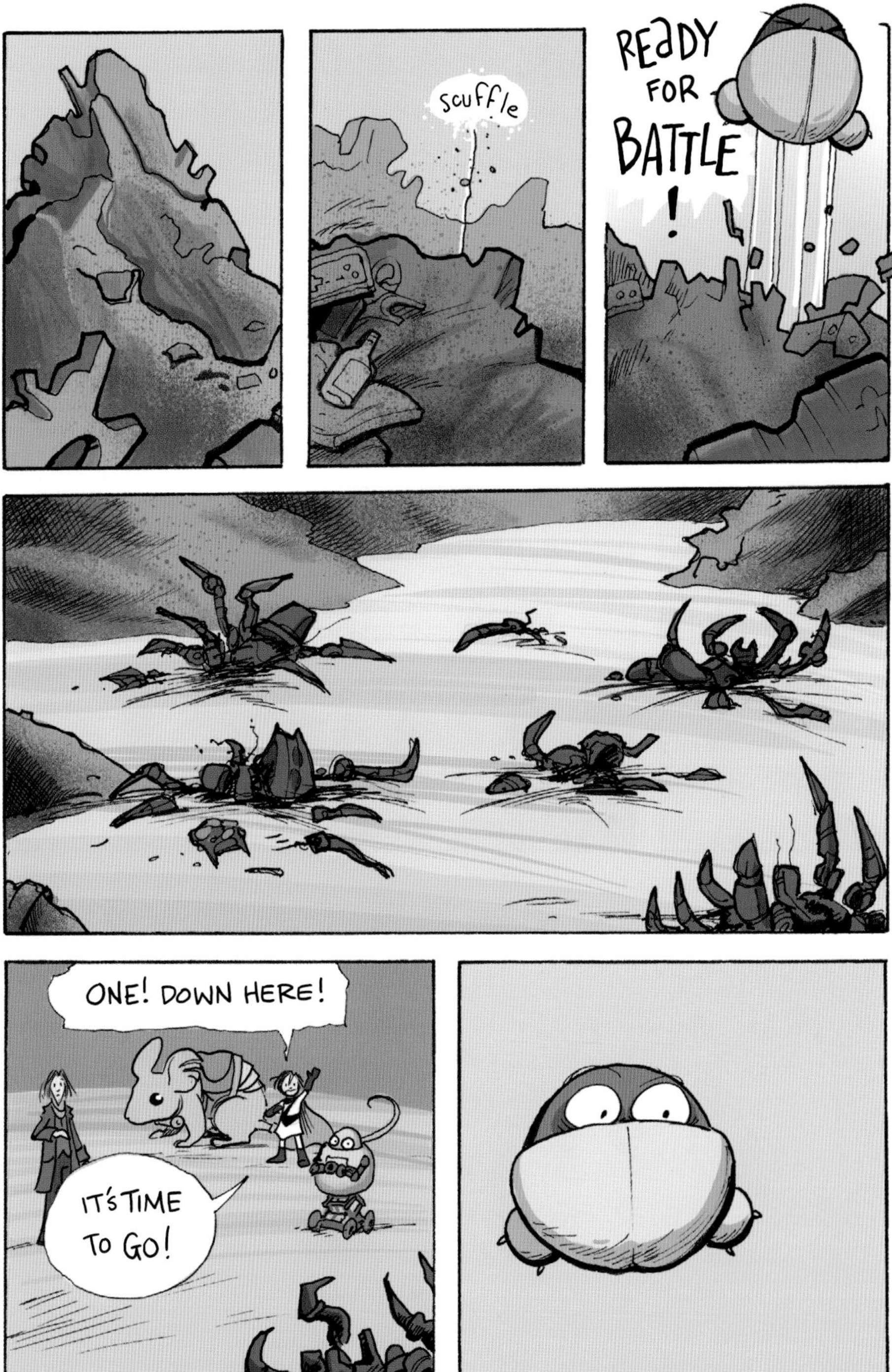
scuffle
READY FOR BATTLE!
ONE! DOWN HERE!
IT'S TIME TO GO!

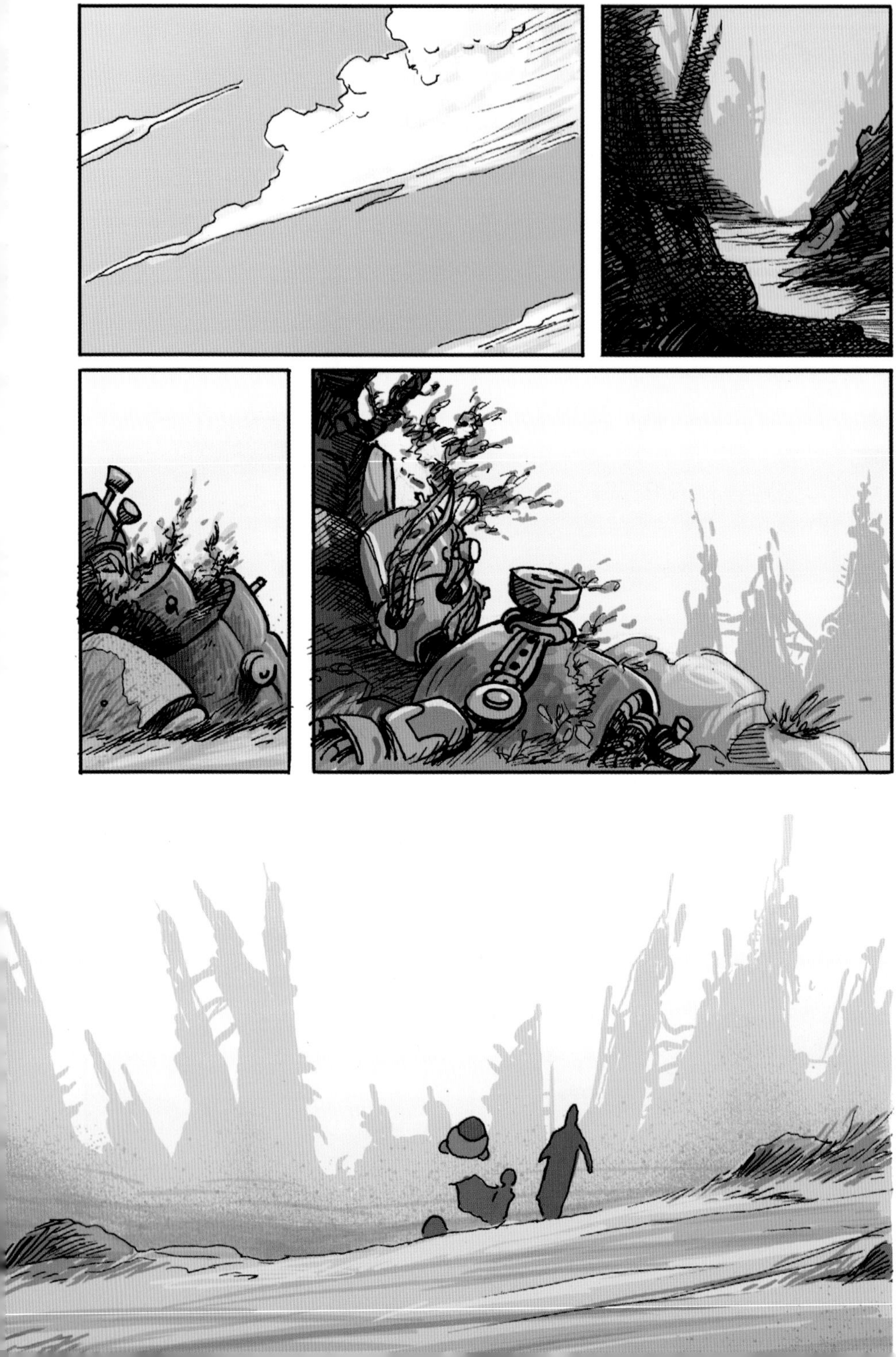

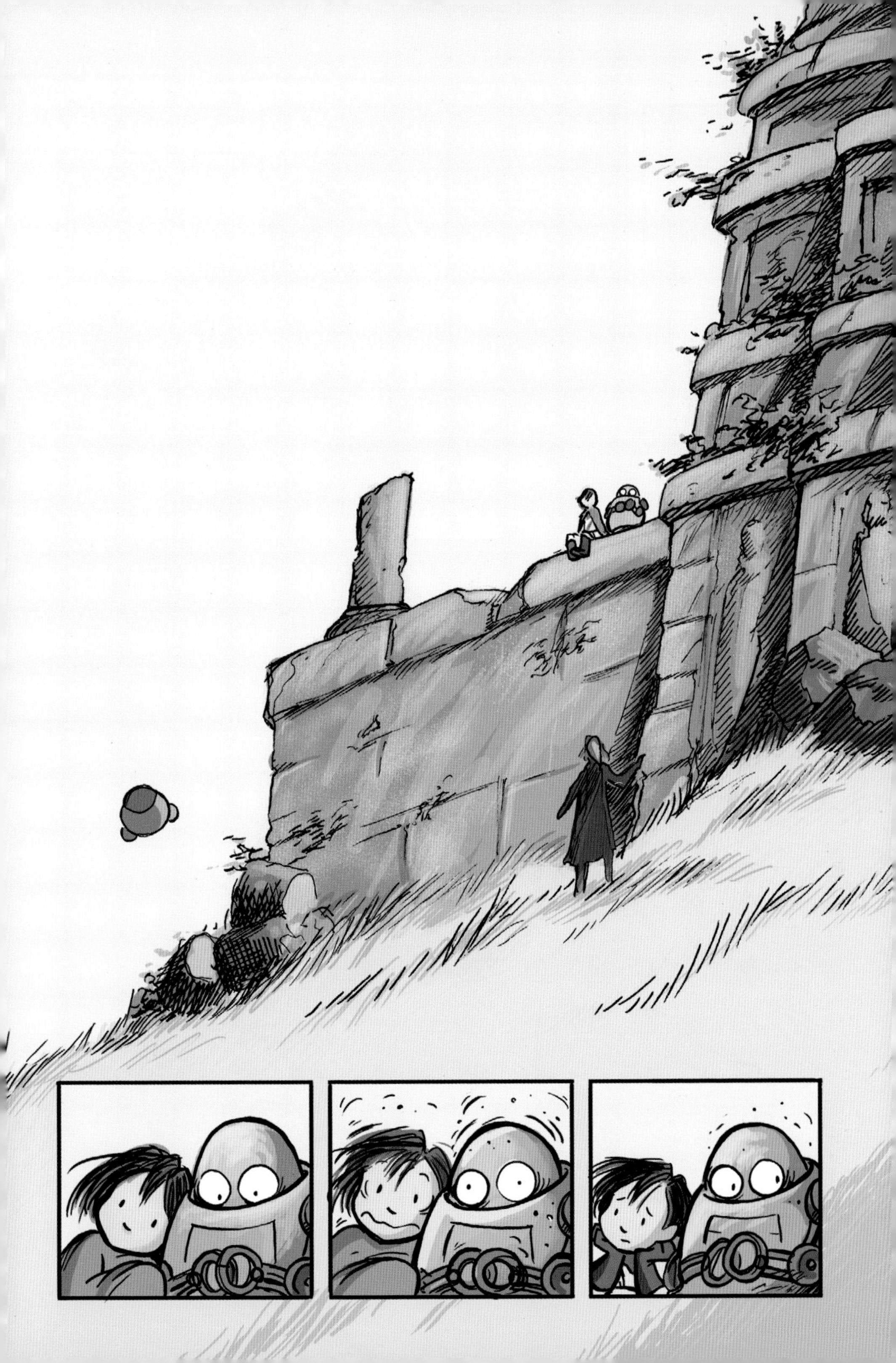

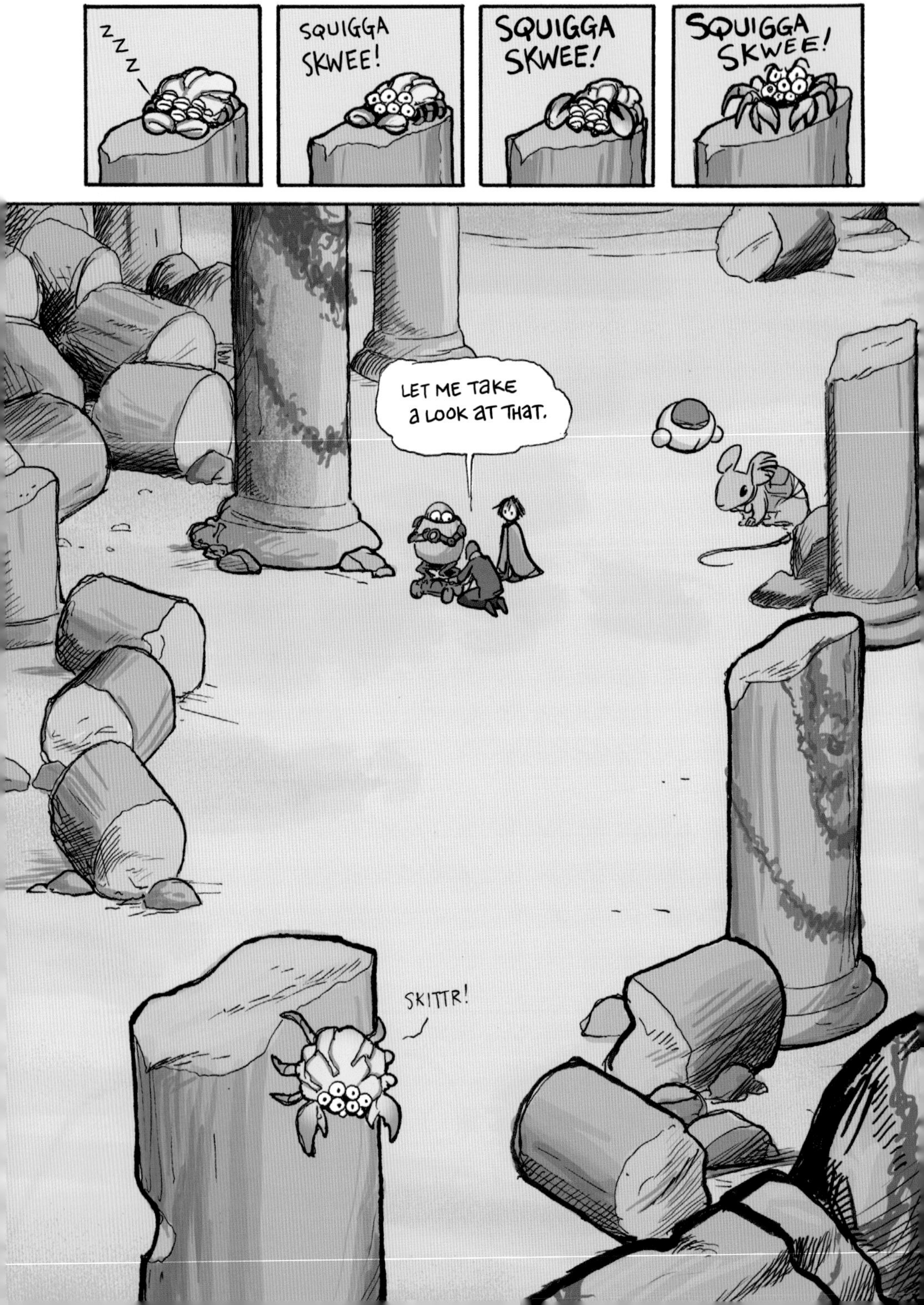
Z
Z
Z
SQUIGGA
SKWEE!
SQUIGGA
SKWEE!
SQUIGGA
SKWEE!
LET ME TAKE
A LOOK AT THAT.
SKITTR!

THERE.

THAT SHOULD FIX THE SQUEAKING...

BUT I DON'T KNOW WHAT'S CAUSING THE RATTLING.

NERVES.

I'VE NEVER BEEN THIS FAR FROM THE SCRAP PILES BEFORE.

WE'RE NEARING THE EDGE OF THE RUSTED WASTES—THE CASTLE IS JUST OVER THAT HILL.

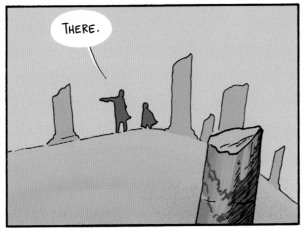

THERE.

NOW DO YOU UNDERSTAND HOW DIFFICULT THIS REALLY IS?

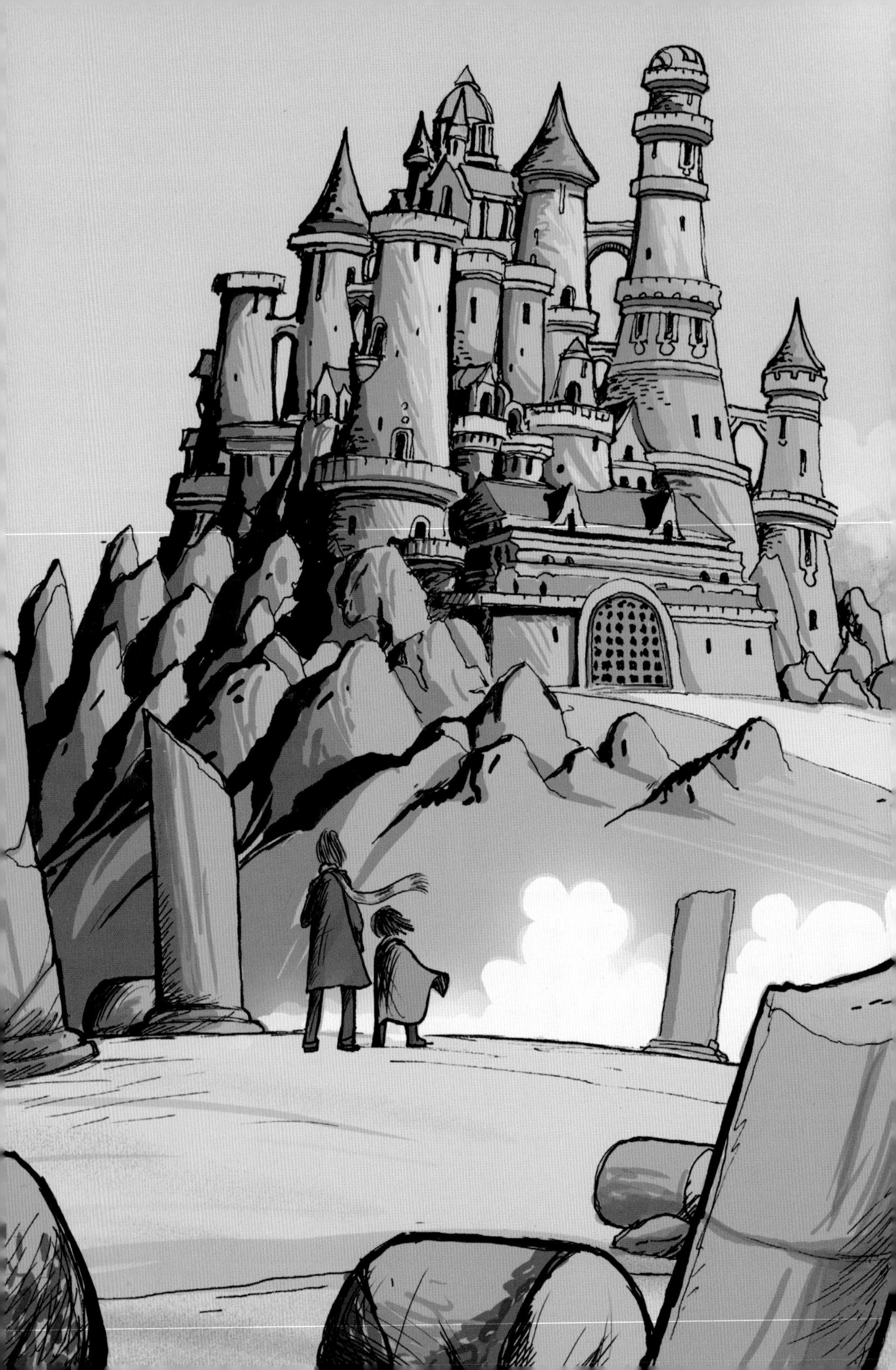

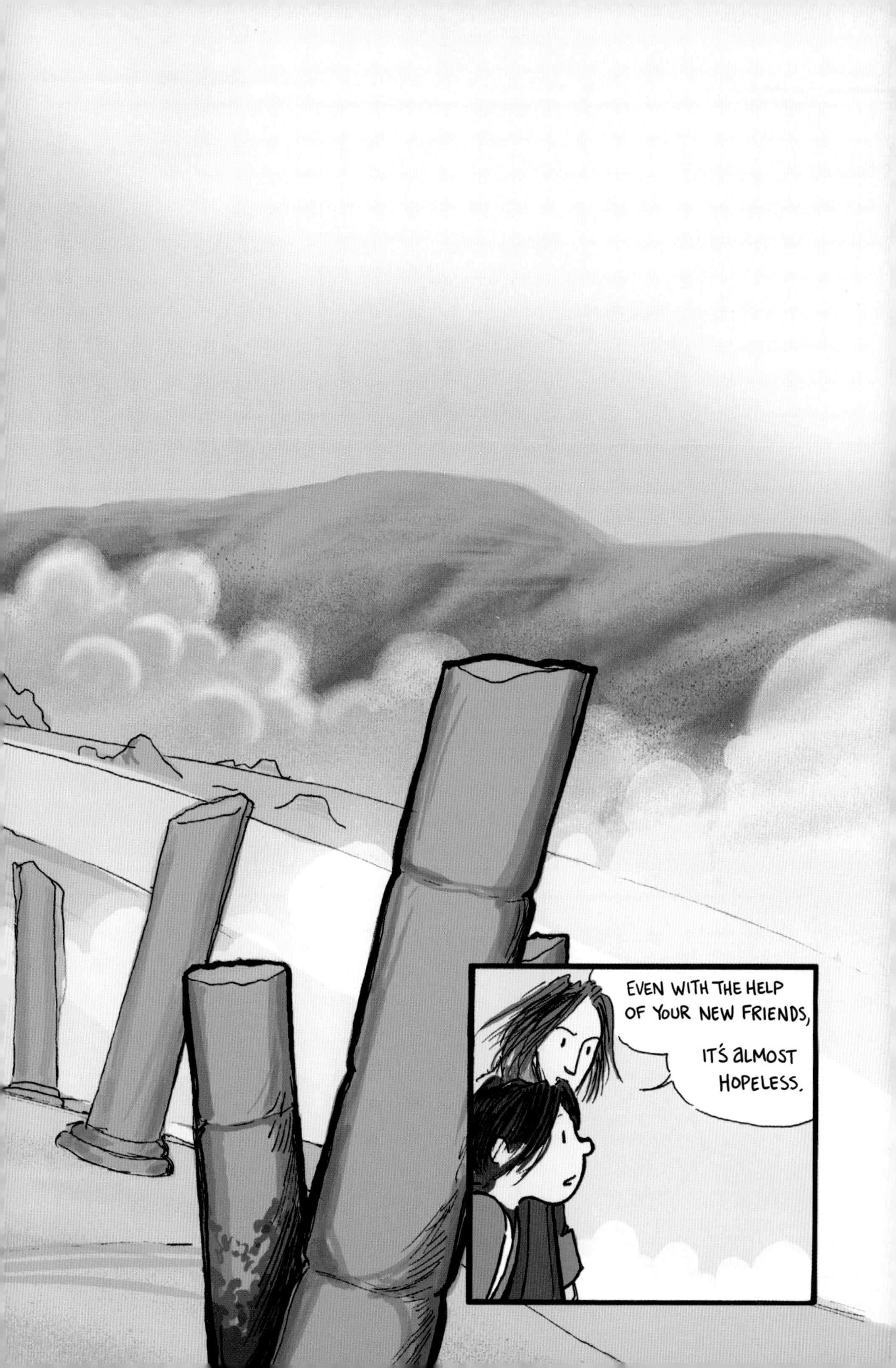
EVEN WITH THE HELP OF YOUR NEW FRIENDS,
IT'S ALMOST HOPELESS.

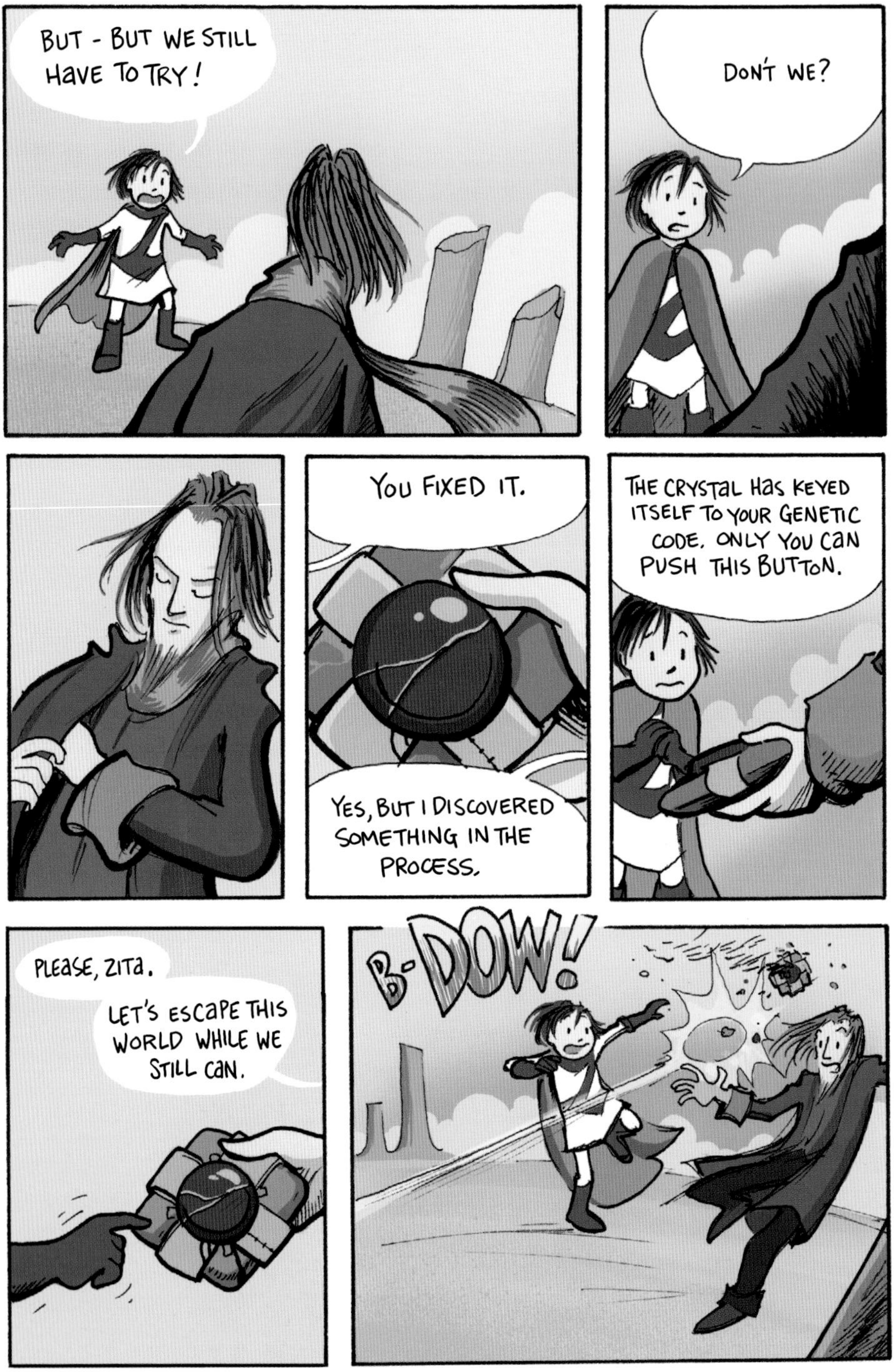
BUT - BUT WE STILL HAVE TO TRY!
DON'T WE?
YOU FIXED IT.
YES, BUT I DISCOVERED SOMETHING IN THE PROCESS.
THE CRYSTAL HAS KEYED ITSELF TO YOUR GENETIC CODE. ONLY YOU CAN PUSH THIS BUTTON.
PLEASE, ZITA.
LET'S ESCAPE THIS WORLD WHILE WE STILL CAN.
B-DOW!

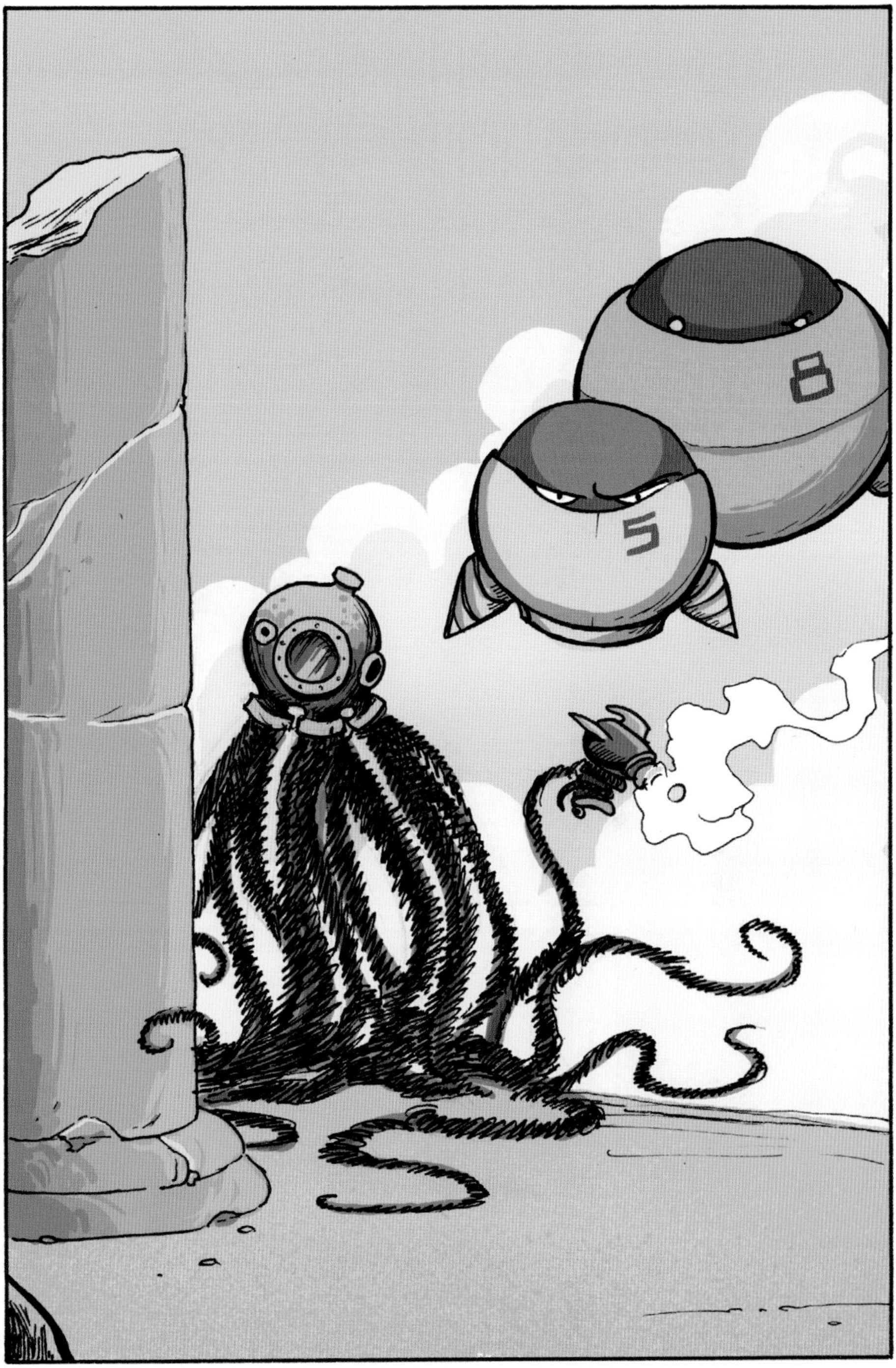

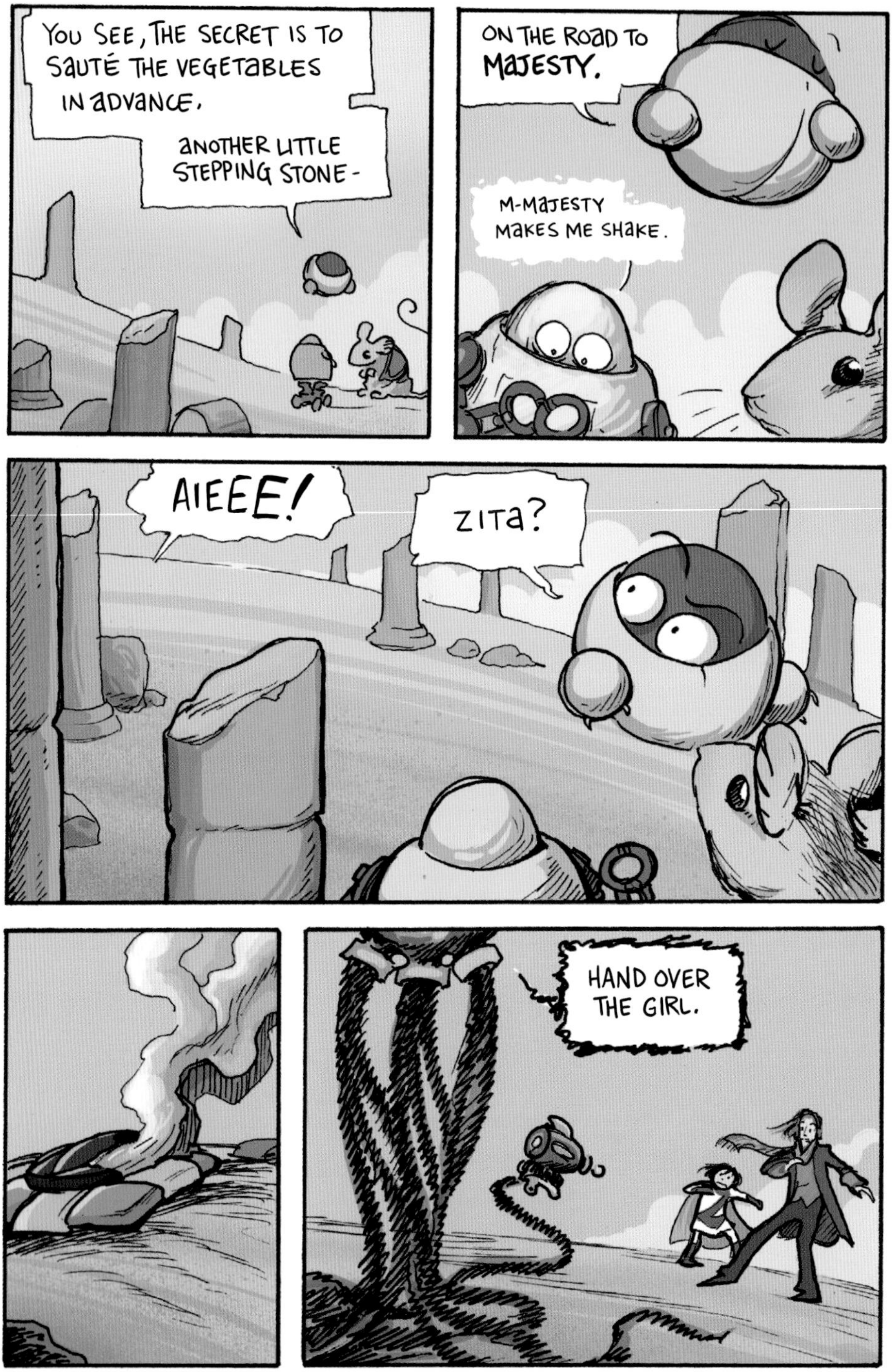
YOU SEE, THE SECRET IS TO SAUTÉ THE VEGETABLES IN ADVANCE.
ANOTHER LITTLE STEPPING STONE-
ON THE ROAD TO MAJESTY.
M-MAJESTY MAKES ME SHAKE.
AIEEE!
ZITA?
HAND OVER THE GIRL.

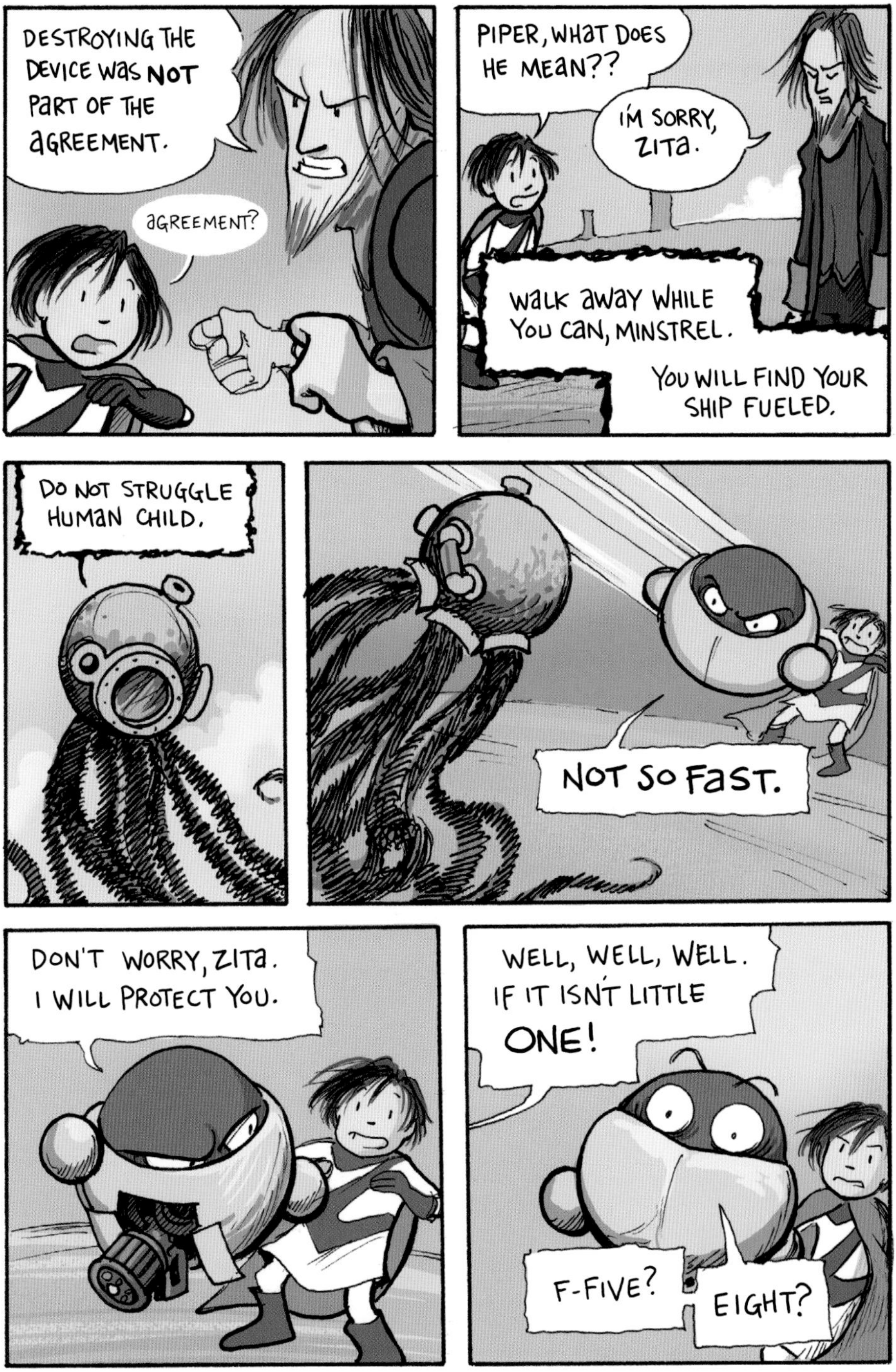
DESTROYING THE DEVICE WAS **NOT** PART OF THE AGREEMENT.
AGREEMENT?
PIPER, WHAT DOES HE MEAN??
I'M SORRY, ZITA.
WALK AWAY WHILE YOU CAN, MINSTREL.
YOU WILL FIND YOUR SHIP FUELED.
DO NOT STRUGGLE HUMAN CHILD.
NOT SO FAST.
DON'T WORRY, ZITA. I WILL PROTECT YOU.
WELL, WELL, WELL. IF IT ISN'T LITTLE ONE!
F-FIVE?
EIGHT?

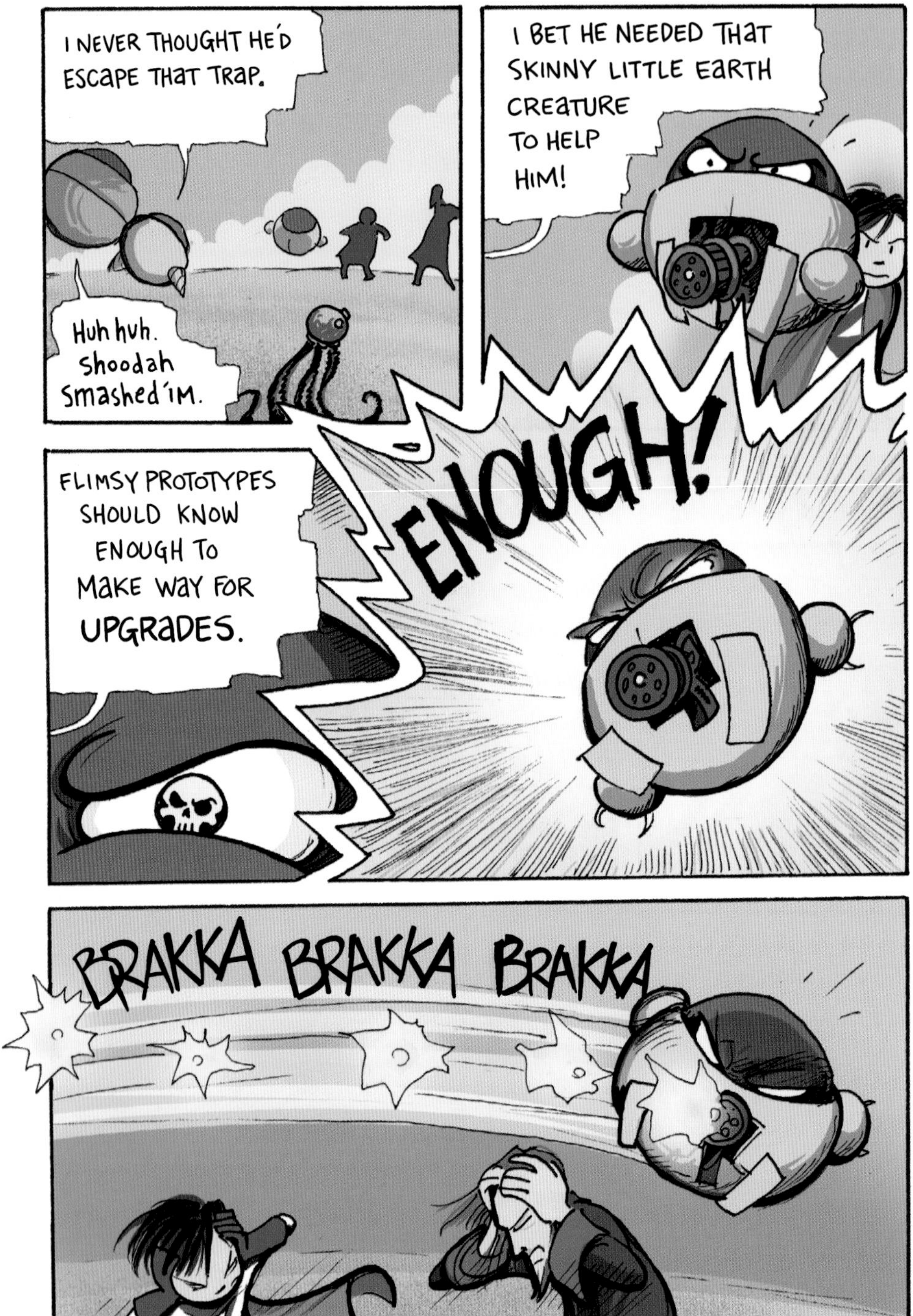
I NEVER THOUGHT HE'D ESCAPE THAT TRAP.
Huh huh. Shoodah smashed 'IM.
I BET HE NEEDED THAT SKINNY LITTLE EARTH CREATURE TO HELP HIM!
ENOUGH!
FLIMSY PROTOTYPES SHOULD KNOW ENOUGH TO MAKE WAY FOR UPGRADES.
BRAKKA BRAKKA BRAKKA

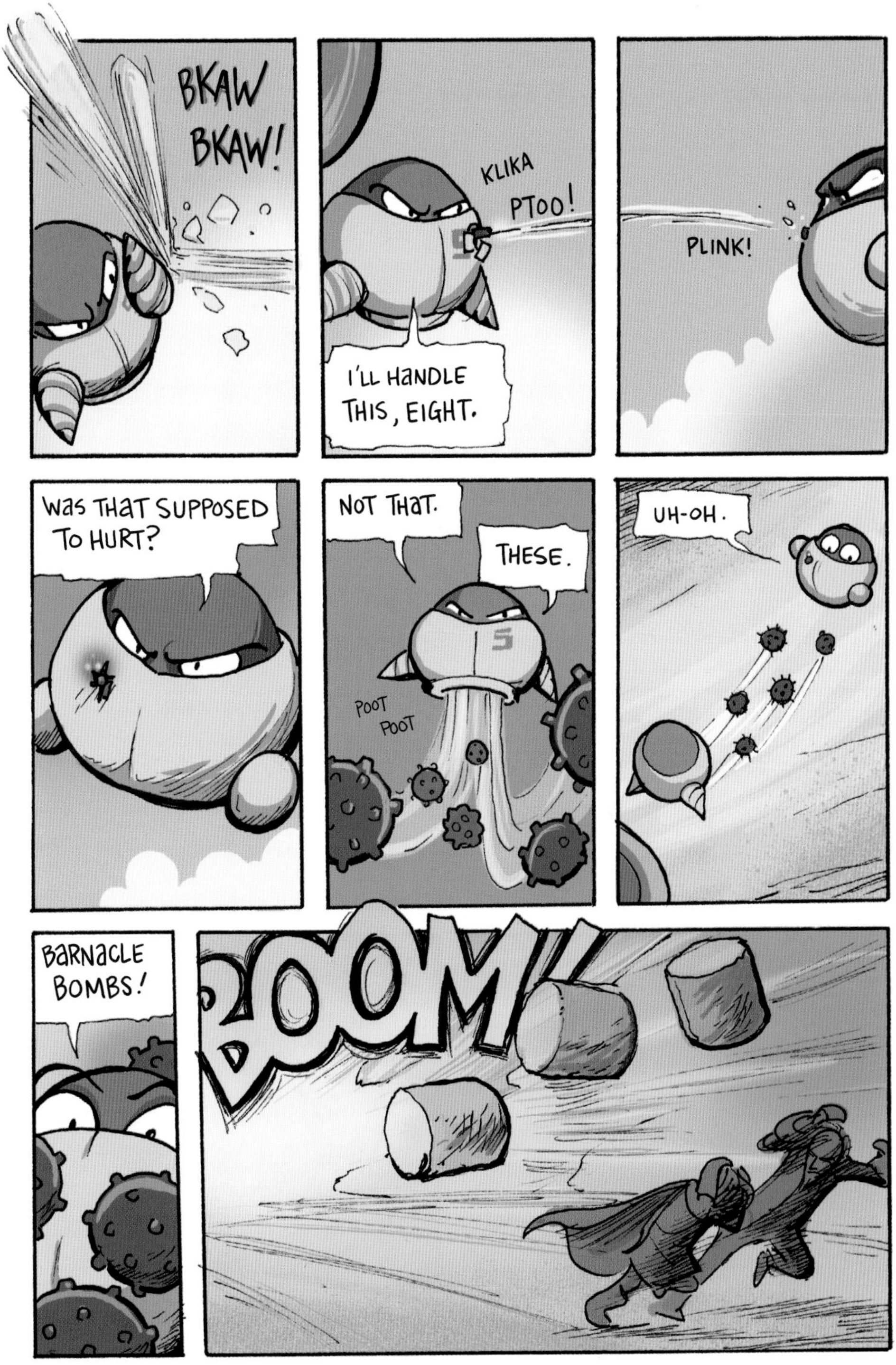
BKAW
BKAW!
KLIKA
PTOO!
I'LL HANDLE THIS, EIGHT.
PLINK!
WAS THAT SUPPOSED TO HURT?
NOT THAT.
THESE.
POOT
POOT
UH-OH.
BARNACLE BOMBS!
BOOM!!

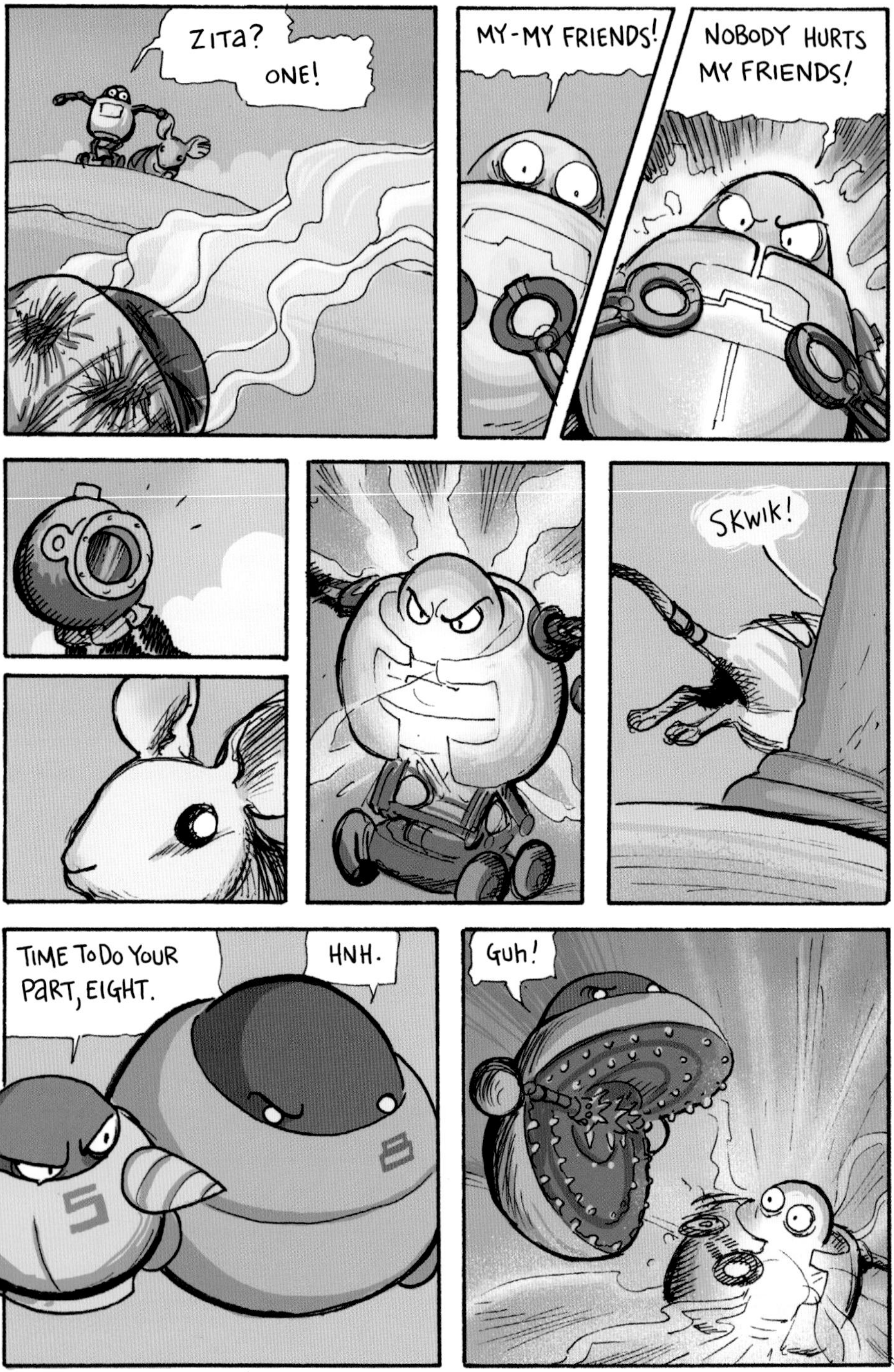
ZITA? ONE!
MY-MY FRIENDS!
NOBODY HURTS MY FRIENDS!
SKWIK!
TIME TO DO YOUR PART, EIGHT.
HNH.
GUH!

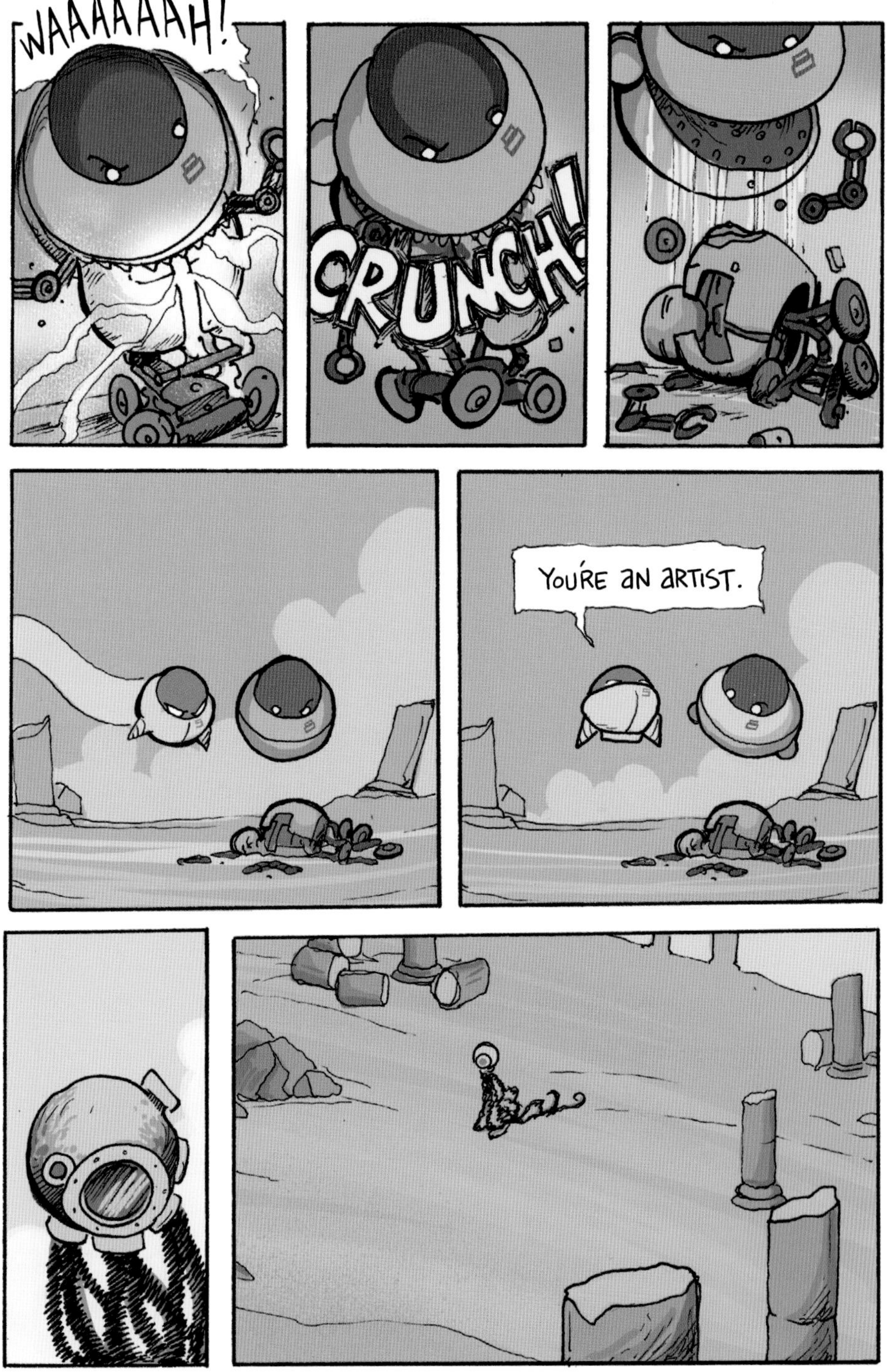
WAAAAAAH!
CRUNCH!
YOU'RE AN ARTIST.

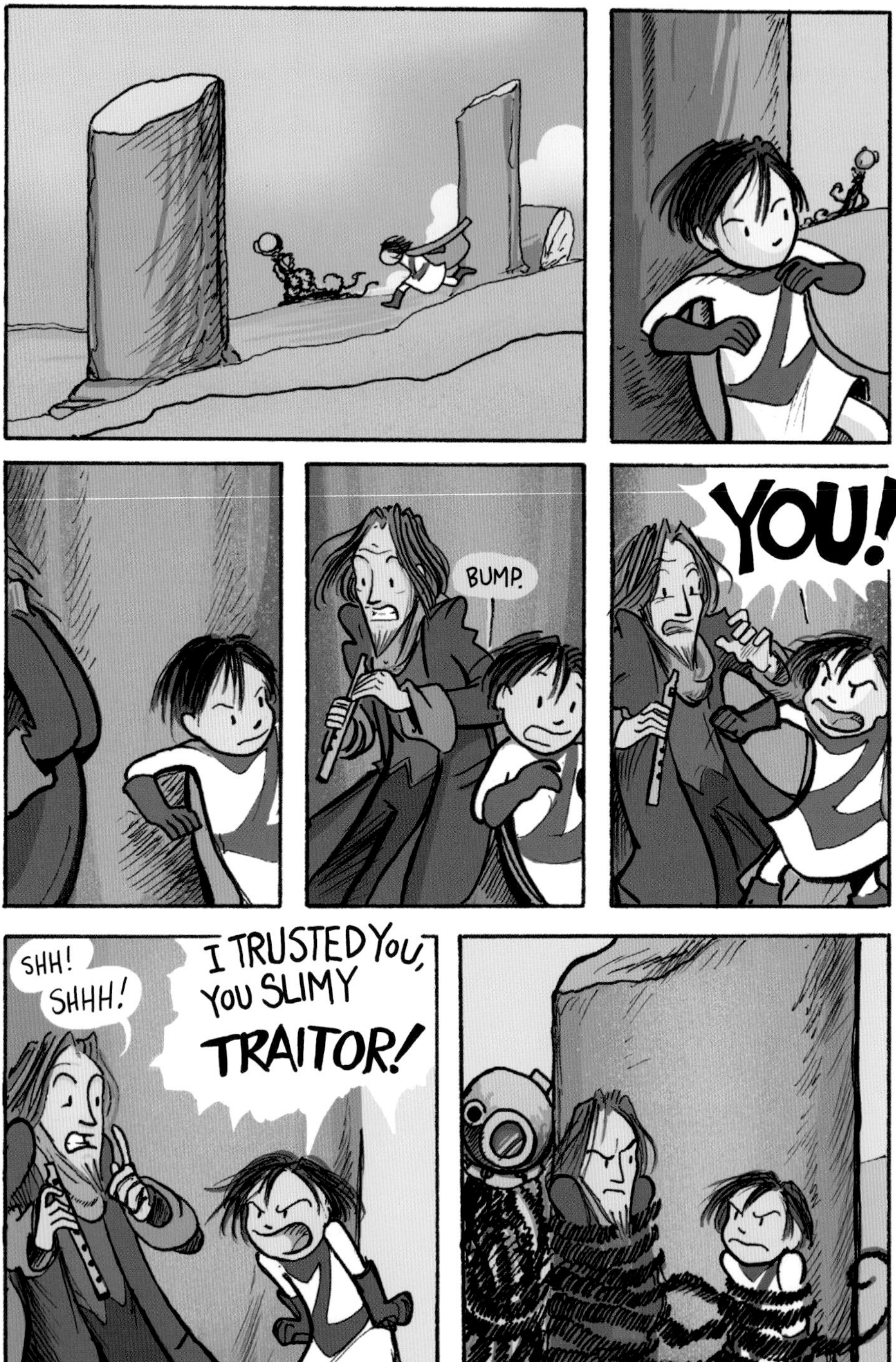
BUMP.
YOU!
SHH!
SHHH!
I TRUSTED YOU, YOU SLIMY TRAITOR!

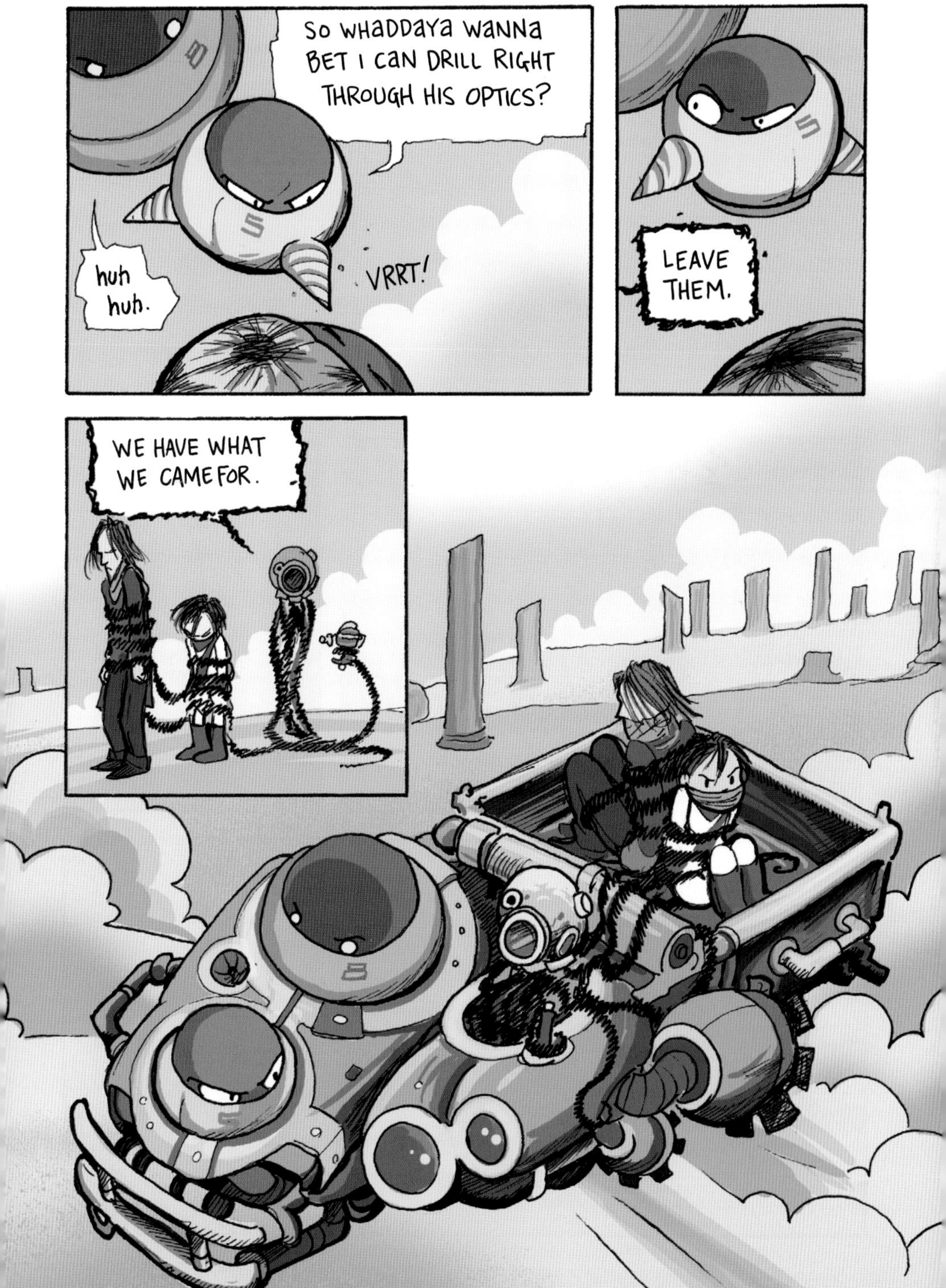
SO WHADDAYA WANNA BET I CAN DRILL RIGHT THROUGH HIS OPTICS?
huh huh.
VRRT!
LEAVE THEM.
WE HAVE WHAT WE CAME FOR.

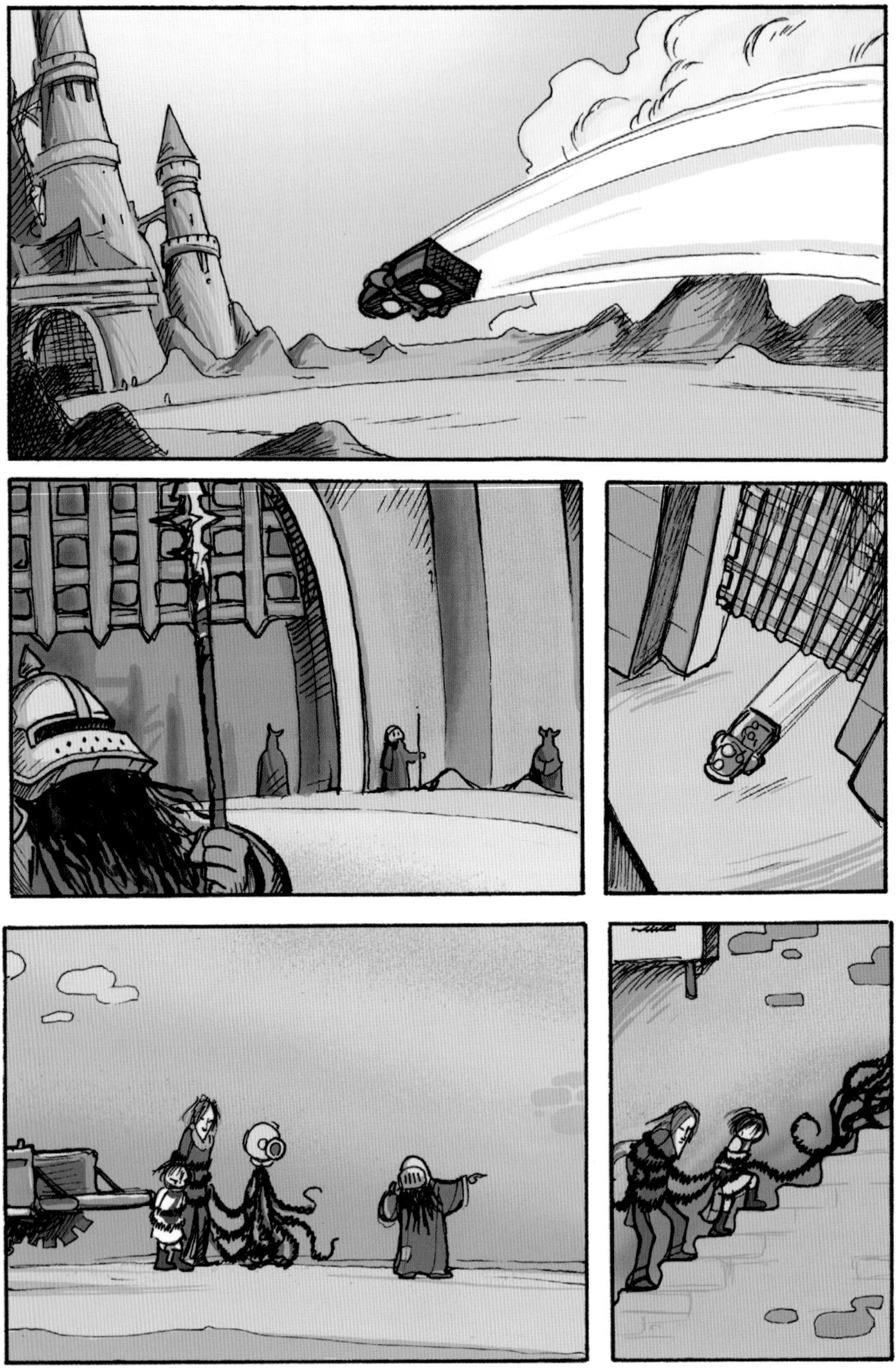

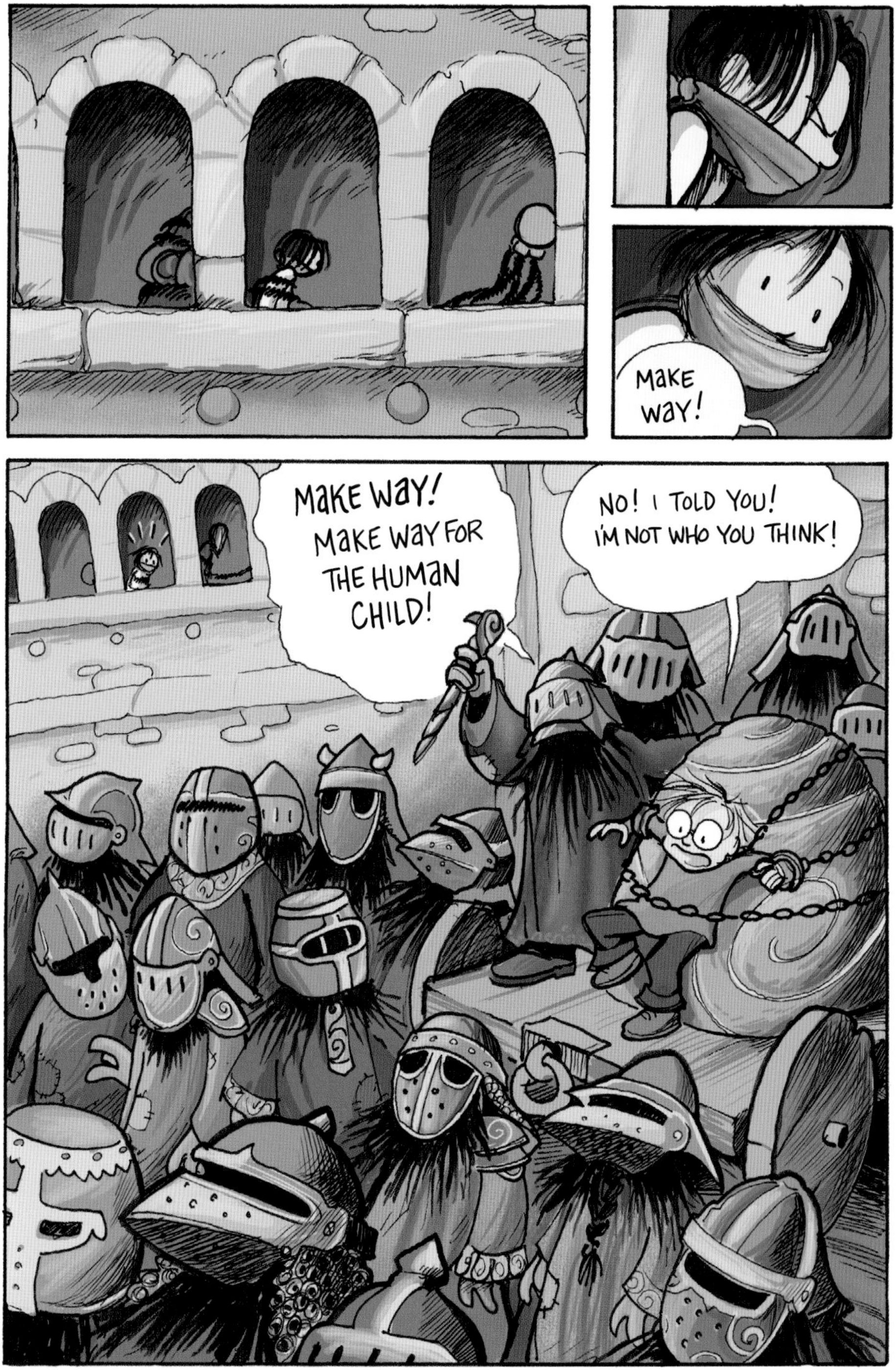

MAKE WAY!
MAKE WAY! MAKE WAY FOR THE HUMAN CHILD!
NO! I TOLD YOU! I'M NOT WHO YOU THINK!

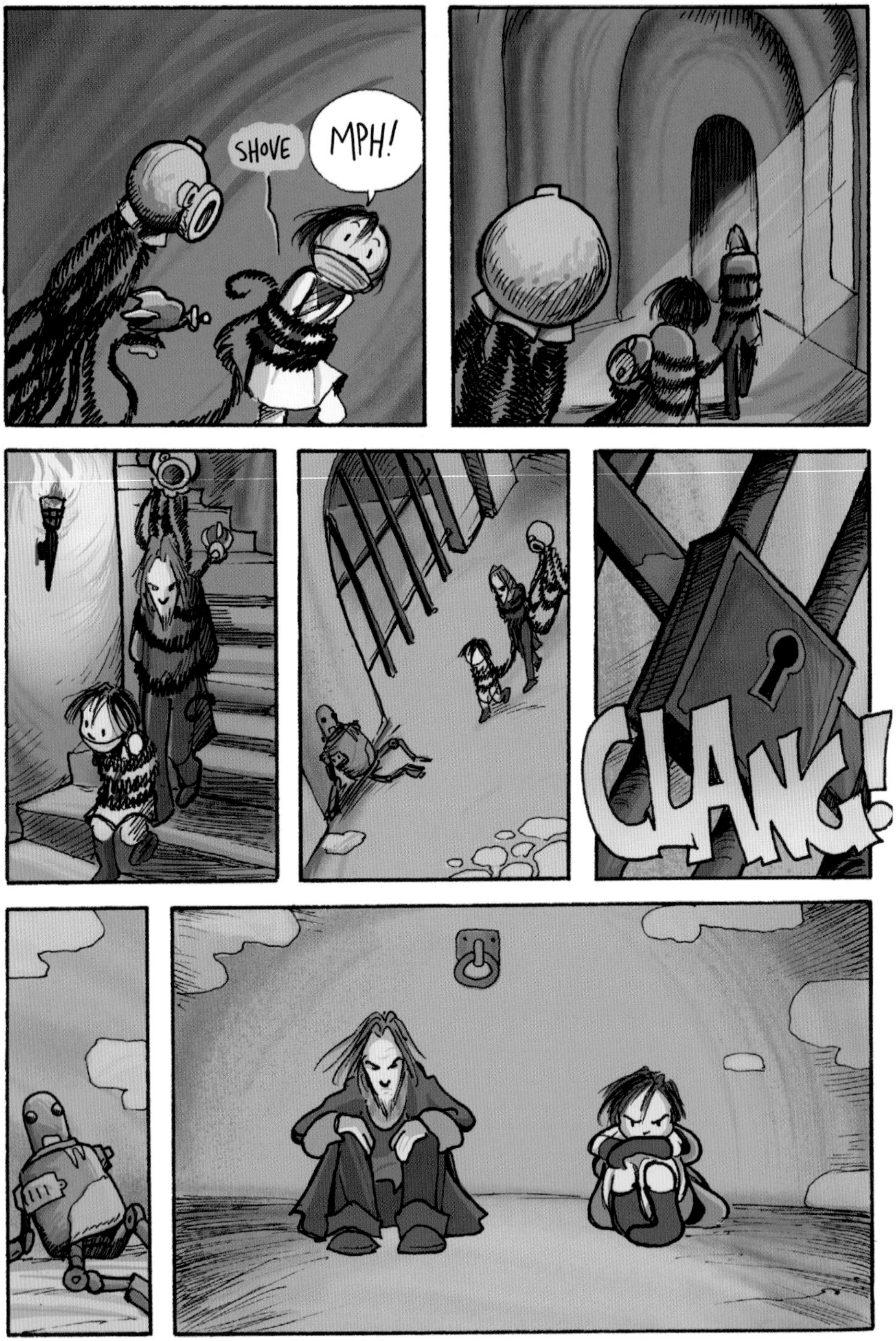
SHOVE
MPH!
CLANG!

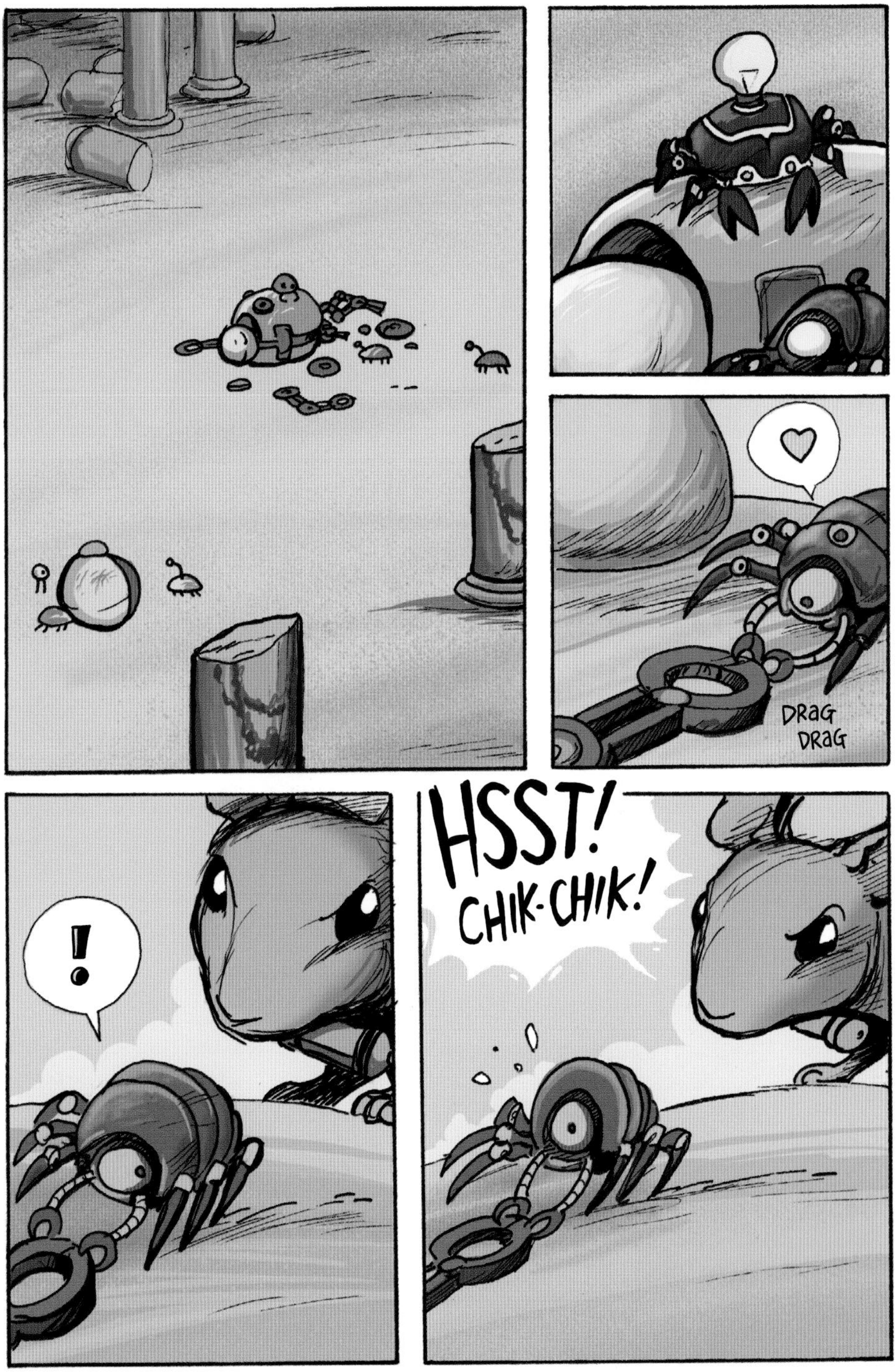

DRAG
DRAG
!
HSST!
CHIK-CHIK!

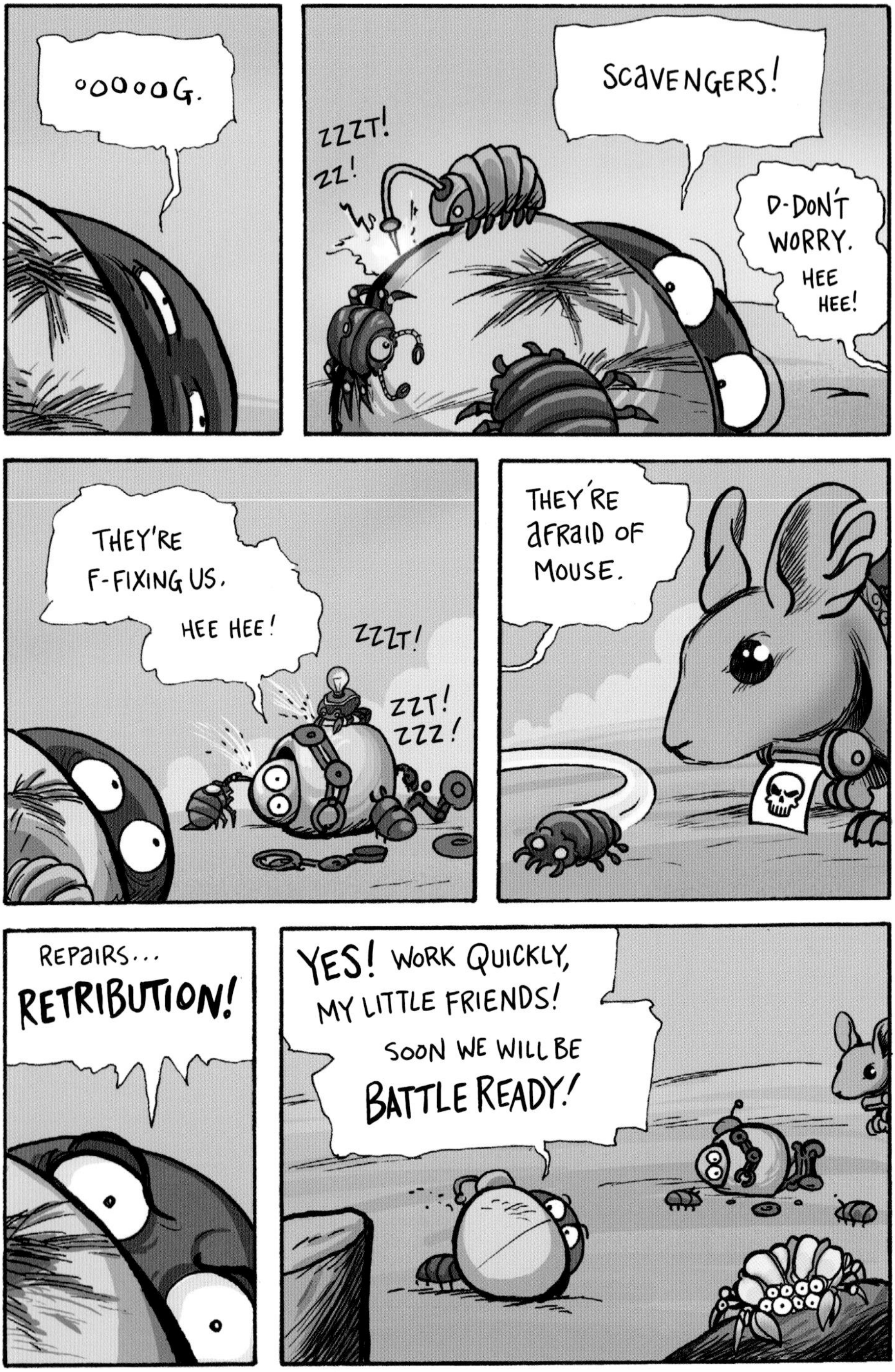

oOOooG.
SCAVENGERS!
ZZZT!
ZZ!
D-DON'T WORRY.
HEE HEE!
THEY'RE F-FIXING US.
HEE HEE!
ZZZT!
ZZT!
ZZZ!
THEY'RE AFRAID OF MOUSE.
REPAIRS...
RETRIBUTION!
YES! WORK QUICKLY, MY LITTLE FRIENDS!
SOON WE WILL BE BATTLE READY!

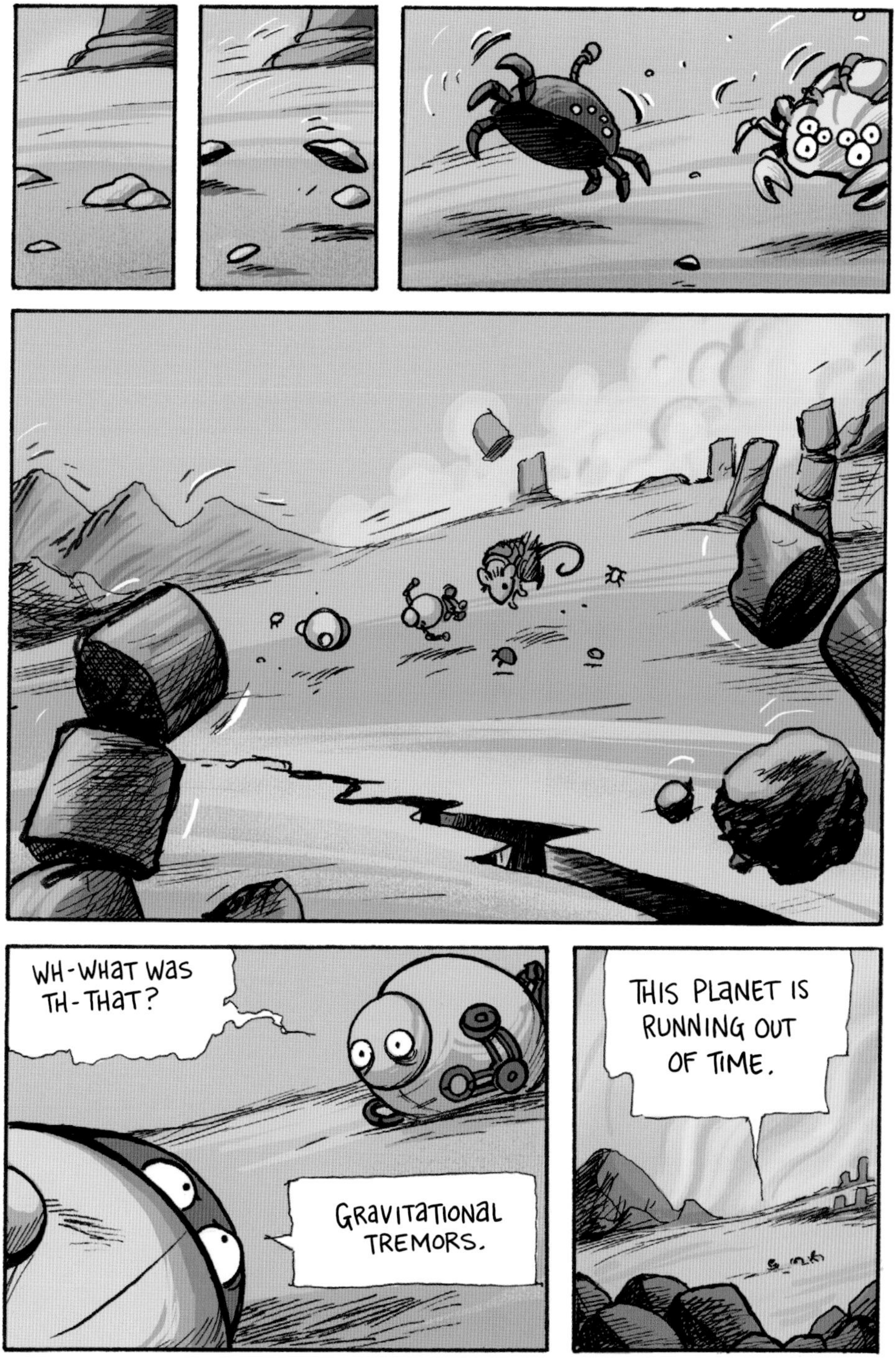
WH-WHAT WAS TH-THAT?
GRAVITATIONAL TREMORS.
THIS PLANET IS RUNNING OUT OF TIME.

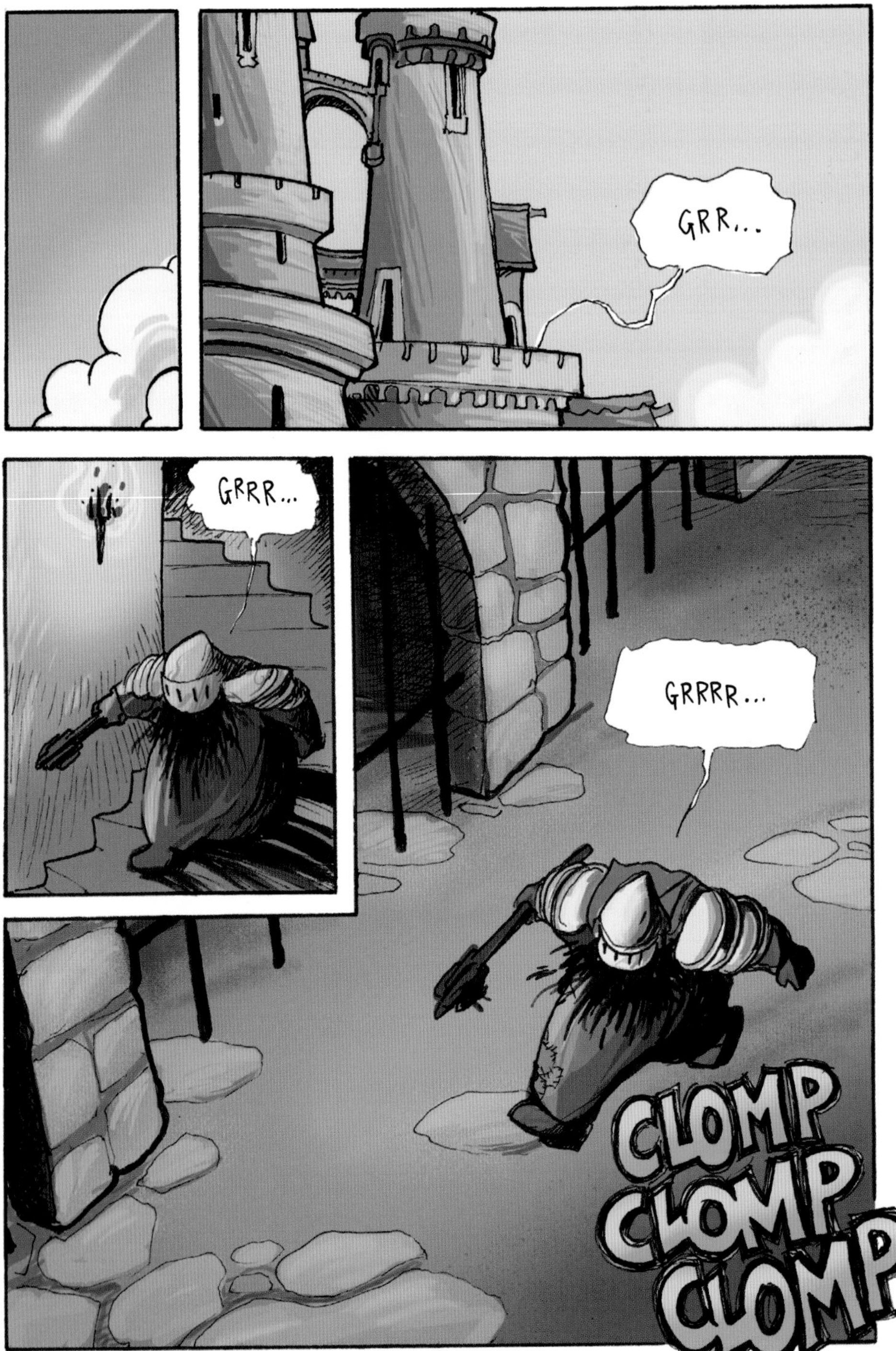
GRR...
GRRR...
GRRRR...
CLOMP
CLOMP
CLOMP

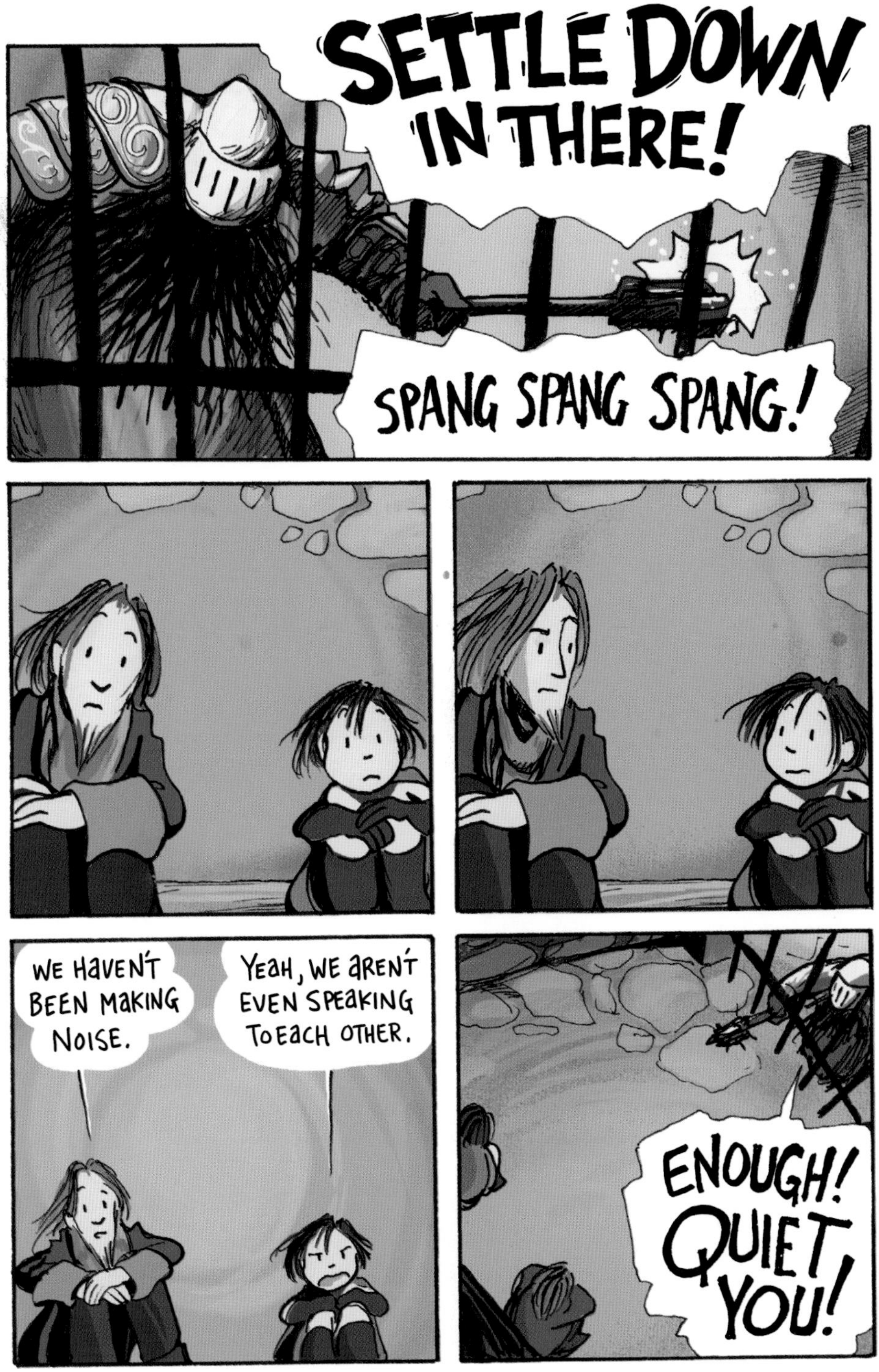
SETTLE DOWN IN THERE!
SPANG SPANG SPANG!
WE HAVEN'T BEEN MAKING NOISE.
YEAH, WE AREN'T EVEN SPEAKING TO EACH OTHER.
ENOUGH! QUIET YOU!

I SEE YOU'RE A MAN WHO TAKES HIS JOB VERY SERIOUSLY.

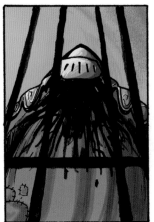

I'M THE DUNGEON-KEEPER!

AND CERTAINLY AN **IMPOSING** ONE.

OH...

THANK YOU.

LISTEN, MY FRIEND AND I WERE WONDERING—

I'M NOT YOUR FRIEND!

RIGHT. THE YOUNG LADY AND I WERE WONDERING HOW LONG BEFORE...

YOU KNOW...

BOOM!

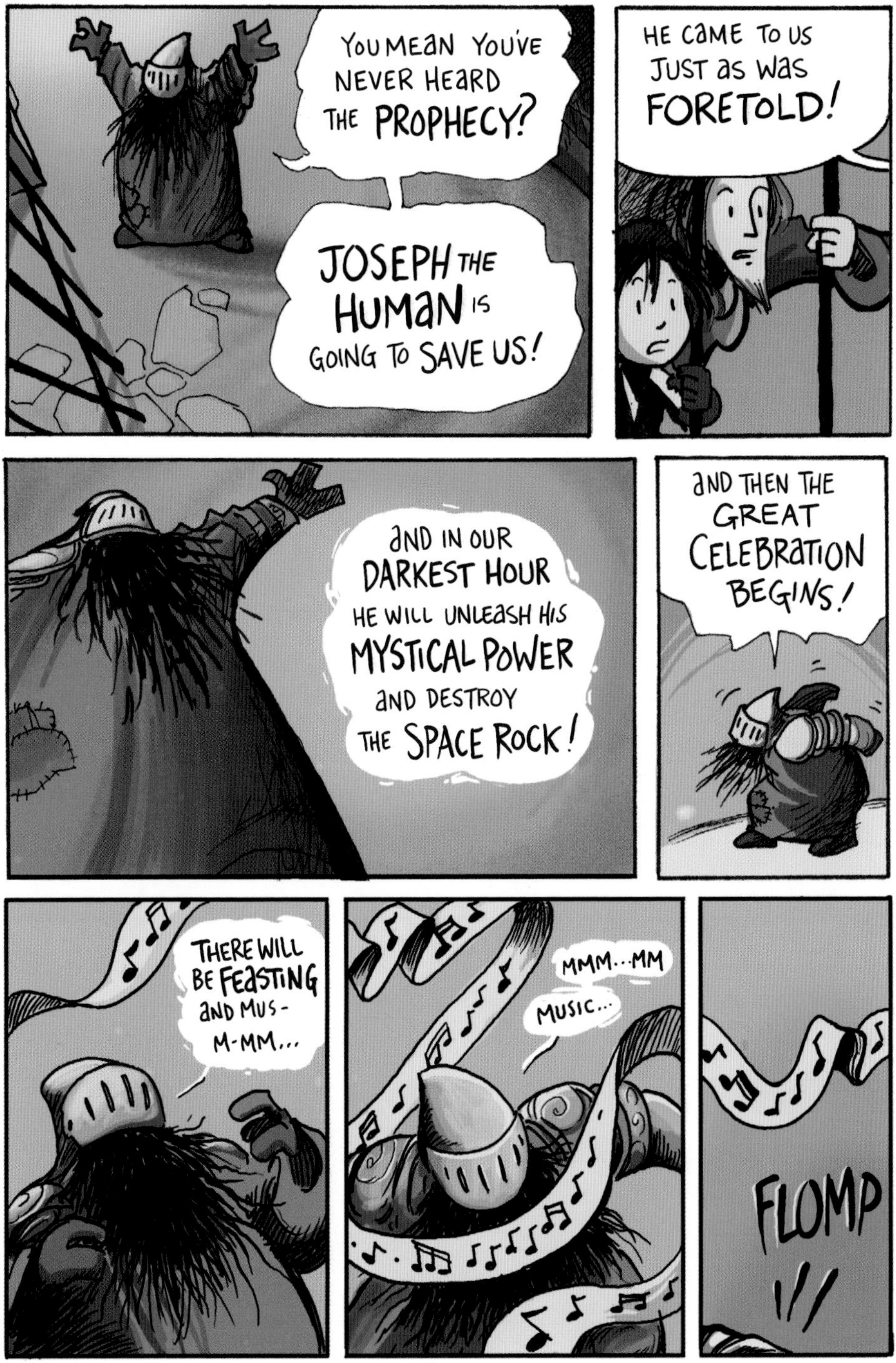
YOU MEAN YOU'VE NEVER HEARD THE PROPHECY?
JOSEPH THE HUMAN IS GOING TO SAVE US!
HE CAME TO US JUST AS WAS FORETOLD!
AND IN OUR DARKEST HOUR HE WILL UNLEASH HIS MYSTICAL POWER AND DESTROY THE SPACE ROCK!
AND THEN THE GREAT CELEBRATION BEGINS!
THERE WILL BE FEASTING AND MUS-M-MM...
MMM...MM
MUSIC...
FLOMP

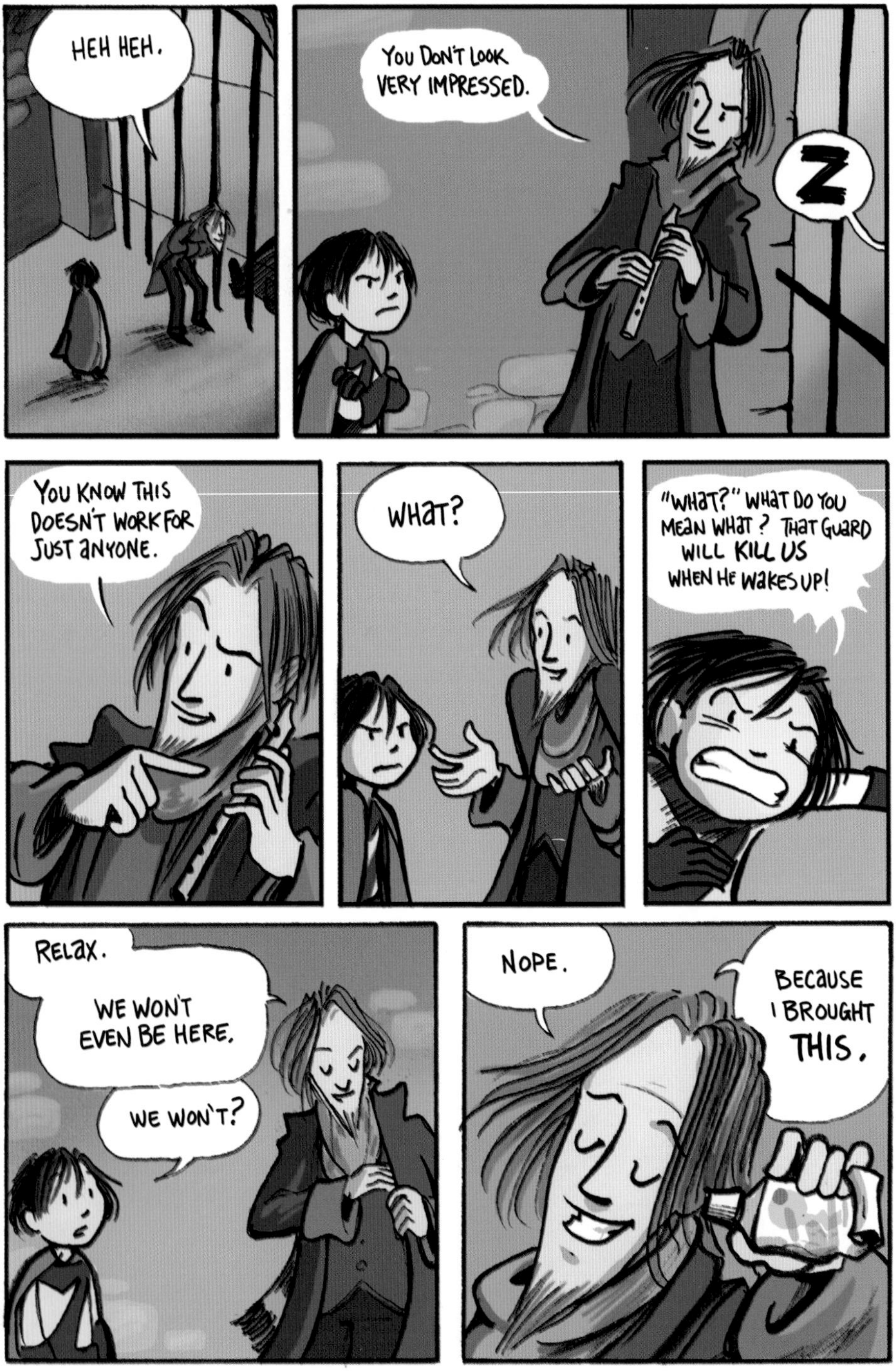
HEH HEH.
YOU DON'T LOOK VERY IMPRESSED.
Z
YOU KNOW THIS DOESN'T WORK FOR JUST ANYONE.
WHAT?
"WHAT?" WHAT DO YOU MEAN WHAT? THAT GUARD WILL KILL US WHEN HE WAKES UP!
RELAX.
WE WON'T EVEN BE HERE.
WE WON'T?
NOPE.
BECAUSE I BROUGHT THIS.

You can get out of jail with toothpaste?

Not toothpaste.

Doorpaste.

The rarest and most valuable paste of all.

After you.

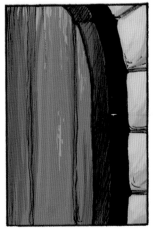

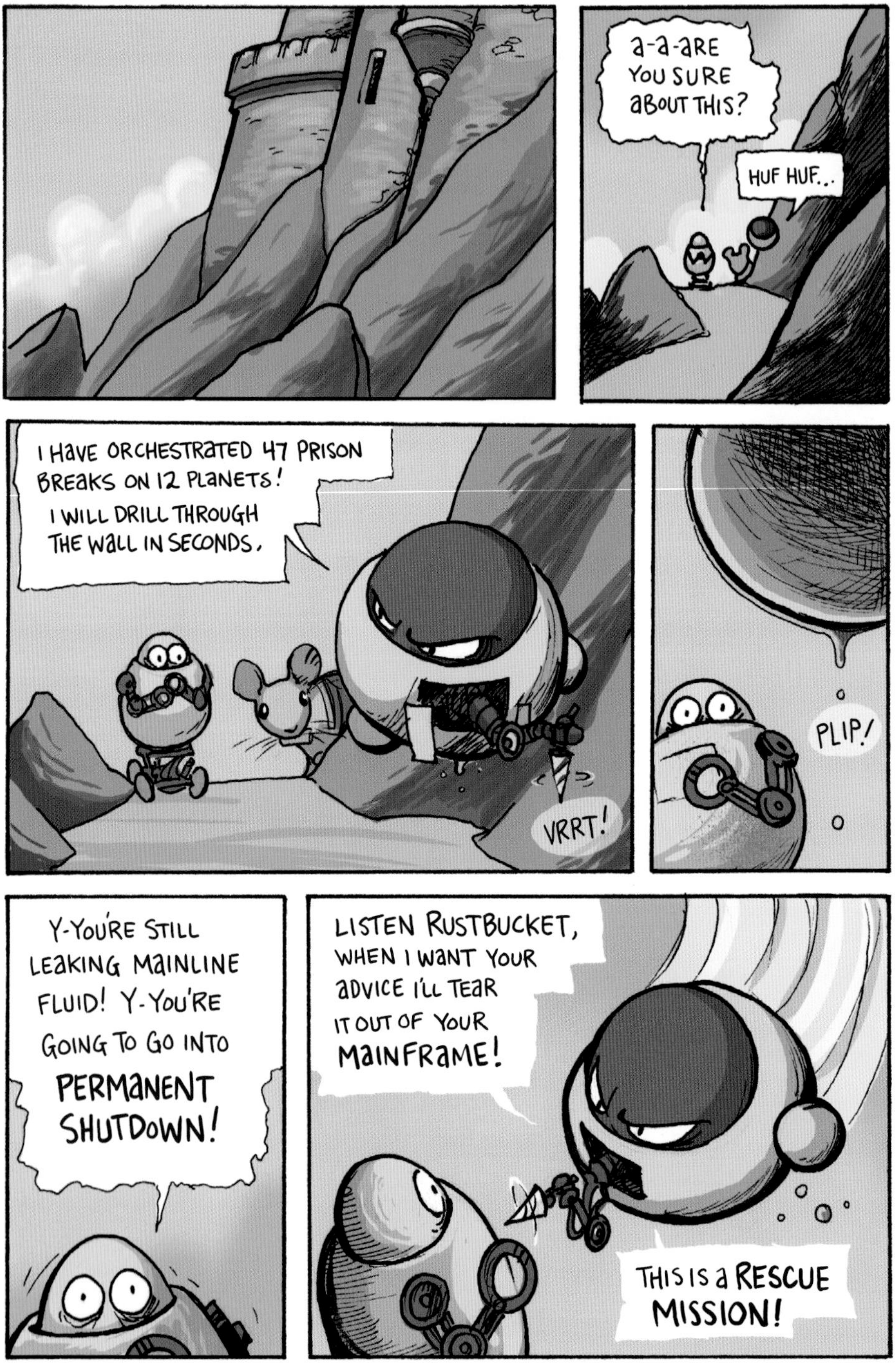
a-a-are YOU SURE aBOUT THIS?
HUF HUF...
I HaVE ORCHESTRaTED 47 PRISON BREaKS ON 12 PLaNETS! I WILL DRILL THROUGH THE WaLL IN SECONDS.
VRRT!
PLIP!
Y-YOU'RE STILL LEaKING MaINLINE FLUID! Y-YOU'RE GOING TO GO INTO PERMaNENT SHUTDOWN!
LISTEN RUSTBUCKET, WHEN I WaNT YOUR aDVICE I'LL TEaR IT OUT OF YOUR MaINFRaME!
THIS IS a RESCUE MISSION!

AND NOT ONE WORD ABOUT MY – eh?

CHIK CHIRRIP!

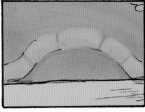

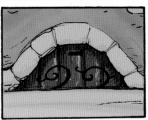

QUICKLY, ZITA! THESE DOORS DON'T LAST LONG.

NGH.

CHIK!

YOU'RE OKAY! HOW DID YOU GUYS FIND ME?

HUF HUF

ONE WAS LOOKING FOR A PLACE TO BLAST THROUGH THE WALL TO R-RESCUE YOU.

AH! THE SWEET BREATH OF FREEDOM!

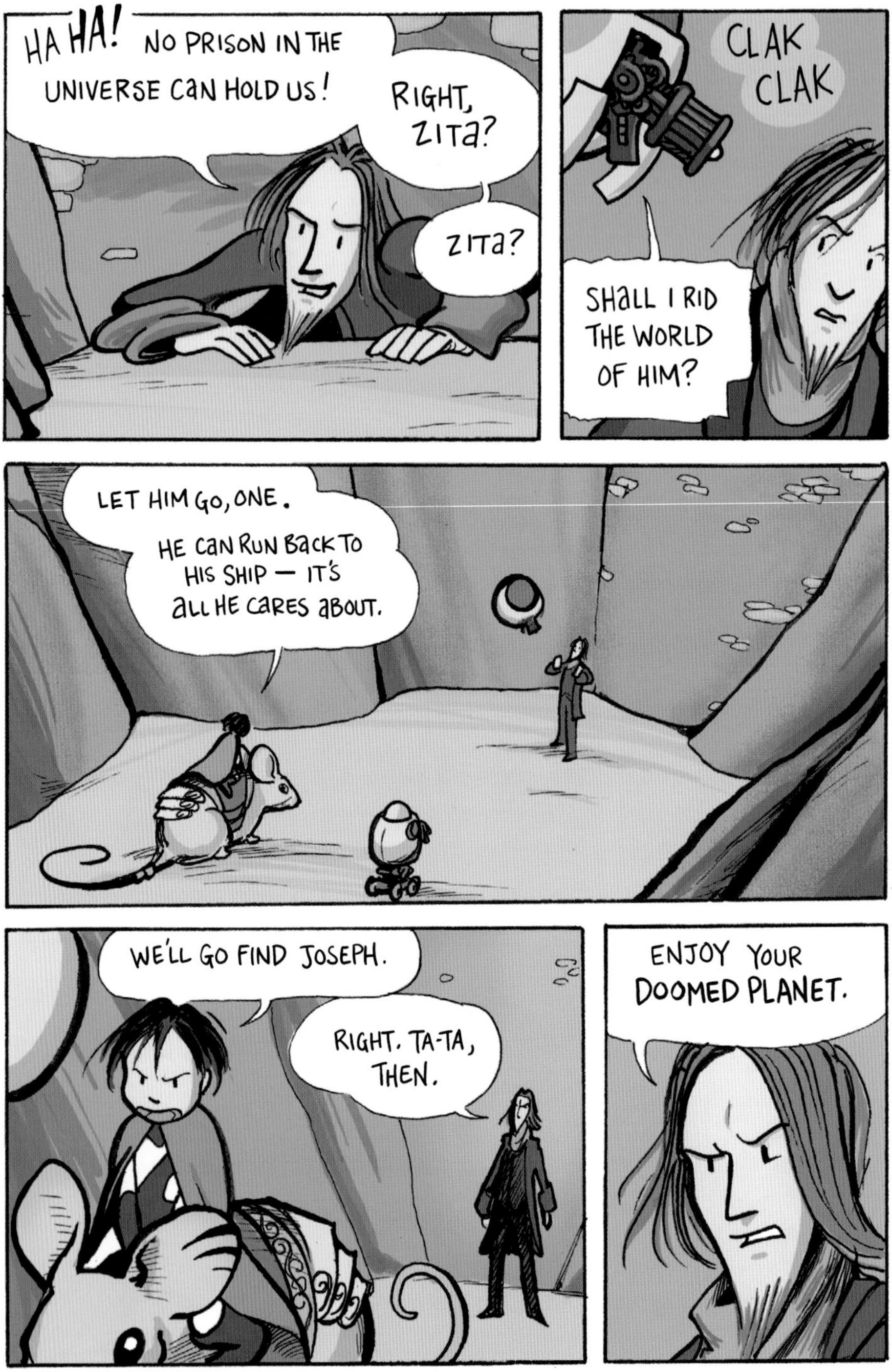
HA HA! NO PRISON IN THE UNIVERSE CAN HOLD US!
RIGHT, ZITA?
ZITA?
CLAK CLAK
SHALL I RID THE WORLD OF HIM?
LET HIM GO, ONE.
HE CAN RUN BACK TO HIS SHIP — IT'S ALL HE CARES ABOUT.
WE'LL GO FIND JOSEPH.
RIGHT. TA-TA, THEN.
ENJOY YOUR DOOMED PLANET.

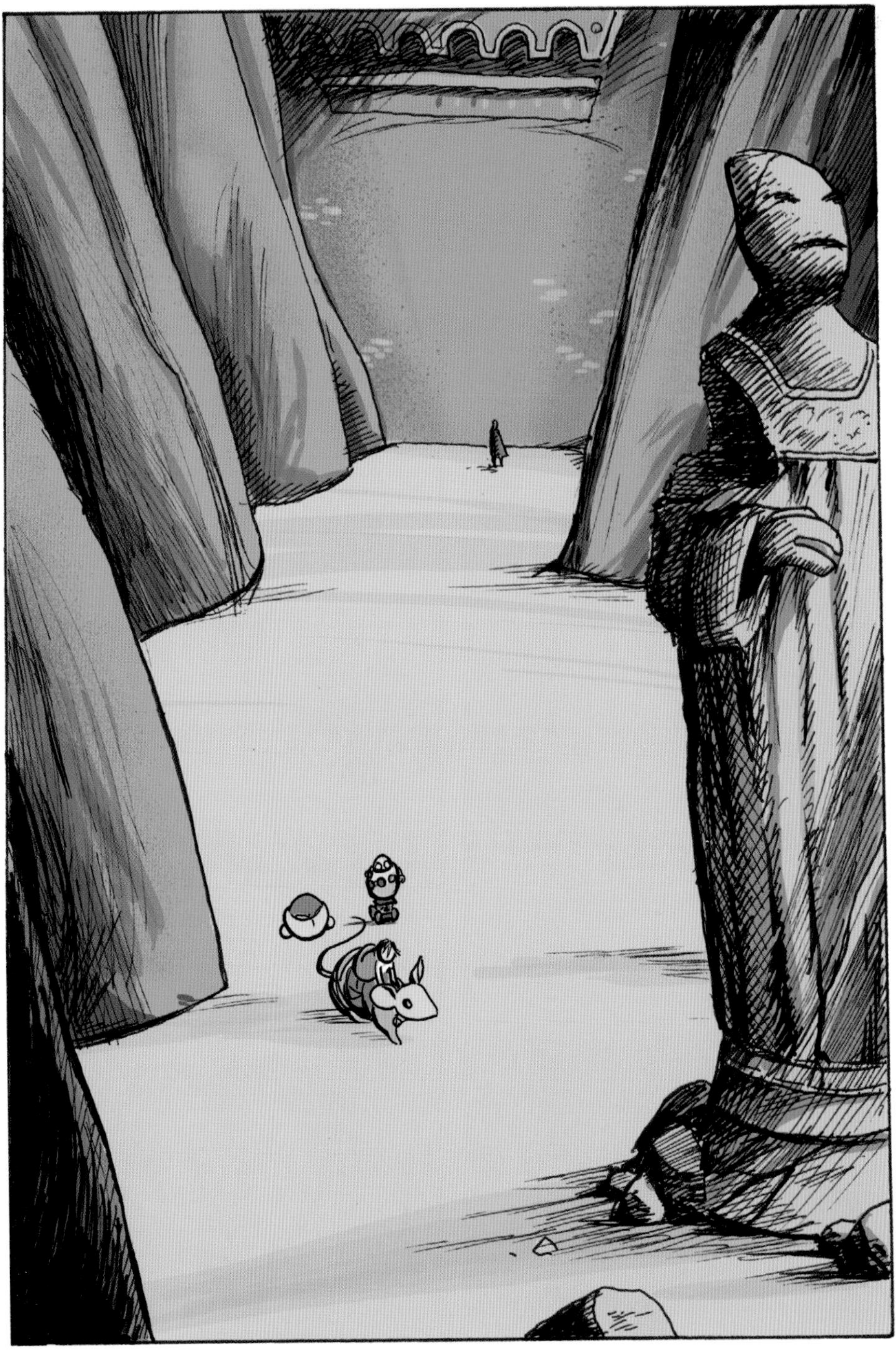

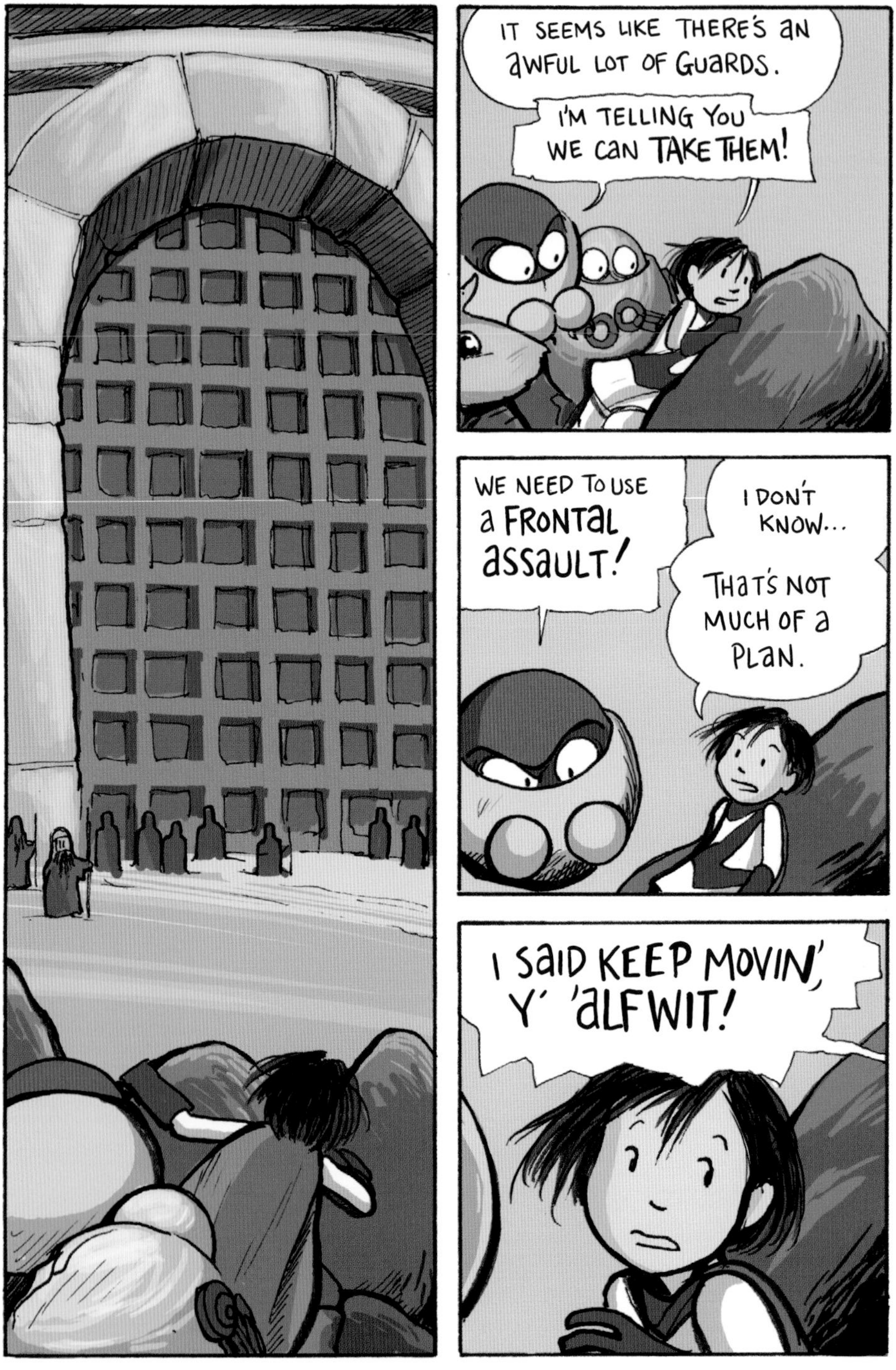
IT SEEMS LIKE THERE'S AN AWFUL LOT OF GUARDS.
I'M TELLING YOU WE CAN TAKE THEM!
WE NEED TO USE A FRONTAL ASSAULT!
I DON'T KNOW...
THAT'S NOT MUCH OF A PLAN.
I SAID KEEP MOVIN', Y' 'ALFWIT!

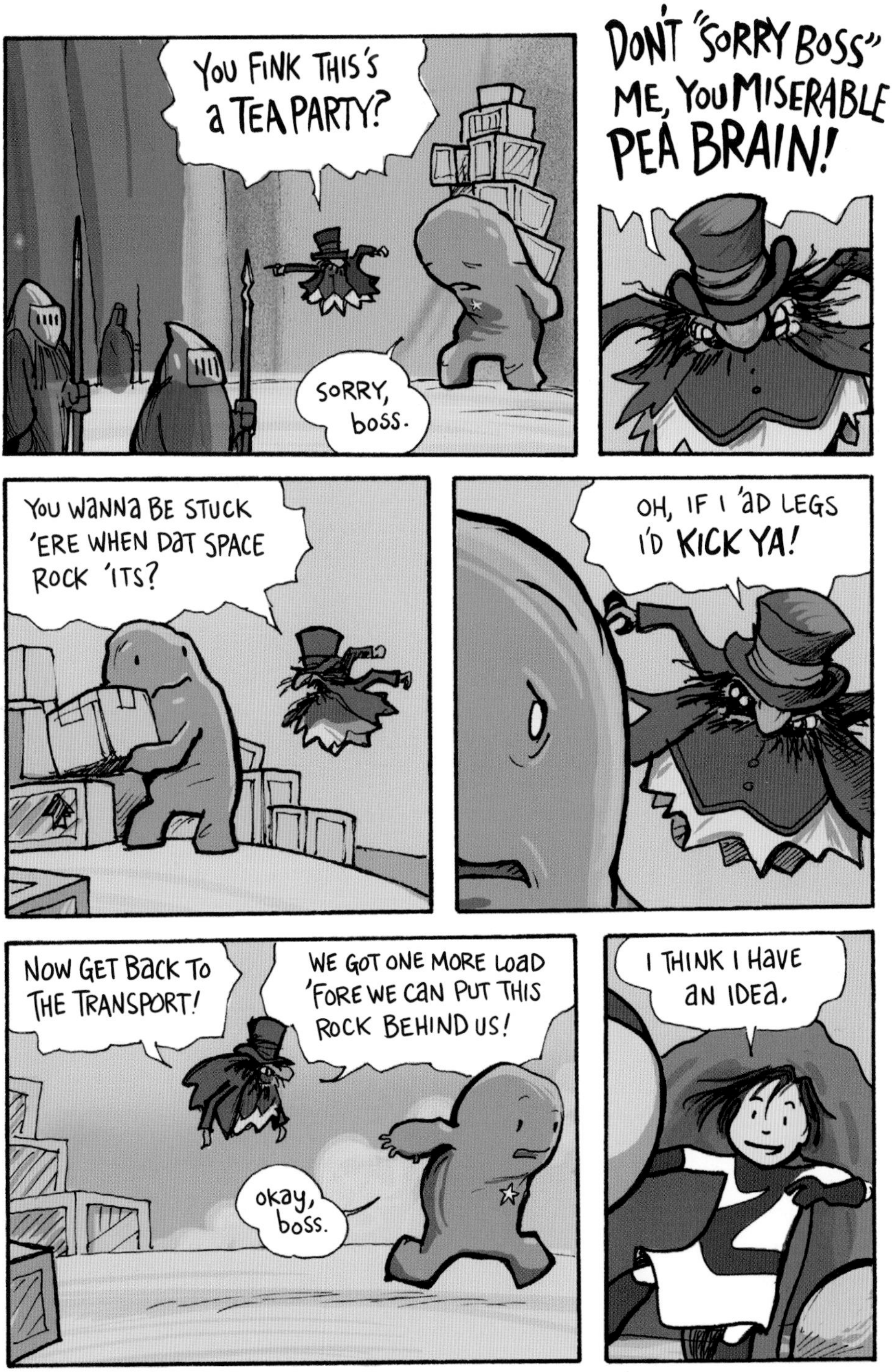

YOU FINK THIS'S a TEA PARTY?
SORRY, boss.
DON'T "SORRY BOSS" ME, YOU MISERABLE PEA BRAIN!
YOU WANNA BE STUCK 'ERE WHEN DAT SPACE ROCK 'ITS?
OH, IF I 'AD LEGS I'D KICK YA!
NOW GET BACK TO THE TRANSPORT!
WE GOT ONE MORE LOAD 'FORE WE CAN PUT THIS ROCK BEHIND US!
okay, boss.
I THINK I HAVE AN IDEA.

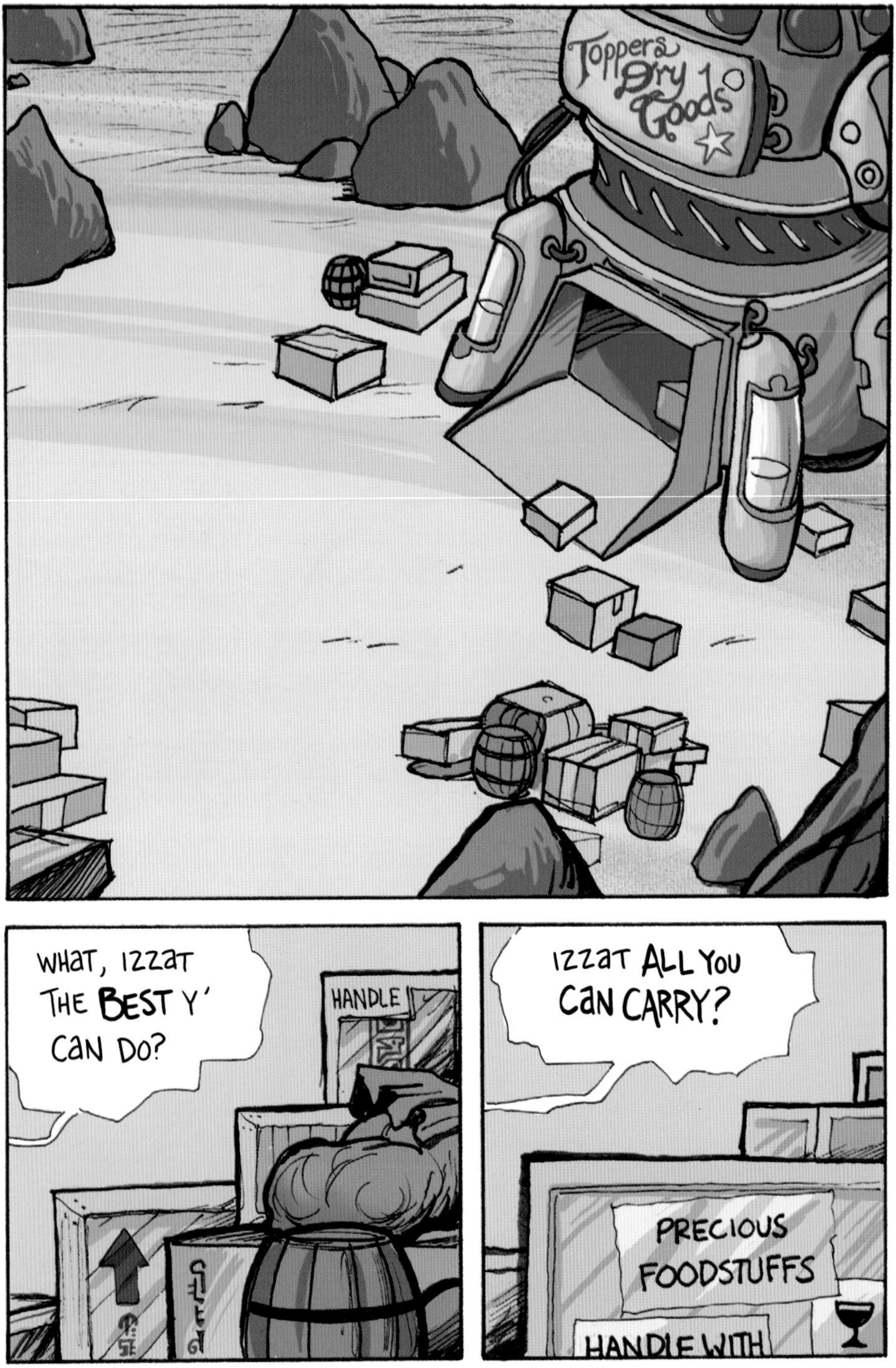
Toppers Dry Goods
WHAT, IZZAT THE BEST Y' CAN DO?
HANDLE
IZZAT ALL YOU CAN CARRY?
PRECIOUS FOODSTUFFS
HANDLE WITH

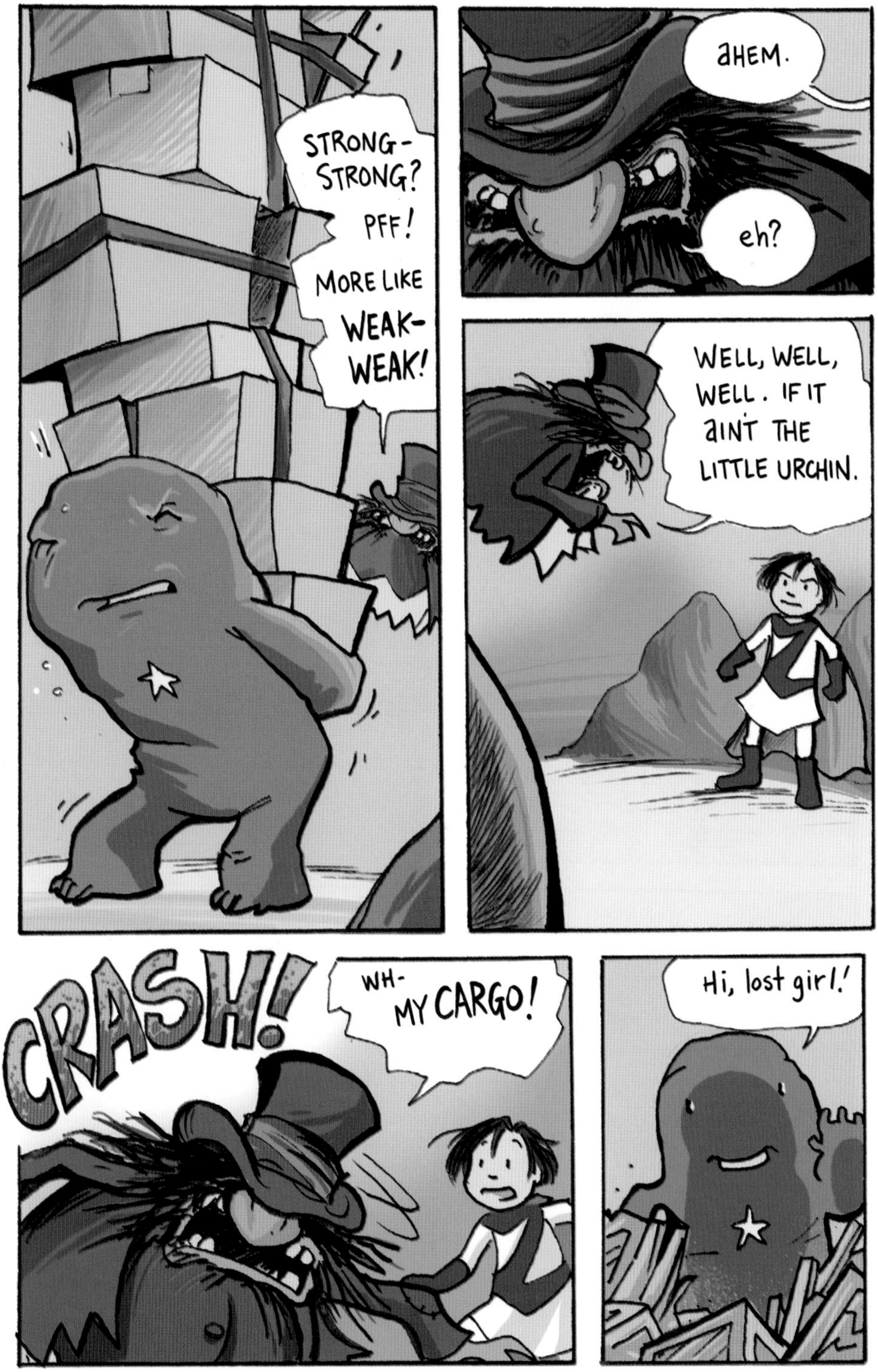
STRONG-STRONG? PFF! MORE LIKE WEAK-WEAK!
ahem.
eh?
WELL, WELL, WELL. IF IT AIN'T THE LITTLE URCHIN.
CRASH!
WH- MY CARGO!
Hi, lost girl!

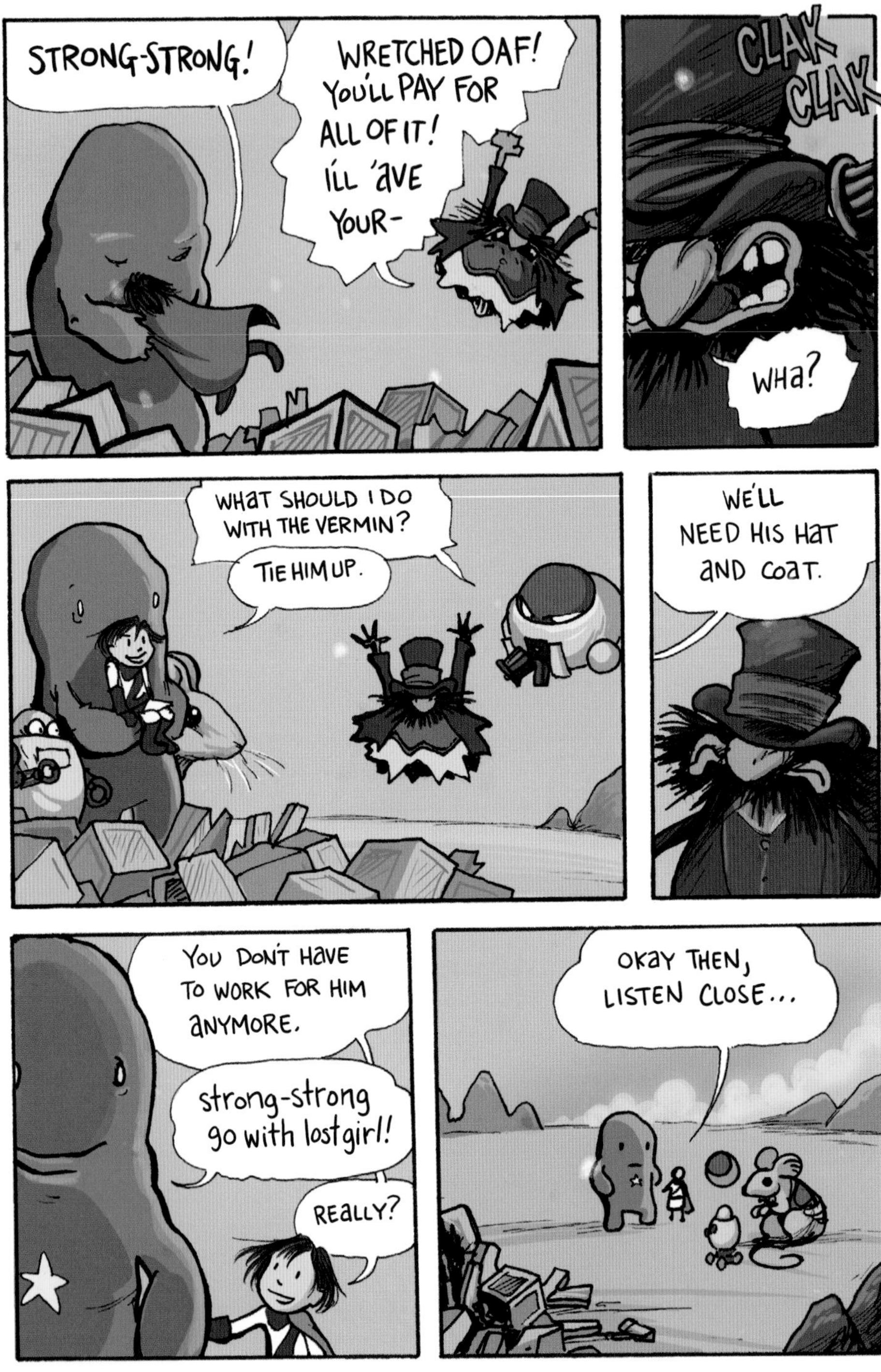
STRONG-STRONG!
WRETCHED OAF! YOU'LL PAY FOR ALL OF IT! I'LL 'AVE YOUR-
CLAK CLAK
WHA?
WHAT SHOULD I DO WITH THE VERMIN?
TIE HIM UP.
WE'LL NEED HIS HAT AND COAT.
YOU DON'T HAVE TO WORK FOR HIM ANYMORE.
strong-strong go with lostgirl!
REALLY?
OKAY THEN, LISTEN CLOSE...

chapter
five

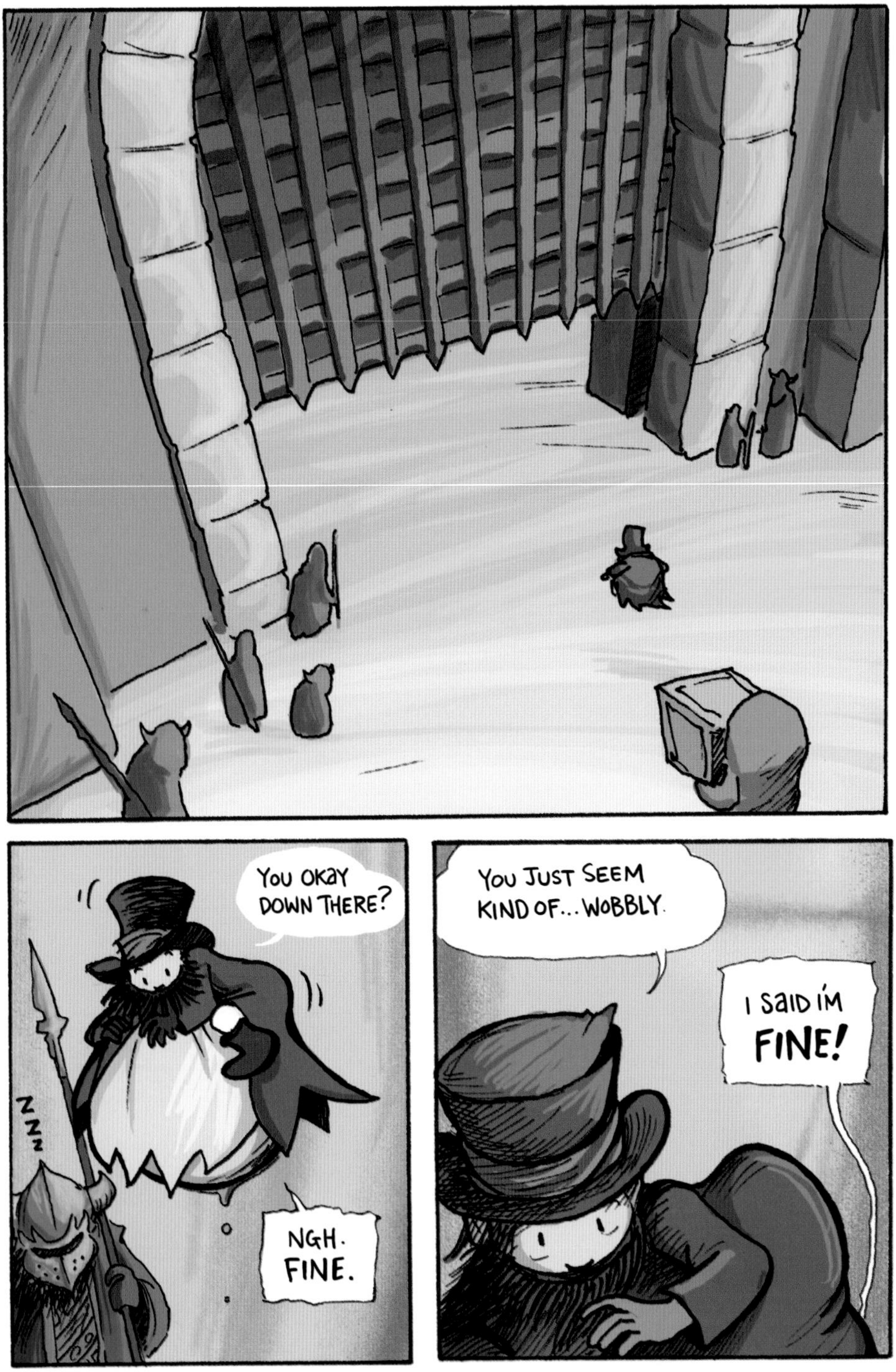
You okay down there?
Z Z Z
NGH. FINE.
You just seem kind of... wobbly.
I said I'm FINE!

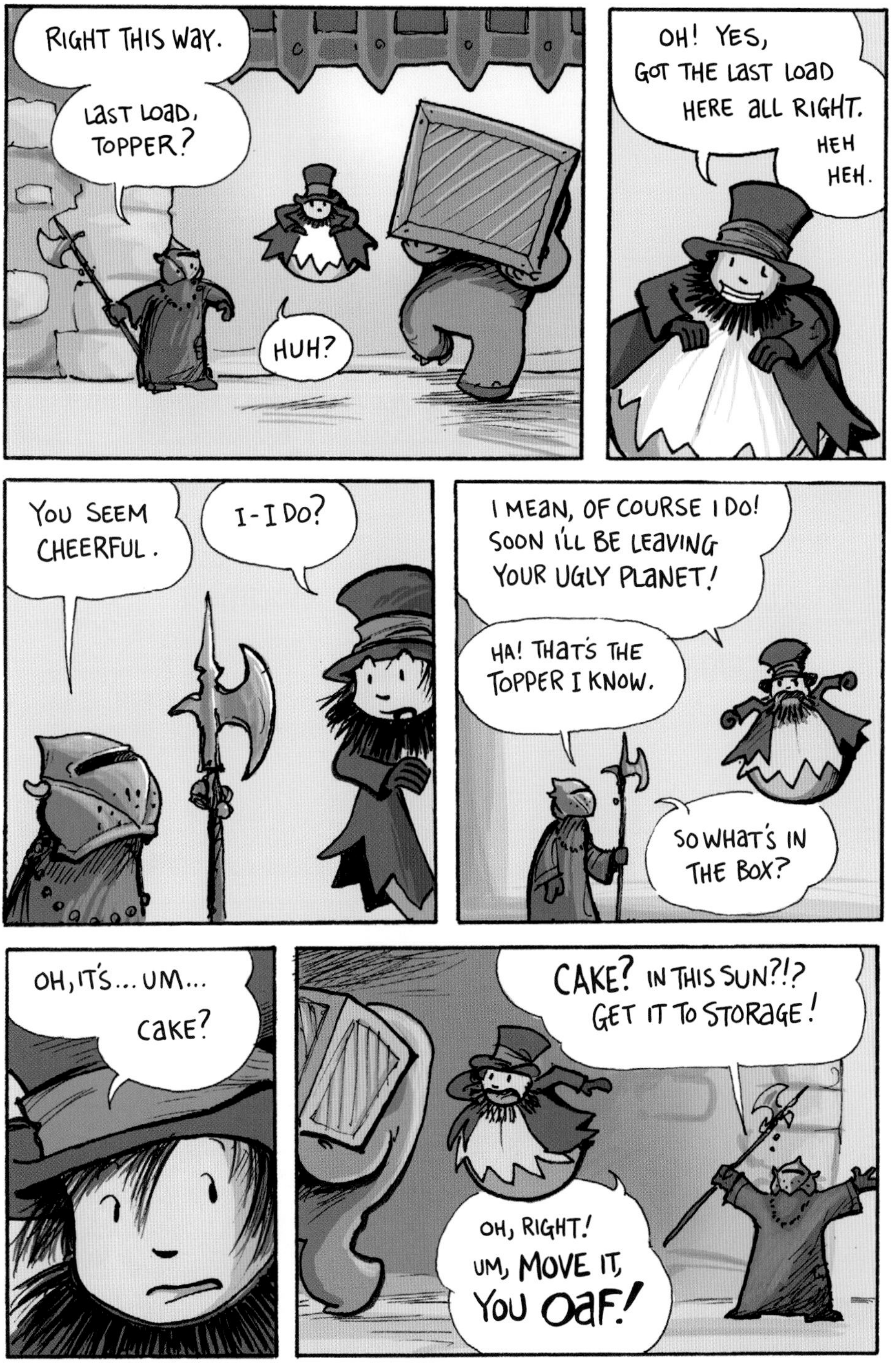
RIGHT THIS WAY.
LAST LOAD, TOPPER?
HUH?
OH! YES, GOT THE LAST LOAD HERE ALL RIGHT.
HEH HEH.
YOU SEEM CHEERFUL.
I-I DO?
I MEAN, OF COURSE I DO! SOON I'LL BE LEAVING YOUR UGLY PLANET!
HA! THAT'S THE TOPPER I KNOW.
SO WHAT'S IN THE BOX?
OH, IT'S... UM... CAKE?
CAKE? IN THIS SUN?!? GET IT TO STORAGE!
OH, RIGHT! UM, MOVE IT, YOU OAF!

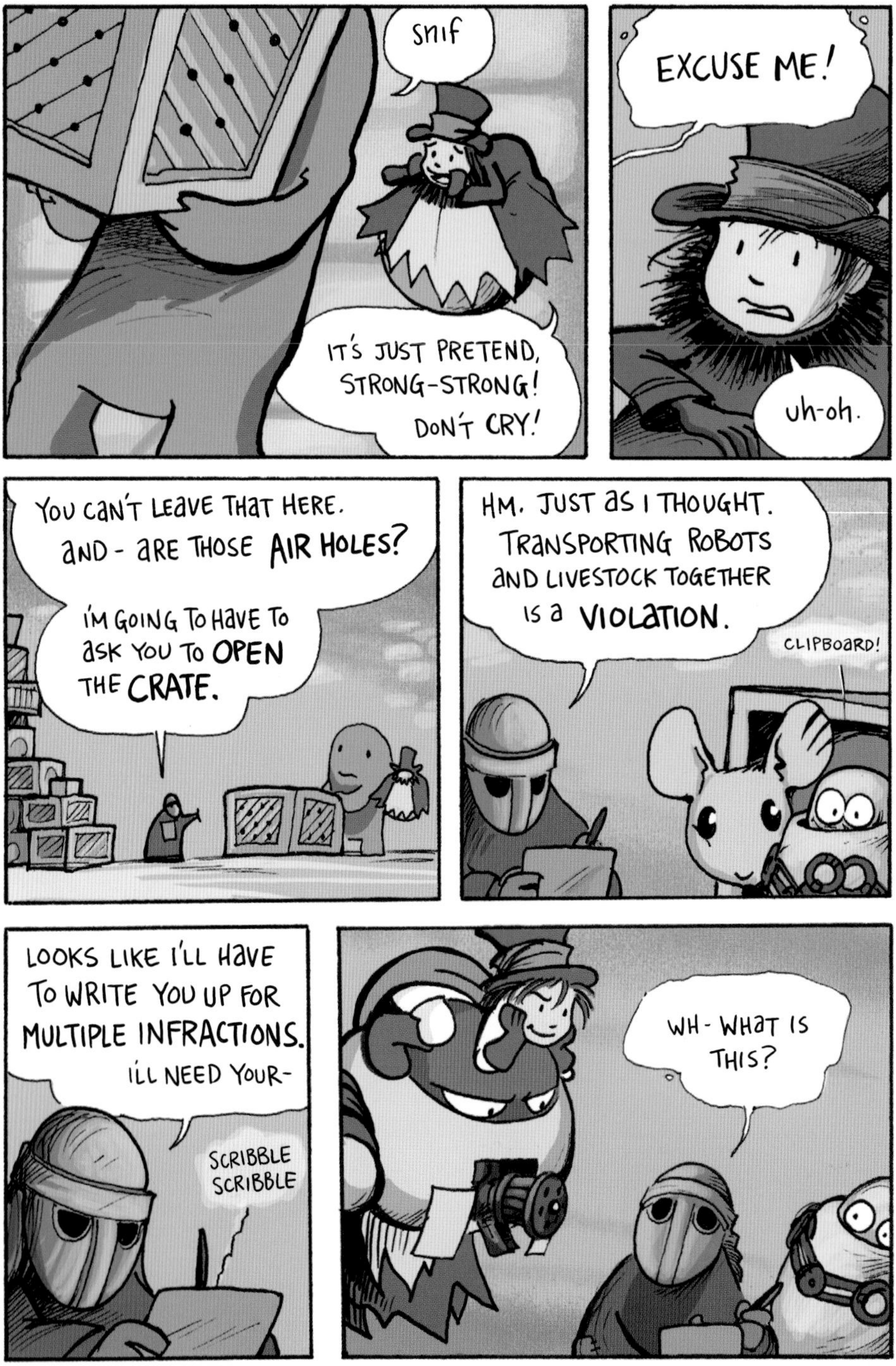
snif
IT'S JUST PRETEND, STRONG-STRONG! DON'T CRY!
EXCUSE ME!
uh-oh.
YOU CAN'T LEAVE THAT HERE. AND - ARE THOSE AIR HOLES?
I'M GOING TO HAVE TO ASK YOU TO OPEN THE CRATE.
HM. JUST AS I THOUGHT. TRANSPORTING ROBOTS AND LIVESTOCK TOGETHER IS A VIOLATION.
CLIPBOARD!
LOOKS LIKE I'LL HAVE TO WRITE YOU UP FOR MULTIPLE INFRACTIONS.
I'LL NEED YOUR-
SCRIBBLE SCRIBBLE
WH- WHAT IS THIS?

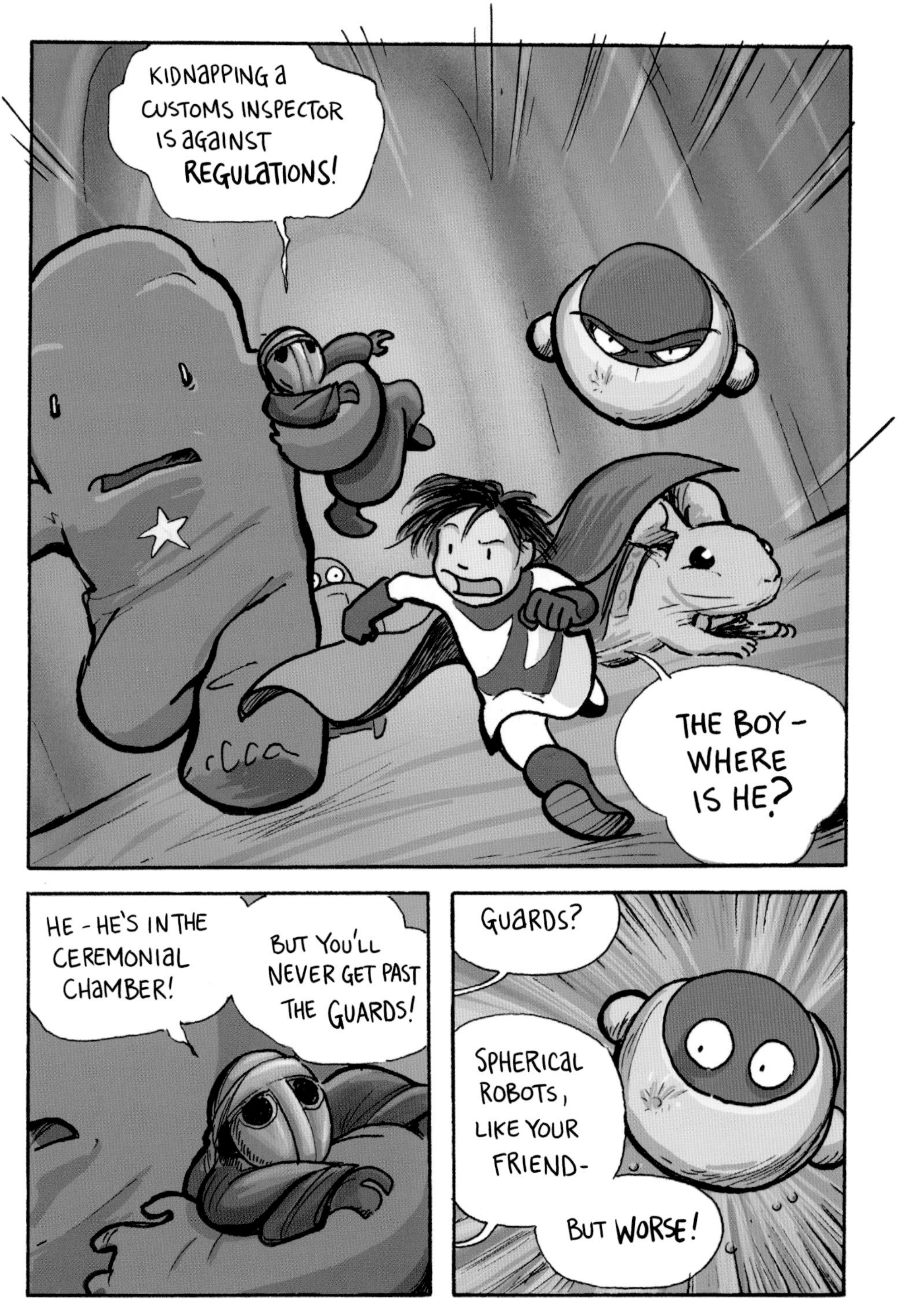
KIDNAPPING A CUSTOMS INSPECTOR IS AGAINST REGULATIONS!
THE BOY - WHERE IS HE?
HE - HE'S IN THE CEREMONIAL CHAMBER!
BUT YOU'LL NEVER GET PAST THE GUARDS!
GUARDS?
SPHERICAL ROBOTS, LIKE YOUR FRIEND-
BUT WORSE!

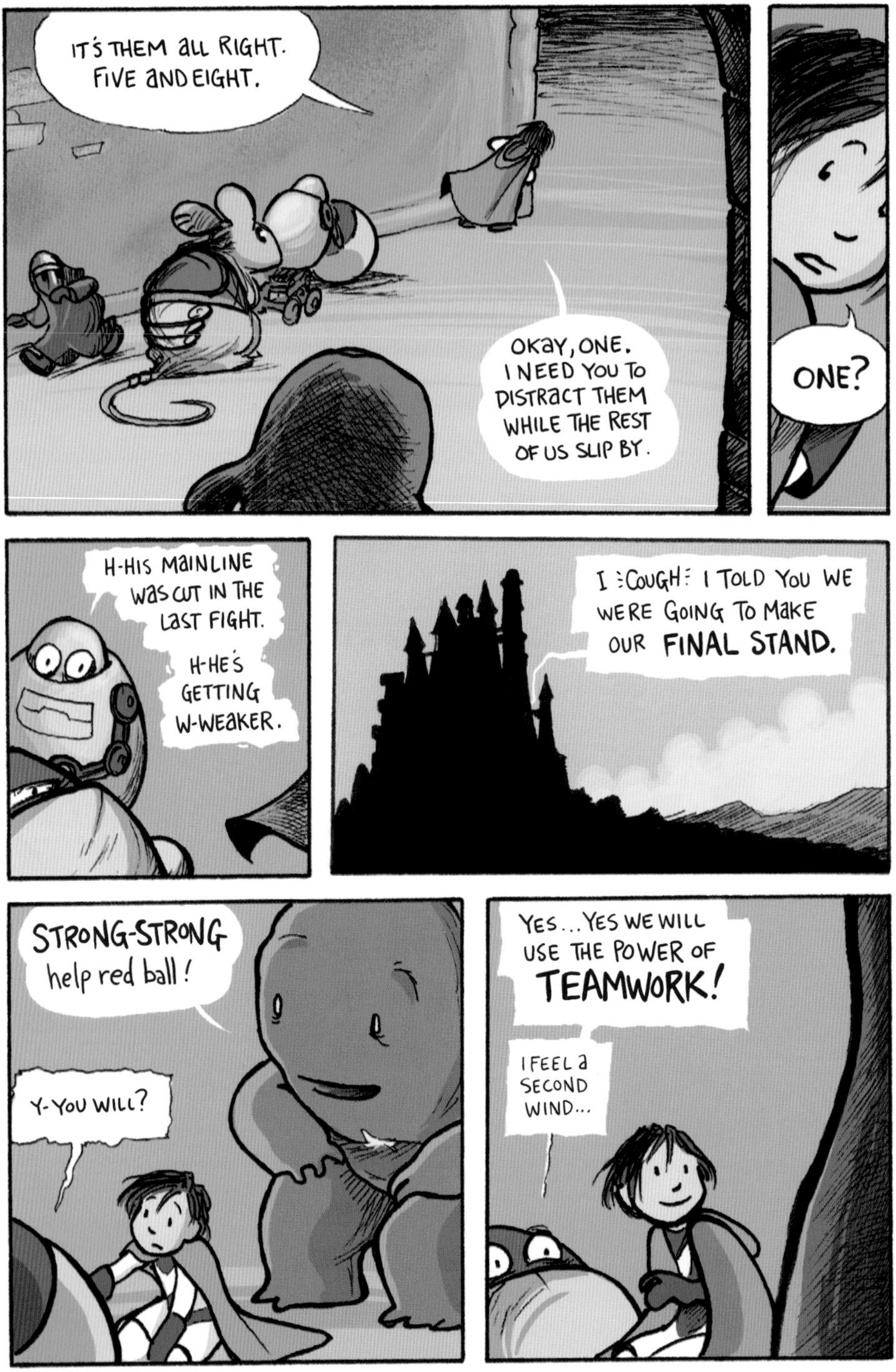
IT'S THEM all RIGHT. FIVE and EIGHT.
OKay, ONE. I NEED YOU TO DISTRaCT THEM WHILE THE REST OF US SLIP BY.
ONE?
H-HIS MaINLINE Was CUT IN THE LaST FIGHT.
H-HE'S GETTING W-WEaKER.
I :COUGH: I TOLD YOU WE WERE GOING TO MaKE OUR FINAL STAND.
STRONG-STRONG help red ball!
Y-YOU WILL?
YES... YES WE WILL USE THE POWER OF TEAMWORK!
I FEEL a SECOND WIND...

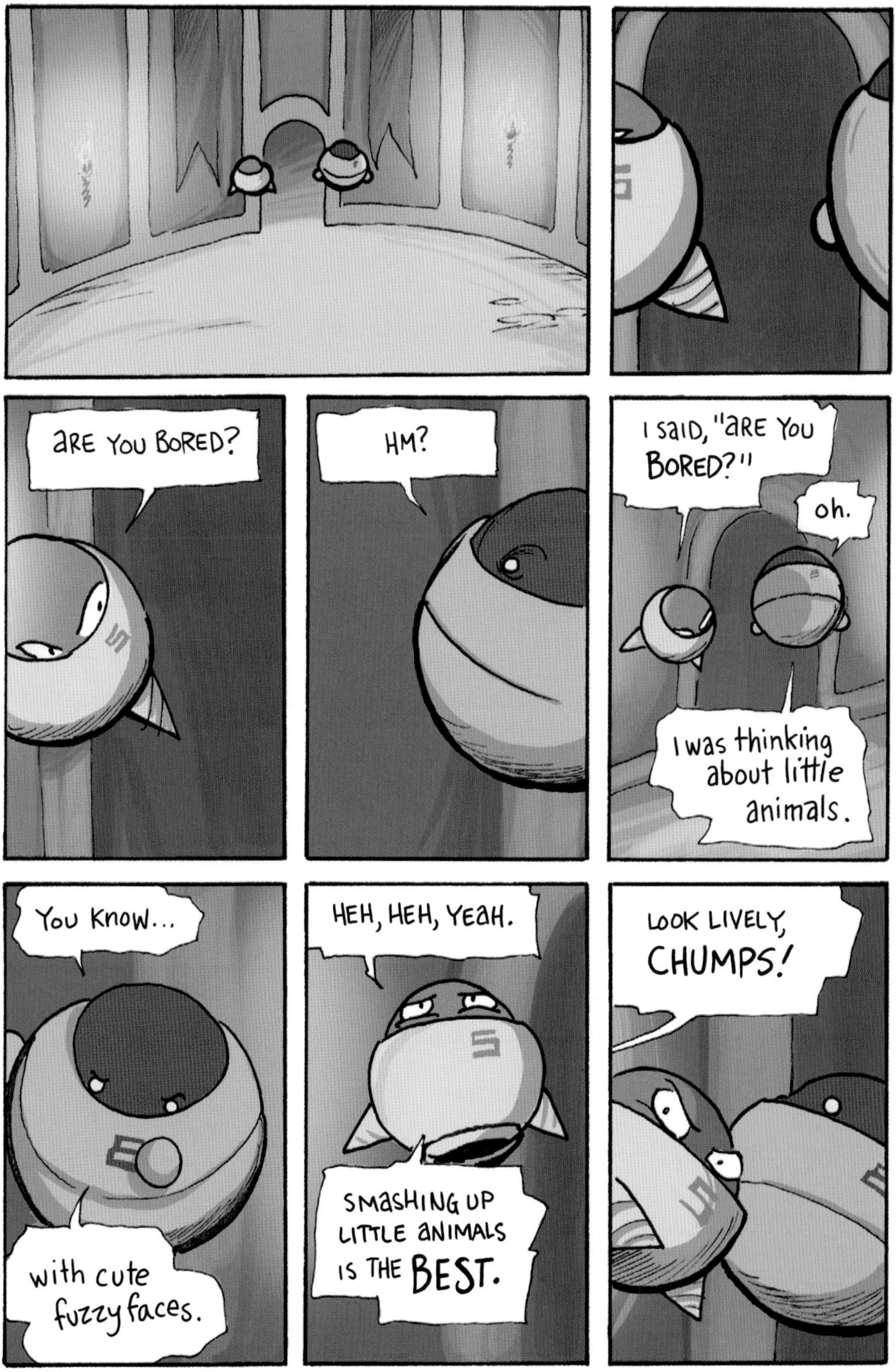
ARE YOU BORED?
HM?
I SAID, "ARE YOU BORED?"
oh.
I was thinking about little animals.
You know...
with cute fuzzy faces.
HEH, HEH, YEAH.
SMASHING UP LITTLE ANIMALS IS THE BEST.
LOOK LIVELY, CHUMPS!

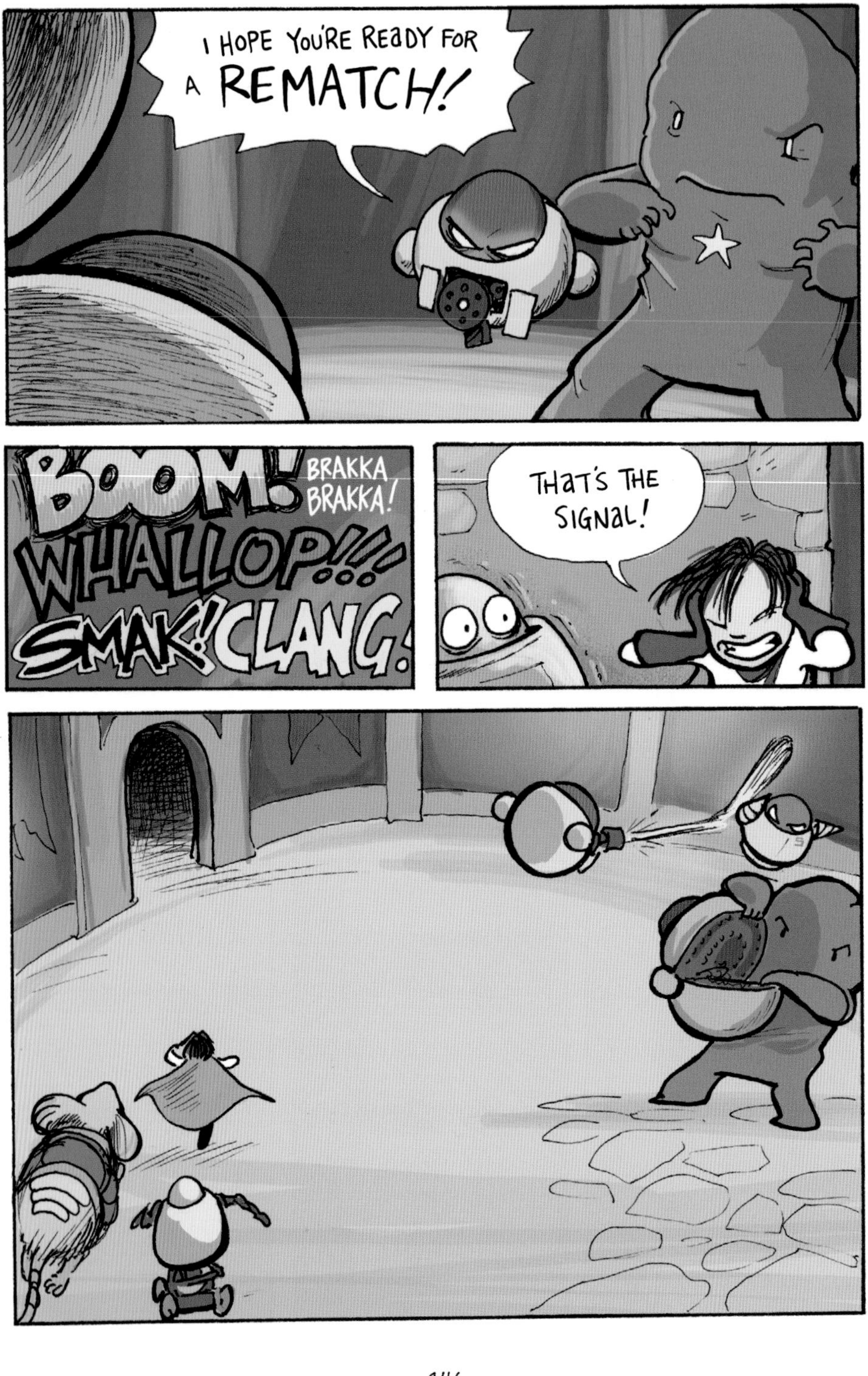
I HOPE YOU'RE READY FOR A REMATCH!
BOOM!
BRAKKA BRAKKA!
WHALLOP!!!
SMAK! CLANG!
THAT'S THE SIGNAL!

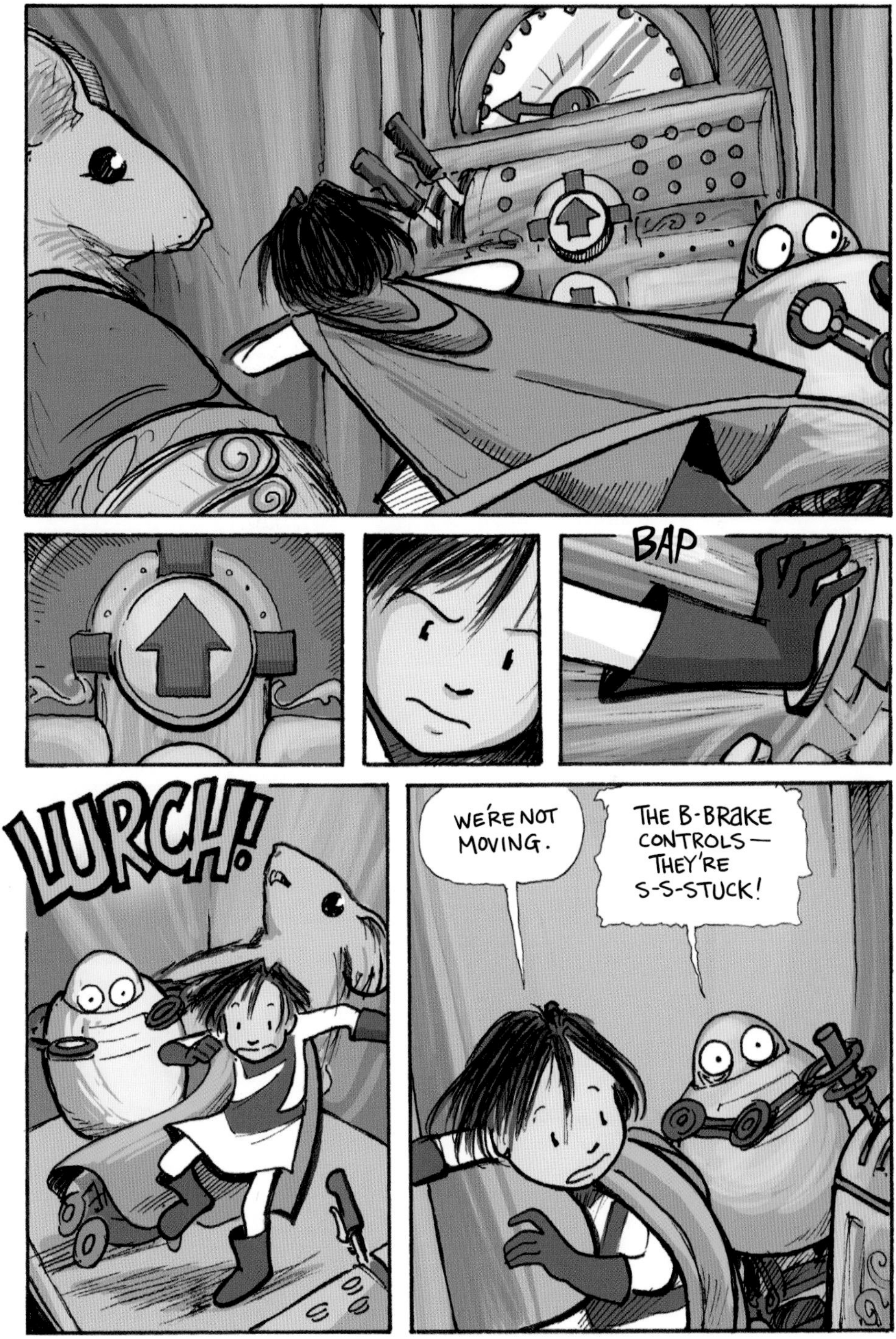
BAP
LURCH!
WE'RE NOT MOVING.
THE B-BRAKE CONTROLS— THEY'RE S-S-STUCK!

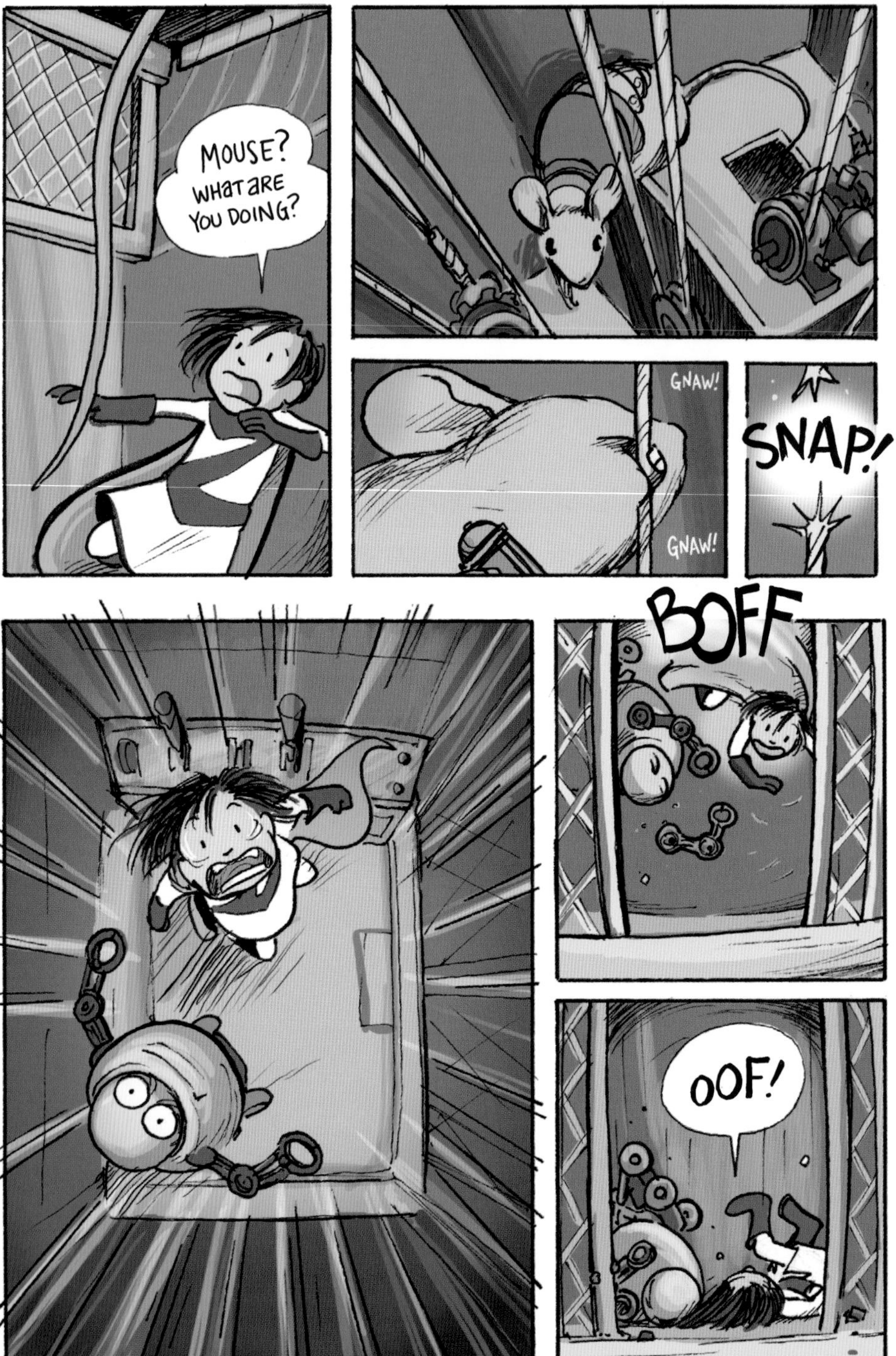
MOUSE? WHAT ARE YOU DOING?
GNAW!
GNAW!
SNAP!
BOFF
OOF!

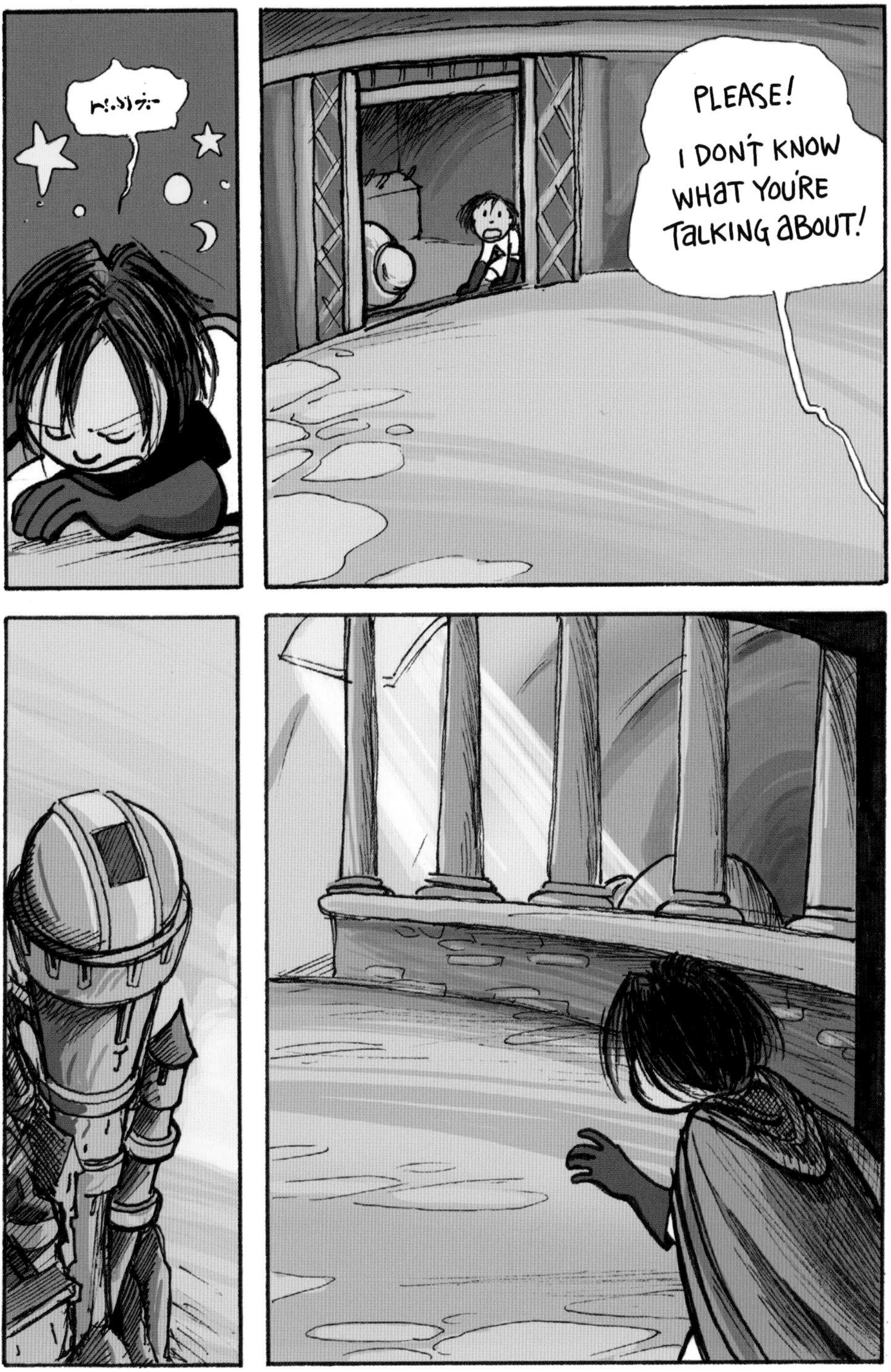
PLEASE!
I DON'T KNOW WHAT YOU'RE TALKING ABOUT!

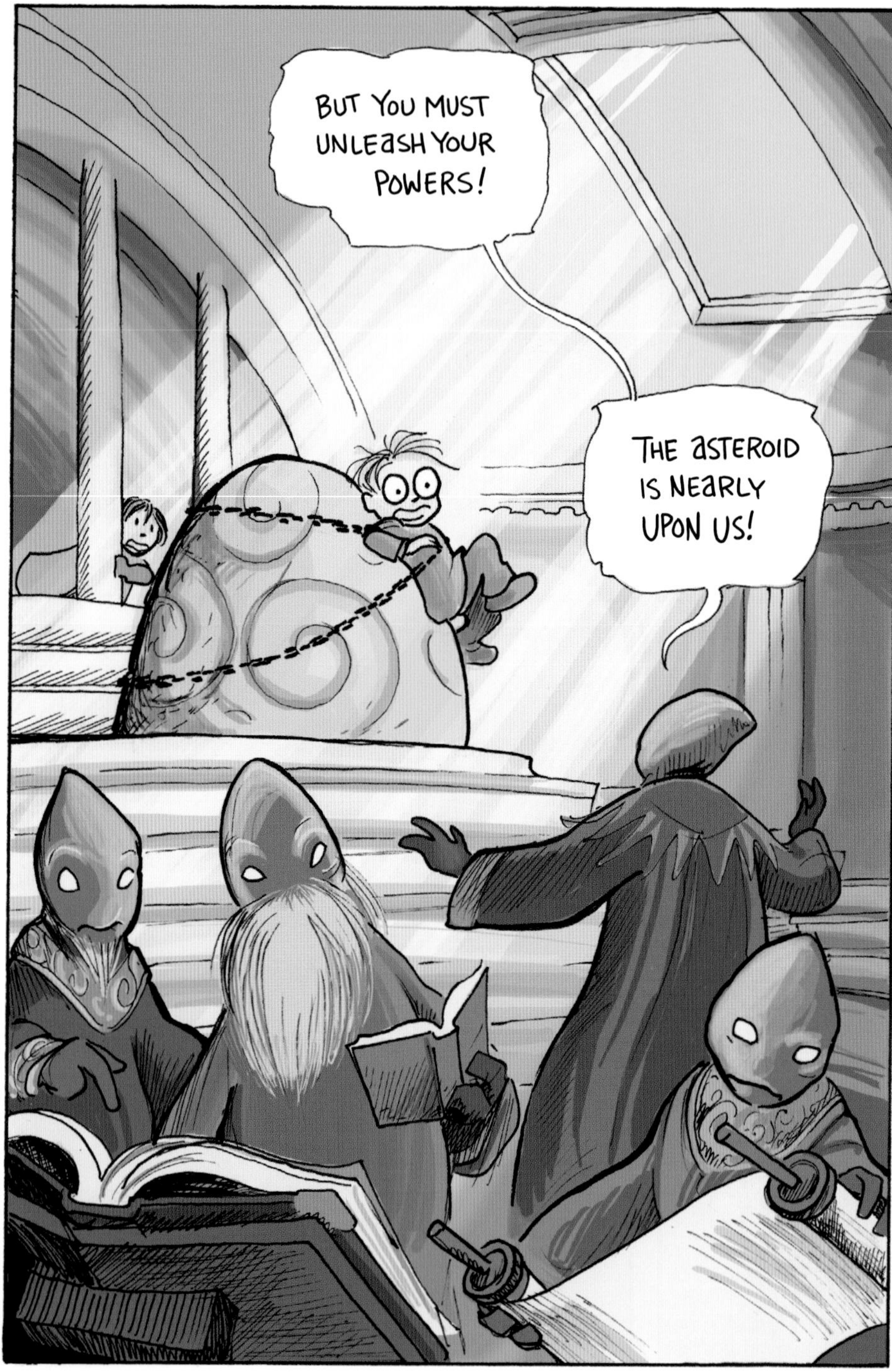
BUT YOU MUST UNLEASH YOUR POWERS!
THE ASTEROID IS NEARLY UPON US!

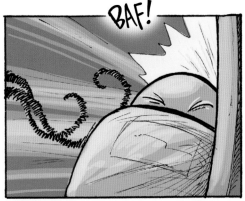

BAF!

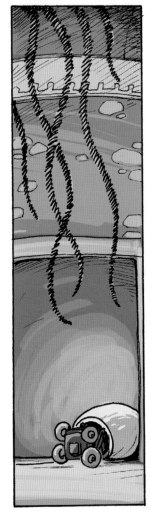

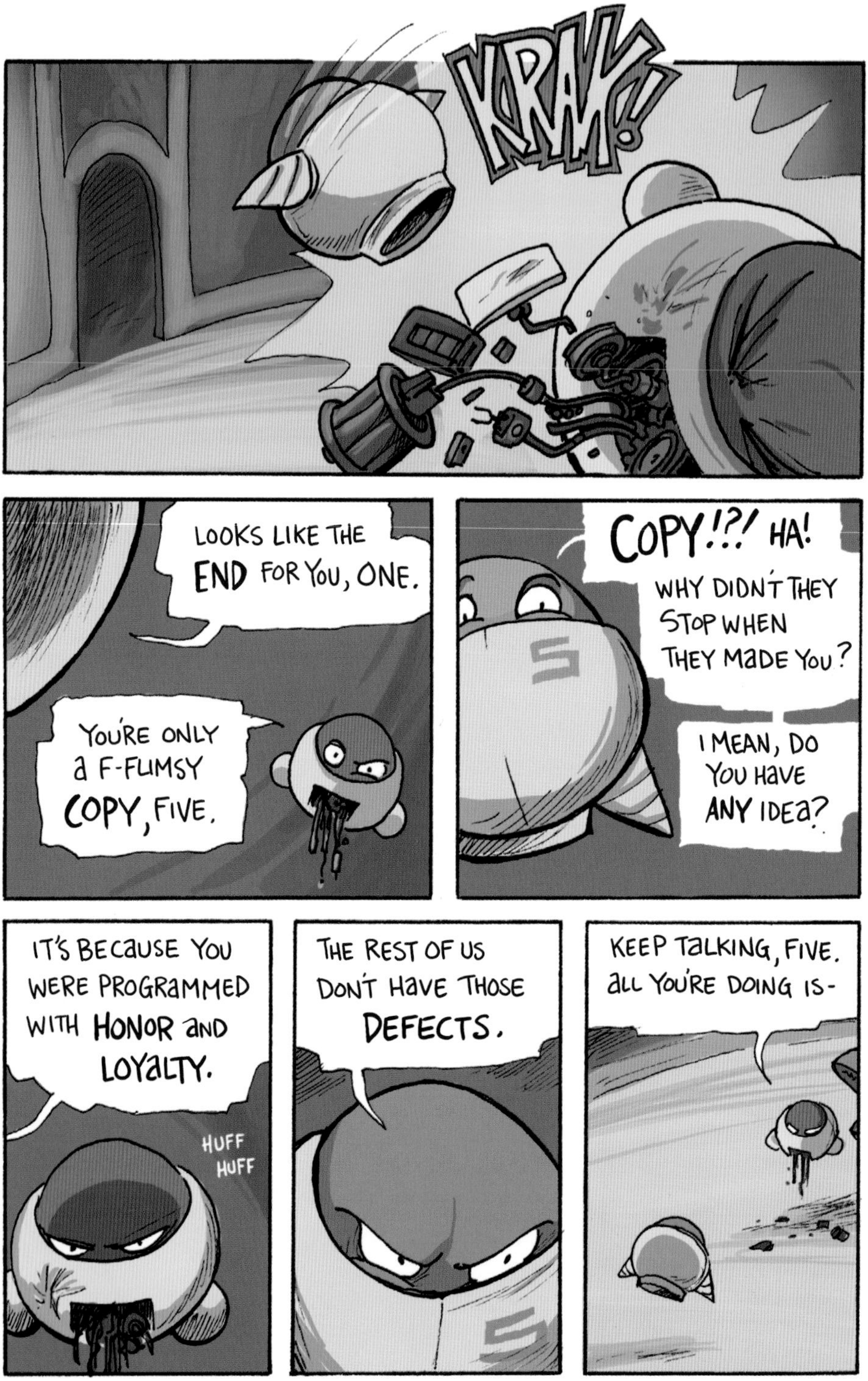
KRAK!
LOOKS LIKE THE END FOR YOU, ONE.
YOU'RE ONLY A F-FLIMSY COPY, FIVE.
COPY!?! HA!
WHY DIDN'T THEY STOP WHEN THEY MADE YOU?
I MEAN, DO YOU HAVE ANY IDEA?
IT'S BECAUSE YOU WERE PROGRAMMED WITH HONOR AND LOYALTY.
HUFF HUFF
THE REST OF US DON'T HAVE THOSE DEFECTS.
KEEP TALKING, FIVE. ALL YOU'RE DOING IS-

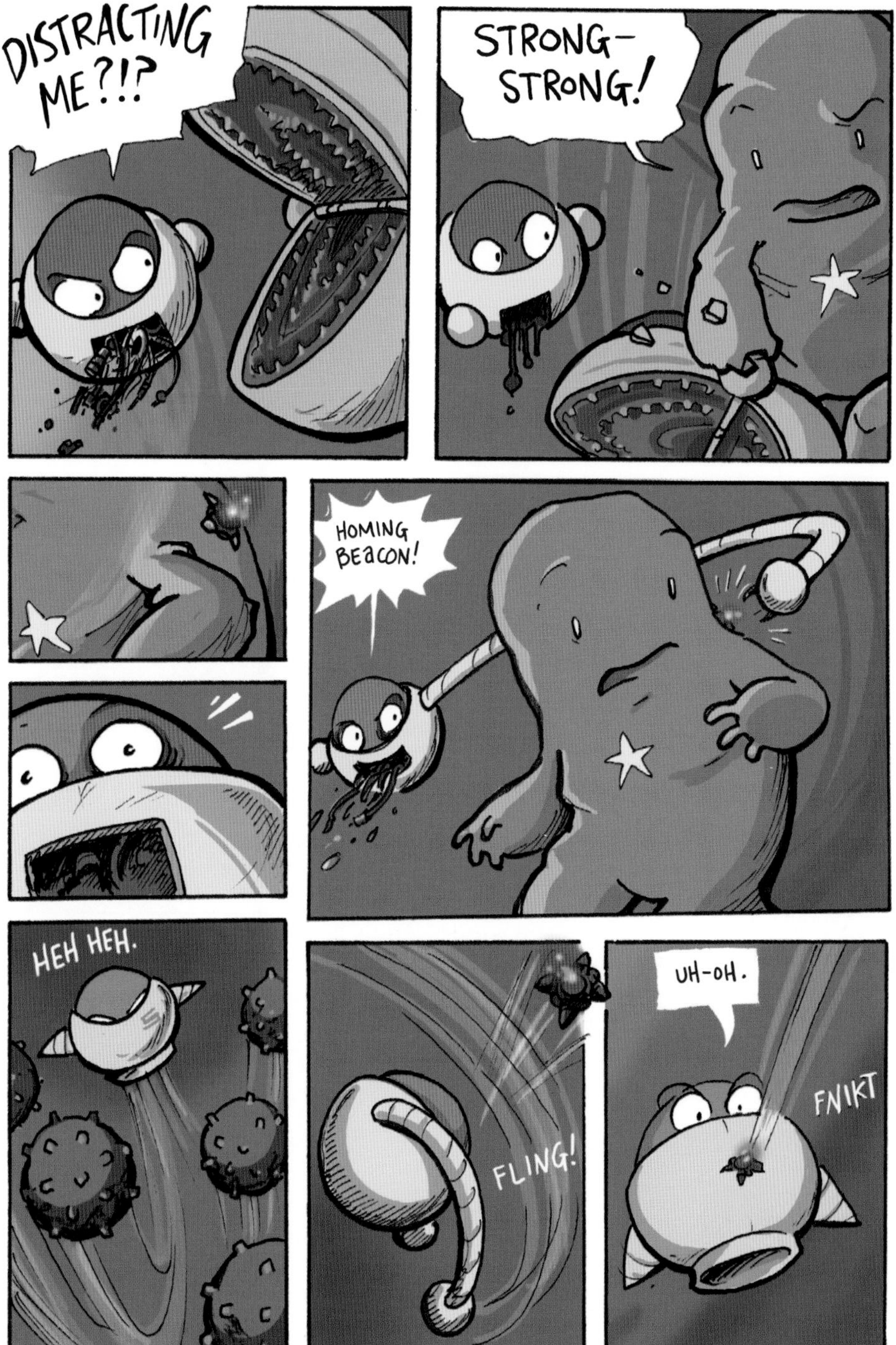
DISTRACTING ME?!?
STRONG-STRONG!
HOMING BEACON!
HEH HEH.
FLING!
UH-OH.
FNIKT

BOOM!

OOOOH.

CLANG!

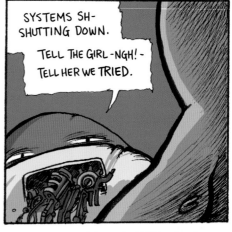

SYSTEMS SH-SHUTTING DOWN.

TELL THE GIRL -NGH!- TELL HER WE TRIED.

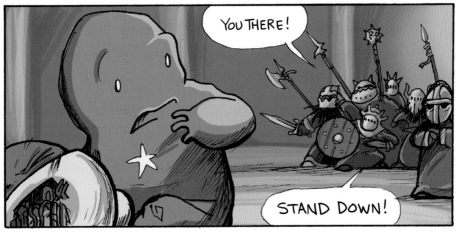

YOU THERE!

STAND DOWN!

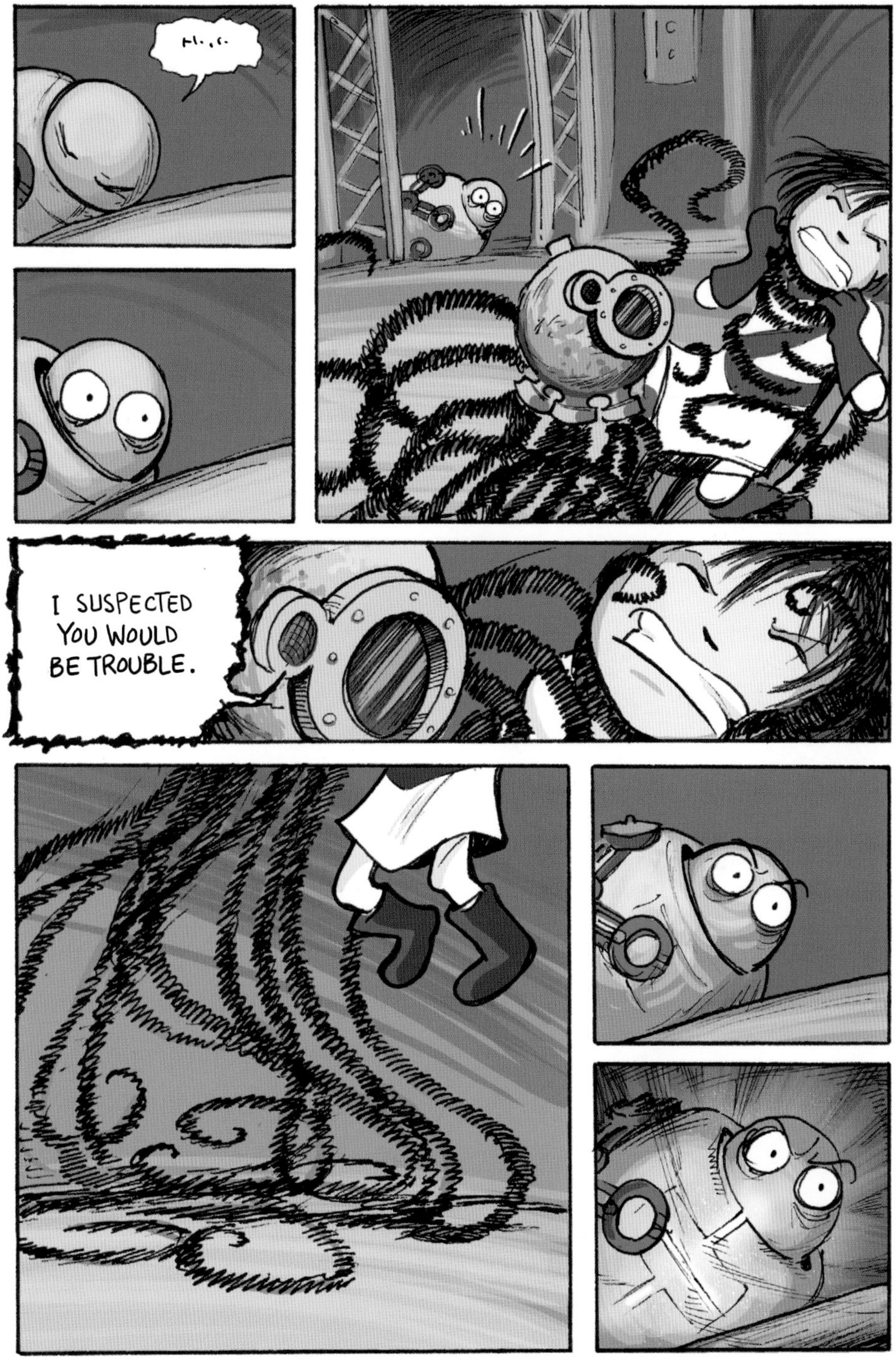
I SUSPECTED YOU WOULD BE TROUBLE.

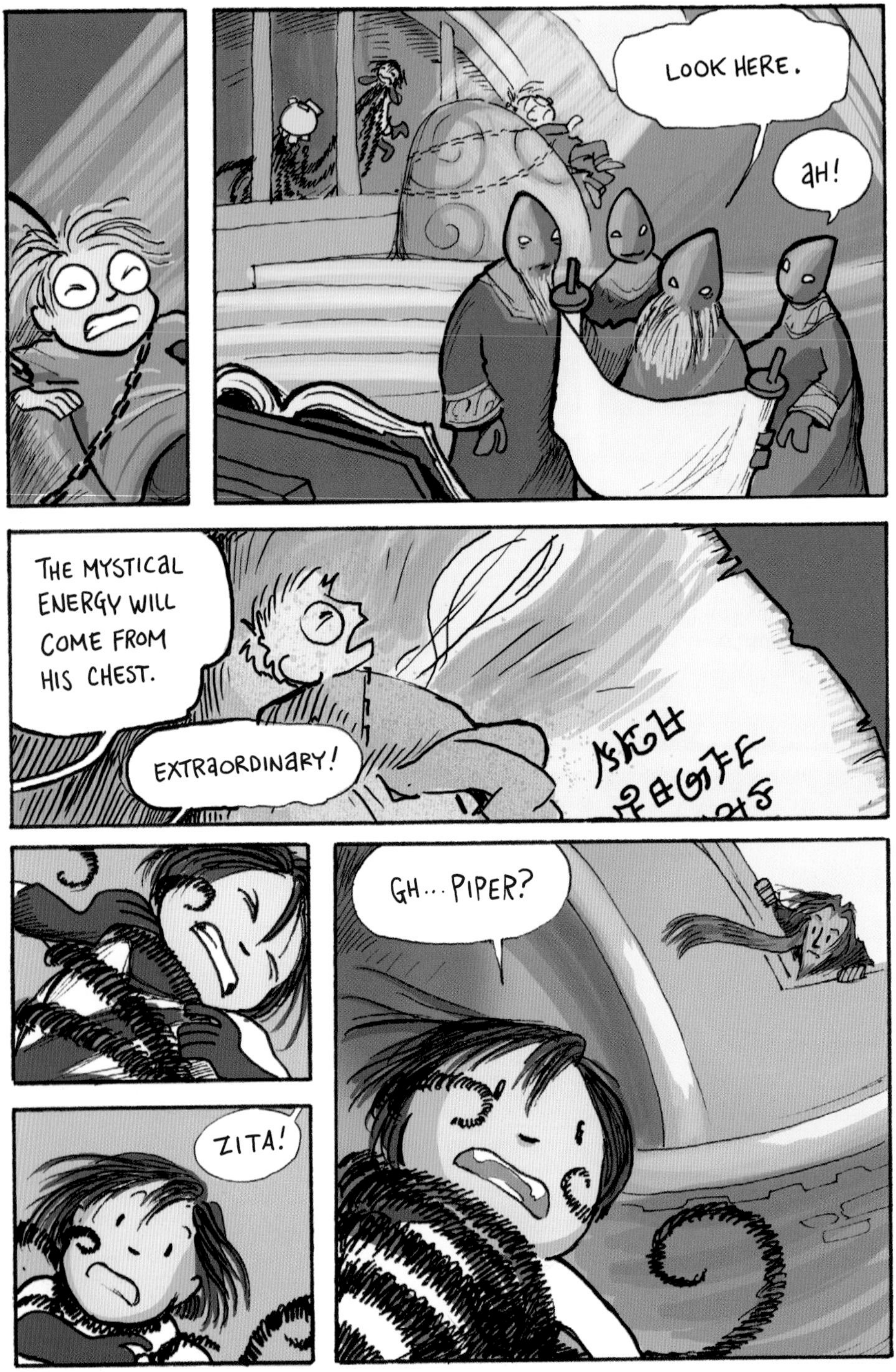
LOOK HERE.
aH!
THE MYSTICaL ENERGY WILL COME FROM HIS CHEST.
EXTRaORDINaRY!
GH... PIPER?
ZITA!

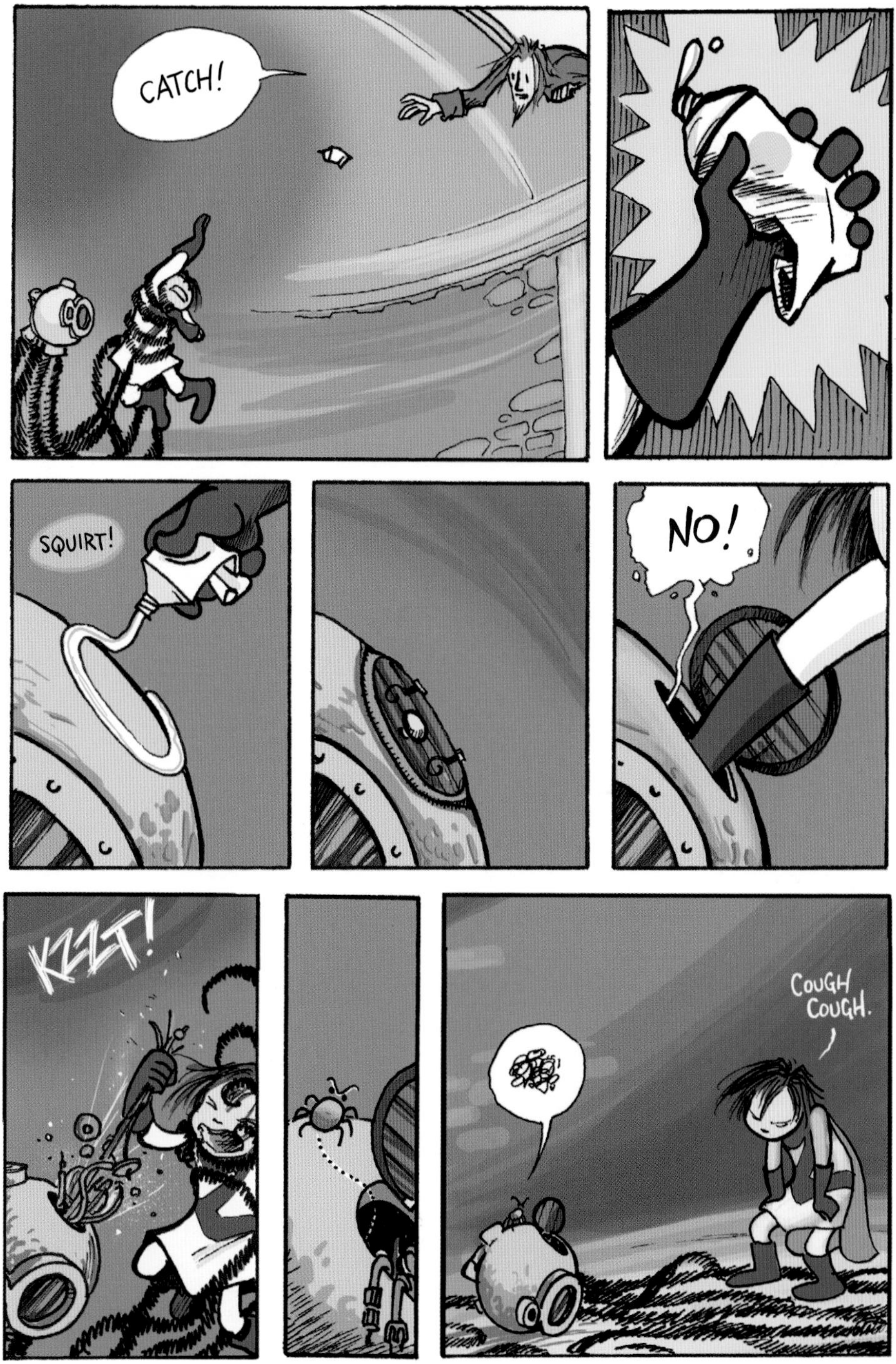
CATCH!
SQUIRT!
NO!
KZZT!
COUGH COUGH.

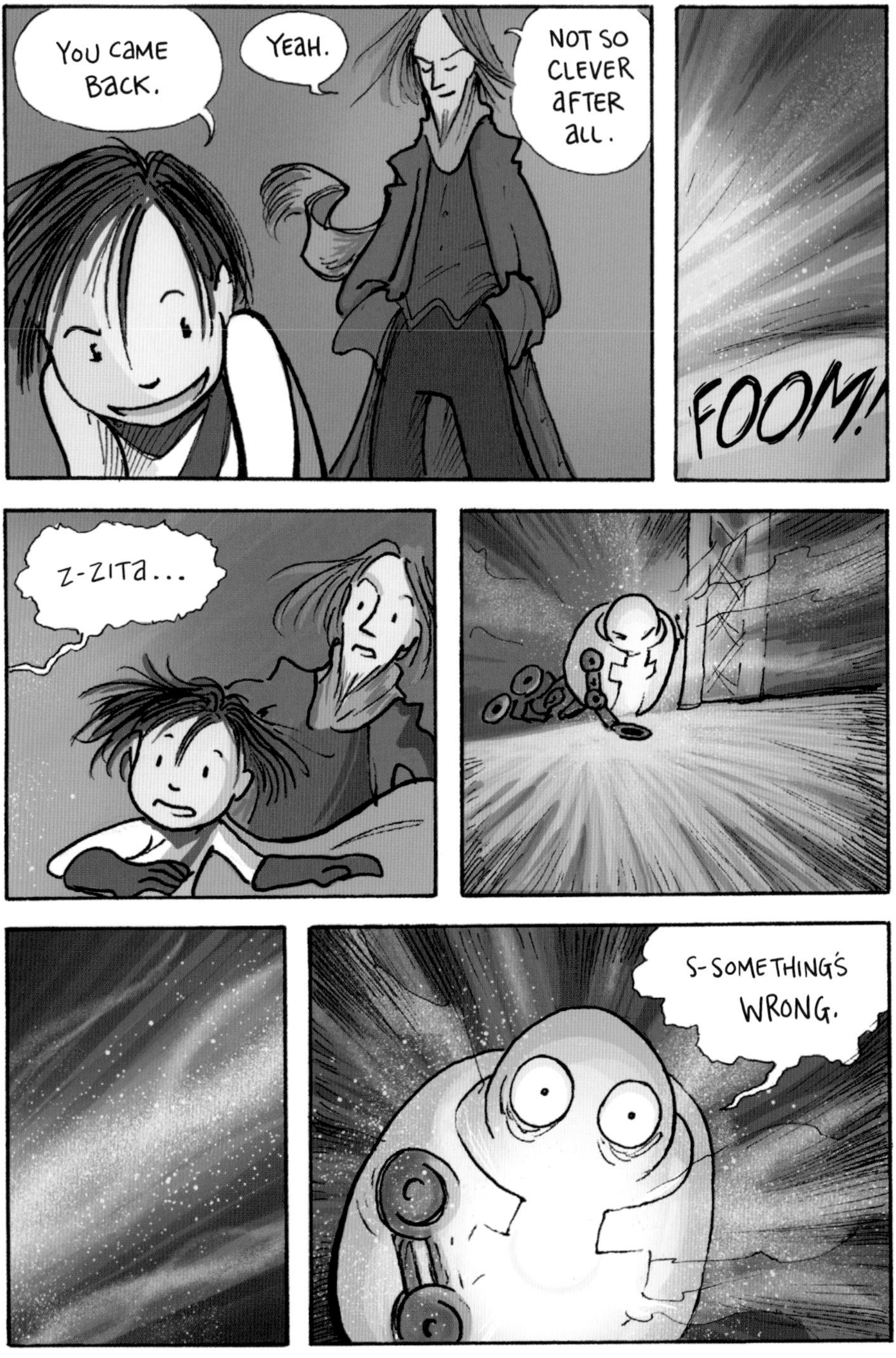
YOU CAME BACK.
YEAH.
NOT SO CLEVER AFTER ALL.
FOOM!
Z-ZITA...
S-SOMETHING'S WRONG.

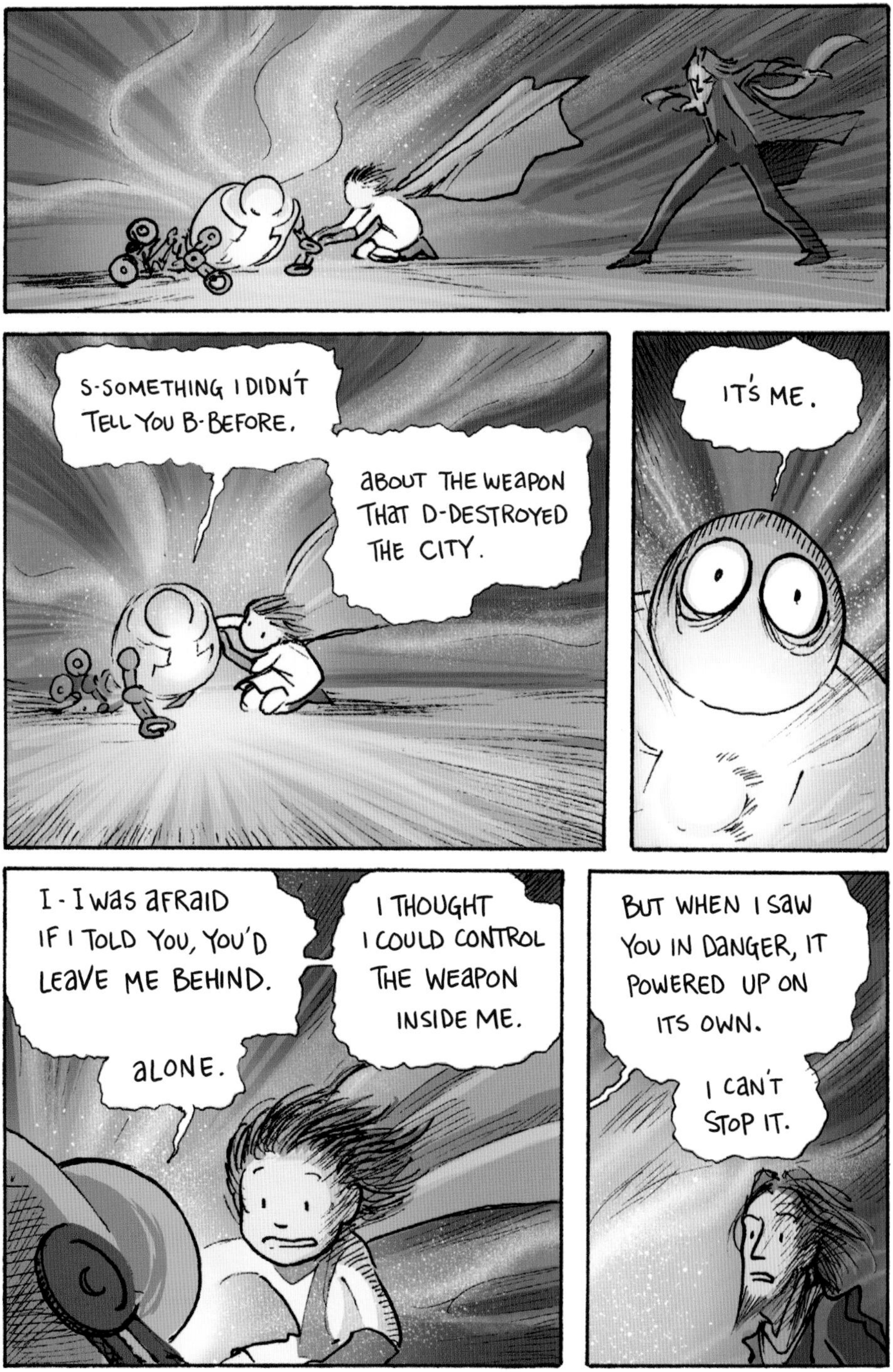
S-SOMETHING I DIDN'T TELL YOU B-BEFORE.
ABOUT THE WEAPON THAT D-DESTROYED THE CITY.
IT'S ME.
I - I WAS AFRAID IF I TOLD YOU, YOU'D LEAVE ME BEHIND.
ALONE.
I THOUGHT I COULD CONTROL THE WEAPON INSIDE ME.
BUT WHEN I SAW YOU IN DANGER, IT POWERED UP ON ITS OWN.
I CAN'T STOP IT.

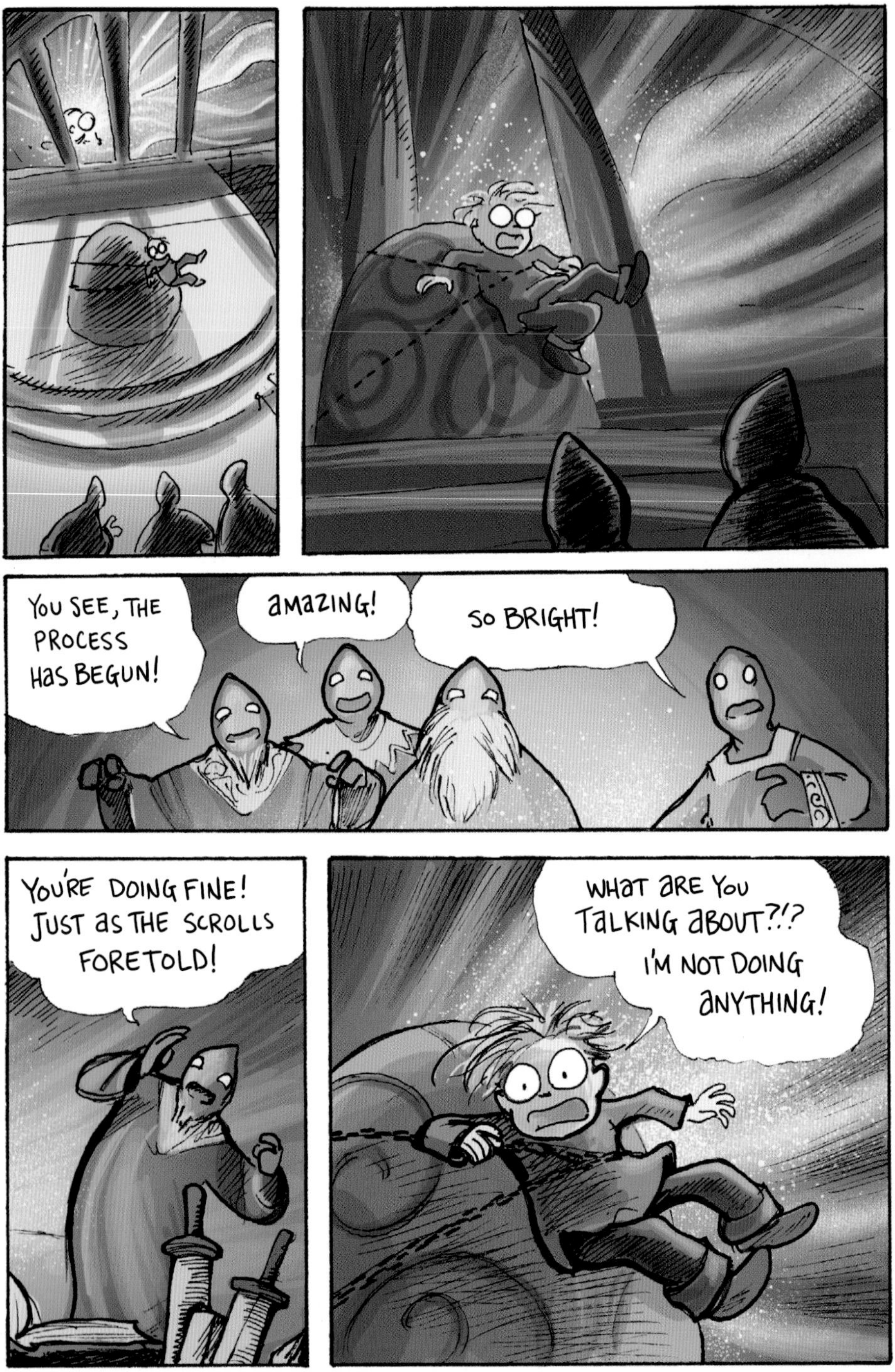
YOU SEE, THE PROCESS HAS BEGUN!
AMAZING!
SO BRIGHT!
YOU'RE DOING FINE! JUST AS THE SCROLLS FORETOLD!
WHAT ARE YOU TALKING ABOUT?!?
I'M NOT DOING ANYTHING!

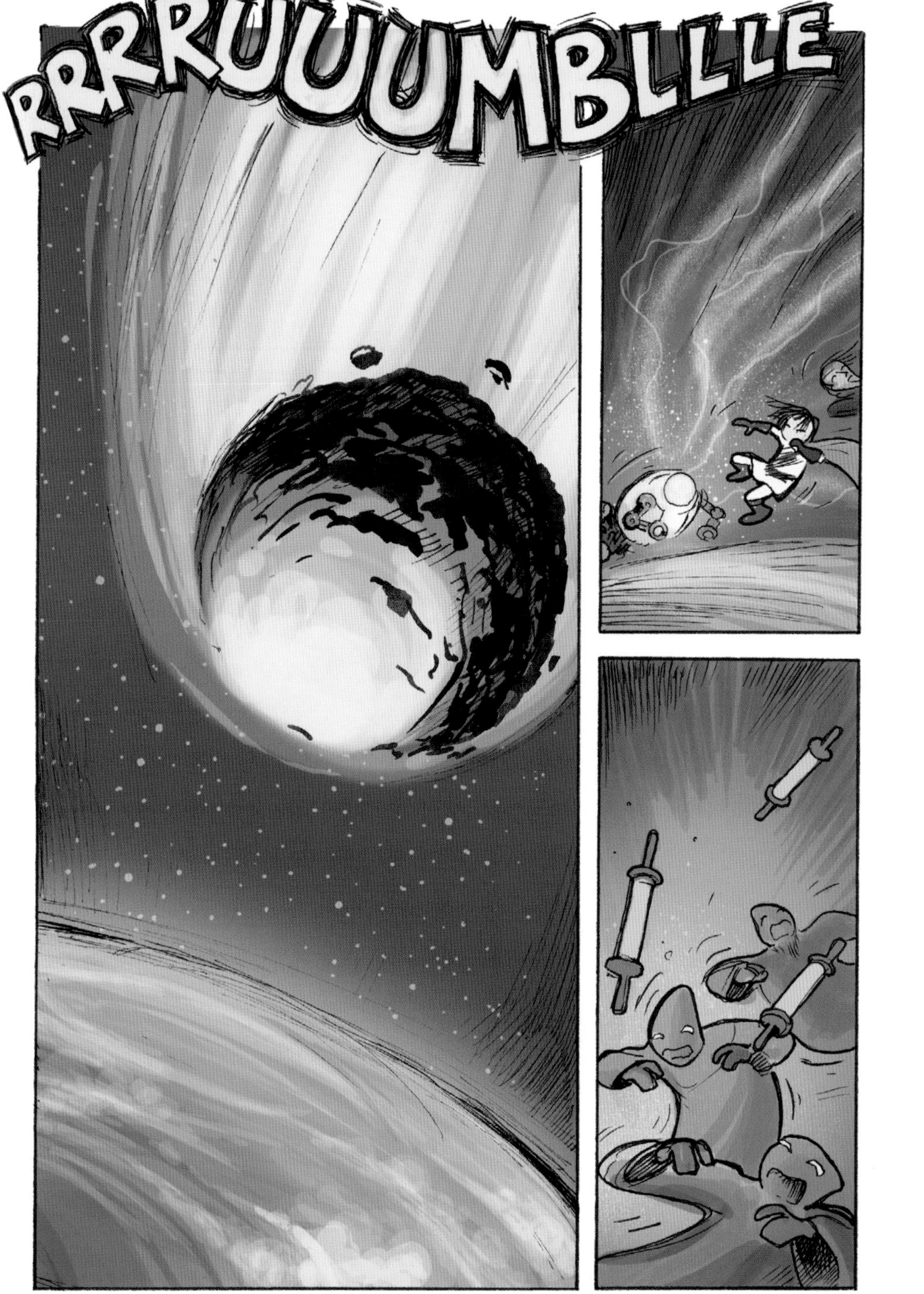
RRRRUUUUMBLLLE

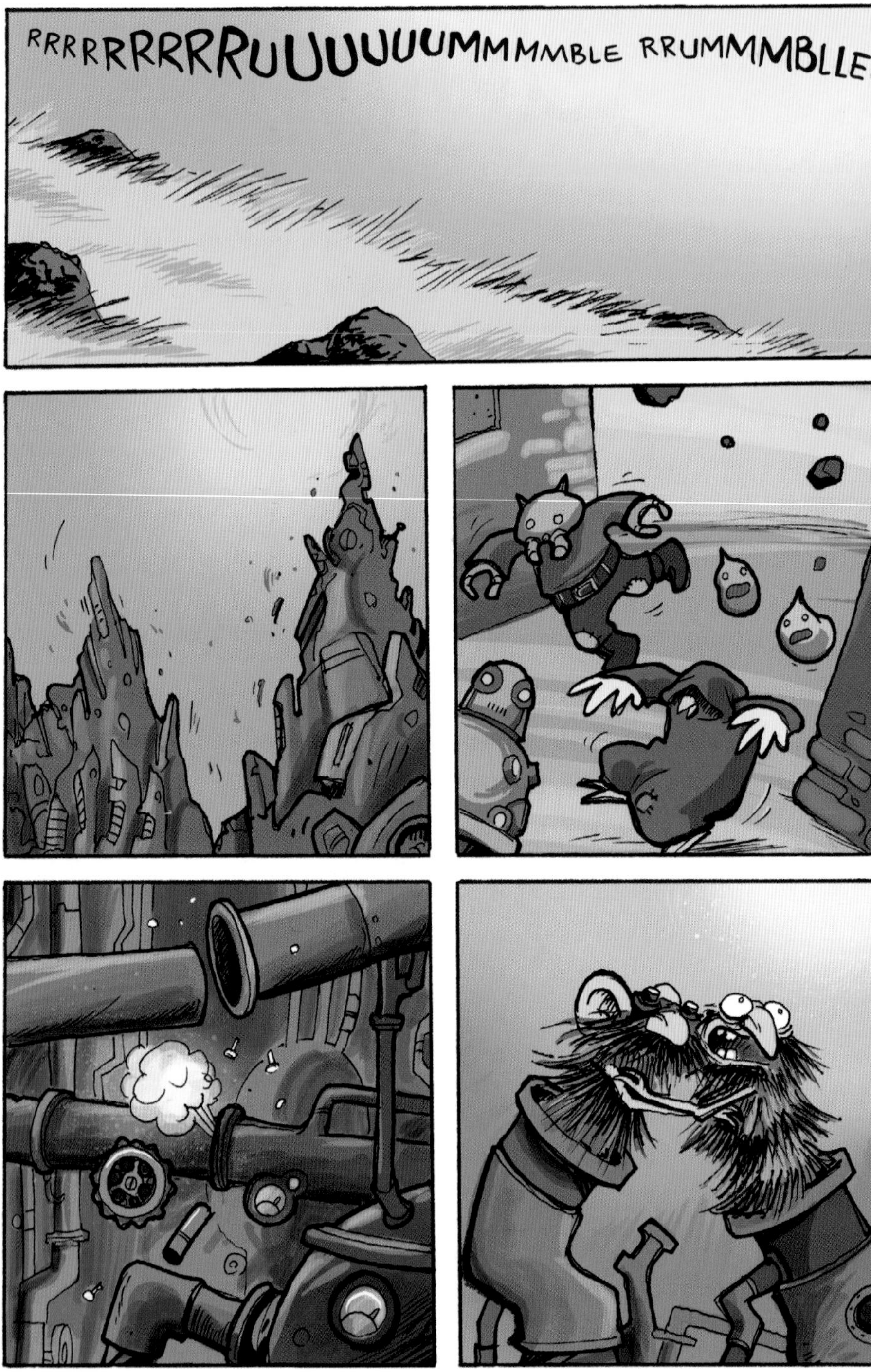
RRRRRRRRRUUUUUUMMMMBLE RRUMMMBLLEE

SO.

WE'RE CAUGHT BETWEEN A MALFUNCTIONING ULTIMATE WEAPON AND A DOOMSDAY ASTEROID.

EVEN IF WE WERE ON MY SHIP, THERE'S NO WAY WE COULD LAUNCH IN TIME.

SO THIS IS THE END.

FOR US, YES.

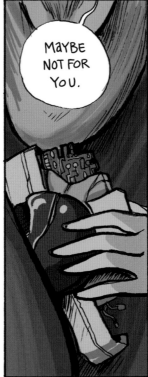

MAYBE NOT FOR YOU.

NOT MANY PEOPLE ESCAPE THE END OF A WORLD.

GO SAVE YOUR FRIEND.

SNRGHT

I WON'T FORGET YOU, PIPER!

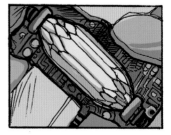

THERE IT IS.

MY MISSING PIECE!

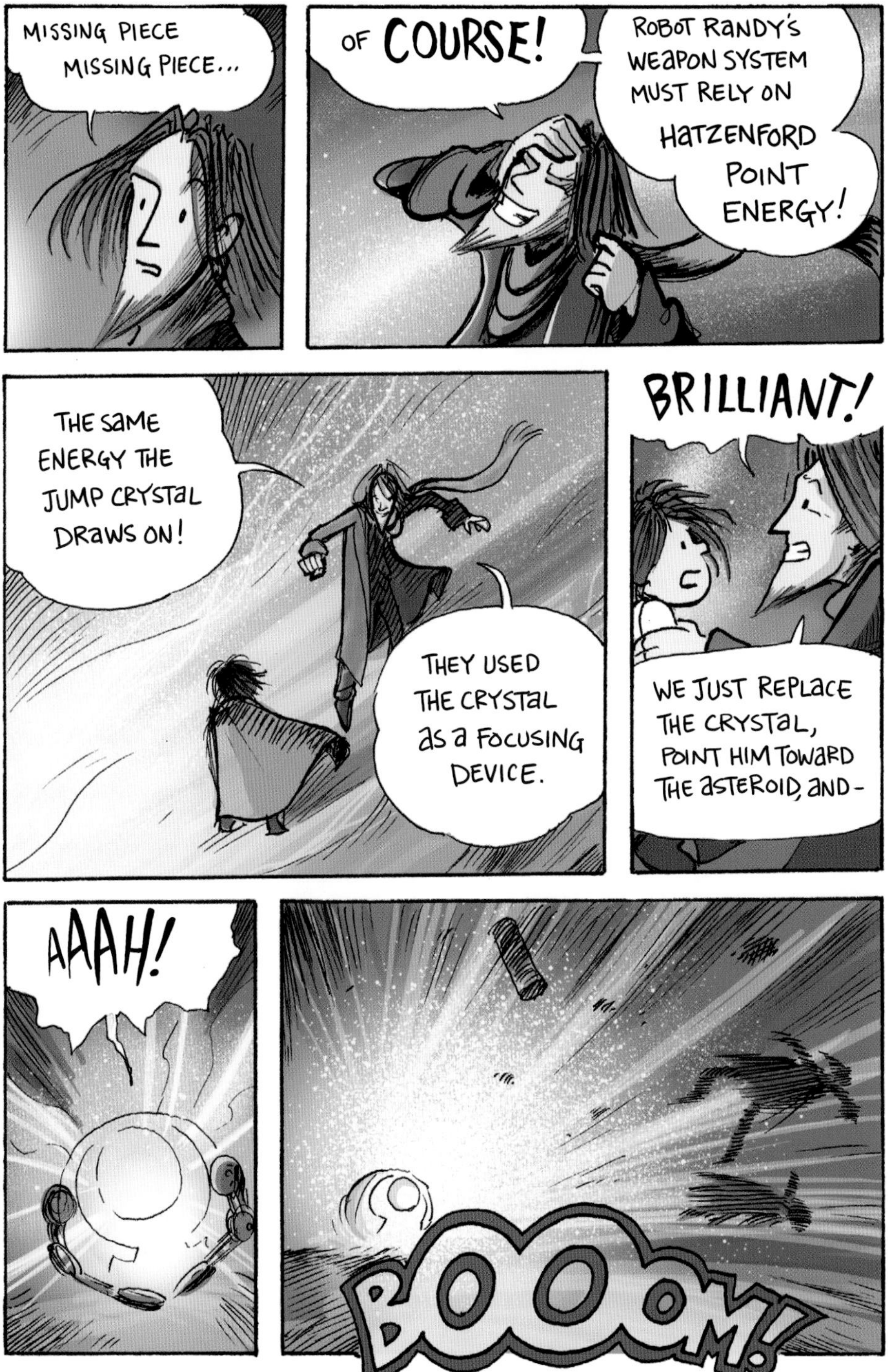
MISSING PIECE MISSING PIECE...
OF COURSE!
ROBOT RANDY'S WEAPON SYSTEM MUST RELY ON HATZENFORD POINT ENERGY!
THE SAME ENERGY THE JUMP CRYSTAL DRAWS ON!
THEY USED THE CRYSTAL AS A FOCUSING DEVICE.
BRILLIANT!
WE JUST REPLACE THE CRYSTAL, POINT HIM TOWARD THE ASTEROID, AND-
AAAH!
BOOOOM!

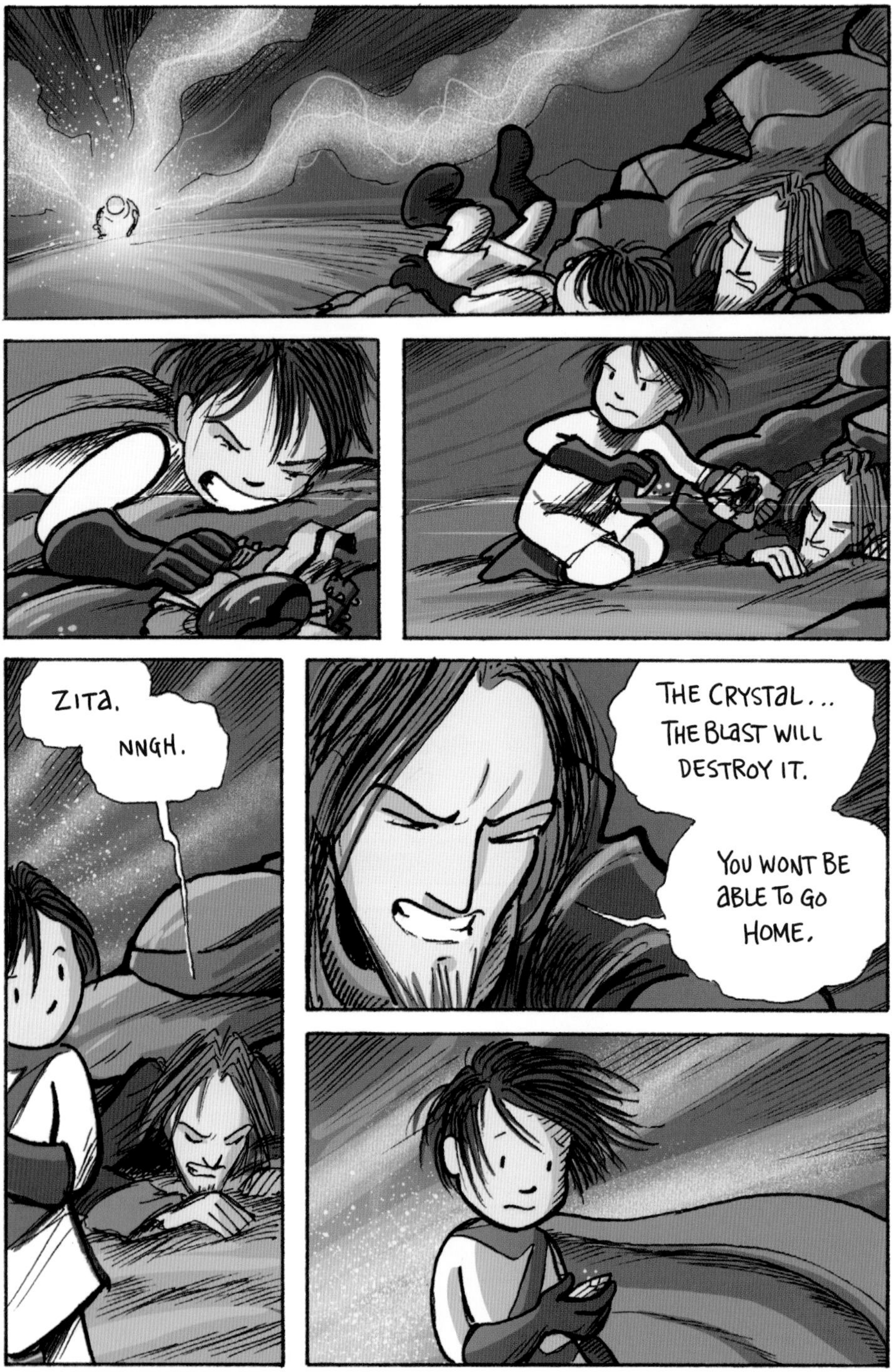
ZITA.
NNGH.
THE CRYSTAL... THE BLAST WILL DESTROY IT.
YOU WONT BE ABLE TO GO HOME.

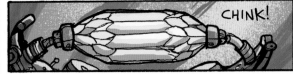

CHINK!

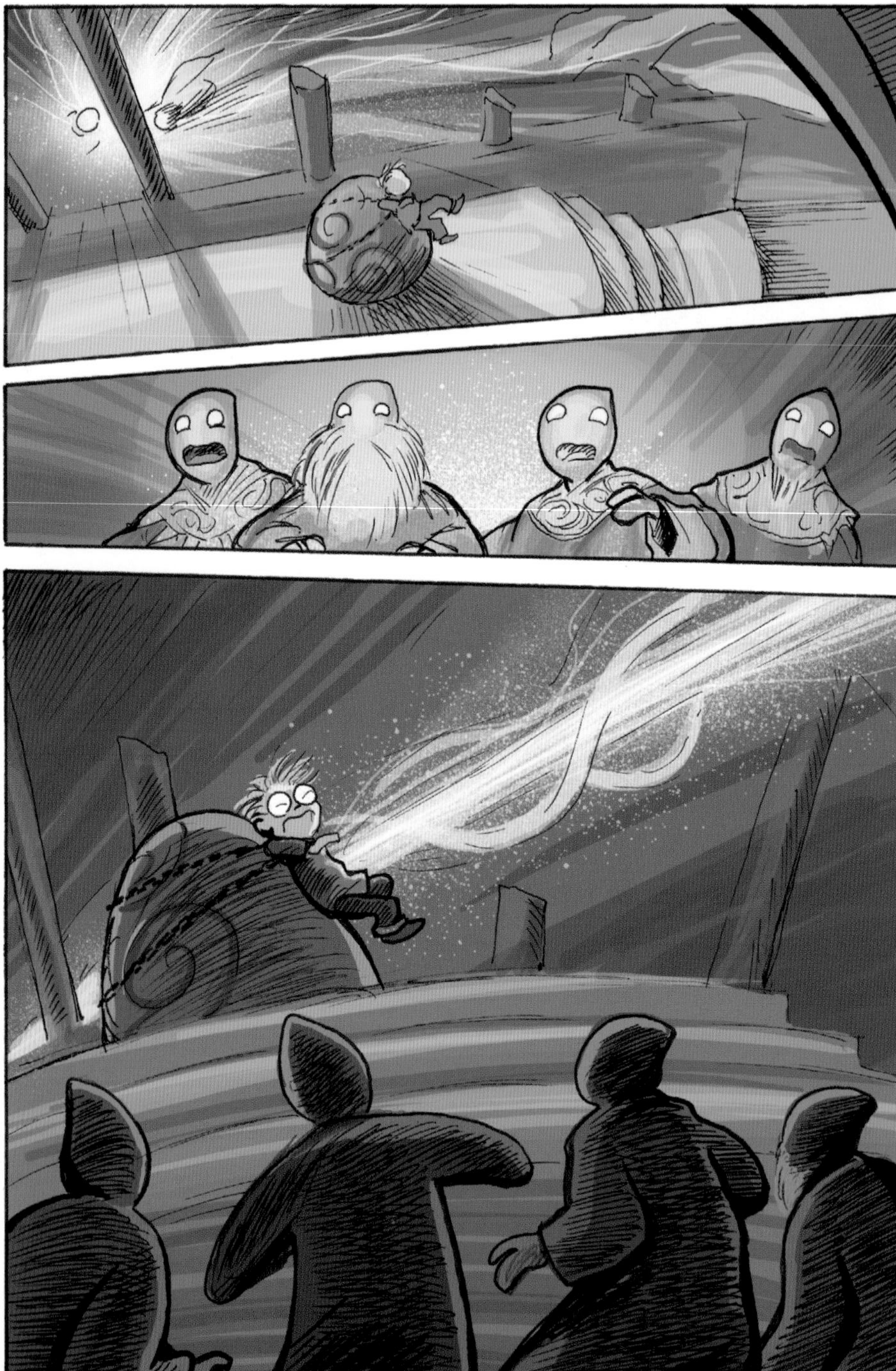

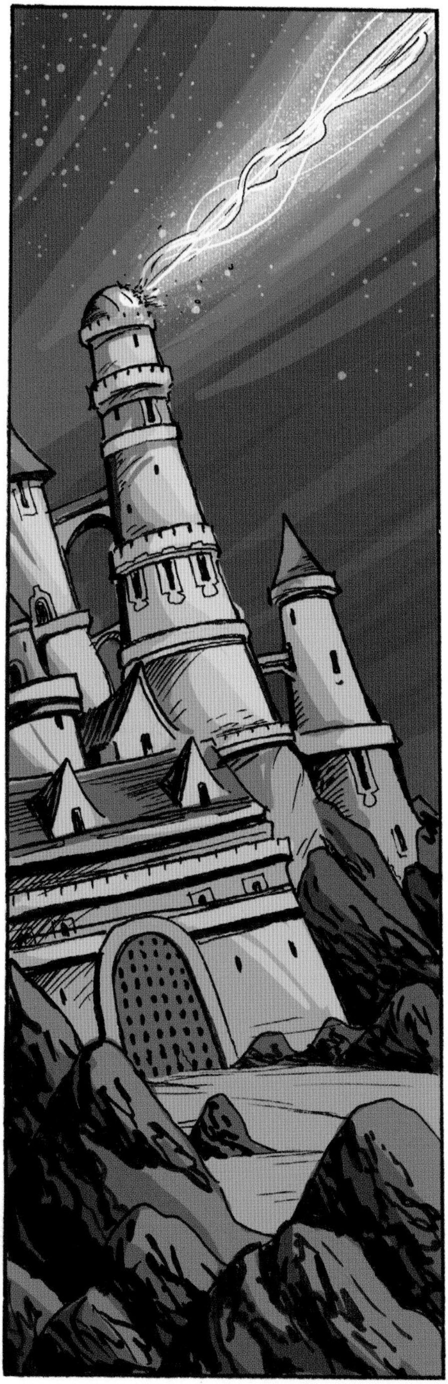

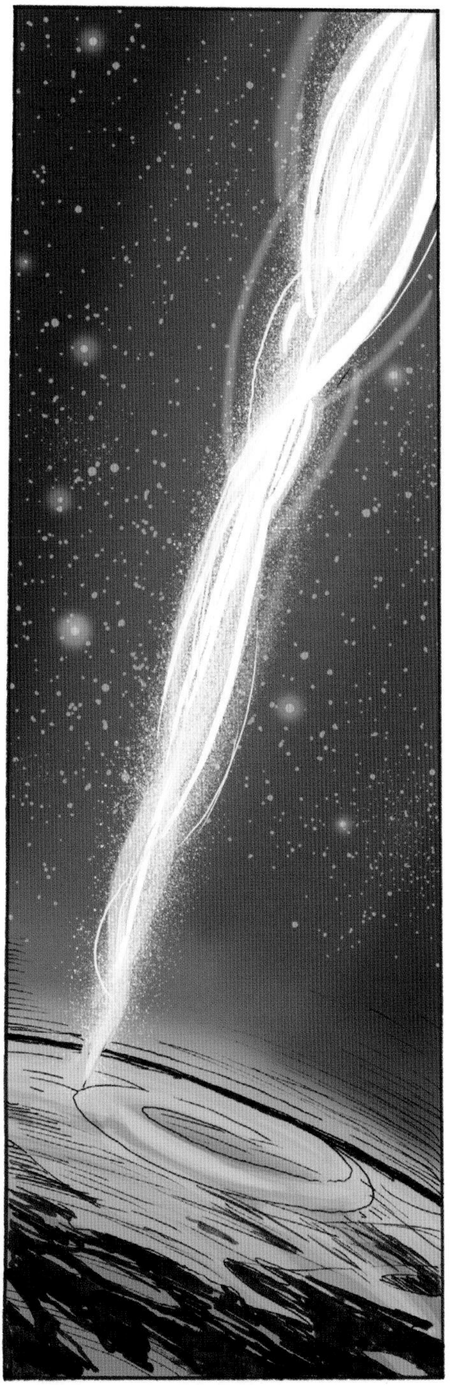

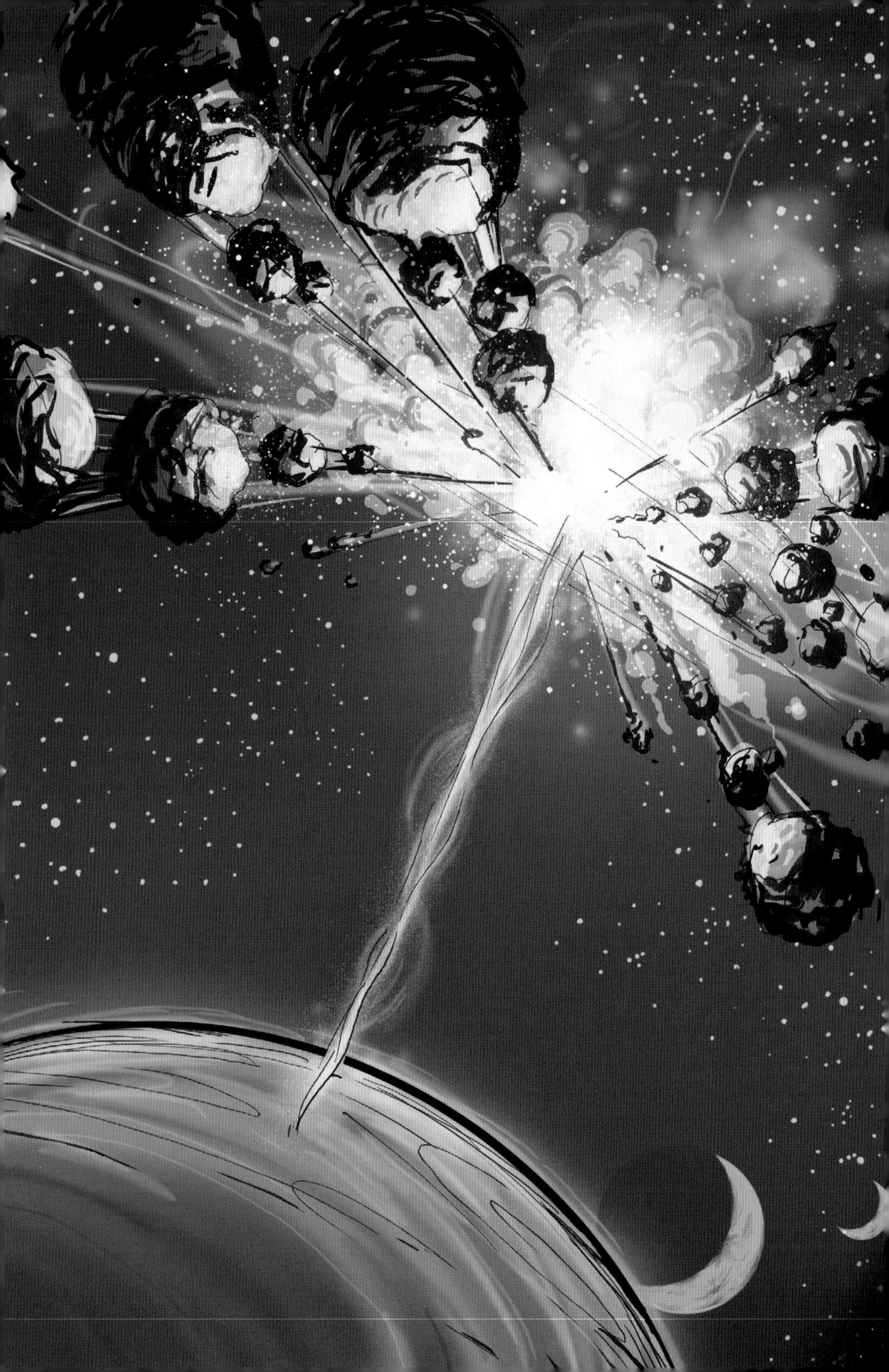

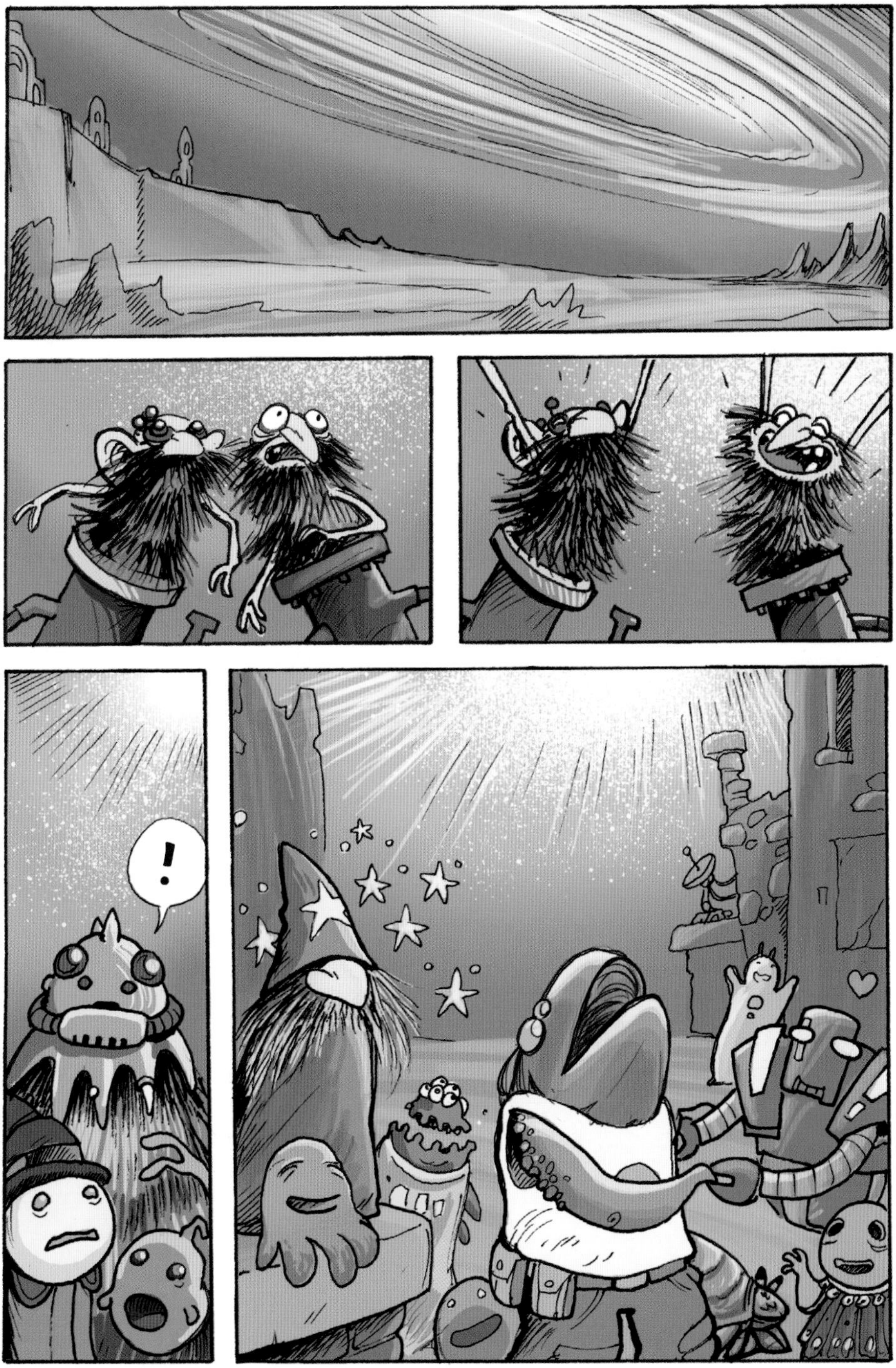
!

THE
END
IS
NIGH!

LAST
SHIP
OUT!
$$$

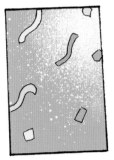

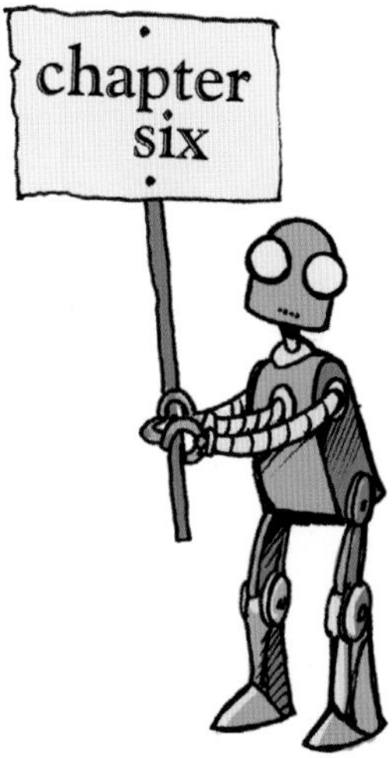
chapter
six

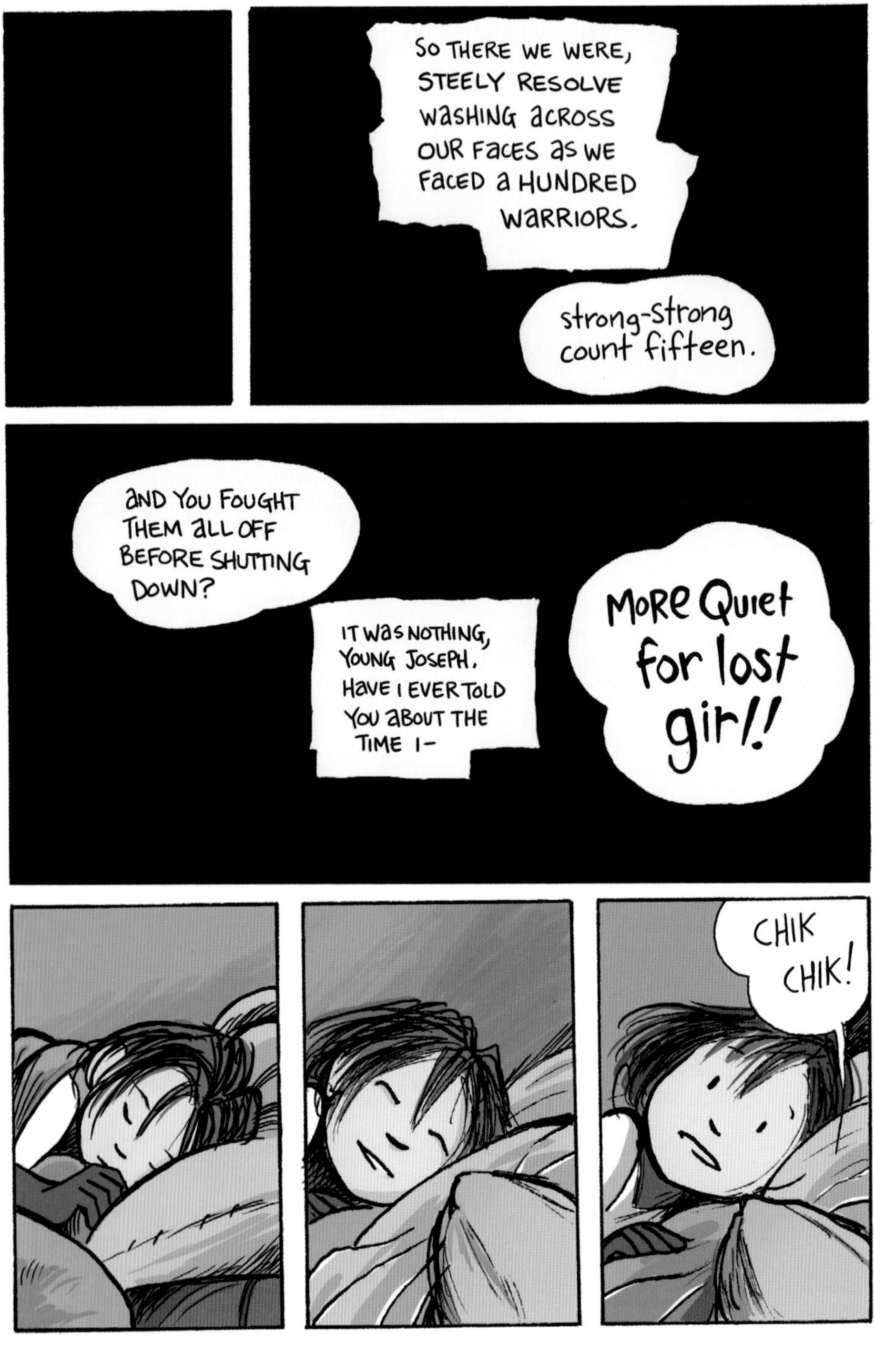
SO THERE WE WERE, STEELY RESOLVE WASHING ACROSS OUR FACES AS WE FACED A HUNDRED WARRIORS.
strong-strong count fifteen.
AND YOU FOUGHT THEM ALL OFF BEFORE SHUTTING DOWN?
IT WAS NOTHING, YOUNG JOSEPH. HAVE I EVER TOLD YOU ABOUT THE TIME I-
MORE Quiet for lost girl!!
CHIK CHIK!

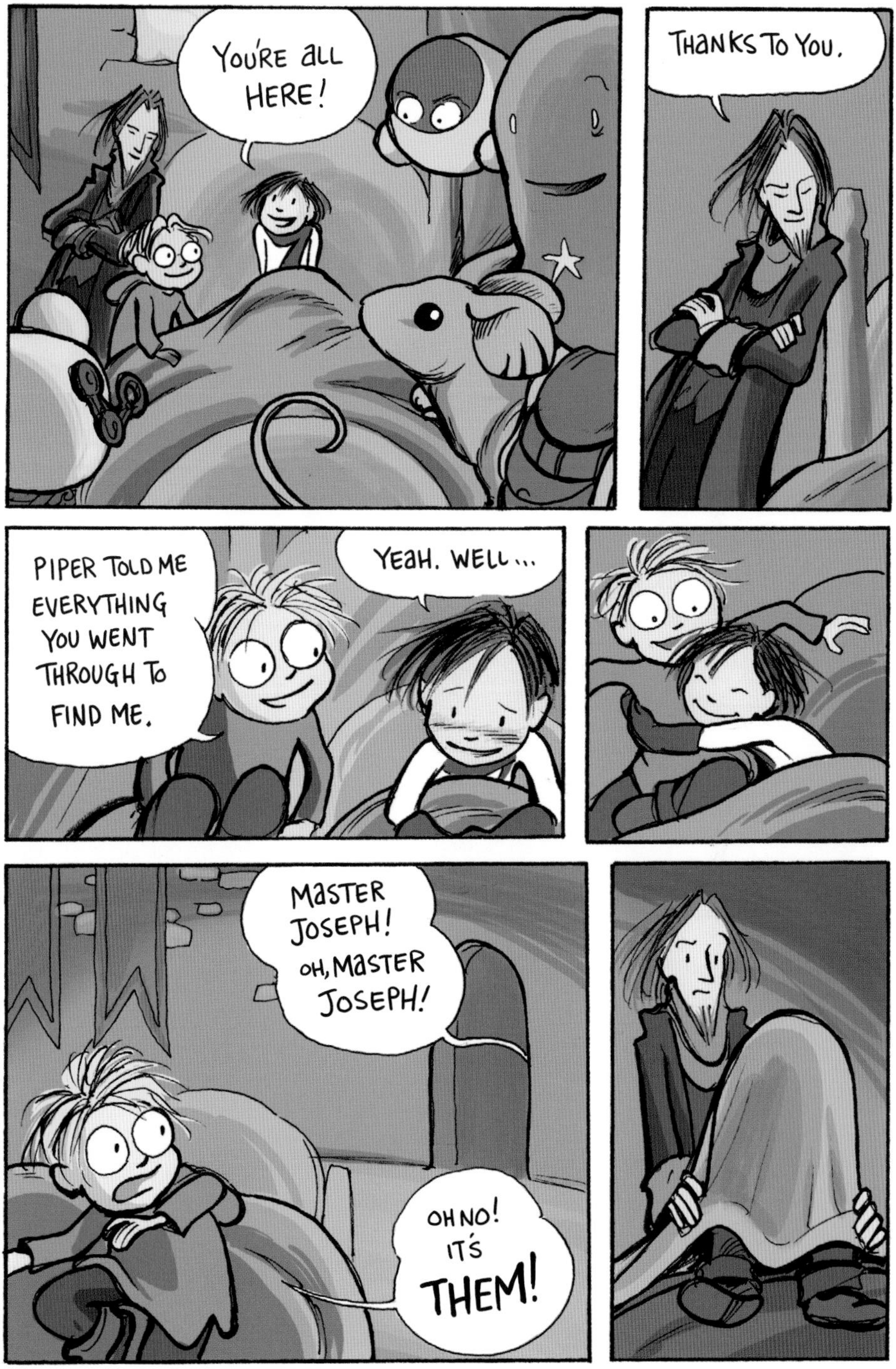
YOU'RE ALL HERE!
THANKS TO YOU.
PIPER TOLD ME EVERYTHING YOU WENT THROUGH TO FIND ME.
YEAH. WELL...
MASTER JOSEPH! OH, MASTER JOSEPH!
OH NO! IT'S THEM!

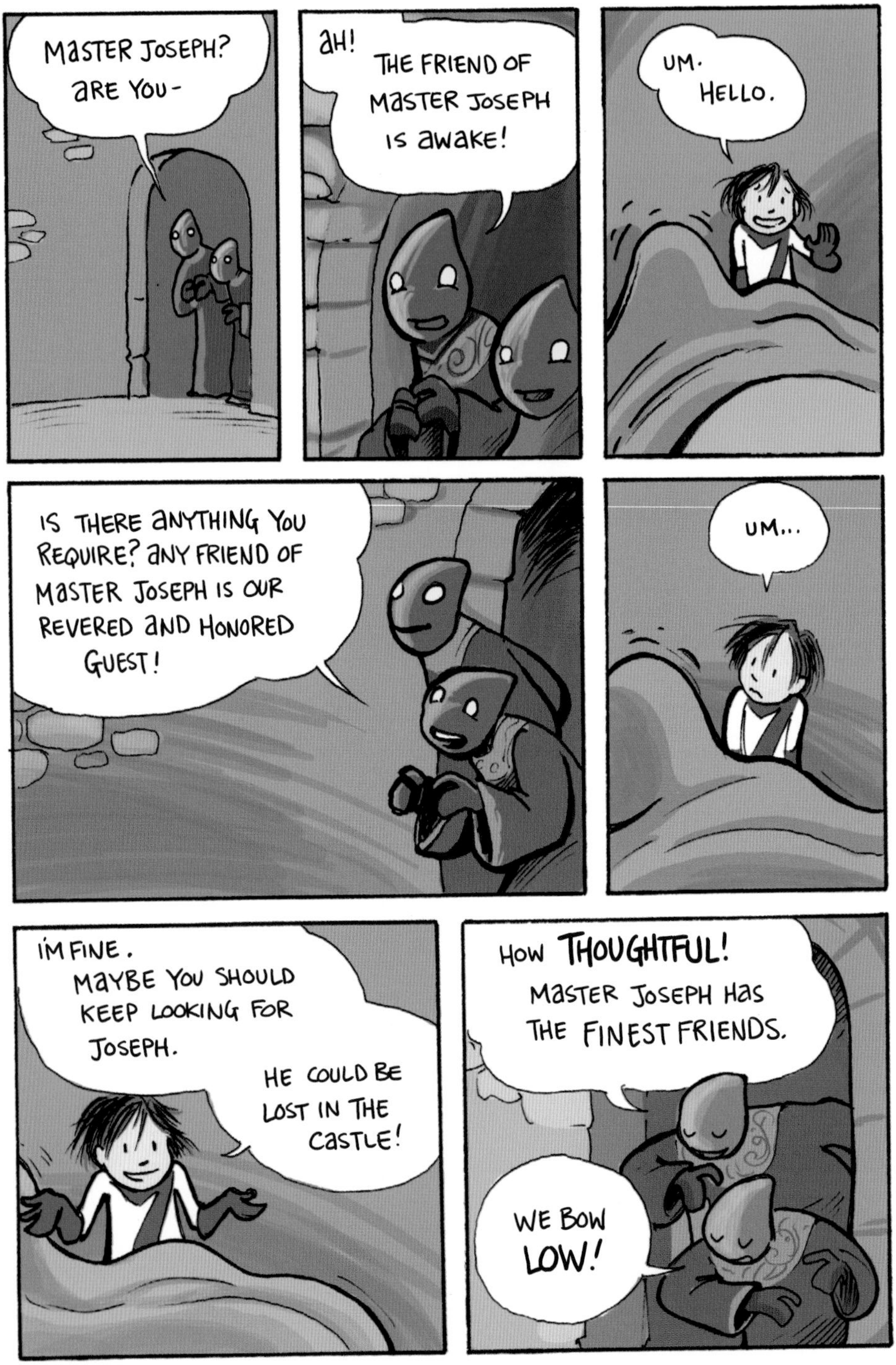
Master Joseph? are you-
ah!
The friend of Master Joseph is awake!
Um. Hello.
Is there anything you require? Any friend of Master Joseph is our revered and honored guest!
Um...
I'm fine.
Maybe you should keep looking for Joseph.
He could be lost in the castle!
How THOUGHTFUL!
Master Joseph has the finest friends.
We bow LOW!

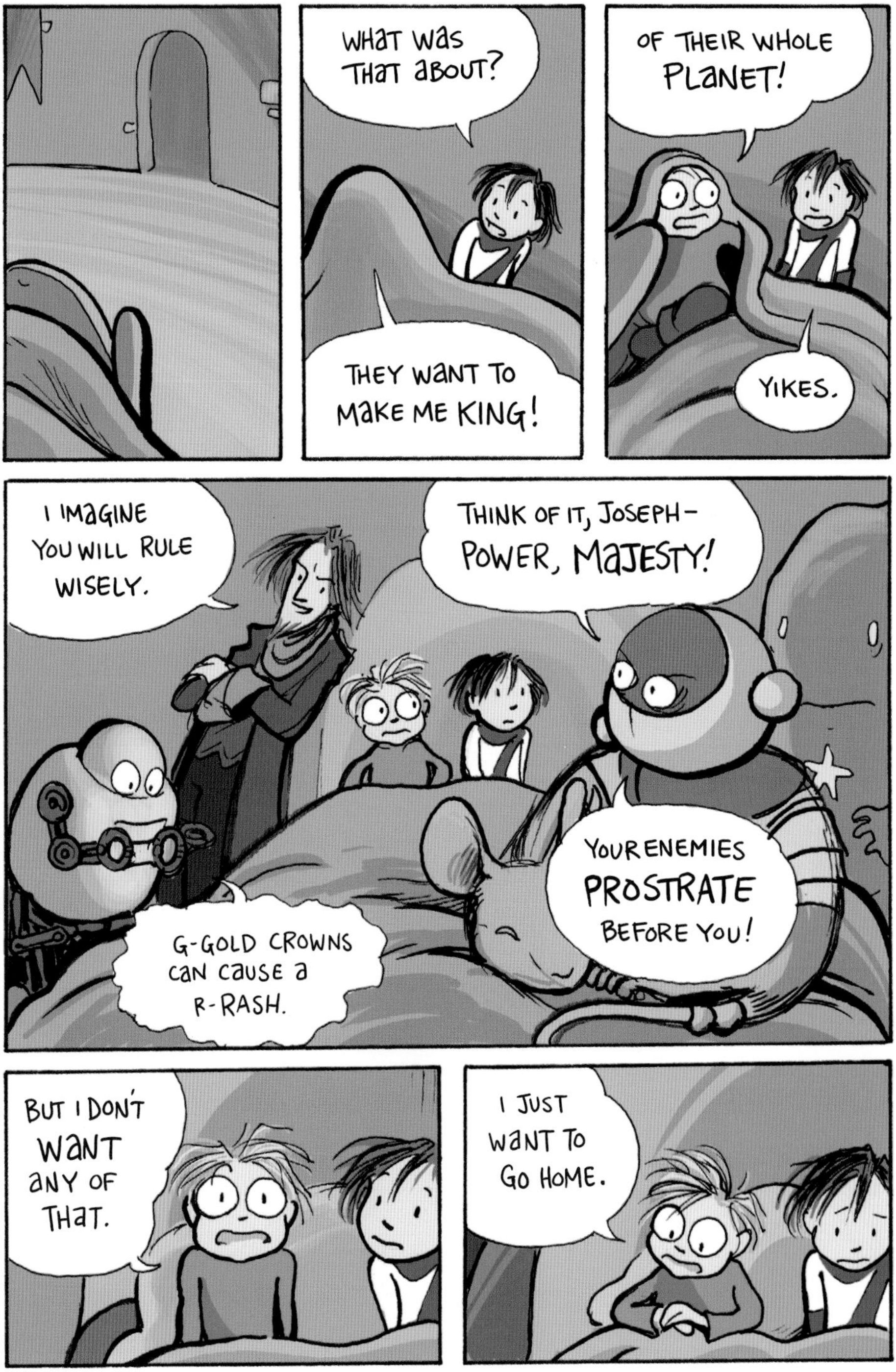
WHAT WAS THAT ABOUT?
THEY WANT TO MAKE ME KING!
OF THEIR WHOLE PLANET!
YIKES.
I IMAGINE YOU WILL RULE WISELY.
THINK OF IT, JOSEPH- POWER, MAJESTY!
YOUR ENEMIES PROSTRATE BEFORE YOU!
G-GOLD CROWNS CAN CAUSE A R-RASH.
BUT I DON'T WANT ANY OF THAT.
I JUST WANT TO GO HOME.

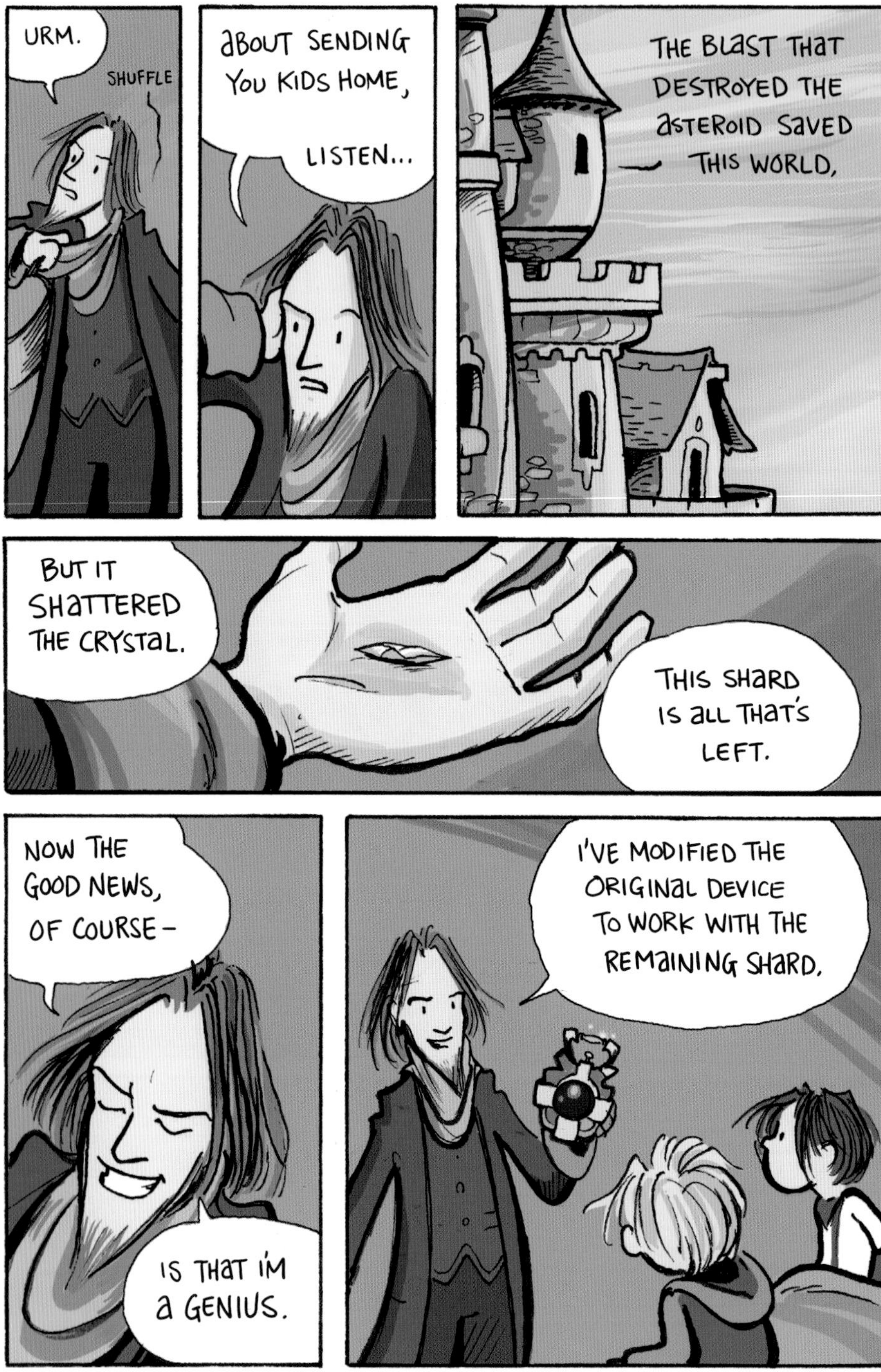
URM.
SHUFFLE
ABOUT SENDING YOU KIDS HOME,
LISTEN...
THE BLAST THAT DESTROYED THE ASTEROID SAVED THIS WORLD,
BUT IT SHATTERED THE CRYSTAL.
THIS SHARD IS ALL THAT'S LEFT.
NOW THE GOOD NEWS, OF COURSE-
IS THAT I'M A GENIUS.
I'VE MODIFIED THE ORIGINAL DEVICE TO WORK WITH THE REMAINING SHARD.

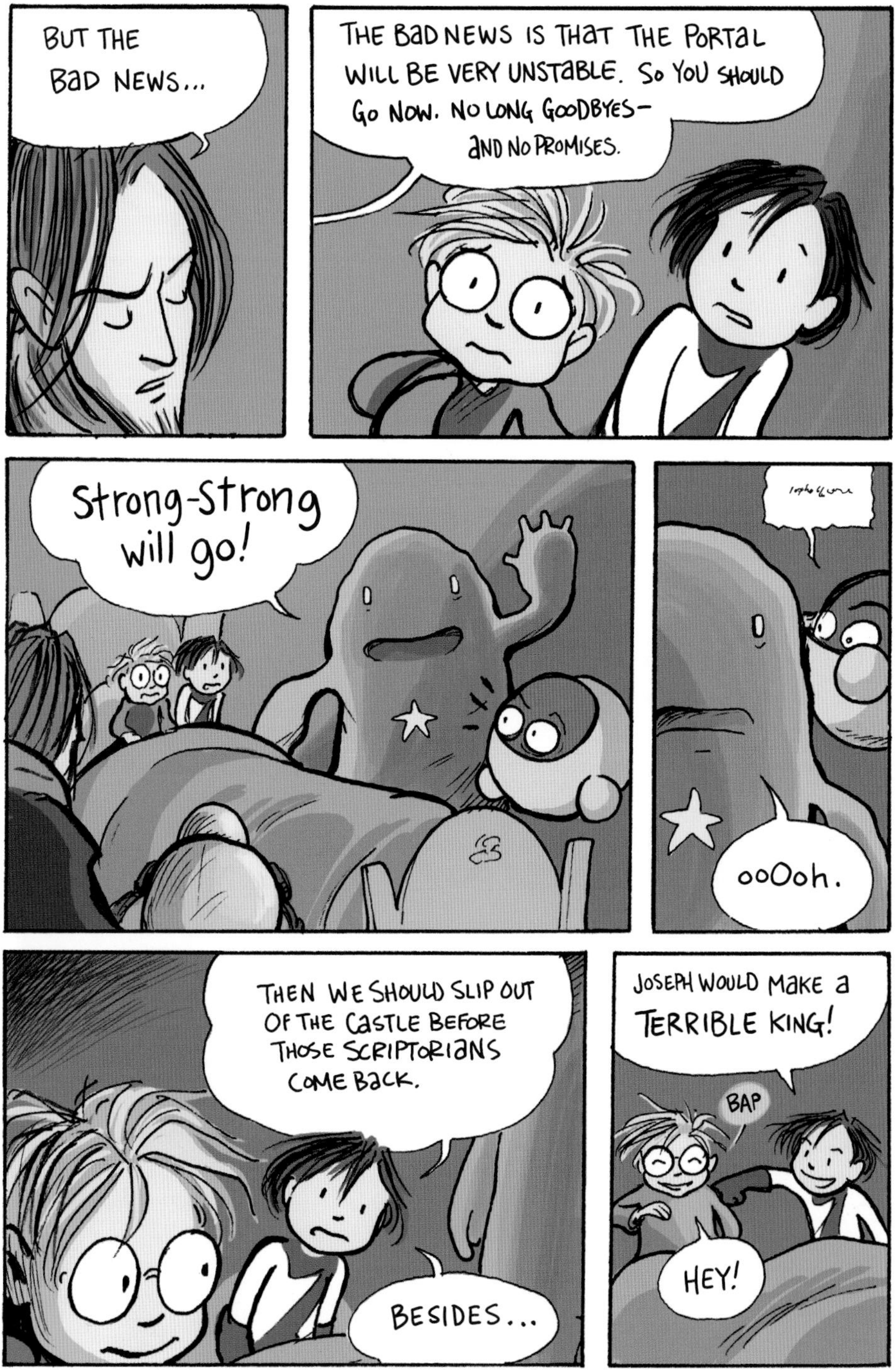
BUT THE BAD NEWS...
THE BAD NEWS IS THAT THE PORTAL WILL BE VERY UNSTABLE. SO YOU SHOULD GO NOW. NO LONG GOODBYES— AND NO PROMISES.
Strong-Strong will go!
ooOoh.
THEN WE SHOULD SLIP OUT OF THE CASTLE BEFORE THOSE SCRIPTORIANS COME BACK.
BESIDES...
JOSEPH WOULD MAKE A TERRIBLE KING!
BAP
HEY!

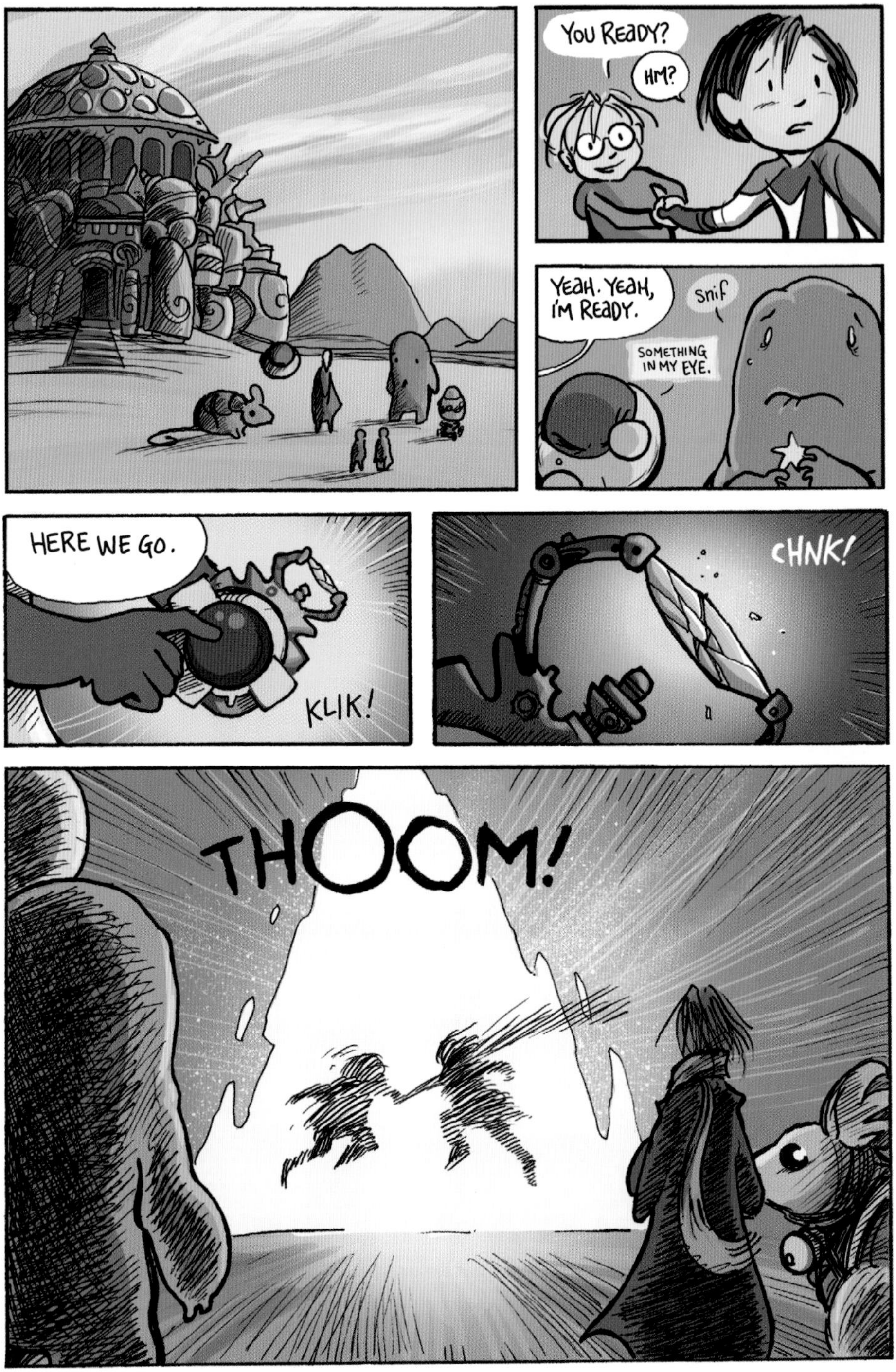

YOU READY?
HM?
YEAH. YEAH, I'M READY.
SNIF
SOMETHING IN MY EYE.
HERE WE GO.
KLIK!
CHNK!
THOOM!

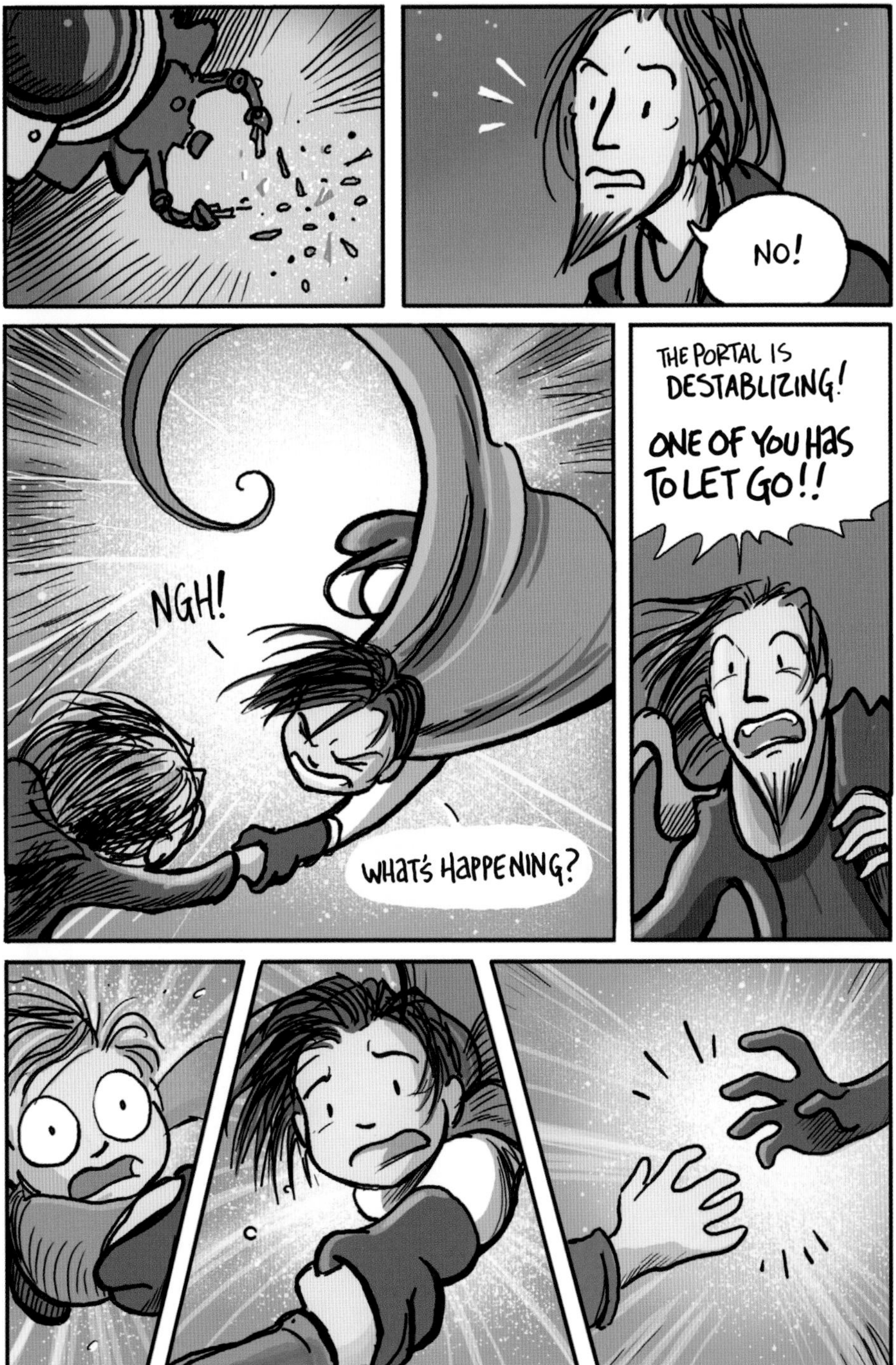
NO!
THE PORTAL IS DESTABLIZING!
ONE OF YOU HAS TO LET GO!!
NGH!
WHAT'S HAPPENING?

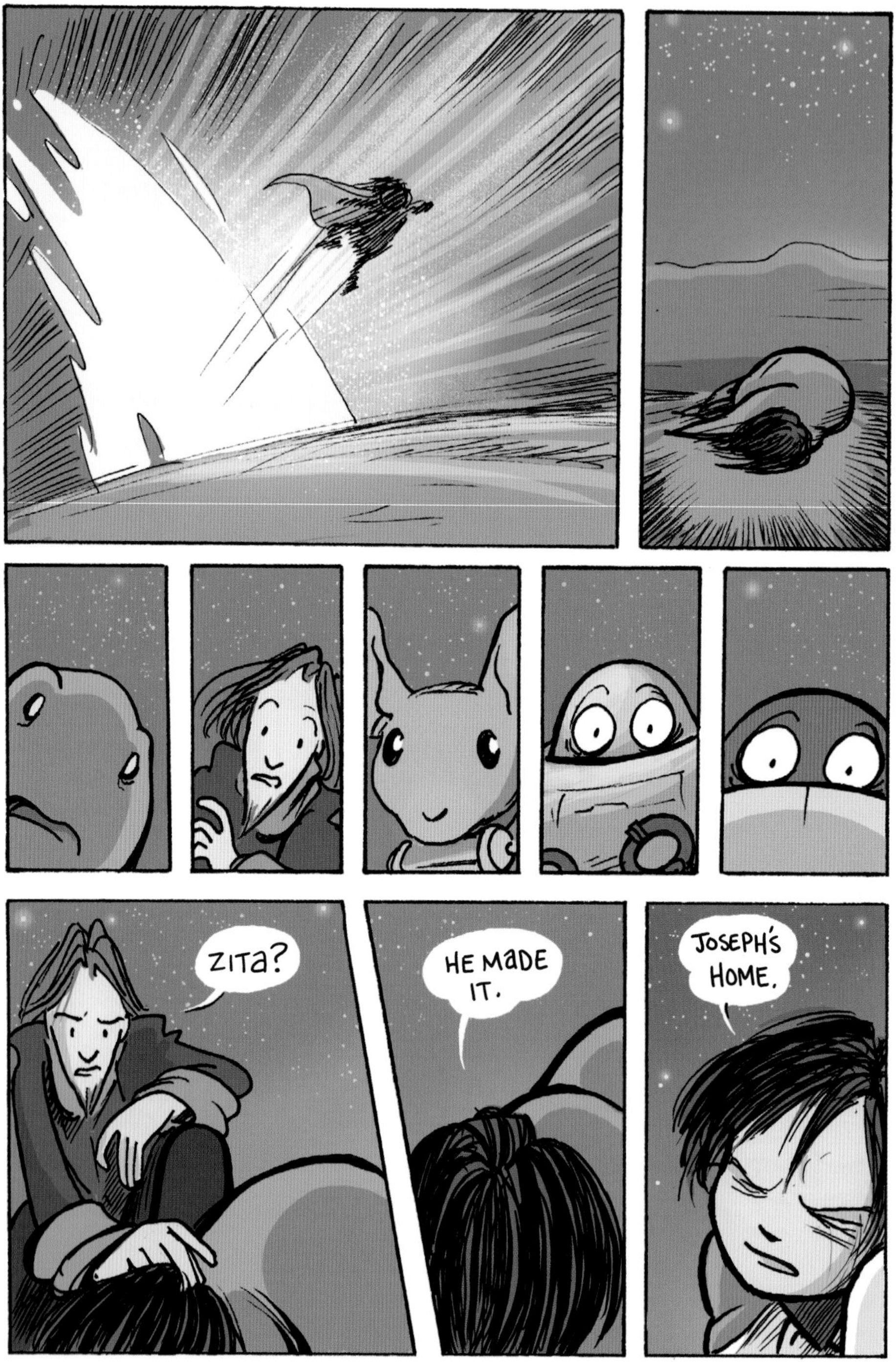
ZITA?
HE MADE IT.
JOSEPH'S HOME.

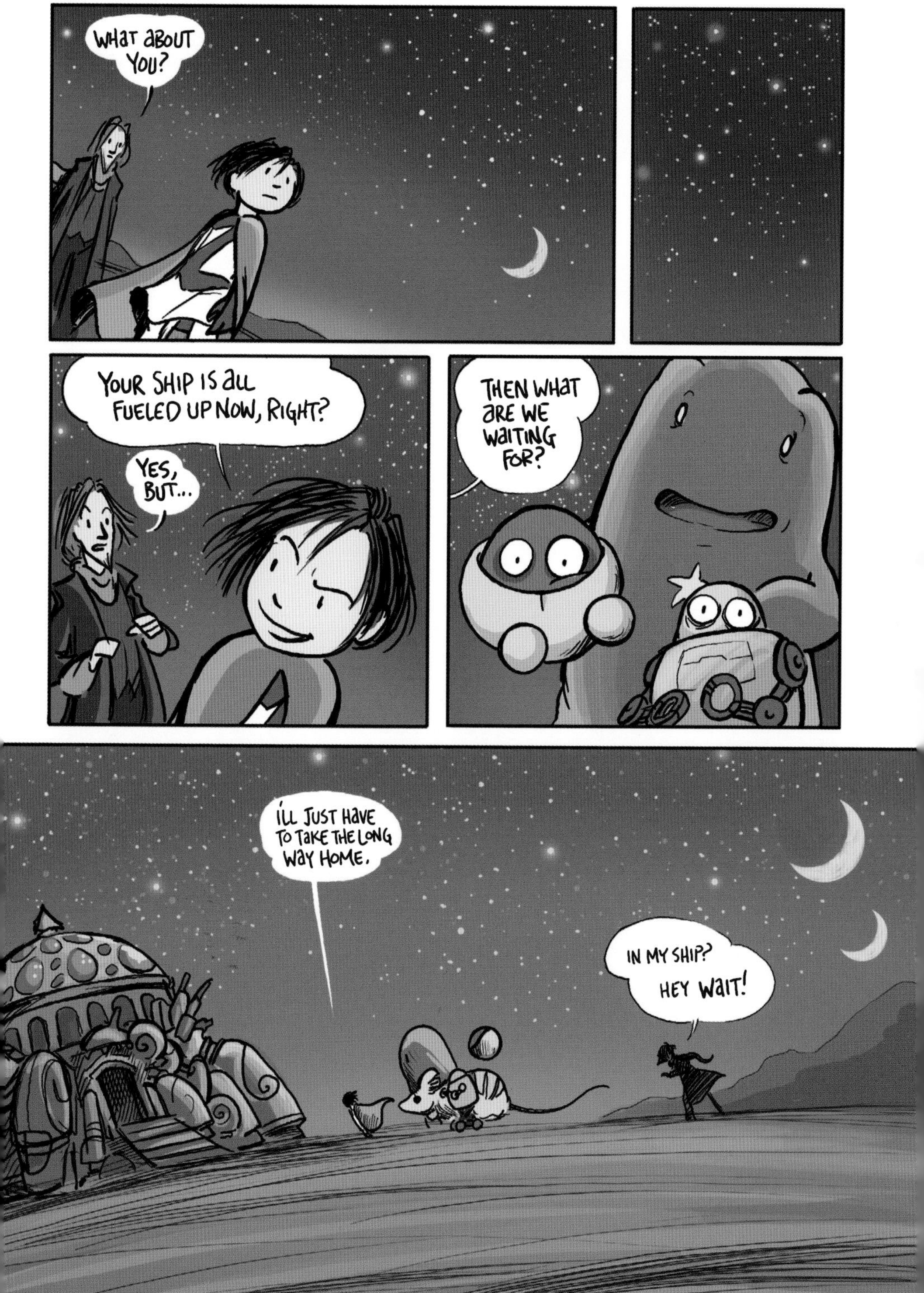
WHAT ABOUT YOU?
YOUR SHIP IS ALL FUELED UP NOW, RIGHT?
YES, BUT...
THEN WHAT ARE WE WAITING FOR?
I'LL JUST HAVE TO TAKE THE LONG WAY HOME.
IN MY SHIP?
HEY WAIT!

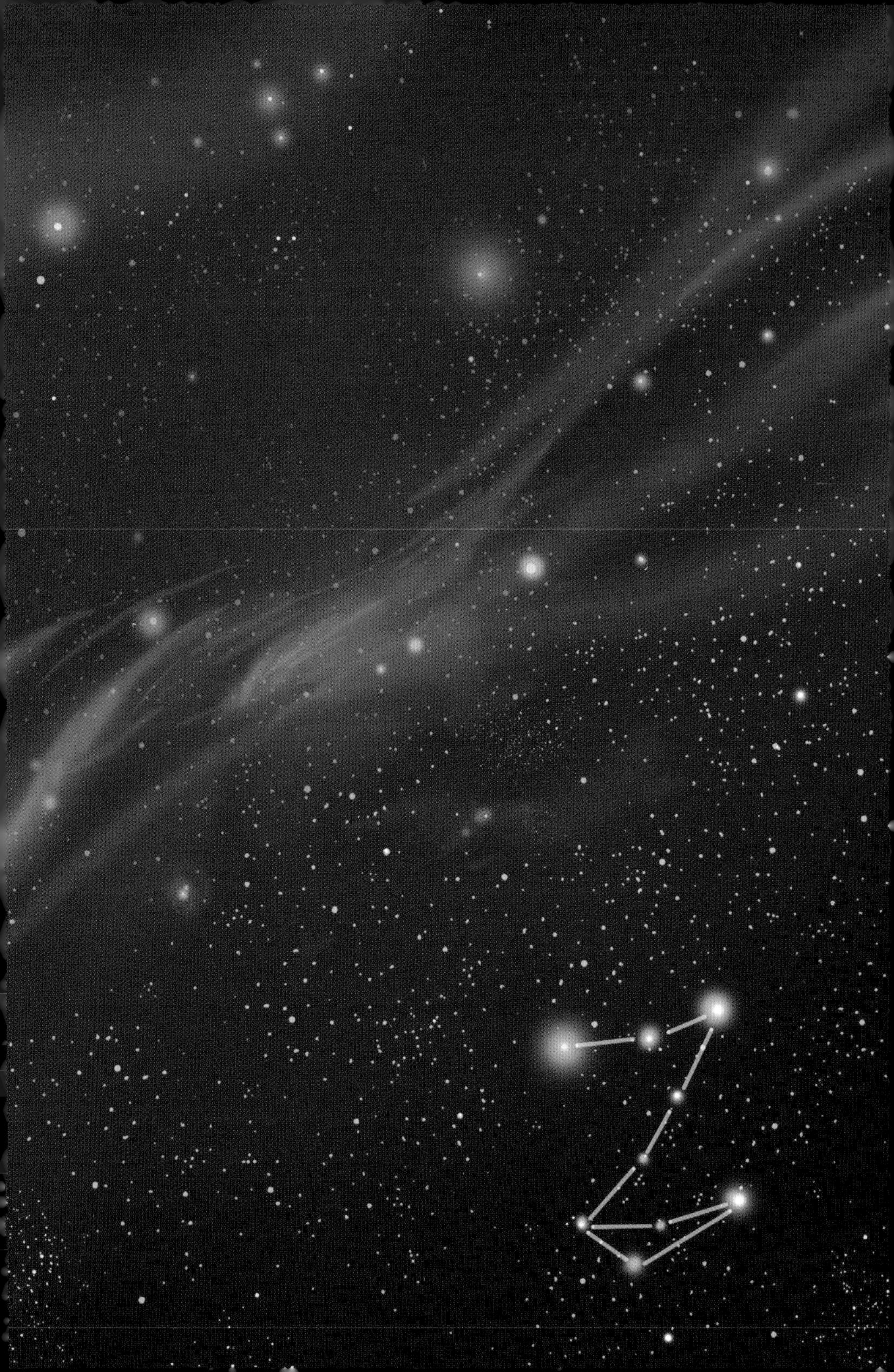

Follow Zita's space adventures in

LEGENDS OF ZITA

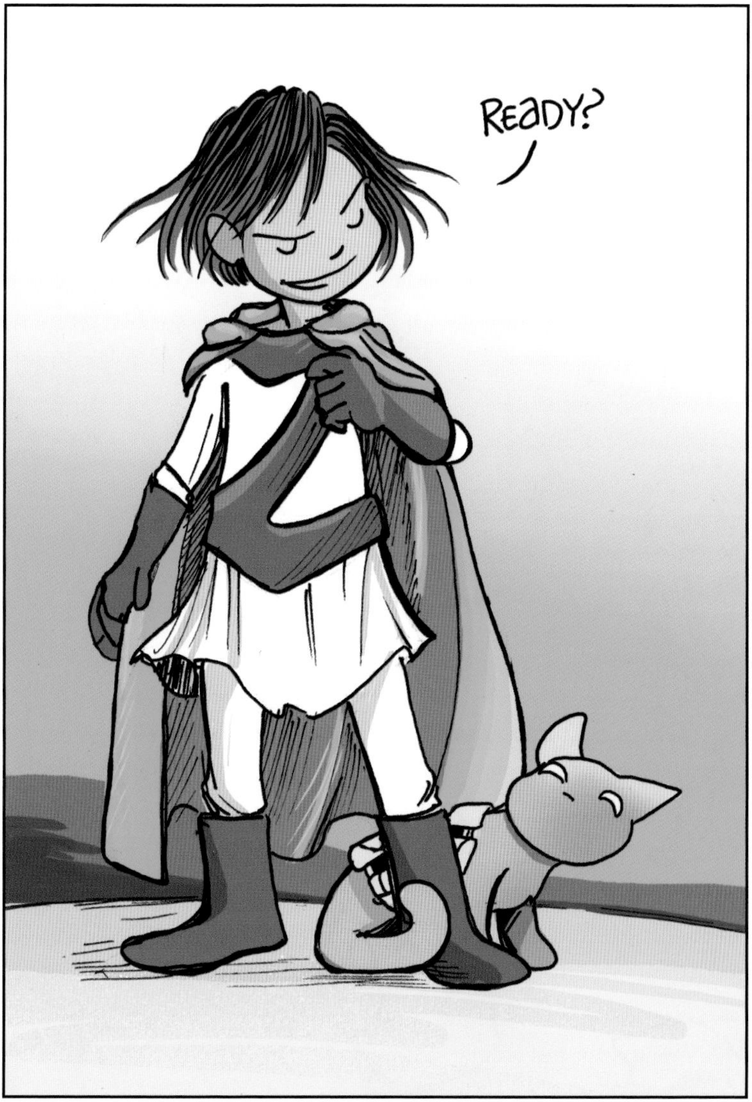
READY?

EARLY ZITA SKETCHES

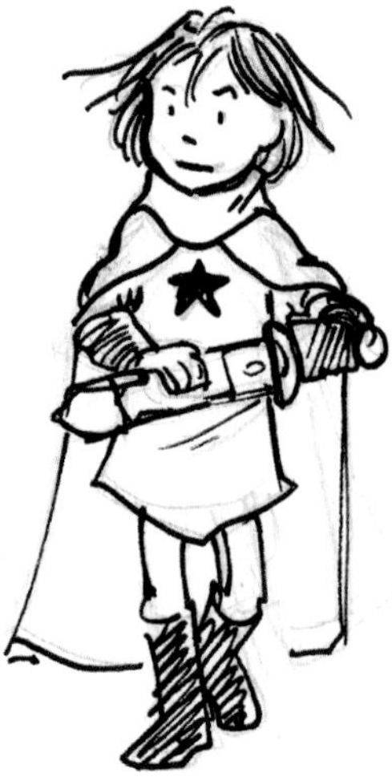

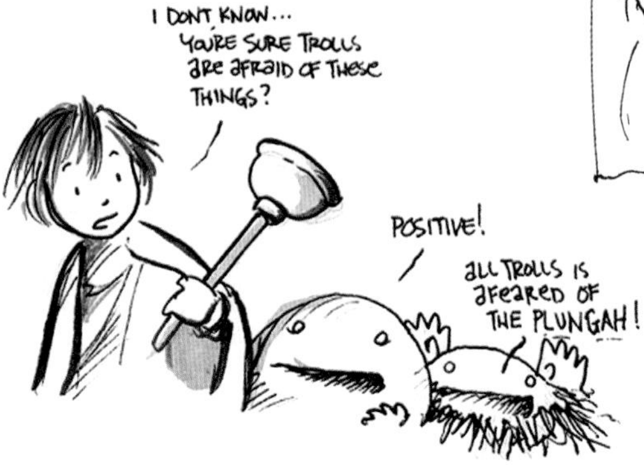

I DONT KNOW... YOU'RE SURE TROLLS ARE AFRAID OF THESE THINGS?
POSITIVE!
ALL TROLLS IS AFEARED OF THE PLUNGAH!

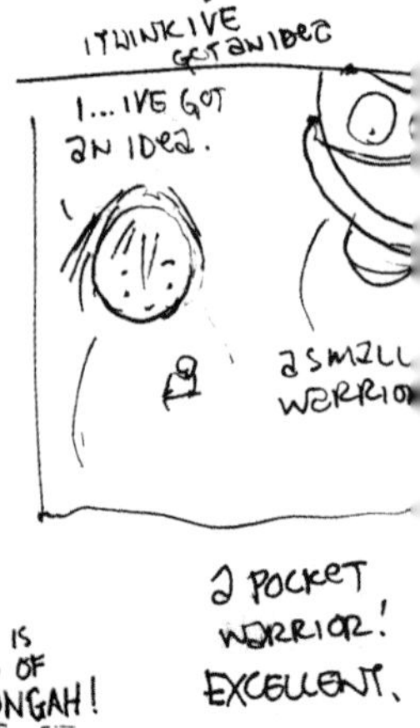

I THINK I'VE GOT AN IDEA
I... I'VE GOT AN IDEA.
A SMALL
WARRIO
A POCKET WARRIOR! EXCELLENT.

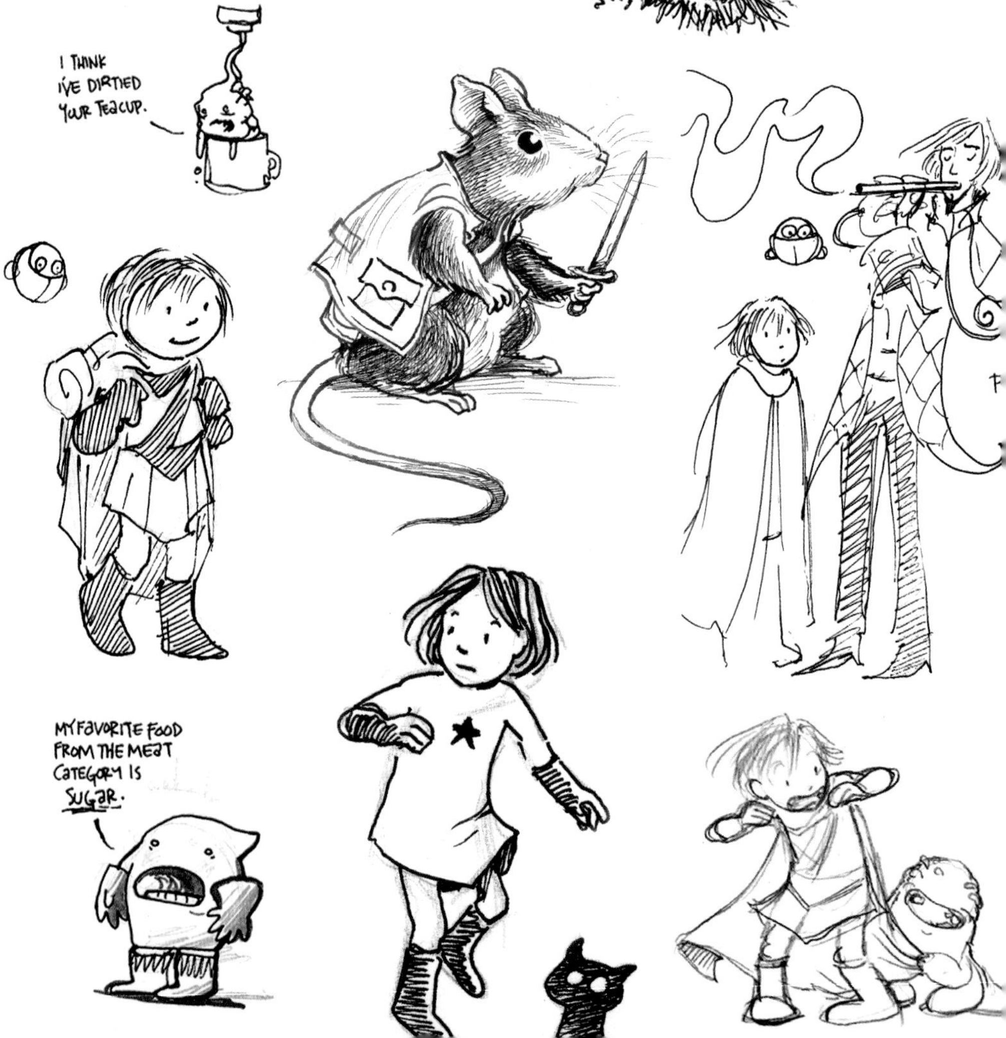

I THINK I'VE DIRTIED YOUR TEACUP.
MY FAVORITE FOOD FROM THE MEAT CATEGORY IS SUGAR.

ACKNOWLEDGEMENTS

They say a tale grows in the telling, and it's surely true with this little book, which went through so many changes in its journey to the printed page. There are a lot of people I should thank.

Special thanks go first to my wife Anna for her great patience, never-ending cheerful support, and so much more. And, with her, thanks to all the people who read through early drafts and were willing to say "I don't get it" or "That's not funny"—especially Ryan, Gwen, and Regina.

In a particular way I want to thank the talented Kean Soo who, when all hope was lost, took me back to the beginning and reminded me what was important. And thanks to my stalwart editor Kat Kopit, who kept up with me through trans-Atlantic address changes and shifting phone numbers. And thanks to my agent Judy Hansen, for her eagle eye and patience with the "artistic temperament."

And to the captain of the First Second ship, Mark Siegel, who gave me that final challenge.

And of course to my three daughters, Angelica, Zita, and Julia, who—when their powers combine—form an unruly pack of pure inspiration.

ABOUT THE AUTHOR

Ben Hatke has published comics stories in the Flight series as well as in Explorer. This book is his first full-length graphic novel. It's a first for Zita, too, but she has many more adventures up her sleeve.

Ben lives in Virginia's Shenandoah Valley with his wife, three daughters, twelve chickens, and a cat. He also enjoys juggling, playing his Irish whistle, and occasionally breathing fire. His work can be seen at www.benhatke.com